Eve's Revelations

- Book 4 in the Abomination Series -

By Felicity Thorne

This is a work of fiction. Names (excluding historical figures), characters, businesses, places, events and incidents are either the products of the author's imagination or used in a fictitious manner. Any resemblance to actual persons, living or dead, or actual events is purely coincidental.

Any trivial references made to real people, places, or media is done so without malice or endorsement.

Enjoy!

The Abomination Series:
Eve's Monsters
Eve's Curse
Eve's Sins
Eve's Revelations

Check out the accompanying Spotify playlist:

The Abomination Series by Felicity Thorne
https://open.spotify.com/playlist/6rVzdKXwm0lk5Bsz1G3SqZ?si=
HgeRqP-KSnyqk7RcltflDg&pi=9X79qnTQQeS8F

"'Everything will turn out all right. You'll see.'
'I can't imagine how,' said Atreyu.
'Neither can I,' said the luckdragon. 'But that's the best part of it.'"

-Michael Ende, The Neverending Story

"The trouble is, you think you have time."

- Jack Kornfield, Buddha's Little Instruction Book

1
You'll Have to Kill Me First

Eve slowly approached Bo and Luc, apprehensive of what they were going to say. Her throat constricted with fear as she kept her eyes cast down to her bare feet moving through the grass. *Left, right. Left, right.* She needed to repaint her toenails. The stubborn remnants of polish on her big toes looked like two pink islands on a map.

The boys' feet entered her field of view, and she stopped. She swallowed hard and furtively glanced up at their faces.

Luc's eyes dropped to the numerous bite marks visible on her neck. He touched a finger to her jaw and tilted her face. "Jesus, Bo," he chastised, glaring at Bo.

"I got carried away," Bo said softly. "I will tend to her." He reached for Eve, but Luc put his arm across in front of her, blocking Bo's hand.

"I think you've done enough, brother."

Bo's wolf eye made a reappearance as he regarded Luc. Eve could see his temples flex and his jaw tick under his mask. "You won't deny me my responsibility," he threatened in a low growl.

Luc met his challenge with flared nostrils and a fierce, icy glare. "She is *my* responsibility."

"She *was* your responsibility, until you let her wander off into the woods…with me."

Thunder cracked overhead, and Eve felt the earth tremble under her feet as she threw herself between them, shoving her arms wide, her hands flattening abruptly against their chests as they lunged at each other.

"Whoa, whoa, easy boys! Take a fucking step back," she commanded with an air of authority. On paper, she had none. She looked like a mouse trying to break up a fight between two bulls. But in reality, she knew she had some semblance of command over them.

And they obeyed, both backing off a pace.

"I think we could all use some space right now," she said. "Maybe we should all retreat to our own corners for tonight."

Luc pressed his chest against her hand again. "No. You aren't leaving my fucking sight again tonight."

Eve sighed, dropping her arms to her sides and lolling her head back to stare at the stars above. "I don't know what the fuck I'm doing." She looked between Bo and Luc. "What the fuck am I doing? What the fuck are *we* doing? Do either of you know how the fuck we're supposed to navigate this?"

There was a long silence.

Luc inhaled deeply. "We will figure it out," he said, his tone surprisingly calm. "We will make it work." After a long pause, he added, "For all of us."

"And if we can't?" she questioned.

Bo spoke up. "We will," he asserted. "There is no other option." He looked at her, determination fortifying his features. "I will do whatever I need to. Whatever *you* need."

She looked to Luc, and he nodded. He took Eve's hand in his and lifted it to his lips, kissing her knuckles. "If you wish to be alone tonight, I will respect that, love." He grinned at her with his dazzling, perfect teeth. "But tomorrow, you and I are going to Grand Rapids to meet with Emma Rose. And, hey, it appears you and I can make the jump together after all. I suppose I should thank Bo for that." But he didn't.

Bo moved closer to her and gently cupped the back of her head, pressing a masked kiss to her forehead while her hand was still clasped in Luc's. "Goodnight, Evie. I'll see you off in the morning." He brushed past her, and on his way by, he brusquely acknowledged, "Luc."

Luc intertwined his fingers in Eve's and slowly headed toward the apartment building, following Bo at a distance, pulling Eve along beside him. "You aren't going to run the second I leave you alone again, are you?" he inquired, and Eve couldn't tell if he was kidding.

She stopped, and he turned to look down at her. She held her wrist out to him. "Mark me. I won't cut it off again, I promise."

"Oh, you'll burn it off this time?" he teased.

"Maybe I'll just cut the whole hand off. You think it'll grow back? Like Deadpool?"

Luc shook his head as he brought her wrist to his lips and kissed it. He held his hand over the place where his old tracking tattoo used to be, and she felt the brief burn of the new mark being forged. "It won't. It'll just heal over into a stump." He lifted his hand, and the little round tattoo was once again imprinted on her skin.

"So, don't do that, then," she concluded.

"Not your best idea. You've had some terrible ones, but that one's right up there." He took her hand and started leading her toward the front door to the apartment building once again.

She swung their arms as she took two steps to every one of his. "You've had some pretty terrible ideas, too. I would make a horrendous mother and wife."

Luc gave her an amused smirk. "I think when the time comes, you'll be exactly what you need to be." Then his smile faltered. "I just hope I will be."

Eve frowned up at him. "What the hell does that mean?"

Luc's pace slowed, as though he were trying to prolong the walk to the apartment as long as possible. "I had a dream when I fell asleep on the couch tonight. We were married, and we had a baby. I left for a quick business trip, but new problems kept cropping up, and I was away longer than I intended to be. When I came home, the baby wasn't a baby anymore. She was a full-grown woman, and she hated me. And you hated me because I wasn't there to help raise her." He gave a short, rueful laugh. "And then I wake up to find out you've bonded to Bo because I failed to fulfil my duties on the one fucking night it really mattered. Because I was *tired*. It was almost poetic."

Eve chewed the inside of her cheek and squeezed his hand. Her eyes burned. She watched their feet as they ambled along slowly. Her bare toes and Luc's gigantic oxfords, the shoelaces untied because he'd slipped them on in a hurry. "Nothing about that was your fault. It…it was an inevitability, Luc."

Luc was silent until they reached the front door. He stopped, but he didn't reach to open it. "You broke your promise," he observed. "You said you wouldn't fall in love with him."

Guilt sat like hot lead in Eve's chest, and she couldn't meet his eyes. Was this the moment? Was this when he would decide she wasn't worth it anymore?

"It was a promise I had no business making. I'm sorry, Luc."

"You already knew back then," he surmised. His voice was strangely soft.

"I don't know what I knew then. Fuck, I don't know what I know now. I knew shit was complicated. And it still is. And maybe it always will be."

"You want to know a secret?" Luc asked thickly. "I knew then, too. I had no business asking you to make that promise, because I knew it was too late." Eve ventured a glance up at him, and he gave her a falsely cheerful smile that didn't reach his watery eyes. He shrugged. "I made you promise, but I already knew."

Eve's eyes dropped to the side, afraid to hold his gaze as a tear rolled down the side of her nose. She whispered, "Is this the part where you dump me?"

His big fingers were suddenly wrapped around her jaw, jerking her face up toward his. He slammed his other hand against the bricks by the door and pushed her against the wall. His lips crushed against hers as he took her mouth possessively. Aggressively.

"Don't you ever fucking say that to me," he warned, his lips hovering above hers, his reddened eyes piercing hers. "You love me, and I love you. You think this shit with Bo changes that? It changes *nothing* between us. Everything I felt before, I still feel, and always will. As I said, Eve: Burn the world. Eat a puppy. Bond to my brother. I don't fucking care. My love will persist. You ever want me to stop loving you?" His hand slipped from her jaw and fisted into her hair as he leveled his gaze with hers. "You'll have to kill me first."

Relieved tears spilled over her cheeks, and she gave him a weak smile. "I don't deserve you," she choked.

"I am pretty fucking great, right?" he joked, grinning, swiping the tears from her cheeks with his thick thumbs. "But Bo is, too. He's always there for you when you need him, when I can't be, in a *way* I can't be. He provides a kind of stability I can't offer you. How can I begrudge him for that? Or you, for growing close to him, even if he is an uptight asshole sometimes? I pushed you two together. I put him in charge of keeping you safe because he's my right fucking hand, and that's a privilege I will forever bestow upon him. I'm not going to promise you I won't get jealous sometimes, but with him, at least I know without question that you will always be taken care of in my absence." Luc gave her an earnest smile. "I know you love him. I mean, he bears a mild resemblance to me, so how could you not love him?"

Eve smiled through her tears. "You are awfully pretty."

"Just so long as you always think I'm the prettiest." He pulled her to him, hugging her tightly against his chest. "But I do have one demand," he announced.

"What's that?" Eve asked, her voice muffled against his shirt.

"I refuse to share my coffin in your closet with him."

Eve laughed. "The closet is all yours, my rotten little sex corpse."

Eve lay alone in bed, exhausted to her very bones, but unable to shut her damn mind off. She craved a body next to her, like an emotional support body pillow that would whisper, "Everything will work out. It'll all be ok."

Alas.

She felt like she was sitting on a powder keg. Could Luc and Bo share nicely? She had her doubts. The dynamic among the group had shifted, and the logistics of it were going to be tricky. She acknowledged that Eoduun had been right when he said that starting something with Bo would change everything.

It had.

But Eoduun had mistakenly assumed that there was some other option. There was never any other option. Bo was her fate, just as Luc was. It wasn't her logic that chose him. She was beginning to understand that it was on a much more molecular level than that.

The Blood of Eve chose Luc.

The Blood of Lilith chose Bo.

And they were going to tear her apart in their battle for love.

2
It All Feels So Arbitrary with You

Eve snapped awake instantly. She had just started to drift off to sleep, but a tingling in her chest, the feeling of ants beneath her skin, jarred her from her slumber. The tingle slowly began to sear, and Eve grimaced, clutching her chest.

No, no, no!

One large hand clapped over her mouth, and another closed over her forehead, and she felt a strange static in her brain, like an interference. She looked up at the bronze eyes and burgundy hair above her, standing next to the bed.

"I can't have you alerting your entourage," Apep explained smoothly. When he removed his hand from her mouth, she opened it and tried to scream for Bo, but her voice was gone. It was like trying to scream in a dream, but all that comes out is a faint squeak.

He grinned down at her, his face contorted psychotically. "Shhh," he shushed her, touching a finger to her lips. "You're completely at my mercy for the moment. Just give me a quick peek into that pretty little head of yours, and I'll grab the grimoire and be on my way."

She tried to call out for Dagon telepathically, but Apep had effectively cut the line. She heard Apep's voice in her head instead.

Just you and me, little devil. Now, where are you hiding that pesky grimoire? She felt him rummaging through her memories, like he was rifling through her sock drawer. He came upon the memory of her *Stranger Things* sensory deprivation trick. *Oh, so that's how you escaped the god realm. Clever girl.*

Bo will scent you and be here any moment now, Eve threatened.

He's trapped in a nightmare of his worst fears until I've retrieved my prize. He may not be much of a threat to me, but he's the one who would alert the ones who are. I don't have the patience to face off against the fertility god, the nuclear reactor, and the dragon right now.

Eve was given pause, and Apep sensed it. *Oh, that surprises you? You didn't know you had a dragon?*

Was he talking about Ramil? Is that what he was? A fucking dragon?

Apep again intercepted her questioning thoughts and answered, *Not just a dragon. A dragon-jinn hybrid. That's a rare but insanely powerful combination. And I don't like it. You should kill it.* Before Eve could respond, Apep stumbled over something she'd buried deep. *You plan to betray Dagon. That's interesting. Use him to help you get rid of me with empty promises, then seal him away, too? Coldblooded. What a gorgeous betrayal. I wonder what he would think about that.*

That's not the plan, Eve lied.

Don't bother lying. Lies have a unique taste that give them away. Apep continued his deep dive. *Looks like you need Dagon for more than just getting rid of me, though, don't you? You want to give the blonde witch her memories back? You're all over the board, aren't you, little devil? Kill monsters, save monsters – it all feels so arbitrary with you. I love that.*

Eve was growing increasingly uncomfortable with everything he was digging up, and all the information he could use against her. But as hard as she tried, she couldn't muster enough power to push him out. *You can clearly see I have no idea where the grimoire is, can't you? Just get the fuck out of here.*

Apep was silent for a moment, and all of Ruth's memories suddenly flashed through her mind's eye. Then she felt Apep's invisible, probing fingers withdrawing from her mind. "Fine. I have what I need," he said aloud.

She tried to speak, but her voice was still suppressed. So she signed at Apep, *What did you find in Ruth's memories?*

He laughed at her hand gestures, but if he understood them, he didn't give her an answer. "Do me a favor. Kill the dragon. I get the distinct impression he could be trouble for both of us." He leaned forward and Eve winced as he planted a kiss on her cheek, running his finger slowly down her jawline. In a low, menacing whisper in her ear, he threatened, "That's not a request, little devil."

And then he was gone.

But the fear and horror crawling through Eve's veins didn't dissipate, and that was when she realized that it wasn't *her* fear and horror that she was feeling.

It was Bo's.

In an instant, she moved through the space between them and was standing in his room, looking down at him in his bed. Even in the darkness, she could see the scowl on his face as he tossed and turned uneasily beneath the covers.

She brushed her hand over his damp hair. "Bo."

He sprang bolt upright, his eyes wild and wide, his pale hair plastered to the perspiration on his forehead. When his sweeping gaze fell on her, he swung his legs over the side of the bed and he dragged her to him, hugging his arms around her waist and pressing his cheek against her chest.

He was shaking.

She hugged him tightly, stroking his hair as she stood over him, curling herself protectively around him. "It's ok. It was just a dream," she soothed.

"He tortured you, right in front of me, and I couldn't fucking stop it," he rasped. "I watched you die the most horrible death, Evie."

"Who?"

"Dagon."

"It was Apep," she informed him.

"No, it was Dagon. Trust me," he corrected her.

"Not in the dream," she clarified. "I meant it was Apep who put that nightmare into your head. He was here."

Bo pushed her back just enough to look up at her face, fear and confusion swirling in gold and blue. Why could she *feel* it so acutely?

"When? Did he hurt you? Is he still here?" he fretted. His nostrils flared as he sniffed the air. Eve did the same, and she could still faintly smell Apep's scent, but it was likely only lingering on her clothes.

"He's gone, I think," she said, her arms draped over his shoulders, her hands clasped between his shoulder blades. "He used his connection with me to pop in when I was sleeping, and he got in my head." She recounted what Apep had found in her memories, then revealed what she'd learned about Ramil. "He wants me to kill him."

Shock colored Bo's features. "Ramil's a *dragon*? I thought dragons were extinct. Do you believe him? It seems like Luc would've mentioned it if Ramil was a fucking dragon."

"Luc doesn't know. Well, he knew he was *something*, but he didn't know what."

Bo was pensive, his eyes shifting away. "Hm." When he raised his eyes to Eve again, he asked, "And then Apep just left? After going through all Ruth's memories?"

"I've been through those memories myself. There's nothing there about where the grimoire is now, and none of the spells from it stuck in her memories. There is *information* from it that Ruth retained, like what was recorded about the Abomination prophecy, but I don't think the spells themselves can be memorized, just as they can't be copied or reproduced from the book. But again, none of that information seems pertinent to Apep. I don't know what he found that seemed to satisfy him."

Bo pulled her against him again, his knees caging her in. "I didn't protect you. I'm so sorry, Evie."

Bo's guilt sat like a rock in her chest.

"No one knew he was here. He made sure of it. But he didn't hurt me."

"This time," Bo added bitterly.

Eve lifted her knee onto the bed and straddled Bo's lap so she could be eye to eye with him. She cupped her hand around the back of his neck and rubbed her thumb along his hairline. "Tell me about your nightmare."

Horror flashed through his mismatched eyes and lanced her heart. "No. I'll never say it out loud. Ever."

"I can feel it, Bo," she disclosed. "Your fear, your horror, your guilt. I feel it like it's my own. And not in a metaphorical way; I literally *feel* it."

He framed her face in his hands, his wolf eye calming back to charcoal. "I'll try harder to keep from projecting. I'm sorry." He kissed her forehead.

"No, I'm not asking you to do that. I was just surprised by it. Is that something we can do now? Feel what the other feels? Do you feel what I feel?"

He grazed one hand down the side of her neck and rested it over her heart. "Yes, I feel it, too. You're uneasy. But I don't have to be bonded to you to know that." He pulled her close and guided her head to his shoulder, his arms surrounding her with comfort.

They stayed like that for a long time, just feeling their heartbeats pumping in uncanny unison, until Eve's eyelids started to get heavy. She forced her head up.

"I don't want to go, but I know I should," she confessed regretfully.

Bo sighed. "Actually, you should probably spend the night with Luc, just in case Apep decides he isn't done with you yet. Luc's a much bigger deterrent than I am."

She felt his jealousy prickle through her heart. "You don't really want that."

"Yes, I do. Regardless of whatever else I feel, I need to know you're safe." He lifted Eve off his lap, and they both stood next to the bed. "I'll walk you down there."

"No, that's ok. You stay here and get some rest. I'll just teleport over and see if I can scare the shit out of him."

Bo chuckled softly. He took her chin in his hand and pressed a chaste kiss to her lips. "Goodnight, Evie. Behave yourself."

She winked at him. "You got it, Daddy."

When Eve moved to Luc's room, she was startled to find him sitting up in bed, papers and lore books scattered all around him. He glanced up at her with surprise, but a beguiling smile quickly curled his kissable lips. His eyes sparked with delight.

"Couldn't stand being away from me?" he guessed.

"What's all this?" she asked, delaying having to reveal the real reason she was there.

He pointed to a stack of papers to his left. "A business proposal for Fagerberg Enterprises." He moved on to a folder next to it. "Last month's financials for The Gutter." With his other hand he pointed to a binder and some loose papers to his right. "Knighco dealings." And finally, he fanned both hands out over the many ancient-looking texts in front of him. "And books I stole from the Vatican archives." He quickly held a finger up and amended, "*Borrowed.* These are all the books that make mention of an 'Abomination.'"

"Jesus, Luc. Don't you have an assistant that can handle some of this?" she asked, sweeping her hand across to indicate the mess around him.

"Of course. I only handle the things I have to."

Eve surveyed the paperwork surrounding him. "And you still have this much to take care of? You're fucking swamped."

"What? Nah. I've just gotten a little behind. I'll catch up."

Eve's heart sank. He was swamped because of her. He was behind on everything because she'd caused him so many problems and started all kinds of fires that only he could put out. And here she was, coming to him with yet another predicament.

"Christ, I'm killing you," she realized.

"You tried the direct route already and it didn't work. What makes you think death by paperwork will?" he teased.

"This isn't funny, Luc." She sat on the edge of the bed. "We don't need to go to Grand Rapids tomorrow. It'll only put you further behind."

Luc waved his hand dismissively. "Nonsense. We're going." He gathered up the papers and books and stacked them high on the nightstand. Then he gestured to her. "Come here. Let me love on you."

She crawled over the puffy comforter and snuggled into his awaiting arms, settling into his chest. "I hate to do this to you, but we have a situation."

Luc rolled onto his back and clapped a hand over his eyes, a sigh heavy on his lips. "Is it Bo again?"

"No, not Bo. Apep. And Ramil."

Luc uncovered his eyes and arched a brow. "Elaborate."

So she did.

Luc was dubious. "No way. Dragons don't exist anymore. Ramil can't be a dragon."

"Just like I couldn't be a monster?" Eve pointed out.

He was given pause. "Hm. Good point." He rolled onto his side and pulled her close again, burying his face in her hair.

"I don't trust Ramil," Eve confided.

"But if Apep wants him dead, it must mean we *don't* want him dead. Enemy of my enemy and all that."

"But he said it wasn't a request. What if he tries to hurt someone else, to use them as leverage to force my hand?"

Luc raked his fingers through her hair and gazed down at her. "I guess we'll have to kill Apep before he can hurt someone else. But he can't get into the compound without you here, so your team should be safe until we get back from Grand Rapids. It'll buy us some time to come up with a plan."

"What if he tries to kill *you*?"

"'*Try*' being the key word." Luc grinned reassuringly at her. "I won't die so easily."

As Eve lay in his arms, she whispered, "I could kill Ramil, though. It would be so easy to get him right where I need him."

Luc hummed sleepily, his eyes already closed. "Easy, my little murder nymph. If he needs to die, he will." He kissed her softly on her temple. "Patience, love."

3
I Want You to Tie Me Up

Luc roused Eve long before she was ready to wake up. His morning wood was like a hot steel rod against her ass as he slowly rolled his hips against her. She groaned as he slid his hand down the front of her shorts, his thick fingers nestling between her legs.

"Luc," she protested weakly, looking at the faint glow behind the curtains. "The sun isn't even up yet."

Luc's voice was sleepy and gravelly as he murmured in her ear, "But I am." It sent a warm tingle straight through her belly.

"Yeah, I can tell. You couldn't sleep in another hour? Maybe two?"

He slipped two fingers inside of her and began to fuck her with them, and she gripped his forearm with both hands as she sucked her lower lip between her teeth.

"Your perfect body pressed up against mine woke me up an hour ago. This is all your fault," he accused, smiling against her neck. "You're lucky I waited as long as I did to wake you. Now, take your shorts off, love. I need my dick inside you right fucking now." His lips caressed the small hollow on her neck behind her ear, and a soft sigh escaped her.

As she pushed her shorts and underwear down over her hips, she wondered, "So what did you do for that whole hour? Just stare at me creepily while I slept?" She kicked her shorts off over the side of the bed.

Luc withdrew his fingers, dragging them along the inside of her muscular inner thigh. "Oh, I stared. And stroked myself. Maybe fondled you a little. You are a dangerously sound sleeper, love." He raised her leg, opening her up to him so he could slide his eager cock into her welcoming heat from behind. She arched her back as he stretched her tight walls, his name rolling silkily off her tongue.

She reached behind her and ran her hand up Luc's neck, feeling the delicious flex of each cabled muscle as he moved, slowly, lazily thrusting into her. "Fuck, Luc…you feel so fucking good." Her other hand fisted in the sheets, and she undulated against him, hooking the foot of her raised leg around the back of his thigh for leverage as she rocked her ass back into him, taking him deeper.

His breath ghosted over her skin as his mouth devoured the soft flesh between her neck and shoulder. She felt his teeth graze her shoulder. His voice was gruff when he said, "His bite marks are still here. Taunting me. Begging me to cover them with my own."

Before Eve could object, he bit into her, and she gasped at the sharp, delectable pain. It wasn't hard enough to draw blood, but it would leave a mark.

"Careful, Luc. Don't make me bleed," she warned.

Luc's hips suddenly rammed against her ass, burying himself deep. "Oh, but I want to make you to bleed," he admitted roughly, his tone threatening as his teeth skimmed her skin. "I *will* make you bleed."

A brief flash of fear caught her breath in her throat.

"I want to give you my power, Eve," he whispered, and she immediately felt foolish for the jolt of fear. "I want you to have that essence of me inside you. Just take it. Please," he begged as he fucked her with hard, deep strokes.

"But last time..."

Luc's hand left her thigh and went to her jaw, turning her face to the side so he could slant his mouth over hers, silencing her doubts with a demanding kiss. "You have *his* power right now, so your curse should be perfectly happy to take mine."

"I don't want to hurt you."

His bright eyes pierced hers, and his pace faltered. "You'll hurt me more if you refuse me. Don't."

Goddamn it.

Eve relented. "Fine. But I want you to tie me up first."

Luc pulled out and sat up. He hiked a brow at her. "Kinky, love. I approve." He moved to his closet and opened a drawer, producing a pair of rather robust metal handcuffs.

"Those look sturdy," Eve noticed. They seemed solid enough to bind even someone as strong as Zeke.

Luc's lips curled into a wide, deviant smile. "They are. They were created to subdue particularly powerful prisoners. Perfect for just such an occasion." When he brought them closer, Eve noticed there were runes etched into the metal all around the manacles. "Once I clasp these around your wrists, I'm the only one who can remove them. I am the only key." He climbed onto the bed and kneeled between her legs, dangling the manacles over her. "Do you trust me?"

Eve recalled that surge of fear he'd elicited only moments ago, and guilt racked her. He'd be devastated if he knew.

"I trust you, Luc. Just don't go dying of a heart attack. I don't want a *Gerald's Game* situation on my hands."

Luc twirled the handcuff on his finger, his face taking on a conspiratorial expression. "Maybe I'm not real. Maybe I'm only made of moonlight," he joked, referencing the story.

Without warning, Luc leaned forward and closed one manacle over her wrist. He flipped her onto her stomach and stretched her arms over her head, looping the handcuff linkage around a vertical bar at the base of the headboard before clasping the other cuff on her other wrist. He tucked a pillow under her hips, angling her ass into the air. He leaned his enormous frame against her back, his rigid cock sliding along between her ass cheeks, and he taunted in her ear, "You can't refuse me now, love." Then, with a low chuckle, he mused, "Let's hope this turns out better for me than it did for the last monster who shackled you."

Eve turned her head to the side and smirked up at him. "I'll just put you in a box in my closet if it doesn't."

"That's my girl," he praised with a chuckle, then smacked her smartly on her ass. He spread her legs wide, settling his thighs between them, and plunged into her.

"Oh, fuck," she moaned into the sheets. The pillow angled her hips perfectly, and he was hitting all the right places as he plowed into her.

His body pressed against her back as his lips caressed the back of her neck. He murmured an incantation as his finger traced over the sensitive spot between her jaw and ear. Pain scorched the flesh beneath his fingertip, and hot blood began to trickle over her throat. The soft warmth of his tongue dragged slowly up beneath her jawline, lapping up every spilled drop, and Eve's core pulsed as pure pleasure surged through her body.

He swelled inside her, and his hips drove him painfully deep, drawing her attention to the fact that she was still a little sore from the savage encounter with Bo the previous night. She gasped and panted, her hands fisting against her restraints, her toes curling as her hips bucked beneath him. The beast stirred, but didn't fully awaken.

The lingering effect of Bo's essence flowing through every fiber of her body kept the monster subdued.

Luc groaned deeply as he sucked her neck, then he whispered dangerously, "I want to keep you shackled to this bed forever." His cock stabbed into her hard and slow, his hips rolling against her ass, drawing another gasp from Eve's lips. The pain from every thrust had intertwined with the pleasure rising in her belly, twisting into the perfect maelstrom of ecstasy.

He fucked her harder as she writhed beneath him. "You know how much it turns me on to imagine it? To have you locked away, at my mercy? I could keep you all to myself and fuck you whenever I wanted to." He tangled his fingers into her hair and lifted her head from the mattress, whispering darkly, "You'd be *all mine*, and you could never run away from me. You could never...*ever*...leave me." His mouth descended on one of Bo's bite marks, and he bit into it and sucked hard, drawing a deliciously excruciating hickey to the surface.

God, he was so psychotically hot.

"You wouldn't," Eve argued, her voice strained as he fucked her into the mattress and gripped her hair.

A low laugh tickled in her ear. "Wouldn't I?" he challenged.

The blooming prickles of fear, the dangerous timbre of his voice, and the glimpse into the dark desires lurking in Luc's heart all cumulated in Eve's core, and her eyes rolled back as that tension detonated, the orgasm tearing through her like a wild, clawed beast.

She hooked her feet over Luc's calves, pressing her ankles behind his knees, pinning his legs as she threw her ass back into him, riding out her pleasure and coaxing his to burst forth inside of her in hot rivulets. She strained against the cuffs around her wrists as he grunted and emptied himself into her, power surging through her like a bolt of lightning.

And then the manacle linkage snapped, and Eve's hand shot up behind her, her fingers digging aggressively into Luc's hair. He slammed his hands into the mattress on either side of her and braced himself over her, a hiss slipping between his teeth.

She could kill him right now. The urge rippled through every nerve-ending, but it was fleeting, receding as quickly as it had swelled up.

He should thank Bo for his life.

Eve pulled his face down next to hers as she trembled and shook in the aftershocks of her orgasm, his chest pressed into her back, and she breathlessly taunted, "You're cute."

He chuckled, the sound warm in her ear. "I'm glad I still amuse you, love." He kissed her cheek. "And you owe me a new pair of enchanted handcuffs."

He helped her sit up, then took her hands in his. The cuffs around her wrists warmed slightly, then popped open, and he removed them, casting them aside like trash. He lifted her marked wrists to his lips and kissed them. His mesmerizing aquamarine eyes slid up to meet hers, and he grinned deviously at her. "I guess I'll have to find another way to trap you."

Eve gazed back at him. "You already have."

"If only." He lay on his back and dragged her down with him, his arms holding her naked body against his. "You didn't try to kill me," he remarked.

"I thought about it," she said flippantly.

"But you didn't. Progress is progress." He brushed his thumb over her arm. "How are you feeling now? Any urge to drain me of all my fluids on repeat in perpetuity?"

She scrunched her face. "Please don't say fluids. And no, my curse seems to be under control."

After a long pause, he apprehensively asked, "Is it because you're getting better at controlling it…or because Bo temporarily lulled it into submission?"

"I don't know."

He wrapped his big hand over her forehead and pulled back, forcing her face to turn up toward his. His eyes searched hers. "Don't lie to me, love. It's ok if it's uncomfortable. I want to know the truth, always."

She averted her eyes. "Bo," she answered.

Luc chewed his lip. "Hm."

"But it doesn't mean anything."

Luc gave a short grunt. "Well, it means *something*. But I know what you're trying to say." He kissed the top of her head. "I love you, Eve."

She rested her hand on his chiseled cheek and squirmed up to reach her lips to his, kissing him softly. "I love you, too." She nestled herself into his side. "Even when you're scary."

He laughed. "Same."

4
He Doesn't Dictate My Bacon Distribution

Eve left so Luc could shower and dress in peace, intending to do the same at her own apartment, but when she walked in, she was surprised to see the anime from last night playing on her TV, Zeke lounging on the couch, Eoduun sitting on the floor in front of him, and Bo sitting at his spot at the kitchen island.

"*Ohayou,*" Bo greeted her. He slid a coffee cup across the counter toward her. "I don't know how hot it is. You came home a little later than I expected." His eyes dropped to the new marks adorning her neck alongside and overtop of his.

She felt his mild tingle of jealousy, but it was overridden by an all-consuming sense of elation at her appearance, the depth of which didn't match the impassive expression on his face. Maybe he was better at hiding his emotions than Eve had realized.

If he had a tail, it would be helicopter wagging.

Zeke leapt over the back of the couch and intercepted her before she made it to Bo. He pressed a quick kiss to her cheek. "Morning, babe." His eyes widened when he saw her neck. "Holy shit, did Luc do that?!" He inspected the fading bite marks. "But those ones look like…" His eyes glanced furtively back at Bo. "Fangs."

"They're mine." Bo said nonchalantly, looking down at his phone. But Eve could feel the pride in his declaration. *She's mine.*

Eoduun stood up and sauntered from the living room, a scowl on his face. He joined Zeke, looking at the marks on Eve. His onyx eyes caught hers knowingly. "I guess only *some* of us are allowed to leave marks," he whispered.

"But that one is definitely a hickey. No fangs," Zeke continued, pointing at another mark on her neck.

"That was Luc," Eve replied. She brushed Zeke's hand away and indicated she was done with the inspection. "Anyway..."

"Bo said you're going on a trip with Luc today?" Zeke questioned.

Eve nodded. "Luc found someone who can tell us more about my biological mother. We're going to see her today."

"I want to make you breakfast before you go," Zeke announced. "You won't need to lift a finger," he added as he headed toward the kitchen.

Eoduun interjected, "*I* will make you breakfast. Zeke will burn your kitchen down." He grabbed her jaw and planted a rough kiss on her lips. In a low voice, he promised, "And when you get back from your trip, we're going to have *you* for breakfast."

A tinge of jealousy churned in her guts. She glanced at Bo, but he sat silently looking down at his phone. The only indicator that he was the source of that jealousy was the blazing yellow wolf eye barely visible beneath his pale eyelashes. His eyes flicked up to meet hers, that golden-yellow warning piercing her from under the scar on his eyebrow. He quickly blinked, burying it back below the dark charcoal.

Eoduun joined Zeke in the kitchen, and Eve snatched up her coffee and approached Bo. She leaned her elbow on the counter next to his, purposely brushing her arm against his. She bumped his thigh with her knee. "You're not going to kill anyone while I'm gone, are you?" she asked as she took a sip of her lukewarm coffee.

It didn't matter that it wasn't hot. Coffee was coffee.

Warm affection spread its tendrils through her as he looked over at her. Was it hers or his?

"Do I *need* to kill anyone?" he asked, raising a brow. He issued it like a challenge.

She rested her chin in her hand and bumped her knee against his thigh again as she glanced at his phone. He quickly blackened the screen, but not before Eve saw an image of two characters kissing. "Looks like you were just getting to the good part. Don't let me bother you," she teased.

"Who are you kidding? You *live* to bother me," he chided, but his countenance was affectionate.

"You love it."

He surprised her by sliding his hand around the nape of her neck and pressing a masked kiss to her forehead – in front of the boys. "I do," he admitted.

Zeke dropped the salt shaker, spilling salt all over the counter. His narrowed eyes bounced between Eve and Bo like he was focused on an intense tennis match. "Something's different," he ventured suspiciously.

"Nothing's changed," Bo asserted. His attention was drawn away as Isaac walked into the apartment, and Eve felt Bo's contempt sizzle in her nerves. "Dammit, I'd almost forgotten he existed," Bo lamented.

"Be nice," Eve implored, nudging his elbow with hers.

He only grunted at her.

"Do you like your new apartment?" Eve signed and spoke to Isaac.

Isaac ignored her question, instead looking between her and Bo curiously, much like Zeke had. He gestured Eve toward him. As she moved toward him, Bo stood from his barstool, watching Isaac distrustfully.

Eve tapped her chin twice with a Y-handshape. *What's wrong?*

Isaac's eyes followed something invisible all the way from her to Bo, across the room. He flipped two D-handshapes from palms up to palms down twice, his brow furrowed, then sawed one flat hand over the other and indicated her and Bo. *What happened between you two?*

Eve touched her temple and drew a Y-handshape away. *Why?*

Isaac watched something she couldn't see. He signed, *Your mists are pulling toward each other like magnets. They're connected.* His eyes widened, then narrowed at her. *Like bonded werewolves.*

Eve held his incredulous gaze. *I don't know what you want me to say.*

Isaac eyed the bites on her neck and signed, *Did he turn you?*

Eve's head snapped in Bo's direction. He was watching them closely. "You can't *turn* anyone, can you?" she asked, a frantic note in her tone.

"What? No," he answered. "You need a full-blooded alpha for that."

She turned back to Isaac and relayed Bo's answer since he couldn't read Bo's lips under his mask, but Isaac seemed dissatisfied. He signed, *I know, but... then how did you bond? That's impossible.*

Eve shrugged, touching her fingertips to her temple and turning her palm down as she drew it away. *I don't know.*

"What's going on?" Eoduun inquired from the kitchen. "You think Bo turned you because he bit you?" He seemed genuinely amused at the absurdity of the idea.

"It's nothing," Eve dismissed. "Isaac's just being a drama queen."

That earned her a look of betrayal from Isaac. He dragged two cupped hands down his torso, palms up, then brushed his thumb under his chin. *I am not!*

"Because Bo bit you?" Zeke asked.

"Something like that," she replied elusively. They didn't need to know about the bond. Not yet, anyway. Especially Eoduun. He would pitch a fucking fit.

Isaac gave her an annoyed look, then pulled *White Fang* from his pocket and settled into his usual chair in the living room.

She raised her hands and flicked her hands from palms inward to palms out and fingerspelled with her brows raised. *Finish* Moby Dick?

He shook his head. *I needed a break from the whale talk.*

Understandable. That book could've been half its size if Melville had stuck to the story. The dude really liked talking about whales.

The entire Smith gang strolled in, and Ruth followed on their heels.

"No Ramil today?" Cassie asked Ruth.

Ruth gave a shrug of her shoulders, but Eve noticed a subtle look of annoyance on Ruth's face. Did she have a falling out with Ramil? Ruth glanced at Eve, and the look of distaste intensified.

"He's hanging out with Veris," Ruth explained spitefully. As she brushed past Eve, she glanced at the TV. "Oh, it's Babhdán's show," she commented.

Eve's eyes widened as Ruth walked past, her willowy form moving to the kitchen to perch gracefully on the barstool next to Bo. The charms on her bracelets rattled against the granite as she folded her arms over the countertop in front of her.

It's Babhdán's show.

That remark unsettled her deeply. Was that…a memory? Or was it something she'd learned again since being here? And the last time she heard Ruth call Bo "Babhdán," she had Eve chained to a wall in Scotland.

"I don't know why this still surprises me," Luc complained as he walked in, his gaze sweeping over the apartment full of people. He appraised Eve. "You haven't showered."

"I have company," she explained.

"This isn't company," he said, gesturing in a wide circle. "They're basically your roommates at this point." He swaggered over to her and grabbed her shoulders, turned her toward the bathroom, then slapped her ass. "Get to it, love. We need to leave soon. Our morning romp put us behind schedule." He made no attempt to lower his voice, and Eve knew everyone heard him. He intended it that way.

Eve rubbed her smarting butt cheek and protested, "But the boys are making me breakfast."

"I'll buy you anything you want for breakfast in Grand Rapids."

"I don't want a bought breakfast. I want Eoduun and Zeke's breakfast."

Luc shoved his hands in the pockets of his neatly pressed black slacks and sighed heavily. He ambled into the kitchen to see the boys' progress, greeting Bo casually as he moved past him.

Eve climbed over the back of the couch and plopped down in the wide-open space between Cassie and Ruger. Cassie was making eyes at Isaac, who was doing his best to ignore her and focus on his book, and Ruger was looking down at his phone. Remi was in the other chair, texting or typing something on his phone.

After a while, Eoduun reached from behind her and lowered a plate of bacon and eggs in front of her face. "Here. Eat."

Eve took the plate, and Zeke came around the couch in front of her and handed her a fork. "I was in charge of flipping the bacon!" he announced proudly, drawing a chuckle from Eve.

"It's beautiful bacon, Z. You did a great job."

He beamed, and Eve couldn't help but beam right back at him. Pure sunshine, that boy.

"Hell yeah, bacon," Ruger said, eyeing Eve's plate. He reached for a piece of bacon, but Zeke's hand shot out and snatched his wrist up with a vise-like grip.

Dagon's voice snarled, "It's not for you!" Vermilion eyes burned with vehemence at Ruger.

Bo and Isaac both leapt to their feet, Isaac fisting the knives in his belt. Luc strode up behind Eve, munching on his own piece of bacon. "Down, boy," he said dismissively, reaching over Eve and tapping two fingers against Dagon's forehead. The red eyes flashed blue, then returned to Zeke's caramel-brown irises as Zeke pressed the heels of his hands against his head.

"Fuck, that hurts," Zeke hissed.

"Keep him under control and I wouldn't have to do that," Luc pointed out disapprovingly.

Zeke wiped his forehead. "You have greasy fingers," he grumbled. He looked apologetically at Eve. "Sorry, babe. Sorry, Ruger. Dagon's being weird today."

"Weird how?" Bo asked, walking up and standing next to Luc.

"Restless, I guess?" Zeke said. "I think he's nervous about letting Eve leave without us. Without him."

Eve scoffed. "He doesn't get to worry about me." She took a piece of bacon and handed it to Ruger, who shoved the whole thing in his mouth before anyone else could stop him. "And he certainly doesn't get to dictate my bacon distribution," she said, keeping a wary eye on Zeke's eyes.

"Yes, help her eat it so we can *go*," Luc encouraged impatiently behind her. She leaned her head back and looked up at him, and he smiled down at her. "Sorry. I'm anxious to have your attention all to myself again."

Eve glanced over at Ruth, who had come from the kitchen to stand on the other side of Luc. She stared at Zeke, not with fear, but with a strange reverence, and it made Eve uneasy.

After a quick shower and change of clothes, Eve packed a small backpack with a change of clothes and some essentials. She returned to the main room with the pack slung over her shoulder.

"I think I'm ready," she announced.

"Excellent," Luc said, pushing off the counter he was leaned against. He held his hand out to her. "Shall we?"

Zeke swooped in and scooped her up in a bear hug. "Not before we say goodbye," he said, his voice muffled in her hair. He kissed her cheek. "I'm going to miss you, babe. Hurry back, ok?"

Eve grinned and squeezed his bulky mass. "I'll miss you, too. I won't be gone long," she assured him.

As soon as Zeke released her, Eoduun stepped in and wrapped one arm around her shoulders, pulling her to him and hugging her briefly against his side. He touched his lips lightly to the top of her head. "What he said," he mumbled.

"Aw, look at you, pouring your heart out," Eve teased, hugging him back.

It earned her a mildly amused grunt.

"Be safe, hon," Cassie said, squeezing her tightly. "I'll make sure these boys behave themselves while you're gone."

A creeping anxiety seeped into Eve's chest. She glanced over at Bo, who was leaning against the kitchen island, surveying her with troubled eyes. He was uneasy about letting her go, but he put on a smile behind his mask, making the corners of his eyes crinkle. He held his hands out at his sides, inviting her to him.

She moved away from the rest of the group and went to him, locking her arms around his ribs. He hugged her around her shoulders and neck, his hand at the back of her head, pressing her cheek to his chest. His cheek rested on her head. "Be good," he murmured. "No running off on your own. You stick to him like glue. Got it?"

"Yes, Daddy," Eve lilted.

"I mean it, Evie."

Eve looked up at him. "I'll be fine. Don't worry about me."

"Fat fucking chance of that." He cupped her face and touched his masked lips to her forehead, and in a tone only audible to her, he whispered, "You are my everything. I'll die if anything happens to you, so if you care about me, you'll keep your cute little ass safe." He touched his forehead to hers, and in the same low voice, he said, "You understand me, little lady?"

Eve looked up into his eyes and smiled. "Well, when you put it that way, how can I refuse?"

He winked his scarred, charcoal eye at her. "That's my good girl," he crooned as he kissed her forehead once more.

Eoduun huffed a disgruntled exhale. "Fuck this," he grumbled to himself, then stormed out of the apartment.

Zeke watched him leave, perplexed at his sudden outburst, then turned back to Eve and Bo. "Seriously, something's different. You two are being weird today."

Luc stepped in and nonchalantly remarked, "They're always weird. Come on, Eve. Let's go."

As Eve turned toward Luc, she caught Isaac staring at her expectantly from the doorway, making to leave. In a V-handshape, he touched his middle finger to his cheek, pointed to Eve, then touched an F-handshape to his chin. *See you soon.*

Eve nodded and returned the gesture, *See you.*

5
Bitches of Babylon

When everyone else left, Eve turned to Luc. "So, where are we going? What am I looking for?"

Luc grinned widely, dimpling his cheeks, and folded his hands behind his back. He bent at the waist, lowering his face toward Eve. "Why don't you take a look?" He raised his pale brows challengingly, watching Eve from behind his round sunglasses.

"How?"

"You have my powers." He touched his first two fingers to his own forehead, like she'd seen him do countless times to Dagon. "Come on in and let me show you."

"But…how?"

"Finger my brain, love. But be gentle, please. It's my first time."

Eve wrinkled her nose. "Ew, Luc. Just…why…"

Luc grabbed her hand and extended her first two fingers, then held them up to his forehead. "I'll even make it easy for you," he offered.

Eve felt an odd psychic ripple, as though she'd just touched the surface of still waters. Echoes of thoughts whispered to her through her fingertips.

"It's like my fingers have ears," she marveled.

"Shhh. Concentrate."

Eve closed her eyes and focused on the whispers, and she felt a mental connection open up where her fingers touched Luc's head. It reminded her of two plastic cups connected by a string in a child's makeshift toy telephone.

A mental image of his erect cock suddenly sprang up in her mind.

Did you just send me a mental dick pic, you fucking pervert?

She heard Luc's laughter bubble into her thoughts. *Just making sure you were fully connected, love. Not so hard, now, was it? The connection, I mean. Not my dick. That was hard.*

Could you just not be you for five minutes and show me where the fuck we're going?

Eve saw a strip of entertainment businesses and restaurants on a busy downtown street. The image zoomed in on one particular building with icy blue lettering over the door. The Iceberg. *I have a club in Grand Rapids. We'll pop up in the manager's office.* Eve saw a small office with a simple desk, filing cabinets, and a minimalist-style couch. *No one should be there right now.*

Eve pulled back, closing the connection, and Luc stood up straight again, tugging at the cuff of his sleeve.

"Ready?" he asked.

"Catch you on the flip side," Eve confirmed, tucking her thumbs under the straps of her backpack. She summoned the image of The Iceberg as she pushed forth the massive effort needed to warp the space around her, and when she saw it before her, she nudged the compression just a little further, opening up her view into the office. It appeared empty. She stepped through.

"We should get a memento to mark this special occasion," Luc said as he popped up next to her. "Our very first jump together."

"Why? We didn't get a memento for the first body we disposed of together, or for the first time you shared your powers with me, or for the first severed head you brought me, and those occasions felt a little weightier than this one."

"I suppose that's true. We've had some amazing times together, haven't we?" Luc commented sentimentally, smiling down at Eve. He laced his giant fingers through hers. "A love story for the ages."

"We're going to end up in a true crime documentary together."

"Well, as long as we're together, that's all that matters," Luc mused as he led her from the office. They made their way through the empty club and exited out the front door. Luc walked up to the passenger side of a sleek black Aston Martin parked at the curb and opened the door, gesturing for Eve to get in.

Eve paused, her gaze dragging from bonnet to boot. "Is this yours?" she asked, lowering herself into the seat.

Luc bumped his sunglasses down his nose, piercing Eve with those aqua eyes. "I keep a car at all my establishments. If I call it a company car, it's a tax write-off," he divulged conspiratorially. "Do you like it?" he asked, resting his elbow on the roof of the car, his other hand on the top of the opened door.

"Nope. Hate it. I bet it's slow as fuck," Eve deadpanned.

"Yeah. I got beat out of the gate by an Outback at a red light last month," Luc replied with mock displeasure.

"It's ok," Eve reassured him. "There's no shame in driving a beater with a heater."

"I should probably just scrap it." He closed the door and came around to the other side, folding his huge frame into the driver's seat. "But, I guess it'll do for now." He rested his wrist on the top of the steering wheel and angled himself toward Eve. He flashed her a dazzling smile and reached his other hand across the space between them, wrapping his fingers gently around her neck. He pulled her face to his and kissed her possessively. When their lips parted, he rubbed his thumb over her pulse point. "Do you want it?" he whispered.

Eve's cheeks flushed. "Right here?!"

Luc chuckled. "The car, love. Do you want the car? Everything that's mine is yours."

Eve pushed back into her seat and admired Luc's beautifully chiseled features as he gazed at her. "I don't need a car, Luc. If I want a ride, I'll just ride you."

Luc's grin expanded. "That's my girl," he said proudly as he slid his sunglasses back in place and started the car.

As Luc weaved effortlessly through the lunch-hour traffic, Eve noticed a faint, niggling tightness behind her sternum. It wasn't necessarily anxiety, but maybe more like…loneliness? She reached over and rested her hand on Luc's solid thigh, hoping touch would ease it.

But it didn't.

What was her malfunction? She couldn't possibly miss everyone already.

She remembered that odd comment from Ruth this morning. *It's Babhdán's show.* Was that what was bothering her? "Ruth said something weird today," she said, then told Luc about it. "It just felt off. I think she's somehow starting to remember."

"She can't *just* remember. You took those memories from her. They're gone from her head. It'd be like trying to remember how to do calculus when you never learned it."

"Then how did she know that was Bo's show?"

"Maybe he watched it when she was bunking with him." Luc arched a brow at her. "And what's the problem? I thought you *wanted* to give her her memories back. We had a little tiff about it, remember? You were willing to take on Dagon's powers just to accomplish it."

"Yeah, but I wanted to give her *select* memories back. If she's somehow gaining access to the whole damn Library of Ruth, I want to know how. And why."

Luc tapped his thumb on the shifter. "I did notice something today," he admitted. "She was wearing her bangles again."

Eve recalled hearing them clinking off the counter this morning when she sat next to Bo, but she hadn't thought anything of it at the time. But, now that she thought about it, it was the first time she'd seen her decked out with all the bracelets since before Eve had stolen her memories.

"Is she stealing her memories back?" Eve wondered. "She's been training with Ramil, learning to use her powers again…what if she's found a spell to get into my head?"

"Or maybe she's just slowly returning to the Ruth she always was," Luc countered. "The Ruth who liked shiny bangles and sparkly things."

Perhaps he was right. It *was* just one silly little comment, and, being that Ruth had spent time living in Bo's apartment with him, it *was* easily explained. If she had her memories back, why would she still be at Knighco, hanging out with people she hated? She would've razed the place and everyone in it.

She rubbed the heel of her hand against her sternum and tried to convince herself that she was worrying over nothing.

Twenty minutes later, they pulled up to the curb in front of a quaint residence in a middle-class cul-de-sac just outside the city. She dug through her backpack and fished out the fake FBI badge she'd been assigned, and clipped it to the waistband of her slacks. When she reached for her door handle, Luc was already outside her door, opening it for her. He held his hand out to her and helped her from the car.

When Luc knocked at the door of the house, a woman Eve's age answered. She wasn't pretty, but she was made up well, with dark, loosely curled hair, immaculate eyeliner, and long, fake eyelashes. Eve was struck at how much she looked like Eve's mother – the mother who'd raised her.

Emma Rose was definitely the baby that was supposed to have gone home with Sylvia twenty-six years ago.

"Emma Rose?" Luc inquired.

The woman looked up at him, clearly awe-stricken. "Yes…"

Luc held out his fake badge. "Special Agent Singer. This is my partner, Agent Mills. We spoke on the phone."

Emma barely spared Eve a glance. She smiled up at Luc. "Yes, yes. Please, come in." She stepped aside and ushered them into her home.

Eve and Luc settled onto a comfortable but worn white couch while Emma brought them each a cup of coffee. She perched on an adjacent chair, angling herself toward Luc.

"You said you had questions about my mom?" Emma posed.

"We've been working through some of our cold cases, and your mother's file caught my attention. I know you were young when it happened, but I was hoping you could walk me through the events leading up to her death. Is there anything that sticks out in your mind? Anything odd, maybe something you didn't feel comfortable sharing with the authorities at the time? I know you were only, what, thirteen when it happened?"

"I was in seventh grade. I'd just turned thirteen – she disappeared on my birthday. Happy fucking birthday to me, right?" Emma said with acidic sarcasm. She took a beat before continuing. "And anything odd? Everything about my mom was odd. Don't get me wrong, she was an awesome mom, and I loved the hell out of her. But she was into weird shit, like, witchcraft stuff, and all her weird friends were, too. I think she got caught up in the wrong kind of coven, if you ask me. I think those nutjobs offered her up in some kind of ritual sacrifice," she spat bitterly.

"I see her body was found in Newbury – that's over three hundred miles away from here. Do you know why she was there?" Luc asked.

Emma shrugged. "I don't know. She traveled around a lot for conventions and craft shows where she sold her herbal remedies, soaps, and lotions, so I just assumed it was something like that. She usually brought me with her, but she left me with my grandma that time so I could help set up for my birthday party the next day. And then she never came back."

"Can you tell us more about her?" Eve urged softly. Selfishly. "About Stacey Rose."

Emma looked at her like she'd only just realized Eve was there. "Well, she was...special. She wasn't like my friends' moms. She never grounded me, and if I needed someone to talk to, or if I had a problem, she was the first person I went to. She was always so understanding and open-minded, free-spirited, and, god, just effortlessly pretty, you know?"

Eve felt a pang of envy. She wanted that. She wished she'd had that kind of relationship with her mother when she was growing up, instead of the passive, stressed-out woman who stood on the sidelines and allowed her stepfather to torment her.

How had she ended up with Sylvia? Was it Stacey who had switched the babies at the hospital, or was it someone else? Did she know *what* she was? How much did Stacey know?

And why couldn't she just have raised her herself? How much different would her life have been if Stacey had kept her?

Didn't she want her?

Didn't she love her?

Or did she know her child was a monster, and couldn't bear to look at her, let alone raise her, so she passed her off onto someone else, like Bo's father had done to him?

Emma shook her head as she continued, "But I think my mom's sweet nature made her a target for people like my dad. I mean, she *did* get dragged into a cult, after all. She was too trusting for her own good. People take advantage of that."

Luc leaned forward. "She was in a cult? When was that?"

Emma waved her hand dismissively. "Oh, that was before I was born. Some crazy religious group my dad was part of. He brought her into it. I don't even remember what they were called. But she got out when she was pregnant with me. She told me they were evil, and that I gave her the strength she needed to finally break free from them and my dad."

Eve heard her phone chime in her pocket, and she mentally reprimanded herself for forgetting to silence it. Should she do it now? She decided to just ignored it.

"Who was your dad?" Eve asked.

Emma shrugged. "I never met him. Mom said his name was Eno, and she joked once that it was fitting because it sounds like the Japanese word for a boar," Emma recounted with a weak smile. "But I didn't want to know him. She didn't talk about him much, but whenever she did, I could tell she hated him. He wasn't a good person. She told me I was the only good thing to ever come from him."

Luc leaned back again and casually crossed one knee over the other. "Do you think it's possible he had something to do with your mother's death?"

Emma shook her head. "No, I doubt it. She hadn't been in contact with him since before I was born." Eve's phone chimed in her pocket again, and Emma glanced at her briefly before continuing. "He didn't even know where we lived. Mom told me he was in Kentucky."

"Do you happen to know his last name?" Luc asked as Eve's phone chimed again. While Eve couldn't see his eyes behind his sunglasses, she knew he was giving her some serious side-eye. She reached into her pocket and fumbled with her phone, finally switching it to silent mode.

"She never told me. She didn't want me trying to look him up."

"Tell us more about the witchcraft," Luc pressed. "You said she had weird friends?"

Emma shared that Stacey belonged to a small group of divorcees and widows that called themselves the Bitches of Babylon, and that she'd been friends with those women for as long as Emma could remember. They would sit around the kitchen table with ancient-looking spellbooks and study and discuss potions and spells and strange-sounding herbs and ingredients, sometimes until the early hours of the morning.

And all the while, Eve could feel her phone vibrating erratically in her pocket. Who the fuck was texting her so much?

"After my mom died, though, only one of her friends stuck around to check on me," Emma said. "She would come see me every week at my grandma's. Her name was Moira MacDougall. She had the wildest red hair I've ever seen and the coolest accent."

Was that the woman Eve had seen with Stacey through Mòrag's memories? "Where is she now?" Eve asked.

"She died about a year after my mom did. She hung herself."

"Oh, Jesus," Eve blurted. "I'm sorry."

"I always wondered why the hell she did it. Was it because of what happened to my mom? Did she know something? From what my grandma said, she didn't leave a note or anything." Emma's eyebrows leapt up suddenly. "Oh! You know what? That reminds me, I do have something you might be interested in. Hold on." She jumped up and disappeared into another room for a few minutes.

In her absence, Luc turned to Eve. "Who the hell is blowing up your phone?"

"Good fucking question," she mumbled as she dragged the device from her pocket. Unread texts, snaps, and messenger notifications littered her lock screen.

Texts from Bo and Isaac.

Snaps from Zeke and Eoduun.

And a messenger notification from Ramil.

…What the fuck did Ramil want?

Before she had a chance to check, Emma returned with a big box in her hands. She plopped it down on the floor by Luc's feet with a grunt.

"I found these papers and records in our attic when I was helping my grandma clean out my mom's house a few years ago. It's mostly just weird witchcraft stuff, but she has a journal in there, too. I started reading it, but it felt too personal. I felt like I was invading her privacy." Emma reached down and rummaged through the papers, withdrawing a well-worn, yellowed journal with a faded flowery design on the cover. She held it out to Luc. "Maybe there's something in it that will help. It's from long before she died, but there's stuff about my dad in there." She gestured to the box when Luc took the journal from her. "You're welcome to take all of it with you. It's not bringing me any closure here in my basement."

Luc and Eve thanked Emma for her time and took the box with them when they left. As Luc dropped the box in the trunk of the car, he plucked the journal off the top and handed to Eve. "You have homework, love," he informed her.

Eve dug her fingers into the achy muscles in her chest as she gazed at the journal in her other hand. This little book contained her mother's words, written by her mother's hand. She was both excited and apprehensive about what she might learn from these pages. She could be holding all the answers to her questions right here in her hands...but she was terrified those answers might destroy her.

6

No Kissing on the Lips

As badly as she wanted to dive into the journal, Eve sat in the passenger seat and scrolled through and replied to the messages on her phone first. She watched Zeke and Eoduun's silly videos and read their nonsense messages, and responded to them with equal nonsense.

Then she opened the text from Isaac, and it concerned her. *Bo's mist is weird now that you're gone. What exactly did you do to him?*

She wrote back, *Is it bad? Is he ok?*

Then she opened Bo's text, and it simply said, *How's it going?*

He didn't seem to be in distress…

She responded, *It's going grand. Isaac is worried about you. Are you feeling ok?*

While she waited for replies, she did a sneaky peek at the message Ramil sent her – viewing it from her notification screen instead of opening it, as she didn't want him to see she saw it yet.

So I hear you are in Grand Rapids? Are you and Luc on a case?

What the hell did he care? It had nothing to do with him. Eve decided to ignore it for now.

A text came in from Bo. *Isaac is WORRIED about me? That's cute. I'm fucking fine. But I'll be better when you're home.*

"Even when I have you to myself, I don't have you to myself," Luc complained from behind the wheel.

She dropped her phone onto her lap. "Sorry. The boys were demanding my attention."

"The zoo just follows you."

"I think maybe I am the zoo."

Luc smirked. "You're definitely the main attraction, in any case." He hit a few buttons on the navigation screen of the infotainment system on the dash and said, "We'll go get some lunch, then check into our hotel. Then maybe we'll see if we can track down some of those Bitches of Babylon." He glanced over at her. "Agreeable, love?"

Eve nodded. "Agreeable."

Eve stared at a menu that couldn't possibly have been in English. "I don't know what any of these dishes are," she whispered to Luc as she absently rubbed her palm over her chest. She felt like an absolute fucking plebeian.

Normally, that wouldn't bother her. But when she was with Luc, she didn't like that feeling. It reminded her of how out of her league she was with a man like him. She felt *unworthy*.

She never felt like this with Bo. He was just as basic as she was.

"Do you want me to extend some suggestions?" Luc offered.

She pulled her phone out and started googling the names of the dishes on the menu, and ignored the new messages and snaps from the boys that popped up in her notifications. "No, I'll figure it out." The last thing she wanted was for him to have to sit there and explain the menu to her like she was a fucking child.

The least they could do was put some damn pictures on the menu.

When the waiter came, Eve ordered by pointing at something with chicken in it that had looked relatively safe in her google search. Luc rattled off his order with such elegance and perfect pronunciation that it made Eve's face flush as he handed the waiter his menu.

Whether it was from embarrassment at her own social failings or because it was impressively hot, she wasn't certain.

Luc reached across the tiny table and held his palm up, and Eve took his invitation, sliding her hand into his. He gazed at her with adoring, beautiful eyes, his sunglasses tucked into his breast pocket.

"What's bothering you, love?"

"What *isn't* bothering me?" she retorted.

"Me, hopefully."

Eve inhaled deeply, then let it out in a heavy sigh. "I just can't shake this feeling that something bad is going to happen. Or something's not right. My chest hurts."

"Is this about Ruth?"

"I don't know, maybe. Or maybe it's about Stacey. Or maybe I'm uncomfortable because I clearly don't belong in a place like this with a man like you. I feel like I should be telling you, 'No kissing on the lips.'"

Luc's brows pinched. "You shut that pretty mouth right now. I never want you to feel that way. I want you to feel special. Worshipped. Loved and adored. I want to give you nice things and fancy meals as offerings to you, not as a display of status over you."

Eve's gaze swept the room, and, as she suspected, several people were giving them sideways glances. "These people can see that I don't belong here. Why can't you?"

Luc's hand tightened around hers. "They won't see much after I burn their eyes from their sockets. You belong everywhere that I do. Why can't *you* see that?"

Eve looked down at her water glass. "I couldn't even decipher the fucking menu."

"How is that relevant? Do I care about that? No. Should you care about that? No." When Eve continued to avoid his eyes, he said, "You're looking at this all wrong, love. You feel out of place because you're not allowing yourself to take up the space you're entitled to. But you have a place, right here with me. Always. Everywhere. Let *me* be your comfort zone. Your safe space. I use you as mine all the fucking time."

Eve's gaze finally rose to meet his. "You do? When the fuck do you ever feel out of place?"

"In your kitchen, when everyone is crowded around and digging through the fridge and laughing and joking and vying for your attention, and Bo's right next to you in his *spot*...I feel like an outsider in the midst of all that. But then I look at you, and I know I'm not. I know I belong, because *you're* there. You ground me." He gave her a beseeching expression. "Let me be that for you."

Her heart squeezed. "But you always seem so at ease, so comfortable with everyone else."

With a mildly rueful smile, he replied, "You know, I'm not social because I like it. I'm social because I have to be. I'm just exceptional at faking it."

Eve hiked a brow at him. "You probably shouldn't admit to me that you're an exceptional liar."

"I didn't say I was a *liar*."

"Didn't you, though?"

"You know I'm not."

She smirked. "Do I, though?"

He leaned back and crossed his arms, narrowing his eyes at her, a playful grin curling his lip. "Are you picking a fight with me?"

Eve shrugged, still smirking.

"That's ok," Luc grinned. "I've come to recognize it's just your love language."

Eve opened her mouth to argue, but closed it again. Shit. He was right.

After their meal, which was annoyingly delicious, they went to the hotel to plan out their next move. As she dug through her pack for her hairbrush, her phone started trilling, notifying her of an incoming video call.

It was Zeke.

She raised the phone and accepted the call. "You just can't live without me, can you?" she teased.

"That's obvious," Zeke said. "But we need you to settle something for us."

Eoduun's face pushed into view. "You need to tell him how fucking wrong he is," he said.

Zeke shoved him away and cried, "I'm not wrong!" He turned back to the phone camera. "In *The Accountant*, they say his real name in it, don't they? Not Christian, but the name he had as a kid."

Eve paused. She shook her head. "I don't think so."

Eoduun pushed back into view. "HA! I *told* you!"

"No, no, but wait," Zeke argued, holding Eoduun at arm's length again. "In the flashbacks to when they were kids, didn't his brother or his dad call him by his name? Wasn't it like Grayson or something?"

"No one says it!" Eoduun yelled back. "They say his brother's name, Braxton, but never his! They only refer to him by his prisoner number."

Zeke looked to Eve. "Really?"

Eve pulled an apologetic face. "Really."

"Are you sure?"

"I'm pretty sure."

"You were so *wrong*!" Eoduun taunted, jabbing his finger in the air at Zeke. "Where the fuck did you get Grayson?!"

"I don't know! I swear I remember someone calling him Grayson!"

As they argued on the screen, Luc stood next to Eve and looked down at the phone. "I see Bo is keeping a tight rein on you two today," he remarked sarcastically.

The boys both stopped and Zeke looked at the phone. "Oh, hi, Luc," he said, waving. "I didn't realize you were right there."

"Go find something to do," Luc replied, then touched the button to end the call.

"Hey, rude!" Eve griped.

"He'll live."

Something caught in Eve's throat, like she'd just remembered something horrible. But in a flash, it was gone.

Did she have a bad dream last night or something? What the fuck was wrong with her today?

Luc sank down onto the plush couch in the living room area of their elaborate suite and pulled out his phone. "Can you check that journal for any names, anyone associated with Stacey that we might be able to track down? I'm going to see if I can find any of these Whores of Babylon."

"Bitches of Babylon," Eve corrected.

"Right. That's what I said."

Eve rolled her eyes and grabbed the journal from the table where she'd left it when they arrived. She reclined on the couch, resting her head on Luc's thigh, and opened the cover.

The first page contained only a quote:

"Please don't expect me to always be good and kind and loving. There are times when I will be cold and thoughtless and hard to understand."

-Sylvia Plath

She flipped the page and started skimming. She was eager to read her mother's story, or at least whatever part of it was represented on these pages, but she was also in a hurry to find names that could be possible leads. Right away, she saw Eno's name.

Well, this is my journal. Eno thinks it would be therapeutic for me to start writing down my thoughts and feelings, so here we go! And Eno, you better not be reading this!

What should I talk about? Me? Maybe I'll read this years from now, when I'm like forty, and remember how cool I used to be when I was 19. Almost 20! Not quite 21. Haha. That won't stop me from ACTING like I'm 21, if you know what I mean. Glug glug. :)

I'm just kidding. Kind of. Anyway, I'm still living at home with Mom and Dad and taking classes at GVSU, but Eno is looking at a place out in Kentucky, so I might be dropping out and moving out there with him. Mom and Dad are not going to be happy about me leaving GR, but I'm a grown woman and I can do what I want.

Eno is the best. He's so damn hot and sexy. I hope when I read this in the future, he's still hot, not all squishy and lazy. You hear that, Eno? Stay in shape! I'm not moving to Kentucky just so you can get soft on me.

The next few entries were more of the same – how great Eno was, how unhappy her parents were about her plans to move to Kentucky with him, and humdrum day-to-day occurrences.

And then there were a couple of entries that made Eve turn crimson, and she understood why Emma had stopped reading. Even though Eve didn't actually know Stacey and Eno, they *were* her biological parents, and it was weird to read diary entries of her *mother* talking about sex with her *father* and how great he was at it. She skimmed past.

Moira is being a major downer. She wants me to dump Eno. She keeps telling me he's bad news, and that the cards are never wrong, but I think she's misinterpreting them. I'm never doing Tarot with her again.

She keeps asking me what a man of his age, with all his money, wants with me. She's afraid he's just using me to pass the time because I'm a hot young piece of ass, but he's not like that. So what if he's a little older than me? It just means he's had time to figure out what he wants. I wish she would at least try to get to know him. Sarah and Lyndsay think he's cool. I don't know why Moira can't just get with it.

Eve shared what she'd learned so far with Luc.

Luc rested his cheek on his fist, his elbow on the arm of the couch, and looked down at her. "Hmm. Emma didn't name a Sarah or Lyndsay when she was talking about the Bitches of Babylon. And I'm not having much luck with the names she did give us." Luc looked at his phone. "So, let's go bother Emma's granny." He held up the screen, showing a GPS map to a red dot just north of GR. "Or, *your* granny, I should say. She may have a better idea of who these Bitches were. Otherwise, I may have to put Celeste on it."

Eve fanned through the pages of the journal. "There's a lot of writing in here. I may still come across something." When she saw a grin quirk the corners of his mouth, she shot a finger up to his lips to stop his remark. "Yeah, yeah, '*that's what she said.*' I know."

His chest shook with a chuckle, and he kissed her finger. "You know me too well. I was actually going to say 'I'd like to come across something, too' but close enough."

She sat up and crawled onto his lap, straddling his thighs and draping her arms around his neck. "You're becoming predictable. What was it you told me when we met? Predictable gets you killed?"

"I did. And it's true. I guess I'm at your mercy."

Eve brought her lips close to his and hovered a hair's breadth away. "You're always at my mercy," she teased.

"Also true." He raked his hand into her hair and closed the distance between their lips, kissing her like he'd been holding it back all day.

Before she could get too swept up in him, she laid her palms against his chest and pushed away. "Sorry, I can't allow you to ravish me right before I go meet my grandma."

Luc groaned. "But you started it," he reminded her.

She gave him a tiny peck on the lips and climbed off his lap. "And I'm stopping it." But it wasn't just the prospect of meeting her grandmother that was quashing her sex drive. It was that persistent, escalating ache in her chest that she just couldn't shake.

Was she homesick already? Was that it?

It was almost beginning to feel like grief.

She checked her phone, and saw she had a text from Isaac in response to her earlier query.

Idk.

Eve gave an exasperated exhale. Helpful, Isaac. Real helpful. She texted back, *What's wrong with his mist? Should we be worried? He says he feels fine.*

A moment later, a reply. *He's lying.* And a follow up, *Are you ok?*

Texting with Isaac was annoying. He completely disregarded the first two questions she asked him. Well, two could play the vague game. She wrote back, *Not entirely.*

Take that, Father Reticence.

She texted Bo again. *Are you sure you're ok? I feel kinda weird myself. Do you feel it too?*

Bo replied almost immediately. *Yeah.*

God, it was like pulling teeth with these guys.

Another text from Isaac popped up. *What's wrong?*

Just feeling uneasy. Don't worry, I'm not going to murder anyone, she assured him.

You should come home where I can keep an eye on you.
Eve rolled her eyes to herself. *Luc will keep an eye on me.*
Isaac quickly replied, *Luc can't handle you like I can.*

7
That's Diabolical

Eve's eyes widened in surprise and she glanced up at Luc to make sure he wasn't anywhere where he could see her phone screen. He was across the room looking down at his own phone, swinging his keys on his finger.

He looked up at her. "Ready?"

Eve quickly backed out of her conversation with Isaac. She approached Luc by the door and slid her shoes on, then almost fumbled the car keys he tossed at her. She looked down at them blankly, then back up at him.

"What? Don't you want to drive?" he asked.

"Fuck no, I don't want to drive!" She tossed the keys back at him. "I don't want to be responsible for something that expensive."

"Are you sure? I don't give a shit about the car," he replied flippantly. "Run it up on the curb if you want. Be reckless. I'm here for it."

"You don't care about much, do you?" Eve commented as she pushed past him out the door, refusing to take the dangling keys back.

"I care about you," he said, following in her wake, twirling the keys on his finger again, his other hand casually in his pocket. "Does anything else really matter?"

Eve scoffed. "A *lot* of other things matter."

Luc simply grunted, slipping his keys into his pocket, and he reached out to clasp Eve's hand in his as he walked alongside her. "Nope. Only you," he disagreed cheerfully.

They stepped into the elevator, and as Luc hit the ground floor button, and the doors began to close, a thick hand invaded its boundaries, forcing them open again. Two young men filed into the elevator, both wearing athleticwear and matching jerseys. They were incredibly well-built and *large*. They were as tall as Luc, but built like Zeke. Football players?

The larger one had short, light brown hair and blue eyes that looked like they were perpetually squinting against the sun. He saw her looking at their jerseys, and he graced her with a cocky, dimpled smile. Christ, he was a big ol' cutie. He reminded her of Zeke. "You a rugby fan?" he asked.

I could be. No, behave. Luc will murder them. "I've never watched it," she said.

Luc surveyed the two titans, and Eve felt the hairs rising on her arms. A tiny arc of electricity sparked between them when his arm brushed hers.

The slightly smaller (but still huge) one had big brown eyes and longer dark hair, and he ran his hand through it as he told Eve, "We're playing at Grand Valley tonight. You should come watch us. We can have them set aside a ticket for you...," his gaze lifted to

Luc's, "...both." He focused on Eve again. "I think we can make a fan out of you," he said confidently.

The bigger one winked at her.

"Tempting," Luc replied, smiling amicably. "But I don't think you boys will be playing tonight."

The two rugby players shared a confused look, then laughed it off. "Oh, we'll definitely be playing."

Luc shrugged his shoulders. "Maybe. But you'll have to clean the shit out of your uniforms first."

The big one crinkled his brow. "Dude, what the fuck?"

The elevator stopped at the first floor, and Luc stepped forward, blocking the young men so Eve could exit first. "Good luck, lads," Luc said as he stepped backwards out of the elevator, running his hand over the entire control panel, lighting up every floor button. He aimed a finger pistol at them, and before they could follow him out of the lift, he made a *pew pew* sound and "shot" the two boys.

They both made a weird strangled sound and collapsed to the floor as the doors closed on them. Luc turned to Eve, a big smile on his face. He happily took her hand and started to lead her away.

"Luc!" she whispered harshly. "What the fuck! Did you just kill them?!"

"No, of course not! I just made them shit their pants," he replied, like it was no big deal.

"Why would you do that?!"

"I didn't like the way they looked at you."

Eve bit back a chagrined smirk. "How did you make them shit their pants?"

"Electric shock to the bowels and lower body. I basically tased them. They'll be riding that elevator in their own shit for the next few minutes until they recover leg mobility."

Eve ran her free hand down her face. "God, Luc. That's diabolical."

"Thank you."

"It wasn't a compliment."

"It was," he asserted as he held the lobby door open for her and followed her out to the parking lot.

When he reached for the car door to open it for her, she quickly grabbed it first. Before she could wrench it open, however, he planted a big hand on it and held it closed.

"Hey, now," he complained, sounding offended.

"I can open my own door," she insisted.

"But I want to open it for you," he countered.

"You've done enough today."

"Not nearly."

As Eve opened her mouth to argue, they both heard a tone of authority shout, "Hey! You, there!" They saw a security officer hurrying from the hotel doors, pointing at them. "You wait right there!"

Luc dropped his hand from the door and allowed Eve to yank it open. "Time to go!" he announced, a hint of delight in his voice as his long legs quickly carried him around the car to the driver's side. He jumped in, turned the key, revved the engine, and took off like a bat out of hell before the chubby security guard made it across the parking lot.

"You got us in trouble," Eve reprimanded.

"Yeah, I did," Luc laughed, clearly proud of himself. He met Eve's look of disapprobation with a sexy grin and returned his attention to the road. "Relax, I'll sort it."

A mile down the road, Eve pointed out, "Those guys weren't an actual threat, you know."

"I know." He bumped his sunglasses down his nose and fixed her with a simmering gaze. "You're *mine*." He smirked and turned back to the road. "But those jocks didn't fully understand that. They required a lesson."

"Maybe I'll just tase the next woman that talks to you or looks at you wrong," Eve threatened. When Luc turned an amused expression her way, she held her hand up. "Never mind. I should've known better. You'd love that."

"Fuck yeah, I would."

Eve sighed and leaned her head back against the headrest. She looked over at Luc. "You're an awful lot of trouble. You're lucky you're pretty."

He smirked. "I know. If I was ugly, you'd have a restraining order and assault charges against me by now."

Eve and Luc sat in creaky wooden chairs at an old table in Sorrel Rose's kitchen while the old woman brought over a plate of cheese and crackers, placing it in the middle of the table.

"Please help yourselves," she urged. She sat at the head of the table and folded one bony hand over the other in front of her. She fixed Eve and Luc with suspicious, pale green eyes. Keen eyes. The woman wasn't tall or physically imposing, by any means, but she was intrinsically intimidating. "Young man, are you visually impaired? Or are the sunglasses simply a fashion choice?" Her lips formed a hard line. "Because I suspect it is the latter, and if that is the case, I would kindly request you remove them so I can look you in the eye while we speak."

An easy laugh erupted from Luc's throat. He slipped off the glasses and tucked them into his pocket. "Yes, ma'am. My apologies."

Her thin eyebrows jumped up when she saw Luc's striking eyes. "Why on earth would you hide those beauties?" she asked in surprise.

"You're too kind. I have a mild sensitivity, that's all. I sometimes forget to take the glasses off."

Sorrel gave a short, "Hmm," but her expression betrayed a sense of skepticism. "So, what do you folks expect I can help you with? It's been thirteen years since my Stacey was murdered. What's changed?"

"We've been looking into her case, and we don't feel that every possible lead was followed. Tell me, Mrs. Rose, did you ever hear

Stacey or Emma talk about, excuse my language, the Bitches of Babylon?"

Recognition lit in her eyes. "Oh, that silly little club Moira started? They thought they were witches, but they were harmless. Those girls watched *Practical Magic* one too many times."

"Witches?" Luc pressed.

"Not the devil-worshipping kind, so put any Satanist nonsense out of your head right now. No, they worshipped nature. They believed Mother Nature extended beyond just earthly elements, and extended through the very fabric of the universe. They believed they could appeal to Her with spells and incantations to alter their lives, to improve their fortunes." Sorrel sighed and rested her chin in her hand. "But, I suppose after that dreadful cult business, Stacey needed something positive to believe in."

"Do you happen to know where the women from the Babylon club are now? We would really like to speak with them," Luc said.

"Moira's gone, rest her soul. Hung herself not long after Stacey was murdered. It made some people wonder if she had a guilty conscience, if she had something to do with Stacey's death, but I never once bought into that. Moira loved Stacey." Sorrel tilted her head toward them conspiratorially. "Maybe a little too much, if you know what I mean. That girl was always a little different. Never showed any interest in the boys." Sadness sagged her aging features as she averted her eyes. "I think she just couldn't handle her broken heart after Stacey was taken from her."

"Were you close with Moira?" Eve asked.

"She'd been best friends with Stacey since she was in middle school, when her family moved here from Scotland. The two were inseparable. Until Eno, that is. But Moira brought her back. I will forever be grateful to her for that.

"The other girls, though," Sorrel continued, "she didn't meet until after she returned from Kentucky. But I have no idea where they are now. They dispersed pretty quickly after Stacey. I heard Kristen got married to some rich asshole and moved to Europe, and a few years back I saw Penny in the breakfast aisle at Meijer. She acted like she didn't know me." Her eyes drifted to the window. "That's what happens when tragedy hits you. No one knows how to interact with you anymore. They don't know what to say to you, so they avoid you. You become a leper, like your grief is somehow contagious and no one wants to catch it."

"I'm so sorry," Eve consoled.

"Me too, honey," Sorrel replied bitterly.

After a moment of silence, Luc asked softly, "Do you have any theories about what happened to Stacey?"

Sorrel cleared her throat and crossed her arms on the table, leaning forward. She seemed to steel herself. "I think it was Eno, but the cops wouldn't entertain it. They said there was no indication that there had been any contact between him and Stacey since she left him in Kentucky all those years ago. But I *saw* the bastard. Two weeks before she left for the U.P., I saw him drive by in a big black SUV. No one believes me, but I *know* it was him. He looked me right in the eye as he went by. It gave me the heebie-jeebies." She looked between Luc and Eve. "That bastard killed my baby."

Luc frowned. "That wasn't in any of the police reports."

"I just said they didn't believe me, didn't I?"

"Well, we will make sure to look into it," he assured her. "What can you tell me about Eno? Was that his real name?"

"It was short for Enoch. Such a strangely biblical name for this day and age, I always thought. Enoch Azra. But I doubt that was his *real* name. I think he picked it to fit in with that fanatical cult. Idiots thought they could start the Apocalypse. They even named themselves after some aspect of the Book of Revelation – The Locusts of Abaddon."

Luc's head jerked up. "Locusts of Abaddon? Are you sure?"

"I wouldn't have said it if I wasn't, son. Why, have you heard of them?"

"Their file has crossed my desk before," he disclosed.

"Then you know what a bunch of loons they all are," Sorrel said.

"And dangerous," he added, furrowing his brow. "But why would he wait *years* to make his move? And why attack in Newbury? What was it that brought them both there?"

Eve knew what was there, and Luc obviously did, too. Her. He was feeling Sorrel out.

"When Stacey escaped from Eno and that cult, she and Moira hid in Newbury for a couple of months. That was where Emma was born, on Halloween night. What possessed Stacey to return thirteen years later, I'll never know. She left Emma with me on October 30th, promising to be back for Emma's birthday party the next evening. I never saw her again.

"But why did Eno wait so long to come after her? I don't have an answer for that," Sorrel said. "If he wanted to find her over the years, she wasn't hard to locate. I've lived in this house since she was a baby, and she bought a house just a few blocks from here." She shook her head ruefully. "I don't have proof that he's behind her death, but I feel it in my gut. I *know* it in my heart."

"Did you tell Stacey that you saw Eno drive by?" Eve wondered.

"Of course. She needed to know that he was around," Sorrel said. "She acted like it was no big deal and told me I had to be mistaken, but I could tell she was as unsettled by it as I was." She glanced at Eve, studying her briefly. "Are you quite all right, dear? You keep pressing your hand to your chest."

Eve quickly dropped her hand, not even realizing she'd been doing it again. "I'm fine, thank you. Just sore from my workout." She ignored the concerned look Luc cast her.

"My Stacey used to do that when she was feeling uneasy. How did she put it? The universe was…unbalanced. I know witchcraft is silliness, but sometimes it did seem like those girls had tapped into some kind of tangible connection." Sorrel leveled a meaningful gaze at Eve. "If Stacey taught me anything, it's to never ignore those nagging feelings that something's wrong. That chest rubbing thing?" Sorrel pointed at Eve. "Stacey was doing that the day she left for Newbury."

8

Fucking Psychotic, Homicidal Asshole

In the car on the way back to the hotel, Luc asked, "Are you having a Don't Think It, Don't Say It episode and not telling me?"

"This doesn't feel like that," she said as she flipped open Stacey's journal. "I don't even know if they're strictly *my* feelings."

Luc gave a short laugh. "Whose feelings would they be?"

Eve avoided his eyes as she looked down at the journal. "Bo's." She could feel Luc looking at her, but she focused on the pages in front of her. She flipped through the dates, looking for October.

"You feel Bo's feelings?"

Eve nodded. "Apparently."

"Does he feel *your* feelings?" Luc wondered.

"Yep."

Luc reached over and took the journal from Eve's hands and tucked it under his leg as he drove.

"Hey!" Eve complained.

"When were you going to tell me this?" Luc asked accusingly.

"When I felt it was relevant. And now it is. Possibly."

"So the bond is real." There was an air of defeat in Luc's tone.

"Of course it's real. Even Isaac could see it in our mists, or auras, or whatever. They pull to each other."

"Hm." Luc reluctantly handed the journal back to Eve. "I should probably check in with Bo, then."

"He said he's fine," Eve shared.

"He always says he's fine, even when he isn't. *Especially* when he isn't."

Fuck. He was right. She should've considered that. Shit, even Isaac said something was wrong with him, and she was quick to disregard it because she *wanted* to believe nothing was wrong.

They teleported from the parking lot to the hotel room to bypass the security guard who was still lingering in the lobby. Luc excused himself to the other room in the suite to call Bo while Eve settled onto the couch with Stacey's journal. She tried not to eavesdrop on their conversation, but it was impossible when she was in possession of Bo's hypersensitive hearing.

The moment she heard Bo's voice when he answered Luc's call, it hollowed her guts. Longing clawed at her insides and sucked the air from her lungs. She yearned to be near him. To feel his touch, to run her fingers over his scars, to hear his voice murmuring low in her ear. The ache in her chest gaped like an abyss, threatening to drag her into its depths.

She heard Bo inhale sharply on the other end of the line, and she knew he'd felt it, too.

Luc began to speak, but Bo cut him off. "Where's Evie? Is she ok?" His tone was frantic.

Luc leaned back and glanced at Eve through the doorway separating the rooms, and found her watching him. "She's here.

She's fine, though she's been complaining of an achy-breaky heart, and she swears it isn't gas."

"Don't make me sound stupid!" Eve chastised, whipping a throw pillow from the couch at him. Luc pivot-turned twice to dodge it, scuffing his shoe on the floor like he was line dancing.

He continued, "And she tells me you two share *feelings* now, so I was curious what you made of it."

"I don't know," Bo replied. "I thought it was just because I missed her, but I don't think that's all it is. I think it's coming from her. It feels like...impending doom."

"Don't Think It, Don't Say It?" Luc supplied.

"Is it that? Did she have a premonition?"

Luc looked expectantly at her again, and she shook her head. "I already told you I didn't think it was that," she reminded him.

"Just keep your wits about you, brother," Luc told Bo as he disappeared back into the other room. "Something could be afoot." Then, shifting the subject, he asked, "Do you remember the Locusts of Abaddon cult?"

Eve finally gave up the pretense and rose from the couch, joining Luc in the other room. She leaned her shoulder on the wall in the archway between the rooms, the journal dangling in her hands. Luc was seated at the small café-style table in the room, his ankle crossed over his knee, his elevated foot bouncing in an uncharacteristically nervous tick.

"Ramil's cult?" Bo said. "How could I forget? Bunch of fucking fruit loops."

"Eve's biological father is, or was, a Locust," Luc revealed.

Eve broke into the conversation. "Wait a minute, that cult Eno was in was the same cult *Ramil* came from? What if Ramil knows something about my mom's death?!"

"It's possible," Luc said, already having put those pieces together. "He would've been sixteen or seventeen, so plenty old enough to have been part of their monster mafia."

"Did you want me to talk to him?" Bo inquired.

"No, I'll interview him when we get home."

"And when is that going to be?" Bo asked anxiously.

"Tomorrow. I have some business to attend to at The Iceberg tonight, since I'm here anyway."

"Send Evie home, then."

Luc chuckled, then replied simply, "No." He rested his chin in his hand and gazed across the little table at Eve standing in the archway. "She'll be accompanying me tonight."

Bo grunted. "Team Delta should be back tonight. I can check in with Zephlyn and see if he has any insights on this feeling of dread."

"Excellent. Have Celeste do a deep dive into LOA for me, too. I want to know what they've been up to since we last threw hands with them."

"Copy that."

"Hold down the fort for me, brother, and we'll see you tomorrow." He ended the call, but kept staring at Eve. "Did you bring your red bottoms, by chance?"

"I didn't think I'd need them," she said. "I don't have any outfits appropriate for clubbing."

Luc tapped on his phone screen, and after a minute, he shoved it in his pocket. "A dress and a new pair of shoes will be here in an hour or two." He stood and stretched, then dipped his head toward Eve's hand on her chest. "You're doing it again. You know, *I* can rub your chest for you if you want," he grinned slyly.

"Ew, stop it. That's not helping." She pushed away from the wall and turned, intending to return to the couch. But Luc intercepted her, catching her around the waist and pulling her back, her shoulder blades pressing against his hard chest.

He squeezed his arms around her, holding her tightly, his cheek resting on her head. "Then just let me love on you for a minute," he begged.

"I don't have a choice, do I?"

She felt him shake his head, mussing up her hair as he squeezed her tighter. "Nope."

Eve smiled. "I think I'm beginning to understand how my childhood cat felt now," she teased.

"I will love you and squeeze you and call you George," Luc retorted, rocking her side to side.

She giggled and relented, relaxing in his embrace. She leaned her head back against his chest, and Luc nuzzled her temple, kissing it lightly.

In a soft, low voice, he asked, "Do you think we should go home tonight? Would it make you feel better?"

Eve didn't answer immediately. It would make her feel better, but the longer she stayed away, the longer everyone at Knighco was safe from Apep.

Apep. Was *he* the one causing her chest ache?

Fuck. The more possible explanations she came up with, the more she realized it could be *anything*.

Or...maybe it was just gas.

Eve glanced down at the journal in her hands. "I need to do my homework," Eve said, waving the journal from beneath Luc's embrace.

Luc sighed. "I know. I do, too. Goddamn it." As he released her, he blurted, "Oh, fuck. I was going to join that video meeting with Sister Fiona and Father Fuckwad tonight, too." He angled his head back and expelled an annoyed groan.

"Father Fuckwad? That's not nice."

"He's not nice. But hey, maybe this meeting will have a happy outcome. Maybe they'll recall him back to the Vatican."

Eve's scowl softened to disappointment. "That wouldn't make me happy."

Luc was surprised. "You don't want them to call off their sanctimonious assassin?"

"Well, obviously I want *that*, but I don't want Isaac to leave."

"He doesn't belong in Knighco, love."

Eve appealed, "He absolutely belongs with us. He checks all the boxes, and you know it. Not to mention the fact that…" Eve hesitated and looked off to the side. "…That my curse responds to him."

Luc held up his index finger. "*Once.* He exorcised your powers *once.* It doesn't make him the goddamn Abomination whisperer."

Eve rolled her eyes. "He's useful."

"Is that what we're calling it now?" he shot back spitefully. "We're not keeping him just because you have a crush on him." He dragged his phone from his pocket and looked down at it.

"But you'll throw him out because of it?"

Luc paused with his body angled slightly away from her. His eyes slid up to meet hers over the rim of his sunglasses, his head tilting toward her. In a deceptively measured tone, he warned, "Careful, love. You're going to get that priest killed, and I won't even feel guilty enough to mention it in confession."

Eve folded her arms and shifted her weight on one leg, popping her hip out. "You wouldn't kill a good man."

Luc turned and faced her, his expression unchanging. "Are you certain of that?"

Eve held his gaze, but didn't answer.

"Because you shouldn't be," he continued. "When it comes to you, there are a lot of questionable things I would do. Downright horrendous things I would do…and have done." A psychotic smile caressed his lips as his aquamarine eyes glimmered with unhinged glee. "Oh, the atrocities I would commit."

Jesus, he was terrifying.

But she toed up to him, because right now, she was stronger than him. She jabbed a finger in his chest and scowled up at him. "You hurt Isaac, and I'll *never* touch you again."

They shared a tense, heated stare-down. Without breaking eye contact, Luc seethed, "He's already causing problems between us. Weaseling his way in. There is no room at our table for *him*."

"I'm not asking you to invite him to the fucking table, Luc. I just want him on our team."

"He will want a fucking seat. Mark my words, love. He *will* want it. He *already* wants it. Don't delude yourself."

Eve threw her hands in the air in exasperation. "So fucking what? Maybe he belongs at the table, too. It takes a lot of fucking teamwork to keep this stupid fucking curse under control, and he is an obvious asset. So what is it, *really*? Are you threatened by him? By the quiet little exorcist with the big dick?"

Luc's eyes blew wide, and Eve felt the earth rumble under her feet. The boring paintings of flowers on the wall rattled against the drywall. In barely a whisper, he growled, "Apparently, I am. And I don't take threats lying down."

And then he disappeared.

Fuck! Fuck! Eve drew from her energy reserves and forced the space around her to warp and bend, and, using the connection between their matching tattoos, she dove through just in time to take Luc down in a spectacular tackle. Luc's sunglasses flew from his face as the pair of them rolled across the floor of Isaac's apartment, smashing into the leg of the coffee table and knocking a ceramic cup onto the hardwood, shattering it. She scrambled onto his back and locked an arm around his thick neck in a rear naked choke, her legs clenched in a vise around his ribs to limit his lung capacity.

Anaconda squeeeeeeeze...

But Luc wasn't staying down. He stumbled to his feet with Eve clinging to his back. He lunged for a wide-eyed Isaac, who had a butcher knife in his hand, crouched and ready to defend himself in the kitchen.

Bracing herself and wringing the last bit of energy she had, Eve ripped through space, dragging Luc's enormous frame through with her, and dropped them both back in the hotel room in Grand Rapids. She fell off of him like a salted leech and lay on the floor, exhausted to her bones.

Luc spun around, sweeping his eyes over the hotel room, then spotted her on the floor. "I don't know whether to be livid or impressed, love," he huffed, then flopped onto the floor next to her, sprawling on his back. "You're a fucking force, you little monster."

"Stop trying to kill my friends," she demanded breathlessly.

"I'll stop trying to kill them when they stop trying to steal you from me."

"Maybe you should focus on what you can do to convince me to love *you* rather than focusing on what you can do to stop me from wanting anyone *else*."

Luc turned to her and smirked. "I can multitask."

She sighed. "You are such an asshole."

"Loveable asshole."

She arched a brow at him. "Fucking psychotic, homicidal asshole."

"Yet loveable, nonetheless."

She rocked her head side to side on the floor in dissent. Her phone was buzzing and ringing from the couch where she'd left it, and she realized she was going to have to explain their latest shenanigans to both Isaac *and* Bo, who likely scented them the moment they made the jump.

She crawled to the couch and grabbed her phone, leaning her back against the front of it as she sat on the floor and checked the messages and missed calls.

Isaac: *WTF*

Bo: *Were you just here???*

Two missed calls from Bo.

Another text from Isaac popped up. *Why is he trying to kill me this time?*

She sent off a text to Isaac: *He's an asshole.*

Then she texted Bo: *Sorry, I had to wrangle Luc. All good now.*

Moments later, she had an incoming call from Bo. She looked over at Luc, still lying on the floor, as she answered. "What's up, Daddy?"

She saw Luc shake his head.

"What the fuck just happened?" Bo demanded.

"Lover's quarrel."

"Evie."

"Your brother's a hot-headed child in Armani."

"What did he do now?"

Luc could hear Bo's voice on the other end cutting through the silence of the hotel room, so he called out, "I was trying to do us both a favor. You should go finish it, Bo."

Eve clarified, "Luc decided, yet again, that Isaac needed to feel his wrath. I intervened and diverted him back to the hotel. No biggie."

Luc rolled onto his side and rested the side of his head in his hand, propping his elbow on the floor. "He wants to take our girl, Bo. Go kill him."

Bo bristled. "Excuse me?"

"Ok, that's enough, killer," Eve told Luc condescendingly, holding up a hand. To Bo, she said, "Nobody wants to take anyone. Ignore him. I suggested something I probably shouldn't have, and he reacted badly. No need to get involved."

Luc clambered over to her and blurted into the phone, "She asked if I was threatened by his big dick, Bo."

A tidal wave of Bo's jealous rage momentarily pushed out the ache behind Eve's sternum.

"Evie!" Bo roared.

Eve threw her head back onto the couch cushion and groaned. "I was irritated, and I chose my words poorly," she explained. "I'm sorry! But please don't take it out on Isaac. He's just over there minding his own business and I don't need you two harassing him because of some dumb shit that *I* said."

"You're right, Evie," Bo ceded. "We shouldn't take it out on him." His voice dropped low, the timbre both threatening and seductive. "We should take it out on *you*."

Luc hummed in agreement next to her. "What an incredibly astute suggestion, brother." Luc leaned over Eve and molded his hand to her jaw. He brought his beautiful lips close to hers. "Someone's been a very, very bad girl."

9
Mine

A shiver of anticipation racked Eve's body, and she almost dropped the phone. She looked up at Luc from beneath hooded eyes.

"Give her hell, Luc," Bo instructed, but she knew the words were more for Eve's benefit than Luc's. Bo ended the call.

But they had both failed to remember one small detail.

Eve tossed the phone behind her onto the couch and raked her fingers into Luc's hair. She pulled his mouth to hers and kissed him ferociously, then pulled back. She spoke against his lips, "You can't punish me, baby. I'm more powerful than you."

A low, amused chuckle rose from Luc's throat and caressed her lips in a soft, staccato exhalation. "Minor detail."

As Luc prepared to dive in for another kiss, a loud knock resonated through the room. Eve froze. Had security finally come to kick them out after the rugby player incident?

"Ignore it," Luc said.

But the knock came again, more insistent this time. And then a voice. A voice Eve *hated*. "Luc! I know you're in there. Security called your father."

Fucking *Mira*.

Luc's whole body stiffened. "Fuck," he spat.

"What the fuck is she doing here?" Eve demanded incredulously.

"I don't fucking know." He drove his fingers through his hair. "He could've just fucking called me himself." He stood up and held his hand out to Eve, but she shook her head.

"Nope. I'm staying right here." She grabbed Stacey's journal and opened it to reinforce the point. "You deal with the bitch."

Luc walked away toward the door, and Eve stared blankly at the journal in front of her. She heard the door open.

"What the fuck are you doing here, Mira?" Luc inquired curtly.

"Your father sent me. He wants me to bring you to the club to speak with him. He's not impressed by your latest antics."

"What the fuck is *he* doing here? He was supposed to be in Florida."

"He was, but then he heard you were running around Grand Rapids with your little gal pal, causing trouble, and he put me on his personal jet and sent me here to fetch you. He had some business to finish up, but he should've made the jump to the club by now."

"And if I refuse to meet with him?"

There was a pause before Mira responded. "I think we both know the answer to that," she said ominously.

Luc grunted. "Well, I can't leave just yet. I'm waiting on a delivery, and then Eve and I will make an appearance. I happen to have business to attend to at The Iceberg tonight anyway."

Eve heard heels clicking on the hard floor as Mira invited herself in.

"By all means, make yourself at home," Luc said sarcastically.

"You know, you used to take *me* to places like this," Mira remarked loudly, and it made Eve's blood boil, just as Mira had intended.

"'Used to' being the key phrase," Luc shot back.

The svelte woman rounded the couch and saw Eve sitting on the floor with the journal, and she gave Eve a disdainful look. It was only then that Eve realized her shirt was stretched, her hair was a mess, and she was missing a slipper flat after her multi-spatial scuffle with Luc.

"I lost my shoe," she mumbled to herself, wiggling her toes.

Eve pushed up off the floor and sat back on the couch, combing her fingers through her tangled mane and straightening her shirt. She kicked off the remaining shoe as she watched Mira gracefully lower herself into the chair across from her, elegantly crossing one long, toned leg over the other, allowing her pencil skirt to ride up her black-stockinged thigh. She watched Luc moving around the room with keen eyes behind her stylish, thick-framed glasses, her manicured hands folded together over her knee.

Eve reached back for her phone, trying to ignore the fuck-me eyes Mira was casting at Luc. She discovered she had three texts from Isaac.

What's going on?

Are you ok?

Eve?

She wrote back, *All good. Sorry about your apartment. And mug.*

Isaac was quick to reply. *Luc's sunglasses are still here. And your shoe. Why was he trying to kill me again?*

Eve sent, *Sorry.* Then she added, *Really. I am sorry. I poked the beast when I shouldn't have.*

"Do you have a rash or something?" Mira asked in disgust, eyeing Eve with an expression even Regina George would wilt under.

She was rubbing her goddamn chest again.

Eve ignored her and read the text Isaac just sent her. *I don't need you to protect me from him.*

She huffed to herself. *You really did. Trust me.*

His texting dots danced for a long time before his reply finally came in. *No, trust ME. I'm fully capable of handling him. Stop putting yourself between us, and maybe he'll learn that I'm not a beast to be poked, either.*

Well. Ok then.

Noted.

Luc passed by Eve and Mira with a binder full of papers under his arm, headed toward the room with the table. As he passed, he said to Eve, "I'm going to sort a few things while I have a few minutes."

Mira jumped up like an eager lapdog. "I can assist."

Luc just shrugged at her as she fell into step behind him.

Eve stared down at her phone, then backed out of her messages and stared blankly at her home screen. She was relieved that Mira was no longer sitting across from her, watching her, but she was also annoyed that she was now sitting across from Luc, out of Eve's line of vision, working closely with him.

Mira was so much more useful to him than Eve was, and it made her feel inadequate. It also made her feel like dragging him back to the bedroom and showing him all the ways in which she was *superior* to Mira.

But then she started to wonder what kind of a fuck Mira was. What if Eve *wasn't* superior? What if Mira was a better lover than Eve, and Luc only chose Eve because of his inexplicable obsession with her? Maybe Mira was a real acrobat in the bedroom. A hoover. Adventurous. Accommodating. Flexible. Submissive? Maybe not. Luc didn't necessarily like submissive. He *liked* it when Eve was a bitch to him. He'd told her as much.

Is that what had drawn him to Mira in the first place? Because, wow, what a bitch.

Did Luc lay with Mira afterward and tell her how beautiful she was or how amazing she'd been? Did he moan her name? Did he sink his teeth into her flesh? Did he tease her and trail his lips over her whole body? Did he tell her he loved the way she tasted after he'd had his face between her legs? Did he like how long and lean she felt under him, wrapped around him, on top of him?

Did he ever miss fucking Mira?

Eve's heart was hammering in her chest as she dropped her phone and hopped up from the couch. *He's mine. Mine. Mine mine mine mine mine....*

She didn't say a word as she stormed into the other room and strode straight up to Luc. He looked up at her, and she caught his face with both hands, holding him in place to lay a demanding kiss on those perfect fucking lips.

She heard the pen he was holding clatter to the table, and his hands were on her and in her hair in the next instant. He held her to him as he stood, hiking her legs around his waist. Without a word to a put-out Mira, Luc carried Eve out of the room, across the living room area, and back into the bedroom, kicking the door closed with a loud slam behind them.

Luc took Eve down to her back on the bed, and Eve made quick work of his belt and fly while his lips seared a path down the side of her neck. She then kicked out of her own pants and underwear, flinging them over the side of the bed.

Luc chuckled, saying, "What's got you all fired up?"

Eve rolled him over onto his back and tugged his slacks and boxers down just enough to release his rock-hard erection. She gathered a pool of saliva on her tongue, then ran it up the underside of his dick, from root to tip. With her lips still brushing his crown, she said, "This is *mine.*" She crawled over him and straddled his hips, taking his cock in her hand and aligning it, notching it at her slick entrance.

As she lowered herself onto his length, he closed his eyes and threw his head back into the pillow. "Fuuuuuck…" he moaned.

She leaned over him as she rolled her hips against him. One hand gripped his hair while the other stretched as far as it could across his thick throat, her fingers leaving light impressions on the sides of his neck. "You belong to *me*, Lucius Fagerberg," she declared, gazing down into his eyes, daring him to challenge her claim. "Every fucking part of you is *mine*. No one else will ever have you again. *Ever. Only me.*"

Luc's beautiful eyes were wild with desire as they locked with hers. "Fuck, Eve. You're the hottest thing I've ever seen. God, I fucking love you." He fisted his hand in her hair and pulled her lips to his, devouring a fervent kiss. "I'm all yours, baby," he promised. "Forever and always. Until I fucking die."

Eve sat up and gyrated her hips, throwing her head back and reveling in the way he stretched her. His palms slid up her belly, and he cupped her breasts, enjoying the weight of them in his big hands. Eve ran her palms up over the backs of his hands and gazed down at him as she rode him, and as he gazed back up at her, mesmerized by the vision of her on top of him, she knew she had him. At least in this moment, he was thinking of no one else. Tempted by no one else. Belonging to no one else.

Hers.

Mira could fuck right off a cliff on a moped.

Luc wrapped one arm around Eve's back and flipped her over onto her back. He lifted her calves to his shoulders and buried himself deep as he leaned over her, folding her in half. He drove into her, hitting just the right angle to draw desperate whimpers from her lips with every thrust as the tension in her core tightened.

Luc lifted her hips off the bed as he rolled her weight onto her back and shoulders, her knees brushing her shoulders as he leaned forward and took her mouth with his, the stroke of his tongue against hers matching the impossibly deep, hard strokes of his cock as he rammed down into her. She moaned into his mouth as her walls clenched around him, an eruption of bliss surging through her as the orgasm broke free and rocked her body.

"And you're *mine*, Eve," Luc asserted with a growl as he poured himself into her, his cock swelling, his frenzied thrusts drawing out a renewed burst of pleasure in her core.

She made sure Mira heard every utterance of her and Luc's exultations.

Eve lay in Luc's arms, her jealousy over his history with Mira remedied for the moment, and stroked her thumb over the sharp angles of his cheek and jaw.

"Such a pretty face," she mused.

"I'm glad you like it. It's *yours*, after all."

"Fucking right it is," she agreed.

Luc ran his finger over her sternum, then splayed his hand over her chest. "Better now?"

Eve wished she could answer in the affirmative, but it would be a lie. "I'm not jealous anymore," she said. "But I still feel uneasy." She looked down at her hand on his face, avoiding his eyes, as she admitted, "I shouldn't have said what I said about Isaac. That jealousy is a shitty feeling. I was being an inconsiderate bitch."

Luc covered her hand with his, drawing her palm to his lips. He kissed it, then held her hand there with his lips pressed to her palm. When he spoke, his lips and breath tickled her hand. "All is forgiven."

"Speaking of, I lost my shoe in Isaac's apartment. And you dropped your sunglasses," Eve recalled.

"I was wondering what the fuck happened to them. They were my favorite pair," Luc pouted. "They're probably broken, you little fucking brute."

Eve laughed. "*I'm* the brute? Sure, ok."

Mira's voice called out with irritation. "Your fucking delivery is here!"

The Iceberg was an entirely different experience at night, bustling with energy and people, music thumping. Eve hooked her arm around Luc's firm bicep as she followed him past the bouncer and through the crowd of party-goers. They drew interested glances as they passed, and Eve tugged on the hem of the microscopic dress Luc had selected for her. He smiled down at her, a new pair of sunglasses hiding the gleam in his eye.

"Stop fussing. Let me show you off," he implored.

"I feel like my ass cheeks are hanging out," Eve griped.

"You're the only one complaining." He stole a sideways glance at Mira who walked in front of them, leading them to the back office, and amended, "Well, maybe not the *only* one. But she's just jealous she can't fill out a dress the way you can." He gave Eve an appreciative appraisal, then loudly declared, "I'm going to fuck you in that dress later."

A blush tinged her cheeks. "Stop. You're fucking embarrassing."

"Don't tempt me. I can be *so* much more embarrassing."

They followed Mira into the manager's office that they'd teleported to that morning, and standing behind the desk was a man that Eve immediately knew to be Luc's father, Victor Fagerberg. She had to dig into Ruth's memories for his name, because she realized she didn't know it. He was as tall as Luc, and there was no mistaking the resemblance. He stood with his arms crossed, and his electric-blue eyes fixed pointedly on Eve. He wasn't *quite* as handsome as Luc or Bo, but Eve still felt her blood heat under his intense gaze.

Luc's father rubbed the trimmed, white beard that covered his jawline, as his eyes lingered on Eve's bare, muscular thighs, then took in her abundant, pink hair. He met her eyes again, showing no remorse for his staring. "You must be the Abomination," he assessed with mild disdain.

"I usually go by 'Eve,' Mr. Fagerberg," she shot back with feigned politeness. "I know it doesn't have quite the same ring as 'Abomination,' but it's the name I would prefer you use from this point onward."

His expression didn't change as he stared at her, unimpressed. He turned his attention to Luc. "You've caused quite a stir, Lucius. The lawyers are *not* happy with your idiotic antics. I can't say I am, either."

"My apologies, sir," Luc intoned with uncharacteristic obedience, and Eve jerked her head up in surprise. The fuck?

10

A Collection of Carefully Curated Personalities

This wasn't the Luc she knew.

"I expect you to cover every last penny spent on the settlement with those rugby players," his father said.

"Of course, sir."

Victor crossed his arms. "What is your business here, Lucius? Are you on a case?"

"We're looking into a monster cult and a murder."

"Just the two of you?" Victor spared Eve a quick, suspicious glance.

"It didn't require the resources of a full team."

Victor sat back in the chair behind the desk and tented his fingers together. He exhaled a heavy sigh of irritation. "You're not a kid anymore, Lucius. You need to grow the fuck up. Your impulsivity is unbecoming of someone of your stature. I expect more from you. Why can't you just be someone I can be proud of for once?"

Rage boiled in Eve's veins.

"I apologize. I will do better, sir. It was a brief lapse of judgement."

"You'd better, or you'll find yourself relieved of your responsibilities at Knighco. Sister Fiona has always favored you, and I think she turns a blind eye to things she wouldn't otherwise. Like this, for example," he said with distaste, pointing his finger between Luc and Eve. "Where is her white collar?"

Eve's brows jumped to her hairline in indignant disbelief. *Collar?!* Her face was hot with fury, her ears burning red. She felt the shift of Bo's wolf eyes shining out from behind her own, and Victor's attention snapped briefly to her face before she could hide them.

"He had a meeting with Sister Fiona, sir."

Wait, did they mean Isaac?

"But he didn't accompany her?" Victor sought clarification.

Luc hesitated, and Mira answered for him. "He didn't, sir," she said. "He is still at the compound."

Victor leaned his elbows on the desk and clasped his hands in front of his chin. He leveled a look of disappointment at Luc. "Lucius."

"She no longer requires a chaperone. She is in full control," Luc reasoned.

"Is that why I just saw werewolf eyes glaring at me from that smug little face? That was control?" Victor retorted. "It isn't your call to make. You need to follow the rules, boy. And apparently you need to make sure your brother is following the rules, too," he added with a hint of venom, glancing at Eve once more. "I know I left Knighco under your supervision, but don't for a moment think I'm not keeping tabs. Frankly, it's disappointing that I still *need* to."

"I'm sorry you are disappointed."

Victor raised an eyebrow and slowly rose to his feet. He rested his hands on the desk, leaning toward Luc. "That's not a proper apology. Don't be sorry that *I'm* disappointed. Be sorry that *you* disappointed me."

"I am sorry I disappointed you, sir. I will work harder."

Eve had tears in her eyes. She felt like Luc had evaporated, and next to her stood some weird shell of him. A robot. Who even was this? She wanted to scream in his father's face for talking to Luc like this, to rip his eyeballs from their sockets, but she refrained. She surmised that insubordination and impertinence in this moment would only make things worse down the road for her and for Luc.

"You're damn right you will," Victor said. "I'm still waiting on the proposal for the ViaCo account, and you're behind on the Beeker Street projections. How close are you to having the Jinwoo presentation ready?"

"It's almost complete, sir. I'll redouble my efforts."

"You'd fucking better. You've been coddled long enough, Lucius, and it's time for you to step up to the plate and earn your goddamn bread. Quit being fucking stupid."

"Yes, sir."

Victor shook his head with disgust at Luc, then waved his hand and turned away from them. "You're dismissed. I don't want any more trouble from you, boy." And then he disappeared.

Luc exhaled and his whole body relaxed. He turned to Eve and grinned. "Want to get a drink?"

Eve just stared at him. In the blink of an eye, the robot was gone and her Luc was back. The flip of a switch.

"I don't like that," she frowned.

"Like what?"

"Whoever the fuck was just standing next to me a moment ago. What the fuck was that, Luc? You weren't *you*," Eve gestured at him.

"I was who I needed to be. You were bound to meet my Straw Man eventually," he explained simply.

"I don't even know where to begin unpacking that."

"Then leave it packed up fucking tight and don't fucking look at it," Luc replied defensively. He took her arm and led her from the office back out into the noisy club.

Eve followed him to the bar, feeling helpless. Useless. She'd just stood there and let that debacle unfold unhindered. Had Luc brought her here knowing she was going to see that? See *him* like that? Did he *want* her to see it?

Her stomach turned.

"I'm going to hit the bathroom," Eve said. "Get me something with a little umbrella, and I'll be right back."

Luc nodded and watched her walk away from him.

In the bathroom, Eve could barely contain her annoyance when she ran into Mira. She tried to ignore her while she combed her fingers through her hair in the mirror, but Mira sidled up next to her.

"Scary, isn't it?" Mira said.

"What? Mr. Fagerberg?"

"Luc's 'good little soldier' act," Mira corrected. "He's always like that when his father reprimands him. And he always will be." Mira touched up her matte red lipstick in the mirror next to Eve. "Luc can be whatever he wants to be. Whatever he needs to be. *Whoever* he needs to be. And that's what's so scary about him. Who is he, really? What's real?" She turned to face Eve. "I've been with him long enough to know that he is an unknowable man. He will give you whatever he thinks you want, but he'll never give you *him*. I don't know if there's even a real person behind those beautiful eyes, or if he's just a collection of carefully curated personalities." As she walked away, she turned a smirk over her shoulder at Eve. "But he sure fucks like a stallion, doesn't he? Can't fake that."

Mira left Eve alone in the bathroom, staring at the closed door. Her chest was being crushed in a vise grip. She pulled her phone out of her handbag and called the one person she knew would bring her comfort.

"What's up, Evie? Everything ok?" Bo asked, concerned.

"No. I just met your dad."

"Oh."

"What the fuck is wrong with Luc?" Eve asked quietly.

Bo sighed. "He's a different person around our father. Don't hold it against him. It's how he copes with the pressure."

"I hated it, Bo."

"I know."

"It wasn't him."

"Nope. He calls it his 'Straw Man.'"

"I want to come home," she whispered, her eyes beginning to burn and water. "I just want to bring him home and keep him as far away from that man as I can."

"You can't save him from our father, Evie. It is what it is. But if you want to come home, come home. What's stopping you?"

Eve tipped her head back and fanned her eyes, trying to dry the tears before they fell and fucked up her makeup. "I can't make a jump just yet. I used up all my available energy when I stopped Luc from killing Isaac. I won't be able to make a jump for at least a few more hours, maybe longer."

After a long pause, Bo confessed, "I miss you, Evie."

Eve smiled to herself. "Are you getting soft on me?"

"Shut up and tell me you miss me, too."

"How can I shut up *and* tell you something?"

Bo grumbled, "I'm sure you'll figure it out, smartass."

Eve laughed, and one of her stupid tears streaked down the side of her face. "I do miss you, Bo. More than you know."

When Eve returned to Luc at the bar, she found Mira perched on a barstool next to him, and it brought Mira's opinion back to the forefront of Eve's mind. She'd dried and removed as much evidence of her tears as she could in the bathroom, but her eyes were still a little puffy, and seeing Mira sitting there smiling at Luc threatened to start the whole process all over again.

Was Luc really just a collection of carefully curated personalities? Was he just showing her the version of himself that he knew best suited her? It was one of Eve's greatest fears with Luc, and Mira had just thrown it out there like it was common knowledge. But, seeing how quickly and easily he could shift between Eve's Luc and Straw Man Luc, it was hard to totally disregard the merit in Mira's claim.

Eve wedged herself between Luc and Mira at the bar and took a long drink of the fruity concoction Luc slid in front of her, downing half of it. She tossed the tiny umbrella on the bar. "Take me back to the hotel," she commanded. "I have a journal I need to get through, and you have work to do."

Luc studied her. "Are you ok?"

"Fucking peachy."

"She's mad at me," Mira supplied. "I told her a truth she wasn't ready for."

"And what truth is that?" Luc asked, frowning.

She shook her raven-haired head and gave a wry laugh. "You're *definitely* not ready for it." She swiveled her stool around and slid off it. "I'll be back at the compound tomorrow night," she informed Luc, then strutted away with that perfect catwalk stride.

"What the fuck is she talking about?" Luc asked, resting his hand on the back of Eve's stool, leaning close to her.

Eve finished off her drink, then picked up the umbrella from the bar and tossed it back in the cup. "Doesn't matter. She's just a dumb bitch." She turned toward Luc and looked up at him. She reached out and snatched his sunglasses from his face and put them on herself, hiding her puffy eyes from him.

Luc graced her with a dazzling smile. "Suits you," he said, then leaned in and kissed her.

Eve caught his face between her hands and stared into his eyes from behind the dark glasses. God, he was beautiful. And god, she loved him. "You better be real," she whispered, then kissed him back, ignoring his confused expression.

Eve lay in the hotel bed next to Luc, his laptop balanced on his outstretched thighs and papers spread all over the comforter around him. She had Stacey's journal opened in front of her. She'd tried to read it so many times today, but the interruptions had been endless. Finally, she was ready to dive in and give it her full attention, especially now that Luc was otherwise occupied. She flipped through the dates, looking for October/November of the year of her and Emma's birth. When she got to where they should be, however, she discovered several of those pages had been torn out.

Fuck.

Stacey's journal picked back up around Thanksgiving, and it merely spoke of her struggles and joys with Emma as a baby, and her efforts in finding a place of her own so she could move out of her mother's house. A week before Christmas, though, Eve found an interesting entry.

> Moira took a trip to check on the little one yesterday. No one is any the wiser, and Mòrag is settling. I didn't think it would work, but Moira is amazing. That bitch can do anything. I only wish I had believed in her true powers before Eno took me to Kentucky. If only I'd known what he was, what he wanted, and what the LOA were really all about, I never would've gone with him. Hindsight, I know. It's a bitch. Some days are better than others, and today isn't one of the good ones. I have so much regret. I feel so stupid. So used. Such a fucking IDIOT!
>
> But I have Emma. My little prize for surviving. I just hope the little one is safe. I hope her family is a nice one. It wasn't like I could pick one out for her. I just hope the fates smile upon her, and I hope she didn't inherit the gift. According to what Eno had told me about the prophecy, she'll have 13 good years, but beyond that, who knows.

I hope she can overcome it. I hope she doesn't have it at all, and that they never find her. But I worry she does, given she was born on All Hallows' Eve, just as the book predicted. I fear they'll figure it out. Someone will talk. Someone will discover it. Please don't let her have it. And god, I hope Mòrag can protect her if she does. I can't imagine what they have planned for her if they ever find her.

At least I know LOA will never want Emma. She's completely harmless and normal. If I can keep them convinced that she is Eno's child, maybe they'll never catch on to the truth. Maybe the little one will be safe, and I'm worrying for nothing. But...I don't dare underestimate LOA again. Fucking monsters. I wish I didn't know things like that existed. I wish I could go back to not knowing. But Moira has a point when she tells me it's better to know and be ready than to live in vulnerable ignorance.

Eve's mind reeled. She hadn't considered that Emma's birthday was actually hers. Eve was born on Halloween, not November 1st.

And Eve hadn't just been cast away as a baby, unwanted. She'd been strategically hidden. Stacey *had* cared about her.

Eve flipped back to the journal entry before the ripped-out pages. It was dated for mid-September of the year of her birth.

I can't do this anymore. This has gotten too fucking insane. Moira is on her way to save me from this fucking place. I don't know where we're going, but that's probably for the best. That little dragon boy might read my mind and tell someone. I've been avoiding him like the plague just in case. He scares the shit out of me. Of all the monsters here, he's the one I worry most about. He's the most inhuman. I need to get out of here. I refuse to promise my baby to that little fucking monster. I refuse to be a part of this plan any longer. I refuse to help them initiate the Apocalypse. I refuse to help them raise Lilith! Even if there is only a sliver of a possibility that this is all true and they aren't just fucking nuts, I have to put a stop to it! And the best way for me to do that is to take away their key ingredient and hide it from them forever! Please hurry, Moira!

"Holy shit, I wonder if that's Ramil," Eve blurted, startling Luc from his concentration on the forms in front of him. She held the journal out to him and pointed out the part about the dragon boy.

"He would've been...three? Four? It's possible," Luc said. He took the journal and read the two entries Eve took interest in. "So, she did know about what you might become."

"She didn't trade me because she hated what I was. She traded me to keep me safe," Eve said with a faint smile. "She and Moira summoned Mòrag to watch over me because she suspected LOA would come after me. The Locusts. And they did."

"I wonder why these pages are ripped out," Luc said as he rubbed his finger over the torn edges.

"I don't know. The whole stay in Newbury is missing."

Luc flipped to the end of the journal. "It stops years before Stacey is murdered. Damn it. I was hoping Emma had been mistaken about that."

"Yeah, I checked that already," Eve commiserated as she took the journal back.

"Well, at least we have an idea of what we need to do next." Eve cast him a questioning glance. He elaborated, "We need to see if Enoch is still in Kentucky, and if he's still with LOA...right after we find out what Ramil knows."

11
Give Him Back

Eve awoke in the dark with her heart pounding, a thin glaze of sweat covering her whole body. Sometime in the night, she'd dreamed of Dagon, the echo of his voice in her head. What had he said? She tried to recall it, but it was gone, overridden by the dreams that had followed it.

The ache in her chest had become as subtle as a sledgehammer. She clutched at her chest, overwhelmed by the worst grief she'd ever felt in her life. She reached for her phone on the bedside table.

She had a DM from Zeke, received over an hour ago.

somethings wrong

That was all.

Luc stirred next to her. "What's the matter, love?" he murmured groggily.

She turned to him, wide-eyed. "Something's wrong." As she held out the phone to show him Zeke's message, she mentally reached out to Dagon, trying to open the connection between them.

Dagon! What's going on?!

Radio fucking silence.

Luc was already on the phone, trying to call Bo. No answer. He called Eoduun as Eve tried to call Zeke, but no one was answering their fucking phones.

"It's happening," Eve announced hauntingly. "Whatever I've been dreading all day…this is it. Whatever it is, it's happening now."

"We need to jump home. Now," Luc ordered, springing from the bed and hurriedly stepping into his slacks.

Eve hoped she had enough energy built up to make the leap. "I'm right behind you," she assured him as she snatched up her backpack off the floor and threw her phone and Stacey's journal in it.

Luc slipped his shirt and shoes on and disappeared.

Eve drudged up all the energy she had and pushed through the wormhole she'd opened, using the connection between her and Luc's tattoos to step out next to him in the war room at the compound.

She gasped at the sight before them. Everyone at Knighco was slumped around the conference table, unconscious. She rushed to Bo, lifting his face to hers. He was limp and appeared lifeless, but Eve could hear his heart pumping in his chest. She could feel his life force binding and tangling frantically with hers again after being separated by too much distance, *fusing* together, and she realized that at least a part of the ache she'd been feeling *had* been from being apart from him.

She didn't know what had knocked everyone out, but she hoped her blood would remedy it. She unsheathed the knife she knew was strapped to his ankle and sliced it across her arm, yanking his mask down and holding the bloody injury to his mouth.

Despite the panic and fear swirling in her head and heart, a violent orgasm tore through Eve's core as Bo's tongue slid over the cut on her arm. She bit back the moan in her throat and clenched her thighs together as Bo groaned, his eyes shooting open and his hands jerking up to grip her arm.

After a tense, heated moment, Bo released her. He looked up at her, recognition registering in his dazed eyes. "Evie…"

Eve brushed the hair from his forehead and pressed her lips to his brow, then hugged his head to her chest. "Thank fuck," she exhaled, relieved.

Luc's voice cut into her moment of relief and severed it. "Where's Zeke? And Ruth?"

Eve's eyes roamed the table, fruitlessly searching for her sunshine boy even though she already knew he wasn't there. She left Bo's side and made her way around the table, holding her arm briefly to each hunter's lips to revive them. "I can't smell either of them," she noted fearfully.

Bo watched Eve as he answered, "Ruthie did this. She must have taken Zeke. She called us all here tonight, claiming she had an urgent announcement that couldn't be discussed in the group chat. Once we were all here, I noticed Zeke wasn't. He was in the compound, because I could still scent him then, but he didn't show up to the meeting. I just assumed he was asleep and didn't get the message.

"When Ruth walked in," Bo continued, "she stood at the head of the table and blew some kind of powder out of her hand at all of us, and that's the last thing I remember." He looked over at the clock on the wall. "She's had Zeke all to herself for over an hour."

Eve's knees were trembling as she continued around the table, and when she touched her blood to Isaac's lips, it took every effort to swallow down the moan, another wave of pleasure crashing over her.

"We need to check for portals," Bo said, rising from his seat.

"What's going on?" Eoduun mumbled after Eve revived him. He looked around. "Where's Zeke?"

"We don't know," Eve replied, panic in her tone.

Luc's eyes widened. "The grimoire."

He disappeared.

Bo sniffed the air, furrowing his brow. "Something's burning," he mumbled. A moment later, realization hit. "Shit, she started a fire!"

Eve and Bo rushed to rouse the groggy hunters around the table, urging them to their feet. They were full of questions, but Eve couldn't focus on them. She needed to find Zeke. She grabbed Zephlyn by his shoulders as he fixed his sleepy eyes on her face.

"Any premonitions? Do you know where Ruth and Zeke are? Do you know what's happening?" she pleaded.

Zephlyn shook his head. "I can't see Ruth at all anymore. It's like she doesn't exist, like there's an interference around everything pertaining to her."

Fuck.

Bo called out, "Evie, go find Luc!" He then directed the other hunters to follow him from the war room to go find and deal with the fire Ruth had set.

Eve realized Isaac was next to her, his eyes frantically scanning mouths, trying to decipher what the fuck was going on because he couldn't read Bo's lips behind his mask. He furrowed his brow and flipped two horizontal D-handshapes twice. *What's happening?*

"Ruth drugged everyone and lit the bunker on fire, and we think she has Zeke," Eve explained aloud, Isaac's eyes fixed on her lips. "They're going to fight the fire. You come with me," she instructed, signing the last part as she spoke it.

Eve and Isaac took off toward the apartment complex on foot, with Eve following the shift in Luc's scent. They crossed the moonlit grounds and burst into the apartment building, dashing up the stairs and rounding the corner to where Luc was standing in the hallway. He held Ruth's apartment door open and stared inside, his nostrils flared and jaw set.

"She fucking took it," Luc confirmed. "She broke into the safe and stole it."

Eve stepped in front of him and poked her head inside, looking around Ruth's apartment, but nothing seemed amiss. Yet she could *feel* it. She stepped inside and kicked away the area rug between the kitchen and bedroom, and there it was.

The sigil. A portal.

And she knew how to get through it, because one of Ruth's memories surged forward, dispensing the information she needed.

She turned to Luc. "Bo and the other hunters are dealing with a fire in the bunker. They could probably use your help."

"Fuck," Luc spat, running his hand down his face, then disappeared.

Eve slid her backpack from her shoulders and tossed it onto the floor away from her, then turned to Isaac, signing, *I have to go.*

She could tell Isaac wanted to argue, but he didn't. He gave her a short nod. Using the sorcerer powers she still retained from Luc, Eve quickly recited the necessary incantation, and fell through the floor, leaving Isaac behind.

The fall ended as abruptly as it had begun, and she found herself in a familiar room. The ranch in Montana. She was in the room where Apep had found her under the bed. Ruth's room.

She mentally called out to Dagon again, but he still didn't respond. She inhaled deeply, and finally caught Zeke's familiar citrusy scent, alongside the perfumy musk that marked Ruth. She drew electricity to her fingertips and bolted from the room, ready to make any monsters that crossed her path shit their pants.

As she rushed through the corridor and down to the basement level, she noticed that the house seemed deserted, yet she could smell them. There were other people or monsters here.

And then she found them. All of them. She stood in an open, dark atrium, lit only by candles on the walls and floor, and she saw what was left of Ruth's army standing in a circle around something. She could hear Ruth spewing an incantation. Something about it tugged at her memory, but the spell itself wasn't in her memory bank.

Familiar scents mingled with foreign ones, and she knew there were, or had been recently, people or monsters here that she'd encountered before, but she couldn't tease them apart to identify them.

She sprinted to the congregation and jostled aside the monsters with human faces until she pushed through to the center. There was a large devil's trap drawn on the floor in blood, and in the center of it lay an unconscious Zeke.

"Zeke!" she screamed, lunging for her sweet jock.

Several rough hands grabbed at her, temporarily stopping her, and she sent a charge through her whole body, electrocuting every creature in close proximity like a pissed, pink-haired Pikachu. When she was free, she whipped around, and the air staled in her lungs.

Ruth had finished her ritual, and was standing by with a demented glee on her face as Zeke rose from the ground. He turned to Eve, desperation and terror in his eyes for a brief moment before they shifted to vermilion. His form began to bulge and contort.

Absolute horror gripped Eve by the throat and held her in place as she heard Zeke cry out in anguish, watching him grow taller than Luc as his muscles bulked out, ripping his shirt to shreds. The tribal-like tattoos on his body swirled and multiplied, covering his torso with artful designs, and his hair turned black and grew out several inches, covering his face. He threw his head back, tossing the hair from his face, and with the sound of a sheet whipping in the wind, two giant, leathery wings burst forth from his back and spread majestically behind him.

Dagon was free.

And Zeke was...gone.

The ground trembled and the walls shook as an inhuman roar filled the room, ripping free from Eve's chest as she threw herself at Ruth. She could barely see through the lightning and flames roiling around her, but she felt the impact of her fury as it struck the witch.

The goddamn piece of shit motherfucking demon whore of a witch.

Eve's grief and rage erupted from her like a volcano, spewing a vitriolic concoction of sorcery, electricity, and raw fucking power at the scrawny, platinum-haired bitch. The very ground crumbled beneath Ruth's feet as she was hit repeatedly by lightning strikes, and with one last wail of wrathful rage from Eve's throat, Ruth exploded into a billion bloody pieces that projected in every direction, covering every surface of the atrium with a fine, red spatter.

Ragged breath rasped past Eve's lips as she turned to face Dagon. He was ripping the heart from the chest of the last of Ruth's monsters. The rest were all a bloodied mess on the floor around him. He looked at the bloody red mass of muscle and cartilage in his hand briefly, then let it fall to the floor with a wet thump.

"Give him back," Eve seethed, moving slowly toward him.

Dagon stared at the bloody heart by his feet, not raising his eyes to hers. His tone was mildly resigned when he answered, "You know I can't, princess."

"You said I could save him." Her steps quickened. "You *LIED!*" she roared as she barreled down on him.

He offered no argument or resistance as she crashed into him, pummeling his body with electrified strikes that crackled and flared like lightning, filling the atrium with a cacophony of thunder. He dropped to one knee and folded his wings back, holding his arm over his face as she hurled her fists into him, but he didn't fight back.

"Fight me, you son of a bitch!" she shrieked, but he made no move against her.

Her strength was fading quickly, and before long, the punches had lost all force. The grief in her heart was threatening to drown her as her legs gave out and she collapsed to the floor in front of Dagon, her face level with his as he remained bowed.

"You killed him!" she cried as hot tears poured down her face.

"I didn't kill him, princess."

She reached out and slapped him across the face. "You let *her* kill him!"

He took the hit. "I couldn't stop it."

"You wouldn't have stopped it anyway, you piece of shit," she hissed. She pulled her knees up to her chest and wrapped her arms around her shins. She couldn't even see Dagon anymore through the blur of tears.

"I didn't want Zeke to die. This wasn't how I wanted it," he said quietly.

A huge hand touched Eve's back gingerly, and she roared at it, but didn't move away from it. Dagon's arms slid around her, and the light in the room suddenly darkened as his big wings enveloped her like a protective cocoon.

She buried her face in her knees and sobbed and keened like a grief-stricken banshee. "I hate you, Dagon. I fucking hate you," she growled at him, but he remained, his embrace unwavering.

12

I Want to Wreak Havoc with You

When Eve's senses returned to her, she pushed Dagon away, bursting up from the shelter of his wings and backing away from him. When she looked around, she suddenly saw Ramil strolling through the epicenter of the giant blood-star Ruth's demise had left on the floor, turning a slow circle as he looked down at it.

"How did you get here?!" Eve demanded.

Ramil turned his copper-green eyes to meet hers, and something in that gaze unsettled her. "Same way as you, I presume. The portal." He gestured to the mess on the floor around his feet. "Ruth?"

Eve nodded numbly. Ramil gave Dagon a knowing look, but Eve quickly corrected his misperception. "*I* did that." Then she pinned Ramil with a suspicious look. "How did you get through the portal?"

"I've been helping Ruth relearn her skills, remember? It was in a spell book she was working with today."

Eve knew which spell book he was talking about, and it wasn't one that Ruth had in her possession when Eve had left yesterday. It had been in Eve's closet, because she'd recently stolen it from Ruth's old room two floors above them.

Ruth must've stolen it back when Eve was gone.

How long had she been planning this?

"I thought you were helping with the fire," Eve said flatly. She didn't want him here. She felt hollow, like nothing was real, and she didn't want to talk to him, let alone explain anything to him.

"They had it under control. I heard Luc mention that you were back at the apartments, so I came looking for you," Ramil explained. "Though your assassin wasn't going to let me get past him. He acts like he doesn't trust me. Good thing I'm faster. I had to make sure you were ok."

"Well, aren't you thoughtful," Dagon interjected sarcastically.

She felt a mild tingle and burning sensation under the tattoo on her wrist, and Luc suddenly appeared next to her.

"Oh, fuck," he blurted when he saw Dagon standing there, and he threw a protective arm across in front of Eve. He glanced around at the carnage, his eyes rising to the blood spattering the ceiling as though he were admiring *The Creation of Adam* in the Sistine Chapel. "Jesus Christ."

"I lost control," Eve explained robotically, her eyes unfocused.

"It's a work of art, love," Luc marveled. Then he hesitated and closed his eyes. "And Zeke?"

The silence was so loud, it echoed off the walls.

When Luc looked down at Eve and saw the blood painted all over her face, arms, and clothes, a spark of something primal stirred in the depths of those aquamarine orbs. But he had enough situational awareness to refrain from speaking it aloud.

Suddenly, Bo popped up on the other side of Eve, startling her. "Well, that's conven...ient..." Bo's voice trailed off as he, too, took in the bloodbath. When he spotted Dagon, his scarred eye shifted, filling with rage.

Eve gaped at him, startled from her dark trance. "How did *you* get here?"

Bo kept his eyes on Dagon as he briefly explained, "Bonded pair. I can find you anywhere."

Eve sagged into Bo and buried her face in his chest, snaking her arms around him and squeezing him tightly. "He's gone, Bo. Zeke's gone," she whispered, taking in a shuddering breath, trying to hold the sob at bay.

"And Ruthie?" Bo asked.

Dagon held up his fists, then burst them open and made an explosion sound with his mouth.

"You fucker!" Bo spat, but Eve fisted the back of his shirt in both hands.

"It was me," she confessed against his chest. "I did it." Then, bitterly, she added, "But I'm not fucking sorry. She did this. She took him from me."

Bo held her to him, hugging one arm around her head, kissing the crown of her head through his mask. She heard him sniffle. "It's ok, Evie," he comforted her, his voice muffled against her head. "You don't have to be sorry. She made her fucking bed."

"Where's the grimoire?" Luc asked, looking between Ramil and Dagon.

Ramil shook his head. "I just got here a few moments ago."

Dagon held his hands out. "I don't have it." He kicked at the cold, sticky heart on the floor. "But Ruth couldn't have orchestrated this alone, you know. She had someone helping her. They must have it."

"Who was helping her?" demanded Luc.

"Apep?" Ramil suggested. "Who else could it be? He wanted that grimoire."

That was when Eve realized she could pick out one of the familiar scents in the room. It was faint and fading, but it was distinct.

In monotone, she said, "Apep was here."

Bo inhaled. "You're right. The scent is faint, but he was definitely here."

Fresh tears pricked Eve's eyes. She could still faintly smell Zeke, too, even though he'd been erased from existence.

Eve heard electricity chittering over Luc's skin as he stared down Dagon. "So, what the fuck do we do about you?"

"I go where she goes," Dagon declared arrogantly, gesturing to Eve. He puffed his chest and spread his wings wider in a formidable display, welcoming Luc to challenge him.

Now that Eve was processing what had happened, observing rather than purely reacting, she realized how incredibly insane she had been to go after Dagon like she had. He was even more intimidating in person than he had been in her dreams and in Zeke's mind. She may have Luc's power, but Dagon had the powers of a *god*.

And those wings. Jesus fuck. She didn't remember them being that fucking enormous.

"You'll stay the fuck away from her," Bo growled, twisting his body to move Eve further from Dagon.

"You want me to cooperate? I will cooperate…for *her*."

"Why?" Eve asked, extracting herself from Bo's arms. The numbness and disbelief was shifting back to rage. "Why haven't you run off already to go wreak havoc somewhere else?"

"I don't want to wreak havoc somewhere else, princess. I want to wreak havoc with you." He gave her an evilly enticing grin. "I'm already bound to you. I have an obligation to you, and you to me."

"I have no obligation to you!" she barked. "You're the reason Zeke is dead!"

"You misplace your blame!" Dagon roared back, taking a step toward her, and she shrank back. Ramil tensed, and Bo and Luc both moved themselves between her and Dagon, earning them an exasperated look from him. "Settle down, children. I am not to blame for this. I was just as blindsided as everyone else. Zeke and I were minding our own business when I started to feel strangely, like I was being cut off from his body, sealed away. I used my last bit of control to connect with Eve and tell her something was wrong. I was sealed before the boy was taken."

"Was it Ruth, or Apep?" Ramil said.

"I thought Apep couldn't get into the compound if I wasn't there," Eve pointed out. "I stayed away, even though I wanted to come home, *because* I thought I was keeping everyone safe from him!" If she had been home, would she have been able to stop this? Would Zeke still be alive?

"He shouldn't have been able to get in," Luc confirmed. "Unless Ruth fucked with the warding."

"I didn't see who it was who sealed me. I wasn't expecting it, and neither was Zeke. It may have been Ruth, or it may have been Apep...or it might've been someone else." He gave Ramil a wary look before turning his gaze to Eve. "But the fact remains, I had *nothing* to do with this." He crossed his massive arms and admitted, "I didn't truly want Zeke to die. I kind of liked the kid. I was hoping you could save him, princess. I had no idea the extraction would be like that."

Dagon suddenly turned back to Ramil. "How the fuck are you keeping me out?"

Surprise colored Ramil's expression. "I beg your pardon?"

Dagon stalked toward him, but Ramil held his ground unflinchingly, even as Dagon towered over him and jabbed his finger to Ramil's forehead. "How are you keeping me out of your head? What the fuck are you?"

Eve eyed Ramil suspiciously as well and divulged, "He's a dragon-jinn hybrid."

Ramil's eyes bulged from his head. "*Excuse me*?!" He shook his head adamantly. "No. No, that's insane." For a moment, the mask slipped, and Eve saw a flash of fear and fury in Ramil's eyes as he looked at her. Did he know? Was he hiding it? But he recovered quickly. "There aren't any dragons left. Everyone knows that. Why would you say that?"

"That's what Apep said," she replied, scowling.

Ramil rolled his eyes, "Well, that explains it. You can't trust anything a god of chaos tells you." He put his hand to his chest. "If I were a *dragon*, I think I'd know." Then he indicated Luc. "And I'm sure Luc and Mira would have figured it out by now, too."

Luc adjusted his sunglasses and made a noncommittal sound in response.

"You're a monster," Dagon insisted. "Dragon or not, you're *something*, and I think you're hiding things."

Ramil scoffed. "Excuse us if we don't put much credence in your assertions and assumptions." He looked to Luc. "What are we going to do with him?" he inquired.

Dagon folded his arms over his chest. "Eve is going to take me home with her, of course. Like I said, I'll cooperate for her. She says jump, I'll fucking jump. She says fuck me, I'll fuck her."

"You won't fucking touch her," Bo and Luc both shot back in unison.

"We can't kill him," Eve said quietly, and Bo and Luc both looked back at her. "What if he's harboring a little bit of Zeke inside of him?" she proposed hopefully.

Dagon hesitated only briefly. "Yes, what if? Best keep me close...just in case."

"Let me take a look in your head, then," Luc suggested. "If he's still in there, I'll draw him out."

Dagon's wings twitched and flexed. "You will keep your filthy hands off me. I don't trust you."

"Oh, but we can trust you?" Luc retorted.

"You? Of course not. But *she* can trust me."

Eve gave a weary sigh, swiping a stray tear from her cheek. The numbness was returning. "I know how to contain him." She pointed to the devil's trap on the floor that was now smeared with blood, corpses, and body parts. "Well, *Ruth* knew how to contain him. I know what needs to be done, but I'm not skilled enough to configure it alone. I'll need help."

106

"I can help," Ramil offered, but Eve ignored him.

Luc's gaze swept over the intricate design on the floor. "All of this work…this knowledge…she must have had her memories back. You were right, love. I should've been more receptive."

Tears once again filled her eyes as the heaviness in her chest intensified. "I should've been more insistent. I should've listened to my stupid instincts when my whole body was telling me something was wrong." This still didn't feel real. When would she wake up from this fucking nightmare?

"You didn't know," Bo said. "You couldn't have known that *this* is what was going to happen. I felt it too, through you, and I didn't take it seriously enough, either."

Eve fought to keep her guts from turning themselves inside out. "How did that stupid bitch get her memories back?"

Bo frowned. "Didn't you say Apep skimmed all of her memories in your head?"

A rock fell in her stomach. It was right there this whole time, and she'd somehow failed to recognize it. "He copied her memories from my head and gave them back to her. Why the fuck would he do that?"

"The grimoire, of course," Ramil contributed. "He had to know that if she had her memories back, the first thing she would do is track down that grimoire."

Dagon narrowed his eyes at Ramil. "You have a convenient answer for everything."

"I have a brain," Ramil shot back. "I'm just connecting the obvious dots."

Eve knew it might be a longshot, but she reached out telepathically to Apep. *What have you done? What did Zeke ever do to you?*

No response.

Eve rubbed her bloody hands over her face and through her blood-drenched hair. "Can we hash this out later, please? I want to go home."

"Sure thing, princess." In a flash, Dagon scooped her up in his arms, and she was suddenly in her apartment. He didn't return her to her feet immediately, though. He held her against the tattered remnants of Zeke's shirt still clinging to his chest, one arm hooked under her knees, the other arm under her shoulder blades.

Eve couldn't help herself – she slid her fingers under the soft, ripped fabric and touched her nose to it, inhaling Zeke's scent. A raw sob escaped her, and Dagon folded his wings into his back and sank down onto the couch in Eve's living room with her cradled on his lap. It creaked under his enormous frame.

"I'm sorry," he whispered in his deep, gravelly voice.

Eve clenched her fists around the fabric and sagged against him, her forehead pressing into his hard, massive chest. "It's all your fault," she bawled. But the rage had passed for the moment, and all that was left was horror and unimaginable grief.

"You know I didn't do this."

"But it's what you wanted. Deny it until you're blue in the face, but we both know it's true. You wanted to be free, regardless the cost." Eve pushed away from him, and for the briefest moment, Dagon tightened his grip, refusing to release her. Just long enough to remind her that he was still Dagon.

She jumped from his lap. "Give me that shirt," she ordered, holding her hand out. "That doesn't belong to you."

He tugged the torn fabric off and deposited it into her outstretched hand. "The pants aren't mine, either. You want those, too?" he challenged her, reaching for his fly.

Eve scowled at him, but her eyes dropped to his lap, taking in the way Zeke's cargo pants stretched across Dagon's muscular thighs. She quickly looked away before her eyes had a chance to wander to where his fingers gripped the button on the waistband.

"Don't be fucking stupid," she gritted.

Eve suddenly scented Bo and Luc...and Ramil. In the next instant, they were bursting through her apartment door, Isaac in tow.

"Goddamn it!" Luc shouted. "I'm out of reserves! I had to take the goddamn portal." He confronted Dagon, "Since when can you do that?!"

"Since I'm free," he replied. "I can use my full arsenal now." He stood up and rolled his shoulders. "It's been *ages* since I was at full power. I look forward to testing my limits." He gave Eve a sideways glance. "And yours."

Eve was so emotionally exhausted, she barely registered his remark. She tucked Zeke's ripped shirt under her arm and flipped Dagon the middle finger, then made for the bathroom. "I'm showering," she announced flatly.

Eve didn't hear what was happening in the other room through the rush of water over her head as she sat on the floor of the tub and let the water beat on the back of her skull. She hugged her knees to her forehead and cried hard, silent sobs until the water ran cold.

Nothing was ever going to be the same. She'd never lost someone. She knew this was a hazard of the lifestyle, an inevitability, but it did little good to *know* it. Now it was real. Zeke was gone, and he was never coming back. She couldn't *fix* it. And she knew he probably wasn't lingering inside of Dagon. She'd had hope when she'd suggested it, still clinging to a state of disbelief, but the cold reality of his death was beginning to settle its weight upon her heart.

She couldn't bring him back, but she could make everyone who had anything to do with it pay for their egregious transgression. Ruth had already paid, and Apep would suffer a similar fate as soon as she could get her hands on him.

But first, she would kill Dagon.

13
Let Someone In

The fire damage to the bunker was severe, and until it could be assessed by a professional, Luc advised that it not be used. Even the cars were moved from the garage.

As such, the reinforced, warded room that had been set aside for Zeke when he was first possessed by Dagon was out of operation. They couldn't be sure it was structurally sound enough to contain him now. As a controversial but necessary alternative, Ruth's apartment was repurposed as a prison cell. Eve and Ramil worked tirelessly, adorning the walls and door with sigils from Ruth's spell books to hinder non-traditional passage and weaken supernatural powers, and painting a devil's trap on the floor using Dagon's (voluntarily donated) blood mixed with their own blood, holy water, and other ingredients from Ruth's sorcery stash.

While they worked, Dagon sat casually in a wooden chair taken from the dining table, placed in the center of the trap, and watched while Bo and Isaac stood guard. He made no complaints, and did everything Eve asked of him, but it only made her more distrustful of him. What was he playing at? She was anxious to finish the warding and finalize the spell to bind him to the trap.

Meanwhile, Luc had gathered the rest of the hunters in Zeke's apartment down the hall to announce the terrible news of tonight's loss. Eve was grateful to not be sitting in on that gathering, as she knew Eoduun was going to be absolutely shattered.

As devastated as she was, he would feel it tenfold.

She couldn't bear to see it.

Luc shared some details, but he left out the fact that Dagon was being imprisoned under the same roof as the rest of them. He only disclosed that Dagon was under surveillance in a secure location. They didn't need anyone playing the hero or taking their shot at Dagon, because they likely wouldn't survive it.

The next few days went by in a haze, one day blurring into the next. Eve locked herself in her apartment and wouldn't let anyone in, and from what she heard outside her apartment door, she gathered that Eoduun was doing the same thing. Luc gave her the physical space she requested, but he texted her repeatedly to check in on her. She rarely replied, even when he texted to inform her he needed to go to New Mexico for a few days.

Will you be all right without me? he wondered. She looked at the message and felt no desire to answer. When he received no reply, he wrote, *I love you, Eve. Please let Bo take care of you while I'm gone. I let you have your space, but you need to let someone in now, love. Please. Please don't suffer alone anymore.*

Then, a few moments later, he added, *Bo needs you, too.*

Bo still came in the mornings, greeted her with his trademark "*Ohayou,*" and left a coffee on the counter for her. It was the only time he forced his presence on her, bypassing her locked door with his abilities, but she didn't see him, since she was still in bed. But she could feel his grief just as palpably as she could feel her own, and she knew he felt hers. She could feel that he longed to be close to her, and she knew *he* needed more from her, but she was incapable of giving anything right now.

She was hollow. A husk.

Isaac came to her door several times a day, sometimes knocking, sometimes not. Sometimes she only knew he was there because the tobacco scent that followed him would drift through the door to her hypersensitive nose, and linger there for several minutes.

The other hunters came to offer their condolences, but she wouldn't answer the door. They sent her messages, and she left them on "read." Cassie was more persistent than the others, but even she, the master of manipulation, couldn't convince Eve to let her in.

The only one who didn't come to see her was Eoduun, and she understood. She hadn't gone to see him, either.

They reminded each other of Zeke.

As for Dagon, he sat in his devil's trap in Ruth's old apartment, patiently biding his time.

Eve wiled away the hours planted in front of the television, rewatching *Boondock Saints* or anime, wrapped up in one of the big t-shirts she'd stolen from Zeke's apartment when no one was looking, or lying in bed with her earbuds in, listening to music while curled up with the tattered shirt Zeke had died in, reading Stacey's journal. Focusing on the mystery around her mother's death and the Locusts was the one thing that successfully distracted her mind from the gaping hole in her heart.

The entries began to get interesting in the December before Eve was born.

I don't know about this church group Eno has involved us with. They call themselves the Locusts of Abaddon, and when I asked him why they were named after a creature of Hell, he told me they weren't, that Abaddon was an "angel of the Abyss." They were named after the locusts in the Book of Revelation that tormented sinners.

Everything they do seems extreme. They talk about working to break the seven seals to begin the Apocalypse, but then they talk about it being to free Lilith from her imprisonment. Eno claims Lilith isn't evil, that she was the first wife of Adam, which makes her a holy creation more significant than Eve. But they refer to her as "the Mother of Monsters," or "the Mother of Abominations," so how is that not evil?

I didn't sign up for all this. I thought he had a little church group. I didn't know he was part of a weird religious cult.

I love him so much. I just hope he comes to his senses and sees these people for what they are: lunatics, not locusts.

Then an entry from January:

I don't even know where to begin today. Eno has really been pushing me to start a family with him, and honestly, the idea has always kind of appealed to me. I've always wanted a family, and the thought of carrying Eno's baby in my belly gave me butterflies. At least, it did. Before.

But last night, shit got weird. At the evening gathering of the Locusts, I was surprised when Eno led everyone in a fertility ritual that involved smearing some kind of blood and ointments on my belly and chanting some weird prayers. I was so weirded out, but at the same time, I felt like it was just his way of trying to help me to conceive. He wants a baby so badly. And then he took me back home and, of course, we did our best to make a baby.

But it was what happened afterward that really freaked me out. As we lay there in bed, he told me that Lilith was real, and that she was his freakin' grandmother. Like, he seriously believes it. And then he told me that our child was going to be the key to bringing her back, freeing her from the Abyss. Something about the blending of first blood, divine blood, fallen blood, and mortal blood. He said the bloodlines represented the four horsemen that "usher in the Apocalypse." Then he went on some tangent about how the Apocalypse will bring a new era of free will.

And then when I told him I didn't think I wanted our child to be any part of that, he said it was already in motion. Then he laughed and said, in a way, I would be like Lilith because I would be the "Mother of the Abomination."

What the fuck! I don't know how much more of this I can take. I love Eno, but he's fucking losing it. These lunatics are poisoning his mind!

A few days later:

This can't be real life. It just can't. I just saw a person...a human woman...change into a fucking werewolf. The Locusts held a ritual under the full moon, and one of the elders bit this girl (Abby), then cut his hand and bled into her mouth. And then she FUCKING CHANGED.

INTO A fucking WEREWOLF.

Just...WHAT.

The journal moved into February:

They're ALL monsters. Every fucking one of them. Eno wasn't lying about anything. He swears they aren't going to try to change me into one of them because they want me to stay a pure mortal, but how can I trust that after what I saw? I need to get out of here.

Two days later:

Eno just told me he's in the Bible. Am I insane for believing him? The son of Cain? He swears his grandparents are THE Adam and Eve, and an angel named Samael and, as I said before, Lilith. He even told me that the big birthmark that covers half of his torso and arm is supposedly the "Mark of Cain," inherited from his father – the mark that was placed on Cain so no one would kill him in retaliation for killing Abel. He said if anyone tries to kill him, they will suffer "sevenfold," whatever that means. I asked him why he's still alive, because he would have to be thousands of years old, and he just gave me a weird smile.

I'm completely bonkers for believing this, right? But, shit, if monsters are real...is this so far-fetched? I feel like I should be running for the hills. I shouldn't be here. This is nuts!

Eve's skin prickled as she read that last passage. She leapt out of bed and ran to the full-length mirror on her wall, flinging Zeke's shirt off over her head, which caught on her earbuds and ripped them out of her ears. They fell with a light clatter to the floor along with the discarded shirt as she swept her gaze over the big patch of faintly discolored skin that she'd developed the summer before she turned thirteen. The dermatologist told her it was probably some kind of late-onset birthmark with a weird medical name she couldn't remember, but she'd been surprised to see it on Eve because it was apparently much more common in men. She said it had likely been triggered by hormones, and assured her it was nothing to worry about. It covered the left half of her stomach and wrapped around to her back, up around her left breast, and partway down her left arm. It was like one giant freckle that darkened when she spent time in the sun, and in the winter, it faded so much it was barely visible. She'd had it so long, she rarely ever thought about it or even noticed it anymore.

One of those situations where you're used to seeing something so often that you stop seeing it altogether.

Was this the mark Stacey was describing on Eno? Did she bear the fucking *Mark of Cain*?

…Or was this all absolutely insane?

Eve threw Zeke's shirt back on, picked up the earbuds, and headed out to the kitchen, deciding to take a break from the journal. Her appetite still hadn't returned, but she knew she needed to eat something. She hadn't eaten more than a handful of chips and a sleeve of Oreos over the past couple of days. But when she stuck the earbuds back in her ears and opened her freezer, reaching for the bag of frozen chicken nuggets, her hand stalled.

"Gone Away" by The Offspring was playing. She withdrew her empty hand and pushed the freezer door shut.

"Pulled away before your time, I can't deal, it's so unfair."

Zeke was everywhere.

Her forehead thumped against the cold, stainless steel, and her body was racked with sobs.

"And it feels, yeah, it feels like, the world has grown cold, now that you've gone away."

It was the first time she'd allowed the despair to spill out since the night Zeke died. She tore the earbuds out and threw them across the room.

Her grief was beginning to catch up to her. Not only was her heart in pieces, and her stolen powers faded, but she was weak from lack of appetite, jittery from too much caffeine, foggy from lack of sleep, and feeling physically ill from neglecting to sate her curse.

So, when Bo suddenly appeared next to her, his arms encircling her and his warm, masculine scent enveloping her, she felt the *need* acutely. Bo knew she had to be at her limits, and she suspected he was simply waiting for her to reach her breaking point, keeping himself available until she was ready.

"It's ok, Evie," he consoled softly, guiding her head to his chest and stroking her hair. "I know it hurts. We all loved him. Just let it out."

"Make it go away," she whispered between gasping sobs. "Please." She reached up to yank his mask down, but quickly realized he wasn't wearing it. He'd come here without it. Eve pulled his face down to hers, pressing a light kiss to his lips. She took a shuddering inhale as she closed her eyes and touched her forehead to his. "Make me forget, just for a little bit."

Bo lifted her wordlessly onto his hips, and she wrapped herself around him, hugging her arms around his neck as his rough, unshaven stubble scratched her tear-streaked cheek. He carried her to her bedroom and sat down on the edge of the bed, holding her on his lap. His lips tenderly caressed her neck, and one hand cradled the back of her head, the other hand on her lower back.

"I love you, Evie," he whispered against her neck. "Give your pain to me. Let me take it. Let me carry it for you." He lifted the hem of her shirt, pulling it off over her head, and his warm mouth descended upon the humble mounds of her breasts, his fangs skimming the soft flesh, his callused hands gently holding her body to him as she threaded her fingers into his hair.

"Please, Bo," she begged breathlessly. "I need you."

He flipped her around onto her back and tugged her shorts off. He grabbed the back of his black t-shirt and yanked it off over his head, then stripped out of his pants. Eve reached for him with greedy hands, and as he settled himself between her legs, she molded her body against his. She dug the fingers of one hand into the muscles on his back, the fingers of the other hand in his hair, holding his head to hers, nuzzling his roughly-whiskered cheek. Her heart ached and swelled at his touch, and she choked out a whimper as he pushed inside of her, a low, desperate moan rumbling in his throat.

She clung to him like she was terrified to let him go as he moved with her, his hips rolling against hers as he pulled out slowly, then drove in deep. He dropped soft kisses to her jawline as he fucked her slowly, his lips traveling up to meet hers. She fisted her hand in the hair on the back of his head and kissed him desperately, like he was the air she needed to breathe, and she rocked her hips more urgently against him.

She wished she could fuse with him. Become one entity with him. Crawl into his chest and live inside of him, cocooned in his love and warmth, forever protected.

Eve didn't need Bo to tell her he loved her. She didn't need the words, because she felt it in the depths of her tainted soul. There was no question in her heart when it came to him, because she had a direct line to his heart. She wasn't afraid he was going to quit loving her or change his mind or grow bored of her. He was a permanent fixture in her life, the beacon of safety her heart relied upon.

Her lighthouse.

He loved her wholly, and she loved him.

Bo cupped the side of her face and kissed her deeply as he thrust harder, interpreting the subtle motions of her body just as easily as he predicted her moves when they sparred.

Fighting or fucking, he read her like a poem he knew by heart, as though he'd memorized every line, every verse that was his Evie. He knew her better than anyone else had ever bothered to.

As her pleasure stirred, the pressure building low in Eve's belly, Bo's lips grazed her earlobe. "I love you so much it hurts," he professed. He feathered soft kisses to the dip between the curve of her jaw and her neck, his arms tightening around her. "I've been drowning without you."

A choking sob caught in her throat as she crested, her orgasm rippling through her with a strange mix of emotions riding in its wake. Tears poured down her face as she was slammed with ecstasy and despair at the same time, like bursting into flames at the bottom of the ocean. She writhed beneath him, her strangled cries smothered by his deep moans when he covered her mouth with his, his kiss tasting of sweet salvation.

14

Time to Reopen the Zoo

Bo held Eve close to his chest as she let all the built-up emotions she'd been harboring wash through her, her body convulsing with cathartic sobs.

"I'm right here, Evie. Just let it out," he whispered against her temple. "It's ok to fall apart. You're safe with me. You're always safe with me."

She allowed herself to visit the memory she'd been avoiding the past few days, because she knew she needed to face it. That last moment. *Zeke's* last moment. It disturbed and horrified her in a way she hadn't been able to explain. It hadn't been gruesome, or drawn out, or torturous. It hadn't been bloody or gory or brutal. It hadn't been a violent death.

It had been quick and clean, and had left no trace of him behind, and *that* was what so thoroughly disturbed her. In an instant, he was gone, as though he'd never existed. Sure, he left *things* behind, like his tattered shirt, but there were no bodily remains. Nothing to mourn over. Nothing to bury. Nothing tangible to prove he was a living, breathing, loving force of flesh. Instead, he'd been swallowed up and repurposed to hold another. And in the fraction of a second when he'd locked eyes with her, in his last moment of life, she'd seen the fear, the questions, the confusion, and she'd stood immobilized, unable to do a fucking thing to comfort him but stare back, mirroring his horror.

Everyone around her knew what had happened to Zeke, but she was the only one who had witnessed it. They knew he was dead, and maybe they felt he was fortunate not to have died bloody, like so many hunters did. And maybe she should agree with them. But the death he got? It felt so...hollow. Like ellipses that should've been a full-stop period. Like a bass drop that never hits.

He just...blinked out of existence.

He deserved more. He deserved more than to just become the clay Ruth used to fashion Dagon's flesh.

He deserved to be saved, and she had failed him. If she had listened to the warning bells her intuition was blaring at her, or if she'd awakened when Dagon had called to her, or when Zeke had messaged her, or if she'd moved just a little faster to heal the hunters in the war room, or if she'd fought the monsters who held her back during the ritual just a little bit harder...

If one thing had changed, she might've been able to stop what had happened. If one thing had been different. If she'd just stayed home, instead of chasing after the ghosts of her past, maybe Zeke would be alive.

She needed to kill Dagon. He needed to pay for his contribution in all of this. She was certain he could've stopped it, if he'd *really* wanted to, but he didn't. If anything was ever going to bring her peace, it was knowing that she'd reclaimed the flesh, the *life*, that Dagon had stolen from Zeke.

Tonight.

When Eve finally calmed in Bo's arms, she realized his finger was tracing a slow trail along the border of her birthmark where it wrapped across her back. He never commented on it, but he was the only one who ever paid any attention to it. She wondered if Dagon had ever noticed it, or if he knew what it could be.

"You might be tracing a biblical relic," Eve remarked, her voice hoarse and broken from crying. She looked up at him, admiring the grizzled, whisker-covered angles of his face. Was he somehow getting even more handsome, or was it just the facial hair he'd neglected to shave?

"Hm?"

"My birthmark. It could be the Mark of Cain," she revealed.

Bo's finger paused in its path as he studied her with cool basalt and ocean eyes. "Why would you have it?" he wondered, the tips of his sharp canines poking out from behind his lips when he articulated the "v" in "have."

Eve rolled onto her back, and Bo's fingers resumed their trek, moving over the slightly differing shades along the midline of her abs. "Well, if Cain is really my grandfather, I may have inherited it." She told him about the journal and what she'd discovered so far. "I don't know if it's even true, though," she admitted. "If it were, anyone who tried to kill me would suffer 'sevenfold' for it. My ex, Adam, tried to kill me years ago, and nothing happened to him."

Bo lifted his brow at her meaningfully. "No? You sure about that? Because I can attest to the fact that he suffered at least sevenfold." When she didn't respond right away, he continued, "But I always thought the Mark of Cain was supposed to be a curse so he couldn't die, so he'd never find peace. That sounds more like a protective blessing."

"Well, Eno wasn't wrong when he called Stacey the 'Mother of the Abomination,' so maybe we need to take this seriously," Eve said.

Bo was thoughtful. "'Mother of the Abomination'…what is that from? I've heard that phrase."

"The Locusts were calling Lilith the 'Mother of Abominations,' according to Stacey's journal."

Bo snapped his fingers as recollection struck him. "The Whore of Babylon in Revelation. 'Mother of Abominations' was written on her forehead or something."

Eve grabbed her phone off the night stand and did a quick search for "Mother of Abominations." The first thing that came up was a reference to a goddess called Babalon from the Thelema religion established by Aleistar Crowley in the early 1900s. She saw terms like, "virgin whore," "sacred whore," "scarlet woman," and read descriptions of a woman riding a great beast, and that she represented female sexuality and sexual liberation. Then she looked up "Whore of Babylon," and found a similar description in the Book of Revelation.

"So, do these Locusts of Abaddon think Lilith is not only the first wife of Adam, but also the Whore of Babylon?" Eve wondered. "Isn't that supposed to be a bad thing? And what the hell did they want with *me*?"

"Maybe we should ask Ramil," Bo suggested. "He was with those nutjobs for a long time. He will know all about their belief system."

"I don't trust Ramil. I think he knows a lot more than he's letting on. Where is he?"

"He's around, but he'll be leaving tonight. Luc assigned Teams Flannel, Beta, and Gamma each to a case. The other two teams have already headed out. We may be in mourning, but the monsters still need to be hunted. And he thought they might be better off outside of the compound for now, with Dagon stewing in the apartment just down the hall."

"Shit, I suppose so. I've been completely out of the loop. What have I missed?"

Bo rubbed his chin, the stubble making a scratching sound against his calluses. "Well, now that Celeste is back, she's been trying to track down who sent you those photos of Dizzy posing as Luc, but she's not having any luck. Zephlyn's been trying to get a read on the location of the grimoire, but he's being blocked. He said the only visions he's getting right now are all jumbled and he can't make heads or tails of them.

"Oh, and the contractors will be starting work on repairing the bunker in the next few days. I'll feel a lot better when we can put Dagon in a confinement chamber."

"Is my bloody floor mural still working to hold him?" With a humorless laugh, Eve mused, "You know, that devil's trap is the first fucking thing I've painted since I got here. You'd think I'd miss it more."

"He's still there, so it seems to be working just fine. Though he hasn't made any attempts to break free of it, either, from what I've seen."

"And Isaac? Did you hear anything about how his meeting with Sister Fiona went? Is he being recalled to the Vatican?"

Irritation flitted over Bo's features. "According to Luc, Isaac requested to extend his assignment indefinitely. Seems he wants to be a *permanent* liaison between the Vatican and Knighco." He gave Eve a knowing look.

Eve allowed herself a small sliver of joy. "Good. I think we're stronger with him."

"He's not completely useless, I guess," Bo conceded. "He has been keeping close tabs on Dagon...when he's not lingering outside your apartment door, that is. I *almost* feel bad for the guy."

Guilt darkened Eve's face. "I knew he was out there, but I didn't have the capacity to care. I wasn't feeling much of anything but grief. I needed to be alone."

"And now?"

Eve rolled to face Bo and laid her hand on the side of his neck. She gave him a weak smile. "Maybe it's time to reopen the zoo. We'll give it a trial run." The smile faded quickly as she asked, "And how's Eoduun?"

Bo shook his head. "He's been locked up in his apartment, too. He's definitely not ok, but I don't know how to help him. He won't talk to anyone."

Eve wondered if it was time for her to reach out to him, or if he would rebuff her attempts. She had to at least try, didn't she? He needed to know she was there, available to commiserate and cry with him, at the very least.

Eve dressed and exited her room, Bo in her shadow. He went to his spot at the kitchen island and started tapping on his phone as Eve went to her apartment door and unlocked it, swinging it wide open, intending to go over and knock on Eoduun's door.

Isaac leapt up from the floor to her right, a book in his hand, his dark eyes full of surprise as they quickly scanned her. He took a quick step toward her, but stopped himself short, as though he thought better of it. He raised his brows and pointed at her, fingerspelling an O and K.

She nodded out of habit, but when her eyes met his, she felt them brimming with tears once more. She shook her head and snapped her thumb and first two fingers together.

Isaac looked at her endearingly, sympathy pouring from his eyes. He pointed to himself and circled his fist over his chest. *I'm sorry.* He gingerly took a step toward her, holding his arms out awkwardly, his eyebrows raised slightly as he invited her into them.

She closed the distance between them and wrapped her arms around his neck, pulling him close as his arms encircled her torso. As she held him tightly, she felt something stirring in her chest, but it wasn't hers.

And for once, it wasn't jealousy.

It was warm. Fuzzy.

She glanced between her bicep and Isaac's chin, one eye giving her a clear view back into her apartment where Bo sat at his spot at the island in the kitchen. He had his elbow propped on the countertop, his hand over his unmasked chin and mouth, his eyes down on his phone. But a quick look cast her way told her he was paying attention.

And, as much as he disliked Isaac, he was comforted by the knowledge that Isaac genuinely cared for her. If there was one thing he was learning about the priest, it was that he could trust Isaac to put himself between Evie and any potential threat.

He just couldn't trust him to keep his dick to himself.

And *there* was that little sizzle of jealousy.

Isaac held Eve in his embrace until she released her arms from around his neck. She stepped back and signed, *I'm sorry for keeping you at a distance. I needed to be alone.*

He pointed to himself and nodded sympathetically, raising his index finger into the air next to his temple. *I understand.*

Eve signed, *Bo told me you're not returning to the Vatican.*

He responded, *For now. I put in a request to stay longer, but it wasn't approved yet.*

Eve smirked at him. *I knew you couldn't leave us. You* like *us,* she signed, exaggeratedly drawing her connected thumb and middle finger away from her chest before touching her finger to each shoulder.

Isaac rolled his eyes and swung his hands alternately back and forth in front of him, brushing his fingers against each other like old Western saloon doors. *Whatever.*

Speaking of 'whatever,' I need to go see Eoduun. Maybe I can get him out of his apartment, Eve signed. *You can wait inside with Bo. I'll be back.*

Isaac curled his upper lip in distaste, but he touched his thumb to his chest, fingers splayed. *Fine.* He brushed past her and went into her apartment, and she watched him flop down in his favorite chair and start reading the book he had with him. *Frankenstein.*

Eve left the door wide open and padded down the hall in her socks to Eoduun's door. She knocked softly, then put her ear to the door. "It's me, Eoduun. Can I come in?"

Nothing.

"Don't make me break this door down," she persisted.

Not a peep.

In her best little girl voice, she sang, *"Do you want to build a snowmaaaaaaaaaaaaaannn?"*

Crickets.

She smushed her cheek against the door and added, *"It doesn't have to be a snowmaaaaaannn…"*

She heard footsteps approaching the door, and she stepped back and saw door handle jiggle. Then the footsteps retreated again. Eve reached out and twisted the handle, and the door pushed open. She went inside.

Eoduun's apartment was dark and smelled like old food and dirty clothes. She waited for her eyes to adjust to the dark, then picked her way over to the window and pulled one curtain back to let a little natural light in. She looked around at the room. It was a mess. It looked like someone had ransacked it in a robbery.

Or in a fit of rage and grief.

15
Swamp of Sadness

She made her way to the bedroom, stepping over a crushed Switch that looked like it had been repeatedly stomped on. When she breeched the border between his dark room and the main room, the sour smell of vomit accosted her. She frowned and pulled her shirt over her nose.

"Eoduun, are you sick?" she asked as she waded through the contents of his closet that were now scattered all over the floor. She went to his bedroom window and pulled aside the curtain.

She heard the rustle of bedding and turned her head just in time to see Eoduun's black hair disappear beneath the comforter. Then she saw the wastebasket next to his bed, dried puke spattering the inside. She went back out to the kitchen and got a fresh trash bag, and changed out the bag in the can. She brought the other bag to the door. She would take it and drop it down the trash shoot when she left.

While she was at it, she grabbed another trash bag and started picking up wrappers and broken things from the floor. "Is there something I can make you to eat?" she asked while she cleaned.

No answer.

"Is there anything I can do? Besides pick up some of this mess?"

Eoduun suddenly threw the covers off and sat up. Wild ebony eyes pierced her angrily from beneath messy, unwashed black locks. "Can you bring him back?" he cried. "No? Then go the fuck away!" He burrowed back under the blankets.

Eve was taken aback, and only then realized she'd dropped the trash bag in her hands. She braced herself and sat down on the edge of the bed. She rested her hand on the mound under the blankets, likely his hip. "I'm not going away, Eoduun. We need each other."

"I don't need you. I never needed *you*. I need *him*."

Those words cut Eve deeply, even if they didn't surprise her, because something inside her told her he was speaking a truth she'd always known.

"It would break his heart if he saw you like this," she whispered.

"I don't give a shit. He broke *my* fucking heart."

"Tell me how to help. Please," Eve implored.

Eoduun rolled over and pulled back the covers so he could look at her. "The only way to help is to take him away. Erase him from my head completely." Desperation spilled from his eyes. "Erase him, Eve. Every trace." He sat up, an odd, dementedly defeated expression on his face. "Just take him out. Extract him." His eyes reddened, and a tear broke free and rolled down the side of his nose. "Erase him before his memory kills me. I can't do this." His voice broke. "I can't go on like this."

Tears pricked at her own eyes, and she shook her head. "I can't do that. I won't let you just throw him away because it's the fast, easy solution." She inhaled a ragged, shuddering breath. "He *deserves* to be remembered. To be grieved. To still be loved. His stories deserve to be told. His antics deserved to be laughed at and reminisced. I won't let you kill his memory. Fuck you for even asking," Eve quavered. She rammed her finger roughly into the side of Eoduun's head, canting it to the side. "*This* is where he lives now." She jabbed her finger against her own head. "And here. I don't give a fuck if it hurts. You *will* hold on to him with everything you have, because that's all we have left of him. This is all we get."

Eve stood up and picked up the trash bag from the floor. "And don't you *dare* fucking disrespect him by doing anything stupid," she threatened. "He loved you. And I love you, too, even if you are a fucking asshole. Maybe we aren't fucking soulmates, but you're one of my closest friends in the world, Eoduun. If you can't drag yourself out of this misery for yourself, do it for me. Do it for Zeke. You deserve better than this." She stormed from the room and headed to the door. Before she left, she yelled to him, "You are *not* to lock this door. I will be back to check on you later."

After Eve tossed the garbage in the shoot at the end of the hall, she returned to her apartment, rattled and furious. Isaac and Bo both read her face like a neon sign. Isaac furrowed his brow and tapped a Y-handshape twice to his chin, and Bo asked the same question aloud.

"What's wrong?"

She noticed Bo had at some point retrieved his mask and donned it while she was at Eoduun's. She wondered if he would've kept it off if Isaac wasn't there.

"Eoduun had the fucking audacity to ask me to erase his memories of Zeke," she relayed as she leaned her hip against the back of the couch, folding her arms across her chest.

Bo exhaled. "I worried he might. Did you set him straight?"

"Of course I set him straight," she answered. "But we're going to need to keep an eye on him. He's…" She shook her head. "He's broken."

"We'll pull him through it," Bo asserted. "We won't let him sink in the Swamp of Sadness."

Eve gave him a funny look. "Swamp of Sadness?"

Bo mirrored her look. "*The Neverending Story*? Artax?"

"I've never watched it."

Shock sent Bo's brows into his hairline. "Are you serious?"

"I was afraid of it. Those old animatronics creeped me out as a kid."

Bo pulled his mask down and looked at Isaac. "Please tell me *you* have seen *The Neverending Story*."

Isaac stared at Bo momentarily, as though in disbelief that he was actually talking to him. He nodded, but furrowed his brow and touched his temple, drawing away a Y-handshape.

Eve filled him in aloud. "Bo referenced the Swamp of Sadness."

Isaac bobbed a Y-handshape in front of him with a knowing expression, then fingerspelled. *Oh, Artax.*

Eve threw her hands out to the side. "Apparently everyone knows Artax but me."

With his mask still down, Bo insisted, "You have to watch it." He looked at Isaac. "She has to watch it, right?"

She and Isaac looked at each other. He fisted his hand and nodded it.

Eve pushed away from the couch. "No, it's creepy," she said and signed.

Isaac pointed to her, held a C with his forefinger and thumb up to his eyes and drew it away, waved a flat, splayed hand behind his other flat hand, touched the palm sides of two A-handshapes together, then rocked a K-handshape between himself and Bo. Then he looked at Bo and raised his brows, stacking two G-handshapes on top of each other.

Bo looked to Eve to translate.

"He says you two will watch it with me. And then to you, he said 'right?'"

Bo gave a small grin, one fang poking out from behind his lip. "Right. It's settled then," he said, then slipped his mask back into place. "Maybe he's not completely awful," Bo said behind the mask.

With her back to Isaac, and moving her lips as little as possible, Eve said, "You mean you aren't going to cut him into tiny pieces and send him back to the Vatican in a barrel of acid?"

Bo gave her a wry look, but didn't answer. Instead, he said, "We should talk to Ramil before we lose our chance. He's coming up the hallway." He rose from the barstool and slid his phone into his pocket.

Moments later, Ramil appeared in her doorway, dressed in a pair of dark jeans and a loose, deep red t-shirt. It made the green in his eyes pop. He was dangerously handsome, but not in an excitingly dangerous way. In a threateningly dangerous way. Eve didn't like it. Something inside her, maybe her curse, wanted to crush that dark beauty.

He paused and looked in. "Have you ended your isolation?" he queried, taking a step inside. He glanced over at Isaac, then at Bo behind her. "May I come in?"

"Please," Eve acquiesced, gesturing him in. "Just the man I was hoping to talk to."

"Me? Whatever for?"

Eve climbed over the back of the couch and plopped down on the middle cushion. She pointed to the other chair across the coffee table from Isaac, adjacent to the couch. "Have a seat. Tell me about the Locusts of Abaddon."

"Oh. That's...unexpected. I haven't thought about them in a long time. Why the sudden interest? Are they causing problems again?" He asked as he made his way across and lowered himself into the chair.

"I just need you to answer my questions," Eve replied.

"Am I being interrogated?" he inquired, only half-joking.

Taking a note from Luc's book, she replied, "Or interviewed. I suppose that depends on you." Then she laughed it off, even though she meant it.

"Please. I'm at your disposal," he replied amicably, holding his palms up. "What would you like to know about them?"

Isaac closed his book and placed it on the coffee table, leaning forward, resting his elbows on his knees and tenting his fingers in front of his mouth, giving Ramil and Eve his full attention. Bo perched on the arm of the couch, not quite at ease, placing himself between Ramil and Eve.

"What kind of religion did they follow?" Eve asked. "Were they Satanists?"

Ramil laughed. "No, nothing of the sort. They worship Lilith as the Mother of Abominations – the mother of monsters. They revere her as a beacon of free will, sexual liberation, and the realization and development of one's true self, one's true nature. A symbol of individual freedom. They believe *she* is the entity to rise again in the Apocalypse to bring liberation to all her children, freeing us all from the arbitrary shackles placed on us by mainstream religions. They believed that Lilith tricked John the Revelator in that cave on the island of Patmos, and she was the one who fed him the prophecy he recorded as the Book of Revelation. They've been doing everything they can to ensure it all goes as they believe it should."

Eve was surprised at her lack of incredulity. "That…that actually doesn't sound as evil as I was expecting," she admitted.

"No?" Bo interjected. "When we clashed with them, it was because Ramil had killed Remi and Ruger, believing them to be the Two Witnesses from Revelation Eleven."

"The Two Witnesses?" Eve repeated.

Ramil elaborated, "Two people who spread prophesy and perform miracles during the Great Tribulation, then are struck down by the Beast of the Abyss. Which, regretfully, they believed me to be. And then, the breath of life returns to them, and they rise from the dead."

"Holy shit," Eve blurted. "I guess I could see why they would think that." She leaned forward. "But wait, isn't the Beast supposed to be the devil? Whose side are the Locusts on?"

"They don't believe in the devil, per se. They don't believe any of the characters in Revelation to be good or evil. Just cogs in a machine that they can use to open the gates of the Abyss to raise Lilith. I was just a character to them. A Beast. A role to fill to bring the world closer to liberation."

"So who was Stacey Rose in their little Revelation cast?"

A brief flash of surprise darkened Ramil's strange eyes, but he quickly replaced it with a look of bewilderment. "Stacey Rose?"

"She was brought in by Enoch Azra. They were part of LOA when you were little, apparently."

"I knew Eno. He brought in most new Locusts. He was the leader, right up until I left. But there was no Stacey Rose that I can recall. If she was there, I must have been too young to remember her."

"Is Eno still there?" Eve asked.

"I wouldn't know." But something in his eyes told Eve he wasn't telling them everything. Eve wished she had the power to get into his mind right now. She made sure to keep her walls up in her head to keep him from probing into *her* thoughts. She didn't want him to know who Stacey and Enoch were to her just yet. He asked, "Why the sudden interest in the Locusts? Did something happen?"

"Possibly. A long time ago," Eve answered vaguely.

"Did you really not know you were a dragon-jinn hybrid?" Bo asked Ramil accusingly, crossing his arms.

"It hasn't been confirmed that I am. If we're just going off what Apep said, you'll excuse me if I retain a modicum of skepticism."

"Why did they yoke you with the role of the Beast, then?" Bo pressed. "Wasn't the Beast supposed to be a dragon?"

"There was more than one beast in Revelation. They assigned me that role because I'm powerful. That's no secret," Ramil reasoned with a shrug.

"What interest would they have in the Abomination?" Eve questioned. "What am I to the Locusts?"

Ramil gave her a wary look. "Have they come after you?"

"No. Just answer the question. Please," she added, forcing politeness. "What am I to the Locusts?" she repeated.

Ramil studied her, mulling over his answer, and she desperately wanted to know what he was thinking. He leaned forward. "If you're the *true* Abomination?" The green in his eyes almost glowed when he said, "Everything."

Isaac raised his brows and signed, *Are the Locusts a threat to Eve?*

Ramil frowned. "Did he just flip me off?" He circled two alternating L-handshapes toward his chin, curled his middle finger in front of his chin, then tapped the fingertips of a V-handshape against his palm horizontally, then vertically, and held his palms up. *What's that sign mean?*

Eve gave a short, wry laugh. "That's my name."

"Oh, well, in that case, possibly. They will be interested in *acquiring* you if they truly believe you are the Abomination."

"Acquire me for what?"

Ramil shrugged. "I'm not sure. I wasn't privy to all the rituals, but I do know that the Abomination is the key to the ritual to open the gates and raise Lilith."

"But what's the significance of the Abomination?" Bo asked. "Why exactly is she 'everything' to the Locusts?"

"The Abomination is the ultimate monster. An entity that can carry any power, resist any curse, and birth an entirely new race of monsters. She can both destroy life and give life. She is the ultimate culmination of dark and light. She carries the blood of all Four Powers – Eve, Lilith, celestial, and mortal. Her birth is essentially like the breaking of the first four seals in Revelation – the arrival of the Four Horsemen. That's where the whole 'Eve is the Antichrist' narrative started with the Vatican, I believe.

"But I think if I had to explain it in the simplest terms," Ramil continued, "I would say if Lilith was God in the LOA belief system, the Abomination would be Jesus."

16
Perfectly Odd...And Oddly Perfect

Ramil made a dismissive gesture. "But this is all according to the Locust belief system. It doesn't mean any of it is remotely true."

"Why didn't you tell us this when the Vatican first started throwing the word 'Abomination' around?" Eve wanted to know.

"Why would anyone care what some obscure cult of monsters believed?" Ramil reasoned. "I trust the resources of the Vatican over the blatherings of those zealots."

Eve eyed him warily. "And you're *sure* you don't know who Stacey Rose was?"

"I don't remember her. Sorry."

Lies, lies, lies, her gut screamed at her.

Ramil leaned closer to her, his eyes trapping hers as his expression darkened almost imperceptibly. In a low, spellbinding tone, he purred, "What is it you *truly* desire, Eve? What do you wish to gain from me?"

His body. His power. To take him and break him. The urge to pounce signaled to her muscles, making them twitch as she tensed.

A loud bang snapped Eve's attention away from those copper-green eyes, and she jerked her head toward Isaac. He had slammed his hand down on the coffee table.

He gave Ramil a deadly look, then chopped one hand onto the flat palm of his other hand. *Stop.*

Bo's eyes bounced from Isaac, to Ramil, to Eve, confused.

Ramil gave an uneasy laugh. "Well, I assure you I meant nothing by the question. I was only seeking a little clarification." He looked up at the clock on the wall. "Well, am I free to go? I have yet to pack. We're heading out to New York for a hunt tonight. Vetala, supposedly."

"What's a vetala?" Eve asked trying to shake off the inappropriate desire for sex and violence burning her insides.

Bo explained, "A vampiric evil spirit that inhabits corpses."

"Zombie vampires? Zompires." Eve simplified.

Ramil chuckled. "Zompires. I like it."

But Eve didn't return his grin.

After Ramil left, Bo asked, "What just happened there?"

"I don't know, but I think he pissed off my curse," Eve relayed.

"Like that time you attacked him in the gym?"

"Kind of, yeah." She turned to Isaac and spoke and signed, "Why did you tell him to stop?"

Isaac signed, *His mist turned black and began to swirl around you.*

Eve repeated it aloud for Bo, and Bo frowned. "He was using powers against you?" Bo asked, livid.

"I don't know. Maybe he was trying to get me to tell him the real reason for my questions."

Isaac signed, *Why are you interested in LOA?*

Eve retrieved Stacey's journal and brought it to Isaac, opening it to the pages she'd been reading. She held up a vertical flat hand and swept the fingertips of a V-handshape down her palm. *Read.*

"I don't want you to be alone with Ramil," Bo instructed her as he grabbed the remote and started scrolling through the streaming services on her TV. "I'm not comfortable with what just happened."

Eve wondered how much of what she'd felt had been transferred to him.

While Isaac settled in with the journal, Bo turned on *The Neverending Story.* Eve curled up next to him on the couch and rested her head on his shoulder.

"Did the dad just put a raw egg in his orange juice?" Eve said.

"Not the point to be paying attention to," Bo replied.

"The kid's mom died, and his dad is essentially telling him to just get over it. Yeah, I didn't miss that, either." Then, a few minutes later, "That bookshop owner has his face way too close to that little boy. He's fucking weir-mmmph—"

Bo's hand clamped over her mouth. "Shhh."

She heard Isaac huff out an amused exhale through his nose, but he kept his eyes on the journal.

Then came the scene in the Swamp of Sadness, and Eve understood Bo's earlier comparison. As Artax sank in the muck, Atreyu screaming for him to care, to not let the sadness overtake him, she saw Eoduun sinking. She saw herself sinking. Her throat tightened and strained, and tears burned in her eyes, but she refused to let them fall. She sank down on the couch and rested her head on Bo's thigh.

It's a movie. It's a fucking movie.

"If sadness makes you sink in the Swamp of Sadness, Atreyu should be sinking, too." she remarked, her throat tight. "He just lost his best friend."

"He's sad, sure," Bo said. "But maybe he still has hope. He hasn't let the sadness overtake him…yet."

But when the terrifying, giant animatronic turtle came onto the scene, Eve recognized the feeling portrayed there, too. That hopelessness. That feeling that nothing matters anymore, that there's no point in caring about anything. *"Not that it matters…"* And then Atreyu did start to sink, all alone in the swamp, the relentless, evil wolf that wants to destroy him closing in on him, the dark clouds of the Nothing overhead.

But the white-haired luckdragon appeared from a glowing cloud and pulled him from his despair, rescuing Atreyu from the fate he'd resigned himself to, carrying him through the endless miles he'd felt he could never traverse.

She wrapped her arms around Bo's leg and hugged it. She recognized that feeling, too.

"This movie is one big metaphor for navigating grief," Eve deduced quietly.

Bo threaded his fingers into her hair and began to gently massage her scalp. "Yes."

The hardest part of the movie for Eve to maintain her composure through was the depressed Rockbiter. *"They look like big, good, strong hands, don't they? I always thought that's what they were. Oh, my little friends. The little man with the racing snail. The Night Hob. Even the stupid bat. I couldn't hold on to them. The Nothing pulled them right out of my hands. I failed."*

Her heart squeezed, and Bo stroked his thumb soothingly over the hairline at her temple.

Eve was quiet through the rest of the movie. (Except for the part when Bastian ate an apple core, because *who does that?*) She wasn't expecting a creepy old children's movie to resonate so deeply. Had she watched it at any other point in her life, she probably wouldn't have thought much of it, but right now? Right now, she could appreciate the significance of the message more profoundly than she otherwise might have.

Eve sat up. "Suppose there's any chance Ramil is a *luck*dragon?" she joked, wiping a stray tear from the corner of her eye as she watched Bastian and Falkor chase his bullies down an alley at the end of the movie.

"Not likely," Bo said. He surveyed her. "Well? What did you think of it?"

"It was perfectly odd…and oddly perfect."

Bo looked pleased. "It was kind of my comfort movie after my mom died. Ruthie hated it, and Luc thought it was weird, so I'd sit in my new room in my new home with my new family and watch it alone." He smiled at Eve from behind his mask. "I'm glad I don't have to watch it alone anymore." Before Eve could think of something to say back, Bo kissed her forehead and stood up. "I'm going to go get us some grub."

She grabbed her phone and saw she had a few messages from Luc. It was time to let him back in, too. She went to her room to FaceTime him when Bo left to get dinner, while Isaac stayed glued to the chair, working his way through Stacey's journal. Eve hadn't expected him to sit and read the whole thing, but she probably *should* have expected it.

Luc's handsome face looked up from her screen at her from behind his new pair of round-framed sunglasses. It reminded her that she needed to ask Isaac if her shoe was still in his apartment from her and Luc's little teleportation scuffle.

A delighted smile split Luc's face. "There you are, love. I've missed you."

"I know," she said with fake arrogance.

"You're in better spirits."

She rolled onto her stomach on the bed, holding the phone in front of her. "A little. Where are you?" She could see a simple, but likely expensive oil painting on the wall behind him and the supple leather upholstery of a fancy chair behind his shoulders.

"My father's office in Albuquerque. But I should be home tomorrow. Have the other teams left yet? I thought you might appreciate a bit of space to breathe."

"Team Beta hasn't left just yet. I was able to snag Ramil for a little interrogation earlier." She gave him the rundown of her discussion with their former-Locust, and Luc seemed intrigued.

"You think he's lying about not remembering Stacey?" Luc asked.

"He's lying about *something*. When I said her name, I saw it in his eyes, some little flash of surprise. I think he knows *something*."

"Hm. But you played your own cards close to your chest, right?"

"Of course. I didn't tell him why I was interested in any of it other than they may have been involved in something that happened a long time ago."

"You think he was using his powers on you, to try to influence you to tell him what you were *really* looking for?"

"I think it's possible."

Eve heard Luc's phone vibrate, and Luc bumped his glasses down his nose to read the notification. "Speak of the devil," he mused.

"What? Ramil?"

"He just texted me, asking if something happened with the Locusts. Seems you piqued his curiosity." Luc's eyes glinted deviously. "Listen, love, I have a little mission for you and Bo. After Ramil has left, I want you to check out his apartment."

"Is there anything in particular we should be looking for?"

"Just anything that seems suspicious or out of place."

Eve saluted the screen. "Yes, sir. Can do."

"How is Bo, by the way? Have you spent some time with him?"

"Yeah. He's solid, as always. He just stepped out to get food." Eve hesitated, chewing her lip. "I'm worried about Eoduun, though. Dude's not pulling through it, and I don't know what to do."

"It's to be expected, though, isn't it?" Luc said. "He and Zeke have been inseparable since the day Zeke arrived at Knighco. Have you spoken to him?"

Eve told him about what happened at his apartment earlier. "I plan to check on him again and bring him a burger when Bo gets back." Her thoughts grew darker. "I'm afraid he's going to hurt himself, Luc. He's sinking."

Luc's expression sobered.

"I don't know how to fix him," Eve lamented. "My blood doesn't fix *this*. And he doesn't want me around him."

"What he wants and what he needs may not align right now. You should recognize that, love. He may not want your help, but he needs it. He needs you."

"I'm not equipped for this."

"It doesn't take any special skills to just sit with someone," Luc pointed out.

Eve promised to do her best with Eoduun tonight, then ended her call with Luc after assuring him that she loved him at least one-third as much as he loved her. She absolutely refused to admit to half.

When Bo returned with burgers from a local fast-food joint, he brought the two paper bags to the kitchen and dropped them on the counter. "Come and get it," he called out, withdrawing a burger for himself.

Eve poked through the bags. "Can I take one of these to Eoduun?"

Bo slid a bag to her. "I got his usual order. See if you can get him to eat it." He grabbed a greasily-wrapped burger from the other bag and turned to Isaac, who was still reading in the living room. "Hey, asshole!" he called, knowing the words were pointless but unable to resist shouting them anyway, and waved the burger in the air.

Isaac looked up, and Bo tossed the burger to him. Isaac caught it in one hand, an expression of pleasant surprise on his face. Bo chuffed a short laugh as he returned his attention to Eve. "He looks so surprised." Bo pulled his mask down and took a bite of his burger, his big canines sinking into the bun.

"He's not used to you being nice to him."

"I'm not. I called him an asshole and threw food at him."

Eve laughed, but the sound pained her ears. "It feels wrong to be laughing just yet."

142

Bo gave her a sympathetic look. "Zeke wouldn't begrudge you for laughing. He would want it. He would want you to be happy."

But she didn't deserve to be happy right now, not when she was the one who failed to save him. Not when Eoduun was closed-off in his room, completely broken. Not when Dagon was still alive, having stolen Zeke's life from him.

And not when she was the one who had given Bo his sister back, only to have to rip her away from him again. She watched him take another bite of his burger, wondering how he was processing the loss of the little girl with the pigtails who hadn't inherited the eyes, despite the monstrous nemesis she'd twisted herself into.

"Your sister...You must be upset that I killed her," she observed.

Bo paused. Instead of answering, he said, "I never should've asked you to revive her at the papermill." His eyes slid up to meet hers. "I'm sorry for that. And I'm sorry you were the one who had to rectify my mistake. And I wish to hell Zeke wasn't the one who had to pay for it."

Eve's face fell. "You can't seriously be blaming yourself for this."

"I've been over it a thousand times in my head, Evie, and the single moment that would've prevented the entire course of events leading up to this, was when I begged you to save her. If I'd just let the dead stay dead, Zeke wouldn't be among their numbers."

"But *I* saved her. I could've said no."

"You wouldn't have saved her if I hadn't asked. *I* put this into motion."

Eve scowled at him. "The only one to blame for this is Ruth. A lot of things could've gone differently to prevent Ruth from having the ability to do this, but in the end, *she* is the one who did it, and *she* is the one to blame."

Bo stared at her. "And she wouldn't have been here to do it if I'd let her die. It circles back to my interference, any way you look at it."

"It's not your fault for having compassion. It's her fault for *not* having any."

Bo gave her a tight smile, then nudged the paper bag toward her. "Take Eoduun his dinner. He needs to eat."

17
Lapdogs

Eve knocked on Eoduun's door, and after a few moments of silence, she walked into his apartment. "Tina, you fat lard, come get some dinner!" she called out in her best *Napoleon Dynamite* impression as she made her way back to his bedroom. She sat next to the mound under the covers and shook the fast-food bag. "Bo got you a burger. Come out and eat. Please."

Nothing.

Eve pulled on the covers, fighting Eoduun until she ripped the comforter from his grasp and threw it back. He growled, "I'm not fucking hungry."

Eve withdrew his burger and unwrapped part of it, then held it to his mouth. "Tina, eat. Eat the food." She pushed it against his lips. "*Eat the food!*"

"Fucking stop!" Eoduun griped, jerking his head away.

"No. You *will* eat, because I won't eat until you do, and I'm *starving*." She leaned over him. "Don't make me chew it up and spit it in your mouth like a baby bird. Because I'll fucking do it."

"Jesus, just go away," Eoduun sighed in annoyance.

"I'll go away if you eat. Just three bites."

Eoduun sat up dramatically and yanked the burger from Eve's hand, taking three big bites in rapid succession. With his mouth full, he scowled at her and mumbled, "There, happy now?"

Eve picked up her own burger and dug in. God, it tasted so good. She hadn't even realized how hungry she was. "Very," she said around her own mouthful of food.

"You said you'd leave me alone."

Eve took another big bite. "I will." She sat there next to him and ate in silence while he glowered at her. She picked up his drink and held the straw to his lips. "Thirsty?"

He snatched the drink from her, and for a moment, she thought he was going to chuck it across the room. He thought about it. But then he took a small sip and slammed it down on the nightstand. To her delight, he took another bite of his burger before he tossed that onto the nightstand, too.

At least he'd eaten *something*.

After polishing off the last of her dinner, Eve went to Eoduun's bathroom and started running a bath.

"What the fuck are you doing in there?" Eoduun yelled at her.

"You fucking stink."

"I don't give a shit."

"I do. You're an affront to my olfactories."

"No one is forcing you to be here," he shot back.

Eve returned to his room. "Exactly." She rounded the bed and started pulling on his shirt. "Let's get out of those smelly clothes and get your ass into the tub."

Eoduun tried to push her away. "I'm not a fucking child!"

She climbed onto the bed and fought him harder. "You could've fooled me!" she argued, finally shucking the shirt off over his head. She moved for the boxers.

"OK! OK!" Eoduun relented. "I can do it myself! God!"

Eoduun rolled his eyes and pushed past her, shuffling through the mess on the floor toward the bathroom. She followed behind him, and when he tried to close the bathroom door in her face, she put her hand out to stop it.

"Get in the tub," she demanded.

"I can bathe myself."

"Prove it." She pushed him toward the bath.

"I can just take a shower. I don't want a stupid bath."

"Maybe I want a stupid bath," Eve replied.

Eoduun was given pause as he turned and studied her. "You...you want to take a bath...*with me*?"

She lifted a shoulder nonchalantly. "Why not? I fucking stink, too." She started stripping out of her clothes.

A flush of color bloomed across Eoduun's face and chest, chasing away the sallowness of his complexion from earlier. He went to the sink, grabbed his toothbrush, and quickly scrubbed it over his teeth, and a small grin tugged at the corner of Eve's mouth.

The first real sign of life.

Eve gestured him toward the tub, and he dropped his boxers and stepped in. As he slowly lowered himself into the water, he grimaced and hissed. "Holy fuck, Eve, are you trying to *scald* the stink off me?" Eve pushed him forward and slid into the tub behind him, and he seemed confused. "Why are you back there?"

"I'm the big spoon today," she replied as she wrang the washcloth out over his shoulders, the hot water running down his back. She lathered bodywash onto the cloth and began to massage it over his shoulders, moving down his back, then down his arms, and around to his chest and stomach.

He sat obediently and allowed her to bathe him.

When it was time to wash his hair, he folded his knees up and slid down into the tub, dropping his head into her lap. As she massaged shampoo into his silky black hair, she looked down at him and mused, "You're very flexible. I didn't know you could fold like this."

Without missing a beat, he said, "I seem to fold myself into all kinds of shapes for you."

Eve gave an amused exhale. She began to use her hands to lap water up onto his hair above the waterline, dragging her fingers back through it to rinse the shampoo out.

He added, "Maybe that's your *real* power."

"Contorting you in the bathtub?"

Eoduun rolled his eyes, then sat up, slicking his hair back and wringing the excess water from it. He grabbed her and swapped positions with her in the tub, causing water to slosh over the side and splash onto the floor.

He gathered up the lengths of her hair and draped them over her shoulder, then picked up the washcloth and slowly ran it across her back. "You twist us into something else," he said ominously.

Eve turned her head to the side, but didn't turn all the way around to look at him. "That sounds nefarious."

"In some ways it is, in some ways it isn't."

Eve looked forward again as Eoduun washed her arms. "And what have I twisted you all into?"

"Lapdogs."

Indignity rose like flames in Eve's chest. She pulled away from Eoduun's touch and turned to face him. "Lapdogs?! I turned you all into lapdogs?"

Eoduun fixed her with a flat look. "Look at me. I'm washing you in a bathtub. When we first met, I would've tossed you into the sun without a second thought."

"I've never sought to make any of you into lapdogs."

"It's not necessarily a bad thing, Eve, because it isn't just *us*. Look at Isaac. You turned your would-be assassin into putty in your hands. Look at Dagon. Up until…" Eoduun swallowed hard, and his hands stalled on her skin. "…Until recently, you were the only person who could somewhat reason with him without using threats."

"Fat good it did us," Eve bemoaned miserably. "He betrayed us anyway. He claims he didn't, but he did."

"Have you seen him? Since…since it happened?"

"No."

"Do you know where he's being held?"

Alarm raised her hackles. Was he going to try to find out where Dagon was so he could go after him himself, to take revenge for Zeke? She would have to keep her barriers up, just in case he tried to read her. With the state Eoduun was in right now, she had to be prepared for anything from him.

"Leave it alone, Eoduun. Whatever you're thinking of doing, don't."

"I don't stand a chance against Dagon. I'm not stupid." He ran his hand around her ribs, then up between her breasts. He fanned his fingers over her throat. "But you can kill him. You turned him into your lapdog, and now you can put him down."

Way ahead of you. "Maybe. I've thought about it."

"Let me help you," he beseeched. He pulled her back against his chest and hugged his other arm tightly around her, resting his chin on her shoulder. His growing hardness pressed up her back between them. "We can kill him together," he whispered, then kissed behind her ear. "For Zeke."

Eve closed her eyes and leaned her temple against Eoduun's, lifting a hand to his cheek. "Maybe," she lied. "But not yet."

"Why?" Eoduun's heart suddenly began hammering in his chest against her back. "Wait…is there still a chance…could he be trapped inside of Dagon?"

"I don't think he's still in there."

"But is there a *chance?*" Eoduun pressed hopefully.

"I can't say there's *no* chance, but I highly doubt it. To be certain, though, I'd have to probe in his head."

"You know where Dagon is, don't you?"

"I wouldn't tell you even if I did."

Eoduun's breath quickened. "Take my power, Eve. Take my power, go find him, and see if he's hiding Zeke."

"The hope that you're clinging to is dangerous, Eoduun," Eve warned. "You're just setting yourself up to have your heart broken all over again. Zeke is gone. I can *feel* it. Can't you?"

Eoduun squeezed her tighter, dropping his forehead to her shoulder. His whole body shuddered, and he sniffled. "I can't just give up on him. Not if there's even a *hint* of a possibility…"

Eve's heart broke for him. She reached back and stroked his wet hair. She sighed and turned her eyes to the ceiling, blinking away the tears. She would regret entertaining this, but she couldn't bring herself to deny him this request.

"I promise to check every dark corner of Dagon's mind, body, and soul before I kill him. But I'm not going to find Zeke, because he's not there."

Eoduun's lips brushed her ear, and he whispered, "But what if he *is*?"

The hopefulness in Eoduun's voice spurred her own, and she tried to tamp it down. Hope in the face of uncertainty is a powerful force that can mean the difference between success and failure, or perseverance and forfeiture. But misplaced hope leads only to darkness. Disappointment. It unnecessarily prolongs the state of denial when the only real path forward is acceptance of the cold, stark truth.

Zeke was dead. Gone. He'd left a gaping chasm in her gut that plagued her every waking hour since that moment in Montana, like someone had scraped out her insides and carved a garish, fake smile in her flesh, like a living jack-o-lantern. Trying to fill that messy void with the glowing flicker of hope would only end up scorching her in the end.

Eoduun was barely surviving the loss of his best friend. To allow hope to take root and grow, only to have it dashed, could spell his ruin. Eve had to protect him, and she had to protect herself, too.

Hope was dangerous.

The sooner she could extract it, the sooner they could work to move on.

The sharp slice of a grooming razor across her shoulder snapped Eve out of her morbid reverie, followed by a crashing wave of pleasure as Eoduun's tongue dragged across the blood that rose to the surface of her skin. Her grip tightened in his hair as she threw her head back against his shoulder, a whimper riding her exhale. His cock throbbed against her lower back.

He slid into a more reclined position in the tub, lifting her onto his lap while she still faced away from him. The length of his cock pressed between her thighs and ass, and she rubbed herself shamelessly along his shaft, the sudden inferno in her core demanding relief.

But this was dangerous. She was no longer in possession of Bo's power, which meant her curse was unmuzzled. She warred internally with the monster inside of her, knowing she should stop this, but when Eoduun notched his cock at her entrance, her body eagerly took him in. She sucked her lip between her teeth, reveling in the connection between them.

Being with Eoduun made her feel closer to Zeke, and for a moment, it felt like exactly the place she needed to be right now.

But as she gripped the side of the tub and palmed the shower wall, listening to Eoduun's moans behind her echoing over the rhythmic sloshing of the bathwater, the monster stirred.

Ruin him.

Break him.

Take his power and hold him under until the struggling stops.

No! Fuck. Shit. Her teeth ached for flesh. It was irresistible. She needed to relieve this maddening tingle in the roots of her teeth that seemed to be inexplicably linked to the pleasure rising in her center.

She grabbed Eoduun's hand from her hip and stuck it in her mouth, biting down on the fleshy part of his palm between his index finger and thumb.

He groaned, a mix of pleasure and anguish. His dick pulsed inside of her and he thrust up into her. "That's it, you little slut. Make it fucking hurt." His fingers dug into her face and jaw, and she bit down harder.

A maelstrom of rage and euphoria swirled in her core and radiated through her body, burning in her thighs, welling in her chest, and tingling in her fingertips. Her inner walls gripped his thickness as she rocked against him, her pace quickening with her soaring pleasure.

Crush him.
Destroy him.
Kill him.

18

Keep Swinging

Eve's will to resist the insatiable desire for violence was fading, the darkness inside her seeping through every pore. She spun around and resituated herself on top of Eoduun, taking him in again as she faced him. She raked her nails down his chest, watching the angry, red welts rise up in his flesh as he sucked air in between his teeth.

"I want to kill you," she warned darkly. Her hips rolled and gyrated, riding him hard and fast. Her hands skimmed up over his collarbones, her fingers curling around his throat.

The passion in his eyes dimmed in resignation. "Do it," he whispered harshly as her fingers tightened, her thumbs pressing into his windpipe, the rage in her belly unfurling.

His submission delighted the beast in her, but horrified the rest of her. "You wanted this," she realized.

He began to slide down into the tub. Before his head dipped under the water, he revealed, "I was counting on it."

She couldn't stop the rush of pleasure that detonated in her core, exulting in the intoxicating thrill of complete domination of his body and spirit. She gasped and moaned as the ragegasm ripped through her, Eoduun's power surging through her as he spasmed inside of her, his hips jerking beneath her as her hands squeezed his throat under water.

No. NO. Don't kill him!

She rose up against the rage, wrapping it in the single most potent emotion in her current arsenal – grief. The vision of Zeke's last moments replayed in her head on repeat until her desire to dominate and destroy dwindled enough for Eve to wrestle back control, dragging Eoduun's head and shoulders up out of the water.

He coughed and sputtered, runnels of water streaming down his face and shoulders. Eve threw her arms around him, hugging his wet body to hers, but the sadistic impulse still ebbed in the aftershocks of her pleasure, and she caught herself squeezing him like a python.

She loosened her hold, pushing him roughly and scooting away from him, a different kind of rage igniting in her chest. "How dare you," she scolded, only now realizing she had tears running down her cheeks. "How dare you use me like that!"

He didn't respond. He only sat in the bathwater that had now grown tepid, his eyes downcast.

Eve opened the drain on the tub and stood up, her wet feet slapping on the tiled floor as she crossed the room to the closet to get a towel. She took one towel and threw it on the floor near Eoduun, then wrapped herself in another and snatched her clothes up off the floor.

"I'm going to change your sheets," she announced angrily, storming from the room. "And then I'm leaving."

She got dressed and changed his bedding, throwing his old sheets in the wash. He still hadn't emerged from the bathroom, so she poked her head in, and she found him lying back in the empty tub. She walked in and stood over him, looking down at his damp body covered in goosebumps, just to make sure she hadn't hurt him more than she realized. He turned his head away from her.

"Get the fuck out of the tub," she ordered. "*Now*."

"You said you were leaving," he intoned.

"I am. But not before you get dressed."

His eyes finally rose to meet hers. "You can quit pretending to care. We both know Zeke was the one holding us together. Without him, we don't work. You don't have to try anymore."

Eve picked the towel up off the floor and dropped it onto his lap. "I'm not pretending. After what you just pulled? I wouldn't still be here if I was only pretending to care. And for the record, Zeke being gone doesn't nullify our friendship. You're still my teammate. And despite how shitty you're being right now, you're still my friend, and I know you'll feel bad about this and apologize to me when you finally get your fucking head right."

He picked up the towel and slowly rose to his feet, wrapping it around his waist. "I didn't plan it. And I didn't do it to hurt you. I just…saw an out."

Eve's hand swung on reflex, the slap echoing off the bathroom walls as Eoduun's head jerked sideways from the force of her strike. "You don't get an out," she seethed. "You're a fucking hunter. You keep fighting. You keep swinging, even when you don't fucking want to. Even when it feels pointless. You are important, and what you do is important. You don't get to just clock out when shit gets hard. You're better than that, Eoduun. Giving up isn't an option. Not for you, not for any of us." She pointed a finger in his face. "Always keep fighting, even when it fucking *hurts*."

Eoduun shuffled past her and she followed him to his bedroom. He climbed into his freshly made bed without fully drying off, curling into the fetal position, and he pulled his covers up to his chin.

"You know, even if I had killed you in the tub, I would've brought you back," she pointed out. "I couldn't bring Zeke back, but I'll be damned if I let anyone else leave me." She tapped the nightstand. "Eat the rest of your burger and finish your drink." She stood up and began to walk away.

Eoduun's voice stopped her. "Are you going to see Dagon? Are you going to do what you promised?"

She didn't turn around. She nodded and said, "Tonight. I'll come see you later, so don't lock me out."

On her way out, she turned on his TV and put on *Napoleon Dynamite* for some background noise. Silence was too depressing.

When she returned to her apartment to reconvene with Bo, she didn't tell him everything that had transpired between her and Eoduun. He didn't need to know that Eoduun tried to get her to kill him, especially with Isaac in her living room, reclined on the couch, watching a true crime documentary. Stacey's journal was on the coffee table in front of him, and Eve wondered if he'd finished it.

"Team Beta headed out," Bo informed her. "Luc texted me and said he wanted us to search Ramil's room. Shall we?"

"Sure." She glanced at Isaac on the couch, then gave Bo puppy-dog eyes while she tilted her head toward the couch.

Bo rolled his eyes. "Fine. He can come, too."

She grinned. "Thanks, Daddy."

Eve stood in Ramil's bedroom, looking around at the strangely decorated space. Everything was gold or shiny or sparkly, to the point of being borderline obnoxious. It danced the line between rich eccentric and tacky. The picture frames were gold. There was a huge jewelry stand in the corner that was filled with at least a hundred expensive-looking pieces. The pens on his desk were gold and silver. He even had a paperweight that Eve was fairly certain was a real raw gold nugget.

Bo entered from the living room and whistled. "Wow. It's even worse in here."

Eve walked around the bed, looking at the gold bedframe, and an ornate, jewel-encrusted headboard. But the foot of the bed drew her attention. It rose up higher than most footboards do, and there were two small holes on the sides with one larger hole in the middle. She noticed two little hooks near the smaller holes.

"What the fuck?" she mumbled as she studied it.

"Who the hell has he been using *that* on?" Bo wondered when he saw what Eve was looking at.

Eve unfastened the latch and lifted the top half of the footboard, and saw that it bisected the three holes…like a stockade. She dropped it back into place. "Oh my god," she blurted, color rising to her cheeks. It wasn't from embarrassment so much as it was from the scenes that began to play out in her mind.

She wondered what it would feel like to be hooked up and bound, trapped in that contraption. Would it be exciting, humiliating, or terrifying? Or all of the above? She, too, wondered who Ramil had been putting in it. Ruth, maybe?

For a fleeting, split second, Eve wondered if he wanted to put *her* in it, and what he would do to her. A dark thrill coursed up her spine that she would never, ever speak aloud.

She pushed the thoughts from her head.

Isaac came in behind them and took in the room. He arched a brow at the bed, but didn't comment on it. Instead, he signed, *You think we'll find a golden gun?*

Eve chuckled and signed back, *I'll be disappointed if we don't.*

Bo went to the closet and opened the bifold doors. Boxes of glittering treasure were tucked into the corners. He dragged one of the heavy boxes from the closet and sifted through it, and after a minute, he lifted a jeweled medallion on a gold chain from the collection. He held it up and inspected it.

"I remember this. A witch we killed last year was wearing it."

"He's keeping trophies?" Eve asked.

He dug through the box again and pulled up an ancient-looking golden figurine. "And this was in a house we raided a while back. We suspected it was a vampire nest, but it was the wrong location.

Just some rich asshole who associated with them." He held up another trinket, a bejeweled mask. "This was there, too."

"So, not trophies. Ramil's just a klepto," Eve amended.

She went over to the bed and looked under it. More boxes of treasure. When she stood up, Isaac was opening the drawer of the bedside stand. He pulled out a chunky golden crucifix necklace. There was a small red gem affixed to the center.

"Hey, I have a necklace just like that," Eve remarked. "It was my grandma's." Then, with a prickle of anger, she rounded the bed and took it from Isaac. The clasp was misshapen, just like hers. When she was little, she'd tried to use the chain for a different pendant, but it wouldn't fit through the loop, so she'd taken pliers and flattened the clasp to try to make it fit. "Hold on," she said, then rushed back to her apartment. She rummaged through the small jewelry box in her room that Luc had brought from her old apartment.

Her crucifix was missing.

When she returned to Ramil's apartment, she pointed an accusatory finger at the necklace Isaac had left on the nightstand. "That *is* my grandma's necklace!" She snatched it up and shoved it in her pocket. "That fucking thief! When the hell was he in my apartment?!" She flung open the nightstand drawer, and inside, she found a trove of items from her apartment. "This is my hair tie! And my sketching pen! And my bookmark!" She cast an anxious glance across the room to Bo and Isaac. "Why would he take *these*? They aren't worth anything. The cross isn't even real gold."

Bo shrugged and shook his head. "Why would he take any of this? It isn't like he's pawning it for cash. He's just hoarding."

Isaac lifted the lid of a laptop sitting on the desk along the wall. The screen lit up and opened to a lockscreen, asking for a password. He turned to Eve with raised brows and signed, *Any ideas?*

She looked to Bo and gestured toward the laptop. "Want to take a crack at it?"

"No, but I know who to take it to." He closed the lid and picked up the laptop. Eve and Isaac followed him down the hall and across to the apartments on the other side of the building.

He knocked on a door, and they were greeted by Celeste's bespectacled, freckled face. "Bo! And company. What's up?" she chirped. She immediately eyed the laptop under his arm.

He held it out to her. "I need you to unlock this."

She took it from his hands. "It looks like one of ours. Whose is this?"

"Not important. I just need to get into it."

Celeste brought the laptop to the messy table tucked in the space between the kitchen and bedroom. She pushed aside a stack of notebooks and papers and sat down with it in front of her. "It would help me if I knew whose it was."

"I'd rather not say," Bo replied.

Celeste looked intrigued. "How long do I have?"

"How long do you need?"

She looked over at the clock on the microwave in the kitchen and twisted her mouth in contemplation. "Hmm...tomorrow morning, probably?" She gave him a wry look. "But you do realize, once I do get in, it'll be pretty easy to figure out whose laptop it is, so you might as well just tell me. I can keep a secret."

Bo's jaw shifted under his mask, and he looked indecisive. With a heavy exhale, he said, "It's Ramil's."

Celeste's eyes widened in surprise. "Why are you trying to break into Ramil's laptop? Is he dirty?" Then with a gasp, she whispered, "Do you think he had something to do with Zeke?"

Bo cocked his head. "Do *you* think he had something to do with Zeke?"

Celeste tucked her chin and chuffed. "Well, it wouldn't be a *leap*. He was spending a whole lotta time with Ruth. Even if he wasn't part of it, I have to think he knew something was up."

"You used to be on Team Beta with him. Has he ever given you reason to think he would do something like that?"

"Please. He's always been uncommonly secretive. Secretive people have secrets." She leaned back in her chair. "Let's just say I wasn't heartbroken when Luc moved me to Team Delta." As an aside, she added, "Plus, Mendal makes an excellent wingman. I swear, bruh can zero in on the hottest girls in a crowd faster than anyone I've ever met."

Bo didn't look impressed. "That tracks."

"Ramil and Veris only ever hung out with each other. And Mira...I don't think that bitch likes anybody but Luc. Although I'm pretty sure she and Ramil were hooking up on the side. I've caught her leaving his hotel room more than once on the road."

Eve grimaced. She couldn't help but make that face any time Mira was brought up. She ventured, "It sounds like you don't like Ramil."

Celeste lifted a shoulder. "I don't *dislike* him, but I never fully trusted him." Then she reconsidered. "Well, maybe that's not wholly true. He was an excellent listener. He'd get you talking, and suddenly you wanted to tell him all your secrets. There were times when I felt like I could tell him anything. Like I *wanted* to tell him secrets I've never told anyone before."

"What kinds of secrets?" Eve wondered.

"Like my darkest desires and wishes." Celeste gave her a flirty grin. "Are *you* trying to learn my dirty secrets, Eve?"

Eve chuckled, feeling a blush rising to her cheeks, and she held her palms out. "No, that's ok..."

Celeste smirked at her. "Relax. You're not my type, anyway." She looked her up and down. "But I am into the muscle mommy thing. Get yourself some tattoos and dye that pink hair black, and then we'll talk," she said with a wink.

Bo stepped in, "Thanks, Celeste. Text me when you get access to that laptop."

On the way back to Ramil's apartment to complete the search, Isaac posed, *If Ramil can make people tell their secrets, maybe he can make them do other things.*

Eve translated to Bo. Then she spoke and signed, "Like Veris? The power of persuasion?"

Isaac alternatingly raised his palms. *Maybe.*

Bo pulled his mask down just below his mouth. "I've never seen Ramil use a power like that."

Isaac started to sign, then paused, looking at Bo's lowered mask. To Eve's shock, he spoke aloud, slowly, so Bo could understand his unique articulation. "Maybe he isn't obvious about it. Have you ever seen him stealing?" he asked rhetorically.

Bo's eyebrow twitched. "Fair point."

Eve was barely listening to the conversation. She just wanted to clap her hands and jump up and down with glee at these subtle gestures that, on the outside, didn't seem like a big deal, but in reality, indicated immense strides in the relationship between Bo and Isaac. One small step, one giant leap.

19
Wings

As Eve, Bo, and Isaac continued the search of Ramil's apartment, Eve considered the plausibility of Isaac's postulation. Did Ramil actually have the power to draw out truths and secrets? Hidden desires? And did that power extend to compulsion? Could he make people do his bidding? Even if he had that power, he wouldn't have needed to use it openly with Veris around. It was possible he could be hiding it, or using it surreptitiously.

Eve could think of only one person…entity…god?…who could have any hope of providing answers to her questions. The one who wanted Ramil dead for unspecified reasons. She didn't want to *summon* Apep, but she wanted to open the telepathic connection. Last time she'd tried, he'd ignored her.

As she rummaged around in Ramil's bathroom, not sure what she hoped to find there, she reached out mentally. *Apep?*

Not a peep.

Had he used the grimoire to break his binding with her?

Or, just as likely, he just wasn't that into her anymore now that he had the grimoire. But what was he doing with it? The god of chaos doesn't come into possession of a monster and mayhem recipe book, *The Book of the* fucking *Damned*, and just sit on it.

Sooner or later, he was going to unleash hell on an unsuspecting world.

"We should be looking for Apep, not in here playing treasure hunters," Eve said as she came out of the bathroom. "Or at least, someone should be."

"What do you think Team Flannel and Team Gamma are doing? They're following leads," Bo replied. His mask was back up again. "Sometimes I think you forget you're part of a whole organization. We aren't the only team. We don't need to see to everything ourselves."

It was true. She did often forget that there was an entire group of people working toward the same goals as her and her team. She'd spent so much of her life without any meaningful support, she'd come to learn that the only one she could rely on to get anything done was herself. She was learning to rely on her teammates, now, to depend on them. But she still had a hard time extending that trust to the rest of Knighco, especially after the incident with Dizzy, Ruth's betrayal, and the questions around Ramil's integrity.

And why the hell did Ramil have so many of her stupid little trinkets?! By the time they finished the sweep, Eve had recovered nine items that belonged to her, including a notebook with her to-do lists and doodles. The creepiest one had to be the cherry Chapstick he'd taken from her bathroom cabinet – it looked like he'd been using it.

She took every one of her stolen items back to her place. She knew it was a dead giveaway that she'd been in his apartment snooping around, but at this point, she felt like it was fair. He'd obviously been snooping in her apartment. Let him confront her about it. She'd love to hear his excuse.

Since she was on a mission to reclaim her lost and stolen items, she stopped at Isaac's apartment on her way back to hers, and he gave her back the shoe that had flung from her foot when she was brawling with Luc. She may have also taken that opportunity to borrow the key to Ruth's apartment he'd left hanging on a keyring next to his jacket by the door. He was using it to check on Dagon, but after tonight, he wouldn't need it anymore.

That night, Eve sent Bo and Isaac back to their own quarters, then returned to Eoduun's apartment to check on him. It was dark when she walked in, except for the glow of the screensaver on the television and the bathroom light. She left those lights on, using them to carefully navigate her way through the mess still littering the floor. She went into his room and crossed to his bed. Instead of just sitting on the edge, however, she climbed wordlessly under the covers with him.

They lay in silence for a while, and she wondered if he was asleep, until she heard him mumble, "I'm sorry."

She scooted closer to him and curled herself around his back, wrapping one arm around his stomach. She was the big spoon today, after all.

"I know."

And that was all that was said. She felt his body tremble and shake as the heartache overtook him, silent sobs and not-so-silent sniffles tearing at her heartstrings, drawing out her own lamentations. Eoduun rolled over and enveloped her in his arms, and they clung to each other and let the tears flow.

Eve awoke with tears in her eyes, the lingering apparition of Zeke's fearful, desperate face burned into her mind. She hadn't meant to fall asleep. She cautiously extracted herself from Eoduun's arms and slipped out of his bed, hoping not to wake him. She wouldn't have his powers long, since she didn't have Bo's powers to help her hold on to them, so she needed to take advantage of them while she could. She snuck out his door and stole down the hall to Ruth's old apartment.

She used the key she'd lifted from Isaac's apartment and let herself in, closing the door quietly behind her.

"I knew you would come eventually, princess," Dagon greeted her. She could hear the sneer in his voice without even looking at him.

The room was lit in a cozy, soft yellow glow from the living room lamp. Ruth had been a fan of those trendy Edison bulbs. Eve cast her eyes over Dagon sitting in the middle of the devil's trap she and Ramil had painted on the floor, waiting for the revulsion to lance through her.

But it wasn't revulsion that struck her.

She slowly stalked around the perimeter of the devil's trap. He sat back casually with his arms tied behind his back, but his vermilion eyes followed her every move from behind long, black locks with enraptured interest. His knees were splayed wide, his massive thighs straining against the fabric of Zeke's black cargo pants, his bare ankles bound to the legs of the wooden kitchen chair. He was still shirtless, his huge muscles flexing and bulging under his deeply tawny, tattooed skin as he shifted in his seat.

Heat simmered between her thighs at the sight of him half-naked and tied up.

At her mercy.

She passed behind him, taking notice of the row of curved gill slits that split the skin behind his ears on the side of his neck, partially hidden by his hair. Her gaze followed the curve of his shoulder, admiring the way his triceps flexed with his wrists bound behind him, and her eyes traveled down his thick, veiny forearms, past the bindings around his wrists, to his enormous hands. Beautifully shaped, enormous hands. He rolled his shoulders, drawing her attention to the way his back muscles bunched together and formed deep ridges in his flesh. Her fingernails longed to leave their mark there.

"Admiring the view?" Dagon taunted.

She looked up, catching his eyes in the reflection of the full-length mirror on the wall near him. "Assessing," she retorted. "What happened to your wings?" she inquired, circling around his other side.

"I tucked them away. Why? Did you wish to see them?" he offered, turning his head to maintain eye contact.

"No. Passing curiosity." Fucking liar. She liked those wings.

No she didn't. She hated him.

He was going to die tonight.

She stopped in front of him, staring him down, her hands casually in her pockets. She wished she had dressed in something more intimidating than pink cotton sleep shorts and a t-shirt.

"Is Zeke still in there?" she asked outright.

"Are you going to kill me if he isn't?" Dagon guessed knowingly. Was he reading her mind?

Her heart sank at the prospect of Zeke's presence *not* still lingering somewhere within Dagon's form, and she only now realized how much she, too, had been hoping for a miracle.

Fuck it. *Just do it.*

An angry black and red haze swirled around the periphery of her vision, like looking down the center of a Christian Louboutin tornado, and Eve cast herself through the tunnel into Dagon's mind.

…And hit a solid wall.

His voice permeated her consciousness. *It's not going to be so easy this time.*

It felt like she was trying to push through a door, and he was on the other side pushing back. The harder she pushed, the more he resisted.

You know what you need to do, princess. Come to me. Give me a taste. Then *you can lord your power over me.*

Her efforts felt futile. She retreated, and the black and red haze dissipated. But since she couldn't get into his head, she felt fully justified in blocking him from hers, too.

"You can keep me out of your head, but good luck keeping me out of…other places," Dagon quipped, his eyes moving down her body keenly. He noticed her bare toes edging up to the border of the devil's trap, but not daring to cross it. "Step inside, princess," he urged in a low, seductive tone. He swayed his knee side to side. "Come sit on my lap and tell me what you want."

"I want Zeke back."

"See if you can dig him out, then."

"Just tell me. Please. Is he in there?"

Dagon leaned forward as far as he could against his bindings, a cruel smile dancing on his perfect lips. "Come. And. See."

She hated his games. She hated even more that she was about to indulge him, and she hated how she didn't hate that half as much as she pretended to hate it.

She stepped one foot over the outer line of the circle, then followed through with the other, bracing herself. But nothing happened. She kept a wary eye on Dagon, now inside the devil's trap with him.

Inside his cage.

"Welcome to the wild side," he said.

Eve shrugged a shoulder and glanced around. "Seems pretty lame, if you ask me."

A chuckle sounded low in his throat. "Is it?" With a quick burst of strength, he suddenly broke free from his restraints, big black wings unfolding from behind him and stretching the span of the devil's trap. In the next instant, he was behind her, blocking her retreat from the painted trap. Her breath hitched in her throat as his gargantuan frame loomed over her, his wings curving around her, casting her in shadow.

Oh, how she'd erred.

She took an unsteady step forward, away from him and toward the center of the circle, and he swept in to fill the space she vacated. He wasn't touching her, but he was close enough that she could feel the heat of his bare chest against her back. Her heart hammered, her knees weak with fear and anticipation.

His finger grazed across the back of her neck, swiping her hair aside. His hot breath ghosted over the skin at the nape of her neck as he bent down, *way* down, and murmured, "Do you want to touch them?"

She cleared her throat. "Touch what?"

His wings furled around her, and her adrenaline spiked at the sensation of being truly trapped. "You know, I don't let just anybody touch them," he said. "My wings are sacred."

She wanted to act aloof, to say she didn't give two shits about that, to pretend she couldn't care less about his wings. But fuck. They're *wings*.

Of course she was going to touch them.

She lifted her hand, slowly reaching out toward the rounded outer edge that arched downward in front of her. Two inches away, she hesitated, but he closed the distance, bumping the edge of it up into her hand. She gasped.

It wasn't at all what she expected. It wasn't *bone*. It was solid, but more like…an engorged cock. It was hot and hard, but also soft like supple leather. She could feel the pulse of blood through it. She splayed her fingers, skimming them down over the thin flaps that stretched between the harder ridges. It was like a kitten's ears without the fur.

Dagon hummed behind her as her other hand joined the exploration. She curled her palm around the smooth, black, claw-like appendage at the apex of one wing.

Traitorous thoughts spilled into her brain. *I don't want to destroy this.*

But she had to deliver vengeance. For Zeke.

Zeke wouldn't want that.

Fuck.

Eoduun wants it, then. And deep down, she wanted it too. Revenge. Retribution. Right?

Right?

Fuck.

FUCK.

Dagon dragged the back of his knuckles down her bare arm, then trailed his finger back up the underside. She yanked her hand back and clamped her arm to her side when his fingertip came close to her armpit.

"Ticklish?" he asked, amused.

"Everyone's armpits are ticklish," she defended, clamping her arm more tightly to her side as his finger teased the seam between them.

"The armpit is an erogenous zone. Did you know that? The increased sensitivity, the scent glands, the proximity to the chest and neck…" His fingers trailed up over her shoulder, arced over her neck, then moved down between her tits, stroking the underside of her breast in its path back toward her armpit.

"Stop it!" she complained, trying to squirm away from him.

His other arm stopped her, pulling her back to him until her back slammed against his chest and stomach. A thick, hard ridge pressed against her lower back.

Her monster stirred, blinking one eye open. The danger he promised, the power he possessed, woke the dark need in her. Without Bo's essence to bring it to heel, it was untethered. Free to wreak havoc.

Dagon shifted toward the center of the devil's trap, and Eve had no choice but to move along with him, trapped between his body and wings. When he stopped and opened his wings, she found herself staring at her own reflection in the mirror on the wall just outside of the circle.

Breakable. That was the first word that popped in her head when she saw herself standing there, Dagon's enormous, godly body looming behind her, a wall of muscle framing her reflection as his eyes bored into hers through the mirror. She looked *breakable*.

But that was her secret. She *was* breakable. She'd already been broken. But, like glass, it had only made her more dangerous.

20

A Girl and Her Hellhound

Admittedly, however, Eve felt anything but menacing as she gazed at herself and Dagon in the mirror. She was reminded of a picture she'd seen once of an innocent little girl with a huge Cane Corso sitting guard behind her. Her protector.

Is that what Dagon was? What he fancied himself?

What *she* fancied him to be?

She watched the reflection of his hand slip around her middle, flattening against her stomach, and he dropped her gaze in the mirror, looking down at her in front of him. "This is where you belong," he asserted.

"In a devil's trap with a demon? Not really my scene." But her voice wasn't as taunting or nonchalant as she wished it to be. She was still fixated on the mirror.

She liked the view. A girl and her hellhound.

She hated that she liked this.

His eyes flicked back up to meet hers in the mirror. "We could rule the world, princess. Just you and me."

"It will never be just you and me."

"'Never' comes to pass all the time. Haven't I already warned you against your confidence in the concept of 'never'?" His hand on her belly slowly inched downward, his fingers dipping under the waistband of her shorts. He leaned down and touched his lips to the shell of her ear, the whiskers of his beard tickling her. "Never say never." His hand plunged into her shorts, and she sucked in a breath when his finger began to circle over the thin fabric of her underwear at the apex of her thighs.

The beast in her belly purred.

That's it. Come closer. Step into my trap.

He curled his finger under her panties, stroking her bare, slick petals. Her knees wobbled, and he gave a satisfied hum. "So fucking wet. Even when you hate me, you want me." He speared his warm, thick finger into her, and Eve swallowed down the whimper that wanted to greet the air.

She hated that she liked this. But, oh, god, did she like this. She watched in the mirror as Dagon shoved her shorts and panties down to her thighs with his free hand, and the tip of one big wing hooked under the waistband and dragged them the rest of the way down.

"Tell me how much you hate this," Dagon taunted, and she lifted her gaze from the view of his hand between her legs to meet the reflection of his vermilion eyes. She widened her legs as he inserted a second finger, and she watched her pelvis grind against his hand, her clit seeking friction against his palm. The motion also made her bare ass rub against the base of the erection straining in his pants, and he groaned. "Look how gorgeous you are, princess. My beautiful little monster," he praised.

The molten heat in her core was rising, bubbling up, threatening to erupt. Her breath grew ragged, panting, and just as she was about to burst...

He stopped fucking her with his fingers, withdrawing them, leaving her unsatisfied.

She growled in frustration, her hips jerking to no avail, the climax eluding her. Her own hand flew between her legs, but Dagon was quick to intercept it, restraining her wrist with an invisible force, disallowing her relief.

"Oh, no, princess. Bad girl," he scolded, tsk-tsking her. He used his unseen power to draw both of her arms up over her head, draping them around the back of his neck and binding them with an invisible tether.

It looked like he was wearing her as a necklace.

"You're a disappointment," she insulted him, shamelessly rubbing her thighs together.

He chuckled. He reached his hands up and, starting at her elbows, began to slowly trail his fingers down the insides of her arms.

Fuuuuck. Her body was already overly sensitive, and now, as his hands inched closer to her armpits, her nerves short-circuited. The tickle was no longer just a tickle. A strange, desperate sort of pleasure prickled in her core, like a deep, agonizing itch that needed to be scratched. She arched her back, straddling one of his muscular legs, grinding her clit back against his thigh. She watched in the mirror as Dagon's fingertips traced the outside of her lats, barely brushing the edge of her armpits, and then...

He dropped his hands to her hips and pushed her away from his thigh.

"Fuck!" she cried out, her eyes beginning to water. She fought against the invisible restraints holding her wrists together behind his neck, but she still had no power over him. Her core pulsed and throbbed, and the beast inside her fidgeted impatiently. If she could get him to taste her blood, it would rocket her over the edge. She just needed to get him to drink from her.

Then she could finish this.

She leveled a glare at him in the mirror while he grinned wickedly back at her. "I'm going to kill you," she threatened.

His grin only widened. "No, you aren't." He ducked his head out from under her arms, but she remained held up by her wrists, like she was shackled from the ceiling by an invisible chain. He circled around in front of her, and she angled her head back to look up at his towering frame. He licked his lips as he gazed down at her, then he made a show of slowly lowering himself in front of her, holding her gaze as he dropped to his knees.

Even though she was only a little taller than him when he was down on his knees, and she was still bound up by his invisible forces, she felt a surge of dominance as she looked down at him. She sneered. "This is where *you* belong. Kneeling before me."

He arched a thick, dark eyebrow up at her, his lip curling slyly. He leaned in and ran his tongue along the side of her neck. "Oh, you'll be on your knees for me soon enough," he promised. He trailed his lips down her collarbone, then lifted her shirt up to expose her soft, unrestrained mounds. His big hands cupped her breasts, lifting one pebbled nipple to his mouth, then the other, while Eve chewed her lip and moaned in frustration.

She needed that mouth somewhere else.

He moved his way down her stomach, following the ridge in the middle of her abs, which also happened to be the ridge her birthmark followed, too.

Did he know what her mark was?

"You've never mentioned my birthmark," she commented breathlessly.

His mouth stilled over her bellybutton, and his eyes traveled all the way up her body to meet hers again. There was a hint of deception swimming in those demonic eyes. "No, I haven't." His lips trailed lower as he kept his eyes trained on hers. He slid his enormous body between her standing legs, nudging them open wider, then leaned back, his wings holding him upright so his hands were free to grip the backs of her thighs. His mouth hovered between her legs. "I wasn't sure if it was what I thought it was." His breath puffed agonizingly against her sensitive flesh.

His mouth was *so* close. She tried to lean forward to close the distance, but he tightened his fingers around her legs.

She chewed her lower lip, trying to control her panting breaths. "What did you think it was?" she managed to ask.

The tip of his hot, wet tongue languidly stroked her clit, and she gasped, but he was quick to pull away again, and the moan that started in her throat turned to an anguished cry. He was relishing in her desperate need.

He answered her question. "I believe you to bear the stain of sin, princess." He tilted his head slightly, allowing his bearded jaw to brush her inner thigh, then blew a sultry, soft breath across her aching center.

And his tongue finally...*finally*...stopped forming words and dipped between her thighs, working in earnest at fulfilling her aching need.

"Yesss..." The drawn-out word spilled like sweet molasses from Eve's tongue. She gazed at their reflection in the mirror in front of her – her body stretched open and trembling beneath Dagon's hands, his face between her legs as she stood straddled over him while he leaned back on his big, black wings, devouring her.

Inside the devil's trap, trapped with the devil.

She hated that she liked this. She hated that she wasn't certain who held the power in this moment, and she hated even more that she didn't give a fuck.

Dagon sucked her clit into his mouth, his tongue swirling quick, tight circles, hitting just the right pressure...just the right tempo...and with a shuddering gasp, Eve was tipped into crashing waves of ecstasy. Her whole body clenched and trembled as she rode the crest, her legs threatening to give out beneath her. Dagon drank every last drop of the nectar he'd drawn from her, gripping his fingers painfully into her thighs.

The next thing she knew, he was on his feet, unleashing his swollen cock. The invisible restraints holding her upright unexpectedly released, and she dropped to her knees at the sudden lack of support. Dagon's hand caught in her hair, his other hand on her jaw. He shoved his thumb between her lips and parted her jaws, like she was a fish on a hook.

"Open that pretty mouth, princess," he commanded.

He slid his cock between her lips, over her tongue, and hit the back of her throat, making her gag. Eve's eyes watered as he fucked her mouth, the thick veins in his cock sliding back and forth over her wriggling tongue, the ridge of his crown skimming dangerously close to her back teeth as he pumped in and out.

She could bite him. She could ruin his fucking day.

…But she didn't.

Dagon withdrew from her mouth and dragged her to her feet, hoisting her onto his hips. He thrust himself inside of her without warning, her core already drenched and primed for him, and she clung to his neck and gasped his name at the way he stretched her.

Varghrir had been rather conservative when he'd taken the form of Dagon for her.

Dagon's pupils were blown wide with desire, the deep red of his irises hardly visible anymore as his eyes roved rapaciously over her body perched atop his hips. His gaze stopped and lingered on her lips. "The way you pant my name is going to live in my head forever," he vowed, then fisted one hand into her hair and attacked her mouth with a voracious kiss, his tongue pushing past her lips with a deep, resonating moan.

And then his teeth sank into her lip, and Eve mewled at the rush of euphoria as her blood spilled like slick copper between their tongues. She pulsed around his cock, clenching her thighs around his waist for leverage as she gyrated against him.

Her curse had awakened fully, and it was whispering to her.

Take him down.

Ruin him.

Make him beg for mercy...

...And do not grant it.

She pulled her mouth away from his, brushing her lips along his jaw, over his beard, and down his thick, cabled neck. She looked over his shoulder and met her own eyes in the mirror.

Her mouth was stained red with her own blood as she grinned at herself, then took in an eyeful of the sight before her – Dagon's massive body rolling and flexing as he pumped into her, her nails digging into the swell of his shoulders just above his wings, her powerful legs wrapped around him, ready to squeeze the life out of him when the time was right.

But those fucking wings. Oh, those beautiful, gothic wings. She reached further over his shoulder and clasped a hand around the thick base of each wing where it connected to his back. It was like holding a giant cock in each hand. Dagon groaned and swelled, stretching her inner walls even more, and it spurred her bloodlust. She watched her reflection bare her teeth, sinking them viciously into Dagon's trapezius.

"Fuck, princess," Dagon purred. He took Eve down to the floor, pinning her back roughly against the hardwood with his enormous body between her legs as his huge hands closed around her neck. He held her down by the throat while he slammed into her, fucking her with every shred of his raw power now that he'd tasted her blood. Now, for him, she'd become unbreakable.

And he'd become her prey.

Own him.

Destroy him.

Pull his wings off like an insignificant little fly.

Her curse was becoming more insistent, but Eve needed to verify one thing before she carried out her dark task.

She had to see if there was any chance Zeke was still alive. With a guttural roar, she drove her hands up between Dagon's forearms and broke his hold on her throat. She locked him in her guard like a steel trap and grabbed his jaw in her hands, dragging his face down to hers. She focused her eyes on his and forced open the swirling black and red tunnel into his mind and burrowed right in.

21
One Final Request

Zeke was everywhere.

Memories she recognized from Texas, Newbury, the cabin in the woods, her kitchen, her couch...memories of him and Eoduun sharing her...memories of watching movies with her, kneading his feet on Eoduun's back while he rubbed her corpse feet...

Zeke! She called out to him, hope gripping her heart.

She saw him trying to sit in Bo's lap, but being pushed onto the floor and lying there, pretending he was so offended, and it made her want to laugh. She saw him leaping down the stairs of the apartment building, meeting her for the first time, and she felt how struck he was by her. She saw him throwing an arm over her shoulder and asking the creepy men in front of the bar if they thought he was pretty. She saw him tossing a hot pink dildo at Eoduun in her kitchen.

She saw memories she didn't recognize, too. Him and Eoduun playing the Switch, and Eoduun getting annoyed that Zeke kept throwing red shells at him in *Mario Kart*. Team Alpha hanging out with Team Flannel at a bar before Eve joined Knighco, and Zeke and Ruger getting on the table to have a drunken belly dancing competition. Zeke and his friend Cassidy running out onto the field to play at Homecoming on a crisp, Friday night.

She waded through all his memories, desperately seeking the man himself. *Zeke! Where are you?* she cried. His memories were all here…he had to be here, too, didn't he?

But as she pushed through the highlight reel, she found herself surrounded by darker, less pleasant memories. Killing the nuckelavee, knowing that Eve hadn't wanted it to die. The horrible desires he'd experienced when he was possessed by the wendigo – how he'd wanted to fuck both Eve and Eoduun *while* he feasted on their flesh, and the nightmares that had plagued him afterward. The dejection he felt when he realized that Eve would never look at him the same way she looked at Luc.

She saw how much it hurt Zeke to keep pretending he didn't know that Eoduun wanted more from him, but he wasn't capable of giving him more because he just wasn't wired that way. He gave him what he could, and he knew it wasn't enough, and he knew it would eventually all come to a head, but he didn't want to lose Eoduun. He loved him as his best friend, and he wished to hell that some day Eoduun would be able to accept it for what it was.

And then she saw that final memory. She saw herself staring back at him as he rose from the floor, confused, surrounded by monsters and strangers. But Eve was there, and even though she was looking at him with such horror, her face still brought him comfort. But then he felt it. Dagon was no longer contained to his own space, and his life force was spilling over into and overriding Zeke's. His body was no longer his own.

With that realization, he also understood the look on Eve's face. He understood why she looked so devastated, and it broke his heart. He had to leave her, and he couldn't tell her goodbye. He couldn't reassure her that it was ok. He couldn't tell her not to be sad. He couldn't tell her not to burn the world down, because he knew that, even if she didn't love him the way she loved Luc, she *did* love him, and this could destroy her. He knew she would need revenge. Someone to blame.

He hoped she didn't kill Dagon out of spite, because he knew this wasn't Dagon's doing. Dagon was a prick, but he couldn't hate him.

It wasn't in Zeke to hate.

And he wanted that for Eve, too – to be able to forgive and not be consumed by hate in the wake of this. In his final moments, he was scared of death, without a doubt, but as he stared back at Eve, he was terrified of what this was going to do to her. To Eoduun. To Bo.

None of them were ready for this.

As his body began to shift and betray him, one final thought poured through directly to Dagon: *I know you aren't evil – I never believed you were. We can be more than the terrible things we've done. How about one last contract, Dagon? One last request before I become you? Show them you* are *more. Keep them safe. Keep* her *safe. Don't let my death be for nothing.*

Those last words echoed around her.

Don't let my death be for nothing.

She couldn't kill Dagon. Eve realized that, while she had to finally accept that Zeke wasn't *alive* within Dagon, some piece of his will had been infused into Dagon. Something of Dagon *was* Zeke, and that's why all of Zeke's memories had become Dagon's.

And they were all here, floating around in the forefront of his mind because Dagon was reliving them, over and over and over while he sat, patiently resigned to his devil's trap.

Eve finally noticed the emotion around her. She hadn't noticed it at first because it so closely mirrored her own. Sadness. Loss. Regret. Dagon missed Zeke, too.

He was a good kid, Dagon spoke to Eve in his head. *He didn't deserve this. He was too good for this world. I don't know when or how it happened, but the little shit made me care about him. Maybe I'm only truly realizing it now that he's dead, but...I've suspected for a while that I didn't resent him the way I should, even though I had every right to. And now I feel like a small, yet significant chunk of me has been ripped out. He's still here, but also...not.*

Eve didn't know how to feel. She wanted to stay there a while longer, roaming from memory to memory, absorbing every bit of Zeke she could, but at the same time, the feral monster inside her gnawed at her focus, demanding she finish what she started.

Take his power.

Take his life.

Kill him!

She withdrew from Dagon's mind, only to find that her body was still very much alive with need. Her own will warred with the will of her curse as she undulated beneath him, his cock still hot and hard inside her. If she tried to stop now, she would end up desperate and out of control, like the time Apep disappeared after she'd already initiated the ritual with him, and Isaac had had to exorcise her. She couldn't let that happen again. It only further proved how weak she was, how much control this curse still had over her.

She had to finish this herself. She had to prove herself.

She threw her arms around his neck and pulled him close, molding her body to his as he fucked her, his pace slowing, his strokes deepening. She needed to take his power. She needed to see it through, but she needed to resist the overbearing urge to tear him to pieces in the process.

"Don't let me kill you, you bastard," she said, gnashing her teeth. The tingle in the roots of her teeth was already driving her mad. "Fight it with everything you have. I don't think I can stop myself as easily with you."

Though she'd told Eoduun she would've just revived him if she had killed him in the tub, she wasn't fully certain that her blood *would* resurrect someone killed by her curse. She didn't want to run the risk if it didn't.

Dagon's hand slid up the side of her face, his thumb hooking under her jaw as his teeth nipped at her neck. "Are you telling me to struggle, princess?"

"You'll die if you don't."

"Tell me. What are you going to do to me, little monster?"

With a surge of fury, Eve tried to roll him over, but he thrust a wing out to stop the motion. She growled in frustration and reached over his shoulders, grabbing the base of his wings.

"First, I'm going to rip your wings off."

Dagon's hands closed around her forearms and, with some difficulty, pulled her hands away from his wings, slamming her arms to the floor by her head. He leaned his weight on them as he jerked his hips, driving into her roughly and making her yelp. His wings suddenly folded in on themselves and disappeared behind his back.

"Nice try. What else are you going to do to me?" he taunted, running his tongue over his smirking lips. His black hair tumbled down over his eyes as his vermilion gaze burned into her, his muscles flexing with every hard thrust.

He was enjoying this.

God, he was hot as the devil. Eve's core pulsed around him as her pleasure mounted. She clenched her jaw and, through bared teeth, she answered, "I'm going to make you bleed."

Dagon's eyes flashed with intrigue. He leaned down close and whispered, "Go on. Make me bleed."

He barely had the words out before Eve closed her jaws over his throat. He groaned, one hand tangling in her hair to try to hold her at bay, which freed one of her arms from his restraint. She shoved his shoulder and thrust her hip up, and this time, she was able to roll herself on top of him, slamming his shoulders onto the floor.

She looked down at him victoriously, then allowed her eyes to slide up to the mirror once again. She saw herself seated atop his hips, her hands pressed against his chest. He still had one hand gripping her hair, the other on her hip, rocking her into motion on his cock. She watched Dagon lift his shoulders off the floor and sit up, then found herself looking up at the ceiling when he tugged her hair back to expose her throat to him. She felt his teeth scrape over her neck, his hot breath on her skin, but he didn't return the bite she'd given him. His hand on her hip urged her into a quicker pace. She could feel him swelling, thickening inside of her, hitting new, delicious depths, and her pleasure rose to meet his.

"I'm close, princess," he panted against the column of her throat. When he loosened his grip on her hair, she leveled her gaze at the mirror again. Dagon noticed. "You want to watch?" He lifted her and brought her right to the edge of the devil's trap, so close to the wall that their reflection filled the mirror. Dagon spun her around and hooked his arms under her knees, holding her back against his chest, facing the mirror. "So watch," he ordered.

Eve reached one arm back and gripped the back of his neck, arching against him as the head of his cock pushed at her entrance. She couldn't pull her eyes away from the view of his girth, slick with her arousal, sliding up into her, then back out again. In, out, in, out…and all the while his huge arms held her so effortlessly, like she weighed nothing. She was fucking a mountain.

"Your pussy was made for me," he crooned, his beard catching in her hair as he spoke, staring over her shoulder at their union in the mirror. "*You* were made for me."

A new wave of euphoric rage consumed her, and she dug her nails into the back of Dagon's neck. "I wasn't made for anyone. *You* were all made for *me*." Her pelvis rolled back against him, the maelstrom of pleasure and thirst for violence quickly building in her core. "Your *power* belongs to me," she panted. She leaned forward and rested her hands on the wall on either side of the mirror, the top half of her body now outside of the devil's trap.

Dagon shifted his arms, allowing her legs to hook back around his hamstrings while he held her up with an arm wrapped around her belly, the other hand tangling in her hair. She felt the rageful tingles spidering over her scalp from the roots of her hair as he pulled on it, and she threw herself back into him even harder, chasing that imminent release.

When she felt Dagon swell and pulse inside of her, a deep, guttural groan erupting from his chest, she clenched her walls around him, and that extra friction was all it took to fling her into violent oblivion. Immense power surged through her in unrelenting waves, and her vision went fuzzy as she slammed her hand against the mirror, fracturing it into shards.

Bleed him!

Kill him!

KILL HIM!

Eve rent a sharp shard of glass from the mirror and, before she even registered what she was doing, she'd twisted around and buried it deeply between his ribs, straight into Dagon's heart. He swore and dropped to one knee, still holding onto her.

Reason had left her.

Finish it.

Finish it!

FINISH HIM!

She peeled herself off of him, then whirled around and tackled him to the floor. She yanked the shard from his chest, blood sluicing from the gash, and her own blood dripped down her arm from the deep slice it had cut into her hand. She touched the point to his throat, and he gripped her arm with both hands to stop her.

But they both knew he couldn't stop her. His immortality meant nothing against her. An injury like the one he'd just sustained would've been merely a flesh wound from anyone else, but from her, in this moment, it was a death sentence.

He was going to die.

She leaned down close to his face, running her bloody thumb over his lips. "I'm not your princess. I'm your fucking queen."

"Evie! Goddamn it!"

22

Lethal, Graceful, Primal Beauty

Bo's voice instantly stopped her, the rage in her soul suddenly cowed. The monster inside her rolled over, showing its belly. She dropped the glass shard in her hand as Bo caught her around the middle and plucked her off Dagon. He quickly stripped out of his black t-shirt and pulled it down over her head, covering her naked form.

"What the fuck, Evie?!" Bo fretted, looking her over, his rough hands worrying over her face and body. He fixed her with an intense gold and blue gaze, his mask missing from his face. He looked like he'd just been roused from bed. "Jesus, I thought you were killing Eoduun. Imagine my surprise when I scented you *here*. Goddamn it, Evie." His voice was stern, but there was an undertone of relief. Eve could feel the lingering panic radiating from his chest into hers.

Dagon groaned and sat up, pressing his hand over the stab wound in his chest to stem the bleeding, but it was already beginning to heal. The blood she'd thoughtlessly smeared on his lips must have been enough to fix him. He licked his lips, then grinned over at Eve. He winked one red eye. "You almost had me." Then, with a smug face, he added, "*My queen.*" He gingerly rose to his feet, scooping up Zeke's old pants from the floor and stepping into them. He looked down at his bare ankles. "Now that I have you here, would it be possible to get me some pants that actually fit?" he asked conversationally.

Bo scowled at him. "That's more than you deserve." He returned his attention to Eve. "You are in so much fucking trouble, little girl."

Eve crossed her arms, avoiding his eyes. "I needed to know if Zeke was still in there," she explained weakly.

Bo raised an expectant brow at her. "And?"

She shook her head. "He's not…not exactly. But…all his memories are still there. He…*became* a part of Dagon." Bo looked contemptuously over at Dagon, and Dagon lifted a shoulder at him. Eve said, "I was going to kill him if Zeke wasn't in there. I was going to get revenge, for all of us. For Zeke." She looked down at the floor. "I changed my mind after seeing in his mind, but by then, it was too late. I'd already started the ritual. I thought I could stop, since I stopped with Eoduun. But not this time." She lifted a defeated look to Bo. "I still can't control it without your power."

She'd failed. Yet again.

She glanced over and saw Dagon eyeing her clothes on the floor near him. She quickly threw her hand out and, using his telekinetic powers, drew the clothes across the floor and into her hand.

Dagon gave her a theatrical slow clap. "Maybe my powers *were* made for you. You take to them like a fish to water."

Eve stepped into her shorts, but when she started to pull off Bo's shirt to replace it with her own, Bo stopped her, giving Dagon a sidelong glance. "Not here. Come on, Evie." He guided her toward the door.

"And what about me?" Dagon called. "You saw in my head, princess. You know what Zeke asked of me. Demanded of me. I don't need to be trapped in here. I'm not going anywhere."

"You're right about one thing," Bo interjected. "You're not going anywhere. Enjoy your comfy chair."

Back at Eve's apartment, after a quick but thorough shower, she wrapped gauze around her hand. It would be healed over in a matter of hours, but it was still bleeding, and Eve could see the way it was drawing Bo's attention. His wolf eye flashed through at her every time he got a whiff of her blood.

The two of them sat at the kitchen island, a bag of rice chips in front of Eve. She told Bo what she'd seen in Dagon's head, explaining that some semblance of Zeke's will was still alive in Dagon, and he was at least partially compelled by it.

"I don't have *proof* that he's not a danger to us, but I felt it, Bo. Zeke might not technically be alive, but he won't let Dagon betray us. Not anymore."

"Small comfort," Bo replied skeptically. "But even if I do trust that that's true, no one else will. Especially not after what happened with Ruth."

He wasn't wrong. Dagon would be a hard sell. An impossible sell. But...

"I'll take responsibility for him," she announced. "I have his power, *and* he's bound to me. I can compel him to behave."

Bo's brows pinched together. "How do you know that?"

She looked at the counter in front of her. "I just know. He'll do whatever I say. He might argue or act like a douche about it, but he'll listen." *Like a good little hellhound.*

"Hm." Bo was unconvinced. "We'll consult with Luc tomorrow."

Eve nibbled at a rice chip. Curiously, she asked, "So, why did you think I was killing Eoduun?"

"Your rage woke me from a dead sleep. I'd heard you go to Eoduun's room earlier, so I assumed you were still with him, and

189

that you'd lost control." He gave an irritated dip of his head. "I was half right."

Eve noticed a distinct lack of jealousy in his emotions, only ire. "You're not jealous?"

He gave her a challenging expression. "Why would I be jealous that you tried to kill Dagon? You weren't fucking him because you *want* him." And then she felt his uncertainty creeping in. "…Right?"

Right?

Right?

…

"Of course not," she huffed out. "I just thought it might bother you, seeing…that."

"For a moment, maybe. And if you weren't actively trying to end him when I walked in, maybe." His wolf eye flashed in her direction. "But there was also a moment, after the initial shock, that I…" His gaze filled with lust. "…I liked what I was seeing." He confessed, "I almost let you kill him. You were a vision, Evie. Lethal, graceful, primal beauty." He cupped his hand under her chin, and in a dark, dangerous tone, he added, "If I thought you were fucking him for pleasure, I would've stood there and watched him die."

Heat kindled in her core under his possessive gaze. She gave him a coy smile. "And then what would you have done? Cut him into tiny pieces, put him in a barrel of acid, and sent him to the Vatican?"

There was no humor in his response. "I would've reclaimed you right there in the pool of his blood and taught you a valuable fucking lesson."

Fuck, that made her insides ignite. She ran her finger up the inside of his forearm. "What kind of lesson?" she prodded.

His nostrils flared. He rested one hand on the barstool behind her and leaned in close, his lips to her ear. "One to ensure you never forget that you belong to *me*."

A shiver of sweet electricity traveled down Eve's spine, making her tremble.

Show me.

190

Punish me.

Own me.

I'm yours.

Bo exhaled against her neck, and Eve wondered if he somehow sensed the submissive, masochistic desires that suddenly consumed her.

"What would that lesson look like?" Eve whispered, her voice low and husky with need.

Bo curled his fingers around the nape of her neck and stretched his thumb out under her jaw. His lips brushed hers. "Do you want me to show you?" he asked, their breath mingling as her heart threatened to break her ribcage.

"Yes."

"Yes what?"

"Yes, please…Daddy."

A low chuckle bobbed in his throat. "I should…I *would*…but you need to rest, Evie. It's late." He pulled back abruptly, grabbing the bag of rice chips from the counter and clipping it closed. He slid off his stool and put the bag back in the cupboard, then returned to Eve, who still sat there, mouth agape at his hot-and-cold act, and held his hand out to her. "Let's get you in bed."

Eve stared up at him, dumbstruck. "You can't be serious."

"You can get into bed willingly, or I can put you there," he warned lightheartedly.

Eve crossed her arms in defiance.

A smile crossed his face. "Have it your way." He scooped her up around the middle and hoisted her over his shoulder.

"Bo!" she grunted as he hauled her to her bed.

He pulled the covers back, then dropped her down onto the mattress. She scowled indignantly at him as he tucked the covers up around her chin.

When he leaned down to kiss her forehead, she fisted her hand into the front of his shirt to hold him there. She lifted her chin. "If you think you're walking out of this room without my scent on your dick, you're absolutely fucking mistaken, Bo."

His wolf eye came alive and his face reddened at her filthy words, and he looked down at her with a predatory hunger. "Haven't you had enough today?"

Eve lifted her head off her pillow to touch her lips to his. She ran her tongue over the tip of his exposed canine. "I can never have enough of *you*, Bo. I'll always want more."

An indecisive, impatient sound rumbled in his throat. "I'm trying to be considerate. You need to sleep. It's 2AM."

Eve gave a fake pout. "Aw, am I making it *hard* for you to be a gentleman?" Her pout transformed into a wicked grin. "You and I both know you're no gentleman."

"Evie," Bo warned. "Go to sleep."

"I need help falling asleep."

"I'll get you that manga you like," he offered, only half-serious.

"Let's act it out instead. I'll be your bunny girl, wolf boy." She slid over and held the blankets open to him. "Get your ass in here. Now."

His brows hiked up. "Someone has her bossy pants on today."

"Come take them off me."

Bo bit back the amused smile teasing his lips. "You're the worst, you know that?" He stripped out of his shirt and kicked out of his pants. "A real fucking menace." He climbed into bed next to her in his boxers.

When she tried to put her hands on him, he intercepted them, then rolled her over, pulling her back against him tightly, spooning her. "Go to sleep, Evie," he commanded.

Eve pushed her hips back, rubbing her ass against the erection she knew she'd find in his lap. "What's it going to take to make you fuck me? You're really making me work for this."

He laughed lightly through closed lips, tucking her even tighter into his embrace. He sighed with satisfaction. "Oh, but you've made it infinitely more entertaining to make you wait. Get some sleep and we'll see if you can convince me in the morning."

Eve exhaled deeply in defeat. "Fucking rude."

"Goodnight, Evie." He kissed the top of her head. "I love you, baby."

Her vexation dissipated in a flash, leaving only a warm glow in her belly. She melted into him. "I love you, too, Bo."

A powerful orgasm rocked Eve's body awake a few hours later when Bo's sharp canines reopened the gash across her hand, a harsh cry tearing from her lungs as her back arched off the bed.

"Bo!" she gasped.

His tongue laved over the blood on her hand once more before he drew it away and twined his fingers through hers, his mouth covering hers, stealing her cries. He was on all fours over top of her, pressing her hands into the mattress, his knees spreading her thighs wide.

He pulled back and took her in, his eyes and expression both wolfish. "*Ohayou*," he greeted her with a rakish grin, his voice low and husky. He kissed down her neck, his breath hot as he instructed, "Be a good girl and wake the whole complex for me, Evie. Don't even *think* about holding back." He pulled her shirt and shorts off, then skimmed his tongue and the tips of his fangs over her lower belly, down to the dip between her leg and pelvis. "I want everyone to hear you screaming my name." Then, with a bite to her inner thigh that made her yelp, he added ironically, "Even Isaac."

She threw her head back, a sensuous moan rolling from her lips as his tongue delved between her legs, devouring the evidence of her orgasm.

His breath shuddered over her sensitive flesh as he praised, "God, you're the best thing I've ever tasted."

Eve buried both hands in his hair, thrusting her hips, grinding herself against his face as he worked her with his tongue. She felt his fingers push inside of her, and he curled them, stroking that textured spot on her inner wall, making her legs shake uncontrollably.

"Oh, fuck, Bo!" she cried, and soon, she was careening into another toe-curling climax, her body quaking and jerking against his face, her fingers tugging at the roots of his hair.

While she writhed and jerked in the aftershocks, Bo pulled free from her grip and released his cock from his boxers. He leaned into her and plunged into her pulsing core, burying himself deep. She moaned as he filled her with his length, his hips digging into her inner thighs as he hooked his hands under her knees, pinning them down to the mattress.

He slammed into her, and she moaned again. "Louder," he demanded with another hard thrust.

Submit.

Obey.

Let go.

But she couldn't help the taunting words that sprang breathless from her lips. "Make me, Daddy."

He bit out a mildly incredulous laugh, as though he were both surprised and amused by her audacity. He wrapped his fingers around her jaw and gazed down into her eyes, a sexy, dangerous expression shadowing his face. "Oh, I will," he promised.

And he did.

He released his grip on one of her legs and tangled his fingers into her hair. He angled her head to the side, curling his lips back as he skimmed his teeth over the tender flesh of her throat. He rammed his hips against hers, driving forcefully into her as he sank his fangs into the base of her neck.

Eve arched against him, throwing her head back into the pillow as a scream of ecstasy tore free, her nails clawing into his back. He growled against her neck as her blood spilled across his tongue, and he rutted into her like an animal singularly possessed. His fingers flexed into the flesh around her knee in a bruising grip as he pinned her down to the mattress, his other fist twisting painfully in her hair.

There was nothing gentle about the way Bo fucked her.

He fucked her like he owned her, because he did.

Eve clung to him as she felt his teeth sink into her shoulder, his name riding on another keening squall as it escaped from her lungs. His hot breath caressed her skin with every pant and rasp as he plowed into her, deep and hard. As she crested another climax, she felt the surge of Bo's power drawing forth. With a deep growl, he buried himself deep inside and found his release, his hips jerking spasmodically, and his essence poured into her.

"Fuuuuck, Bo," she groaned, holding him tightly to her as they both came down.

He exhaled a satisfied hum against her neck. "I'll never need anything more than this," he confessed contentedly. "Even when everything else has gone to shit, when the world is falling apart, I know I'll find peace right here with you."

Peace. Eve ran her fingers through his hair, brushing it from his forehead. She nuzzled the side of her face against his, her eyes welling with tears, and wondered if she'd ever feel true peace again. How could she feel peace when she was terrified of having him ripped away from her, like Zeke had been?

She loved him too much to know what peace was anymore.

23
Oh, the Beautiful Screams

As she lay curled up next to Bo, Eve glanced down at her birthmark, and she was reminded of what Bo had said about making her ex suffer.

"You never told me *how* you killed Adam," Eve remarked.

"I never intended to tell you I did it at all," he replied, somewhat sheepishly. "I shouldn't have told you. You didn't need it burdening your heart or mind."

Eve remembered all the horrible things Adam had said and done to her. She remembered all the terrible names, the bruises, the degradation, the assaults, and the night he tried to kill her. She thought she had loved him once, but now that she knew what love truly felt like, she realized it was never love. It was an emotional attachment she'd mistaken for love.

She'd never fully put Adam behind her. Even now, after she'd been told he was dead, she still felt his presence weighing on her soul, like she was swimming in the ocean with an empty backpack hooked to her ankle. It wasn't dragging her under, but it was enough to be a constant hindrance as she tried to move forward.

Maybe just *knowing* he was dead wasn't enough.

"Show me," Eve requested.

Bo looked over at her with concern. "You don't need to see that, Evie. You don't *want* to see that." He turned his eyes to the ceiling. "I was...not myself."

That's right. It had happened close to the blood moon. "Or maybe you were more yourself than you've ever been," Eve countered. "Let me see, Bo. Let me see all of you. I know the man, now let me see the monster."

Bo buried his fingers in his messy silver locks. "You won't look at me the same way once you see it. It was brutal."

"Do you regret it?"

"Not for one second," he replied quickly. Darkly.

"Then show me."

Bo's expression was tortured. "You can look, but only if you promise to still love me after what you see."

Eve smiled warmly at him as blue and gold began to swirl around her, like crashing waves in a whirlpool. "I love every monstrous part of you, Bo. The dark parts are the best parts."

Bo lay in his hotel bed with Zeke and Eoduun, fuming at the fact that Evie was lying next to *Isaac*. She should be next to Bo. She should *always* be next to Bo. He wanted to hurt someone. He was still riled up after running into Eve's douche of an ex, and he just wanted to curl up with Evie and let her tame the rage singeing his nerve-endings.

The rage. It was getting worse as the super blood moon approached. But other urges were beginning to slip from his control as well. He glanced over at Evie, and that monster inside of him pulled at its chains, wanting nothing more than to ravage her over and over and over again.

Make her writhe in ecstasy beneath him. Make her scream. Make her cry. Make her bleed. Make her beg him to stop, then beg him for more.

Make her *his*.

He loved her more than he'd ever loved anything, but the beast inside wanted to *own* her. Chase her down, break her, then put her back together.

She should belong to *him*.

His hands twitched as his mind returned to that piece of shit Adam they encountered earlier. That fucker had had his Evie before him. He'd been inside of her. Tasted her. Pleasured her.

And then he'd hurt her.

He was still hurting her. Bo saw it on Evie's face in that bathroom. That asshole's existence alone was causing her pain.

Bo couldn't have that.

The moment he noticed she was asleep, and Zeke and Eoduun returned to their own room, he was in the Toyota, following the navigation screen to an address he'd found using Knighco resources.

He sat parked in the street in front of the house, staring at Adam's stupid, smug face through a window. He was feeding a toddler, and a woman walked through with a diaper bag over her shoulder. Bo couldn't help but notice the fresh black eye she sported.

He watched the woman lift the child from the booster seat, then a few tense words passed between Adam and the woman. Moments, later, she was storming out the door with the child in her arms, Adam hot on her heels. She put the kid in the backseat, then rounded the car, and Adam shoved her into it.

The rage boiled up again, and Bo's hand reached for the door handle.

The woman pushed him off, then got into the car and backed out of the drive, Adam yelling as she accelerated away.

Bo got out of the car and looked around. No one was in the street.

He whistled, and Adam looked around, his eyes finally catching Bo's. A deep scowl etched itself into Adam's face, and he stalked toward Bo.

"The fuck are you doing at my house, *freak*?!" Adam bellowed as he came at Bo. Adam swung at him, but Bo dodged his fist, his hand shooting out and catching in Adam's hair. He pivoted his torso and used Adam's own momentum against him, slamming his head into the Toyota with tremendous force.

Adam slumped to the ground, groaning, barely clinging to consciousness. Bo popped the trunk, glanced around once more, then moved all the weapons and tools from the trunk to the backseat. He hefted Adam into the empty trunk and closed the latch.

The town was small, so it was only a mile or two before Bo found a secluded patch of road surrounded by woods. He pulled Adam from the trunk and dragged him into the woods. Adam was starting to come around, and he began to thrash against Bo's grip.

Bo tossed him onto the forest floor, withdrew his knife, and slashed both of Adam's Achilles tendons, rendering him unable to run. Adam screamed, grabbing at his useless ankles.

The sound was music to Bo's ears. Adrenaline pumped through his veins, making his breath shaky with anticipation as he watched the pathetic heap on the ground begin to crawl toward him.

He liked watching him crawl.

Adam's voice was full of venom as he shouted, "I'm going to kill you, you piece of shit!"

Bo pulled his mask down and grinned, showcasing his horrible canines. He swung his boot, catching Adam's chin in a devastating kick, and Adam fell face-first onto the ground with a pained grunt. Bo stood over him, reveling in his position of power over him.

"You're going to die," Bo informed him. "But not until you beg me to kill you."

Adam rose up onto his hands and knees again, his hand grasping at Bo's knee. He yanked, trying to take Bo to the ground with him, but Bo shifted his weight to the other leg and put added force to his bent knee, driving it straight into Adam's face. He reached down and grabbed Adam's hair, flipping him onto his back.

He unholstered the gun in his waistband and, with a demented grin curving his lips, he pointed the gun at Adam's kneecap and pulled the trigger.

The screams. Oh, the beautiful screams. The predator beneath his skin relished in those delicious sounds of suffering.

Death's prelude.

He shifted his aim and blew out the other kneecap, then holstered his gun. He stuck his knife between his teeth, then dropped down and straddled Adam's ribs, fighting his swinging arms until he had one pinned to the ground. He took the knife in one hand, held Adam's hand down with the other, then plunged the knife through Adam's hand, staking him to the ground. He unsheathed the knife at his ankle and did the same with Adam's other hand.

Bo closed his eyes and basked in the screams.

"What's your fucking problem, man?!" Adam demanded, spittle on his chin, tears streaming down his face. "Is this because of Eve?"

Rage surged through Bo's chest, and he gnashed his teeth at Adam, his hand squeezing around his throat. "You don't ever say her fucking name again." He again pulled the gun from its holster and shot Adam's elbow. Then the other.

Then he pointed the gun to Adam's left shoulder and obliterated that, as well. He holstered his gun and pulled the knife from Adam's left hand. He would need it for what came next.

"You touched her beautiful body with these fingers," Bo hissed. "Then you *hurt* her with these hands." He then stabbed the knife through the base of each finger, severing them one by one, until all ten digits were littered loosely around Adam's palms.

He slid his knife into Adam's mouth, slicing it along where his jaw hinged, severing the masseter muscle on each side. Adam's mouth fell open, slack. Bo reached into his mouth and pulled out his soft, slimy tongue.

"You tasted her with this tongue. Then you *berated* her with it." His sharp knife slid cleanly through it, and Bo tossed it aside. "You looked at her body with these eyes. Then you watched her *suffer* through them." His knife slipped between the orbital socket and the eyeball, and he popped Adam's eyes from his skull.

Adam wasn't even screaming or writhing anymore, but Bo didn't notice. He was too absorbed in his vengeance.

He stood up and grabbed at Adam's pants, tugging them down to his thighs. "I don't even want to fucking know everything you did to her with this." Bo severed the appendage, then shoved it into Adam's gaping mouth.

Bo stood over Adam, looking down at his work. Adam wasn't moving, and Bo could tell his heart was no longer beating. He died too quickly, robbing Bo of the chance to make him beg for death, but the monster inside him was satisfied, nonetheless. Eve would never have to worry about Adam again. He couldn't hurt her anymore.

Then horror crept through him. If she saw this…if she knew what he'd just done…she would never look at him the same way. She would be disgusted with him. Repulsed by him. Maybe even a little afraid of him.

She may have accepted what Luc had done to Dizzy, but…this was so much worse. He remembered the way Eve had looked at Luc when she saw him standing at the door, Dizzy's head hanging from his grip. The shock. The fear. The horror. He didn't want to imagine her face if she ever saw this.

He looked down at his bloodied hands, and they began to tremble. She would never let him touch her with these hands again if she knew what they'd just done.

He pulled his phone out and called Luc.

"I fucked up," he announced when Luc answered.

"Is Eve ok?" Luc worried.

"Evie's fine. But she won't be when she finds out what I just did." He told Luc what had happened.

Luc laughed. He *laughed*. "Bring her his head. She'll love it."

"No! My control is slipping, Luc. This is worse than it's ever been." He looked back down at the mutilated body. "I worry what I might do to *her* when the blood moon rises."

"You think you'll *hurt* her?"

Bo screwed his eyes closed. "You don't want to know what I want to do to her, Luc."

"You do *not* have permission to eat my Little Red Riding Hood," Luc threatened.

"Then keep her away from me. I don't trust myself."

Luc sighed. "Clean up your mess. Wrap up this case quickly, and get home. I'll make sure to be home and keep her with me when the time comes."

In a quiet, beseeching tone, Bo pleaded, "Please don't tell her about this. She doesn't need to know."

"Whatever you say, brother. But, for the record, I think she can handle more than you're giving her credit for."

"She shouldn't have to handle knowing this."

He shoved his phone back in his pocket. He bent down, picked up all his bullet casings, and yanked his other knife from Adam's right hand. He wiped his knives on Adam's shirt to clean them, then sheathed them.

He went to the car, grabbed a shovel, and dug a shallow grave. He didn't have time for anything more than that. He rolled Adam's body into the hole, kicked all the severed parts in on top of it, and covered him with dirt.

Bo returned to the hotel, and he was glad to see that Eve was still asleep. Isaac barely spared him a glance as he went straight to the bathroom to clean himself up. He washed the blood from his hands and face, and was thankful to see that whatever blood got on him was hardly noticeable on his black clothing.

Then he heard a light moan coming from the other room, and his blood heated. Evie.

When he emerged from the bathroom, he found Eve wrapped around Isaac, her body moving slightly against his, her lips parted with another airy whimper. Isaac's eyes met his, and he just sat there, allowing her to rub up against him while Bo watched.

The wolf raged against its chains once more.

Eve withdrew from Bo's mind. She gazed into those tormented, mismatched eyes, and she ran a finger lightly down the vertical scar over his eye.

His eyes searched hers, and she knew he was sensing her feelings, seeking out that bit of horror he was expecting. But he didn't find it. "You're not disgusted with me?"

Eve smiled softly at him. "Quite the opposite. Now I know why my monster is so obsessed with yours."

Relief washed over him. "You still love me." It wasn't a question.

Eve laughed, then kissed him, feeling his smooth, wolfish fangs against her lips. She ran her fingers through his hair and gazed at him adoringly. "Now more than ever. You'd have to do a whole lot worse than a little grisly torture to make me ever look at you with anything but love."

24
Too Many Spinning Plates

The ruckus of Celeste banging on Bo's door down the hall roused Eve and Bo. Bo groaned and slid out of bed, pulling on his clothes, then looked around and realized he didn't have a mask here.

"Shit," he grumbled, scrubbing his hand down his face.

Eve guessed what he was fretting over. "It's not a big deal if you don't have your mask on, Bo."

"It is to me," he said. "If you had to wear your curse on the outside as a constant reminder to everyone who looks at you, it would be a big deal to you, too."

Eve threw back the covers and flourished her hand over the faintly discolored birthmark on the side of her torso. "Does this count?" She took on a falsely serious demeanor. "'This is the skin of a killer, Bella,'" she deadpanned.

He exhaled a laugh. "Not quite the same effect as these, Twilight," he said, baring his teeth. He sighed and turned away. "I'll be back."

Eve watched him walk out the bedroom door, then she, too, got up and got dressed. When she went to her apartment door and opened it, though, Celeste and a masked Bo were both walking up the hallway, so she held it open and let them walk through.

Celeste went to the kitchen island with Ramil's laptop under her arm. She set it on the counter and opened it, leaning against the ledge as she logged into it. "I know you didn't ask me to snoop," she jittered, clearly overcaffeinated, "but you know I can't help myself. You won't believe what I found." She opened a folder, then angled the laptop screen toward Bo and Eve.

Eve was staring at the scandalous pictures of Dizzy impersonating Luc. Not just the ones that had been sent to her phone, but a folder full of them. Videos, too. She'd only been sent the highlights.

"Wait, does this…does this mean what I think it does?" Eve sputtered, looking between Bo and Celeste.

Celeste turned the laptop back toward herself. "If you think it means Ramil sent you those texts, then I think all signs point to yes."

"Why?" Eve wondered. "Why would he do this? Did he put up the cameras, too?"

"It's hard to say," Celeste responded. "But judging by the timestamps on some of these videos compared to the dates they were downloaded or modified, I would say it heavily indicates he had remote access to the cameras that were recording them." She left the laptop on the counter and stepped back, and Eve dragged it over to look at it again. "As for why he would want this footage? You'd have to ask him. I have a hard time understanding why people do the shit they do," Celeste said frankly.

Bo was on his phone, calling Luc, while Eve sat next to him at the kitchen island, browsing the photos and videos on Ramil's laptop. How long had Dizzy been posing as Luc? Even knowing these photos weren't Luc…well, *trusting* that none of these photos were Luc, they still turned her blood to lava. A possessive flame scorched her insides.

Bo put Luc on speaker when he answered the phone, and he filled him in on what Celeste had just found on Ramil's laptop. "What do you want us to do?" Bo inquired.

"Celeste?" Luc called out.

"Here," she answered, leaning closer to the phone on the counter in front of Bo.

"Install some spyware on the laptop and monitor everything he does. Don't say anything to anyone else," Luc instructed.

Celeste saluted, even though Luc couldn't see it. "Yessir."

Celeste swiped the laptop from Eve, then left the apartment with a quick little wave of her fingers. On the phone, Luc said, "Bo? You and Eve need to get some cameras from the tactical supply room and put them up in Ramil's apartment. I'm going to send the jet and recall Ramil on the pretense that we need him to help monitor Dagon. We'll watch him for a few days while we decide what to do with him."

"Bring him *back* here?" Eve sputtered.

"Oh, hello, love," Luc's voice suddenly became sugary. "You're up early."

She pressed on. "If he's coming back, I'm putting cameras up in my apartment, too! He's been stealing my shit!" She told him what they found when they searched his place. "I took it all back. He's going to know we've been in there as soon as he goes to use my chapstick and it's gone." As an afterthought, she added, "Maybe I should just erase his memories of taking my stuff."

Luc made an intrigued sound over the line. "Do you have Eoduun's power right now? Do you think you could get into his head? Eoduun could never read him very well."

Eve was brimming with power – Eoduun's, Dagon's, and Bo's. "I'm pretty stacked at the moment," she said vaguely. She didn't want to get into a discussion regarding her recent rendezvous with

Dagon over the phone. "I think I could get in and do a quick scan if he had his guard down." Maybe.

"That's a risky move," Bo objected. "What if he senses it? What if he gets suspicious?"

Eve winked at him. "I'll dazzle him with my tits. I mean wits."

He looked unimpressed. "I'm serious."

Luc chimed in, "Love, you have permission to use whatever tactics you deem necessary to get the task done. Ramil's loyalty as a Knighco hunter is officially in question, so protections against specialty use afforded to members no longer apply to him. Dazzle away. Just don't kill him…yet."

"I don't like this plan," Bo grumbled.

"You don't have to like it," Luc retorted. "But someday you're going to have to admit that our little *Evie* isn't a fragile little flower that needs to be sheltered."

"Yeah," Eve jumped in. "I'm a peacock, Bo…"

"You gotta let her fly," Luc finished for her.

"When are you returning?" Bo asked Luc, changing the subject.

"I'll be back before Ramil returns. I don't want to leave you and Isaac playing babysitter to Dagon *and* Ramil. How is our winged Darth Vader faring in his little Death Star, anyway?" Luc inquired, referring to the star-shaped lines that comprised part of the devil's trap that confined Dagon.

Bo looked to Eve, unsure of how to answer. "Uh, he's fine, I guess."

"Behaving?"

"For the most part," Bo replied.

Luc sighed. "What the fuck are we going to do with *him*?"

Bo and Eve looked at each other, and Bo shook his head at her. But Eve opened her mouth anyway.

"I think he should take Zeke's place on our team," she ventured boldly.

Luc scoffed loudly on the other line. "If it were anyone else who'd suggested that, I would be laughing right now, because obviously they'd be joking. But not you, love," he said with a breathy exhale. Luc's voice softened. "I know Zeke left a huge hole in your heart. But don't try to use Dagon to fill it. He isn't Zeke. He will never be Zeke. He'll only wreak havoc."

"I can keep him in line. Please, Luc. He's the closest to Zeke that I'll ever get. He holds all Zeke's memories, and a part of Zeke's will has fused into him." She again relayed what she'd discovered in Dagon's mind.

When she finished speaking, Luc sought Bo's input. "Bo?"

Bo was sitting with his chin in his hand. "No one will accept it," he opined.

"It'll start a riot," Luc agreed. "And Eoduun will disown us all."

Eve swallowed. Eoduun would be pissed. But if Dagon let him in his head, let him *see* how much of Zeke still pervaded his mind, maybe he would come around. "Let me handle Eoduun," she requested.

"I think you have too many spinning plates, love."

"What the hell does that mean?"

"You know, the circus trick when someone is balancing poles with plates spinning precariously on top of them?"

Eve slapped her hand on the counter. "Well, it's a good thing I'm somewhat of a freak, then. Circus tricks fit well within my wheelhouse."

"You're taking on too much," Luc said bluntly.

"But I'm a peacock."

"You absolutely are. However, you are but *one* peacock, my love."

"So, what, we're just going to leave Dagon locked in Ruth's old apartment in a fucking devil's trap forever?" Eve argued.

"Evie." Bo nudged her arm, but she ignored him, focused on the phone in front of her.

"I was kind of hoping he would starve to death at some point," Luc replied, and Eve wasn't sure if he was joking. "But, sadly, he doesn't seem to require food."

"Just let me have him. Please," she begged. "I can control him."

"*Evie*." Bo nudged harder.

"He's not a pet," Luc said.

"I know. He's a *weapon*. We can *use* him," she pointed out, still ignoring Bo.

"A weapon with a will of his own," Luc countered. "A weapon we can't trust."

Eoduun's voice startled Eve, and only then did she realize she'd picked up his scent a minute ago, but hadn't registered it. "He's *here*?" he quietly accused, pinning Eve with a lethal glare from the doorway.

That's why Bo had been elbowing her.

Eve didn't answer him. She looked back down at the phone. "Any news on Apep's location?" she asked Luc, quickly changing the subject, wondering just how much Eoduun had overheard.

"Apep? Not yet. He's fallen off the face of the earth, it seems," Luc said. "Is that why you want to keep Dagon around? You're hoping he'll save us from Apep if he comes knocking? Because I wouldn't count on it."

Eoduun stalked into the room, an invisible black cloud hanging over him.

"We'll call you back later, Luc," Bo said, then ended the call.

"He was here this whole time, and you didn't tell me?" Eoduun seethed through clenched teeth, his eyes jumping between Bo and Eve.

"We didn't tell anyone," Bo explained. "We didn't want anyone getting any foolish ideas. But he's safely contained."

Eoduun fixed his gaze on Eve. "You didn't kill him. Does that mean…?"

Eve let the unfinished question hang in the air as she held his gaze. She watched the range of emotions parade across his face in the pregnant silence, until it finally settled on betrayal.

"You were supposed to kill him if Zeke wasn't there."

"It's not that simple." She explained the complex situation with Dagon's mind for the third time, feeling like she should just make a PowerPoint presentation at this rate.

By the time she was finished talking, she'd expected the look of betrayal to leave Eoduun's face, but it was still there, furrowing lines in his features. "All you're telling me is Zeke's not there," he said. "Zeke isn't a part of Dagon any more than Ruth is a part of you. They're just memories."

"It's not the same," Eve argued. "Ruth and I didn't coexist in the same body. And Zeke left behind more than just memories."

"Erase those memories from Dagon, and tell me what's left. Erase him and take Zeke back. Keep his memories safe with you, Eve, and then...get rid of Dagon once and for all."

Eve looked to Bo, but he didn't offer any assistance. He seemed to be considering Eoduun's stance.

"No," she said firmly.

Eoduun shook his head with a cynical, humorless smile. "No? Just no, huh?" He leaned across the kitchen island toward her. "You want his power. That's it, isn't it?"

Eve scowled in offense. "That's bullshit, and you know it."

"Then why?" Eoduun demanded, slamming his fist on the counter. "Why won't you kill him?"

Bo rose from his barstool and spread his arms wide on the countertop, one hand planted firmly in front of Eve in a protective stance. He leaned forward confrontationally. "She *was* going to kill him. I stopped her. So leave her the fuck alone."

Eoduun slowly shook his head. "Why the fuck would you stop her?"

Bo clenched his fists against the counter, his jaw ticking. "Because you can't just unilaterally decide something like that. It isn't *your* decision to make. It's a Knighco discussion, at the very least. And, as Eve pointed out, he is a weapon – one we've benefitted from in the past. We may not want to be too hasty to off him," he said, a hint of reluctance in his tone.

Eve gave Bo a surprised look. "I thought you said no one would accept it."

"They won't. Not at first." He sat back down on his barstool. "But in time, if he were to prove himself, they might. Maybe."

"I'll never accept him." Eoduun declared. "Never. I will never work with him. If he's part of this team, I'm not." He looked to Eve with pained eyes. "Zeke is no longer with us because Dagon *is*. That's the bottom line. He took Zeke's life, and I'll be fucked if I let him live it. I won't let him replace Zeke."

"No one can replace Zeke," Bo said softly. "We're not trying to replace him. We're just suggesting that maybe – just *maybe* – Dagon is more useful alive than dead."

Eve tried to shift the subject. "We can discuss the Dagon problem more when Luc gets home, ok?" She gestured at Eoduun and said, "Let's talk about how glad I am that you left your room, instead." She forced a smile.

Eoduun rolled his eyes in genuine disgust. "Yeah, and I wish I hadn't." He turned and stormed out of Eve's apartment.

"One step forward, two steps back," Eve lamented, burying her face in her hands in defeat. She whispered, "I'm trying so hard with him. But he's just so hard to *like* right now, as awful as that is to say."

Bo stroked his hand over her hair. "Unfortunately, people are the most unlovable when they need love the most," he said.

"He acts like he's the only one who lost Zeke. We *all* lost him. We're *all* still reeling from it." Eve swiped a lone tear from her cheek with the heel of her hand. "Doesn't he understand? That's exactly why I *can't* kill Dagon. That's exactly why I want Dagon to join us. *Because* of Zeke."

25
Sit

Later that morning, after Eve and Bo had finished putting up cameras, they collected Isaac (who immediately saw the change in Eve's aura and gave her grief about her recently acquired powers) and headed to the gym to train. They knocked on Eoduun's door on the way to invite him along, but, unsurprisingly, he wouldn't answer.

When they walked into the gym, Eve saw that Zephlyn, Mendal, and Celeste had the same idea. Zephlyn saw them enter, and he finished his set and strolled over to Eve as she was warming up with some light dumbbells.

He gave her an inquisitive look. "You're harboring some major firepower, aren't you?" he said, surveying her.

Eve was instantly uncomfortable under his appraisal, and she shifted her weight on her feet. How much could he infer? Did he sense Dagon's power radiating from her?

Isaac was suddenly near her, looking at the dumbbell rack as though he were trying to decide which weight to select. He gave Zephlyn and Eve a sidelong glance, assessing the interaction.

Zephlyn looked at Isaac. "I'm not a threat," he said amicably, intuiting the real reason Isaac was standing there. "Just curious." His eyes returned to Eve. "Your power fascinates me – I've never encountered someone naturally immune to my foresight. How are your powers of premonition coming along?"

Eve dipped her head to the side. "I'm still working on understanding them."

"You sensed something was wrong when Ruth was planning to release Dagon, didn't you? Even when I couldn't see it, you sensed it." When Eve gave him a surprised look, he explained, "Bo asked me if I could decipher why you might be feeling off that day, but I didn't see it. I assumed I couldn't see anything because it was regarding *you*, but I now suspect Ruth did something to block me out."

Eve walked past where Isaac was still lingering to exchange her weights for heavier dumbbells. "It didn't do us any good, anyway. It didn't change a fucking thing."

Zephlyn followed her to the bench as she set it to a 45-degree angle. She straddled it and began a set of incline presses as Zephlyn continued the conversation.

"I had a vision this morning," he disclosed.

She paused with the dumbbells in the air. "Why are you telling me?"

"Because even if I can't see you, I feel like you play a part in it. Maybe you can help enlighten me."

Eve lowered the dumbbells and rested them upright on her thighs.

Zephlyn continued, "I saw wilderness, and a cave in the mountains filled with beasts. There was a snake, a dragon, and sea monster all pouring something from their mouths into a goblet. When it was full, a man took the goblet and poured it out into a fiery pit in the ground, and strange, horrific creatures began to climb out of the hole."

Something about Zephlyn's description triggered a hint of recognition in Eve's brain. Did Zephlyn know Ramil was a dragon? Is that who the dragon in the vision was supposed to be? "That's some Revelation-style shit," she commented. "How am I a part of it?"

"I don't know. I just get the sense you're involved somehow."

Eve looked to Isaac, who had been raptly watching Zephlyn tell his vision, but Isaac offered no insight.

Bo came up behind her. "That's cryptic," he said.

"The more symbolic the vision, the less certain it is," Zephlyn explained. "So whatever it means, it's only a possibility right now. But it's a possibility I'd rather not see come to fruition, because it's obviously nothing good."

Bo suggested, "The creatures climbing out of the hole in the ground reminds me of what happened at the papermill. Ruth had portals buried, and she summoned her army through them."

Eve added, "And maybe the creatures are new creations, like Ruth was making with the grimoire." Her eyes widened. "If Apep has the grimoire, does that mean he's using it to create more monsters? Is that what he's planning? To unleash his own army of chaos on the world?" And though she didn't want to say it in front of Zephlyn, she had to assume the dragon could mean that Ramil was somehow part of that plan.

But...if that were the case, why would he have asked Eve to kill Ramil?

Zephlyn noted, "The monsters might not even be literal monsters. They could symbolize something else. For all I know, it could represent Dagon being drawn out of Zeke – a warning that that event might be the catalyst that brings out untold horrors." He made a wary face at Bo. "He is still safely contained somewhere, right?"

Bo nodded. "He's contained."

Relief softened Zephlyn's features. "Good. Let's keep it that way."

"But it might not have anything to do with Dagon," Eve countered. "What if we need Dagon to help fight whatever it actually is? If we have to go up against Apep and an army of monsters, I'd feel a lot better having Dagon fighting alongside us."

Skepticism narrowed Zephlyn's already narrow, dark eyes. "What makes you think he would fight alongside us? He could be on Apep's side."

"He's not," Eve insisted. "Dagon wouldn't let anything happen to me."

"You trust him," Zephlyn remarked, surprise coloring his tone. "Why?"

"I don't know about *trust*, but I've been in his head, and I've seen his intentions. He's on our side. And he might get pissed at me for sharing this, but he cared about Zeke, too. He's not going to betray us because it would mean betraying Zeke. And me."

Zephlyn crossed his arms over his chest. "Huh." His expression was loaded, but he didn't give voice to whatever thoughts were behind it. It made her wonder what he was "keeping under his hat." He looked at Bo. "Do you think he can be trusted?"

"I think there are a lot of factors at play here, and I don't know if *trusting* him is necessarily part of the equation. But I trust Evie's intuition."

Zephlyn arched a dark brow. "You should've been a politician. That was an excellent way to say 'no' while making it sound like 'yes.'"

Eve hoisted her weights back up to her shoulders. "Regardless of whether we trust him or not, it would be smart to keep our options open. I'm sure you can agree with that," she said, then finished her set.

Through the rest of her workout, Eve considered Zephlyn's vision. It could mean so many different things, could be interpreted so many different ways, but she failed to see how she was any part of it. How could he be so sure that she was?

Maybe she was one of the creatures climbing out of the pit.

An Abomination.

On their way back from the gym, as they made their way up the corridor toward their apartments, Isaac suddenly moved ahead of them, holding his hand up to her and Bo as he locked his eyes on Ruth's apartment door. Bo held his arm across in front of Eve, on high alert, while they watched Isaac approach Ruth's door. Isaac reached out and pushed the door open.

It wasn't latched.

Fuck.

Bo lurched forward, and Eve was right behind him.

Ruth's apartment door handle was broken, and when they pushed inside, they found Eoduun standing just outside the devil's trap, his hateful gaze fixed on Dagon.

Isaac threw his arm out in front of Eve, shielding her and blocking her from coming any further into the room.

Dagon was standing just on the other side of the trap border, staring right back, his wings extended menacingly, his vermilion eyes filled with loathing. Without looking away, he growled, "Remove this pissant from my quarters before I lose my patience with him and paint the walls with his blood."

His threat sent Eve's blood into a furious boil. Bo sprang forward and grabbed Eoduun, dragging him away from Dagon. "You touch him, you die," Bo snarled, putting himself between the two.

Eve shoved past Isaac and Bo, storming straight into the devil's trap, squaring up against Dagon's massive form. She jabbed a finger into his solid chest and moved into his personal space, scowling up at him. "You will *not* threaten a member of this team!" she shouted.

"He threatened me first!" Dagon bellowed back.

Eve pointed at his chair at the center of the trap. "Go sit down!"

"But—"

"Sit!"

216

Dagon's nostrils flared as they had a tense battle of wills, staring each other down.

"Evie! Get out—" Bo began, but she held her hand up behind her, decisively signaling for him to stay the fuck out of it.

Dagon's jaw clenched, and with an angry growl, he retreated, dropping heavily into his wooden chair, crossing his arms like a huge, petulant child.

Eve turned her back on Dagon, still within the bounds of the devil's trap. It was a risky move, because you *never* turn your back on an enemy, but it was also a display for everyone in that room – a move to show that she had no fear of the monster behind her, because she *knew* he wasn't a threat to her.

He wasn't an enemy.

She pointed an accusatory finger at Eoduun. "What the fuck were you trying to do here?!"

"I had to see it for myself!" Eoduun snapped back. "How could you keep him here? Look at him! He's a fucking *demon*! Just kill him!"

"I'm a *god*, you fucking shit stain!" Dagon bellowed.

Shut the fuck up, Eve spoke directly into Dagon's mind. *You're ruining any headway I've been trying to make to get you out of here.*

Dagon huffed in irritation, but didn't reply.

Isaac signed frantically at her, *Get out of there! You're not safe!*

"Dagon, tell them I'm safe in here," she directed. "Tell them we're all safe. You're not going to hurt anyone." When he didn't speak, she turned and raised her brows at him.

He sighed and glared back at her. "You're all fucking safe," he spat. "As you command it, princess."

"Thank you." She turned back to Eoduun. "What did you say to him?"

Eoduun gave her a hard stare. "I wanted to see Zeke's memories."

"And I'm not a fucking moron," Dagon retorted. "If I let you in, you'd try to steal them. You can't fucking have them!"

"You don't deserve them!"

"They're mine!" Dagon argued.

"Zeke was *mine!*" Eoduun cried. "*He* should be here right now, not *you!*"

"I know!" Dagon's admission echoed off the walls, and he rose from his chair. "You think I don't know that?! But here I am! If you want any part of Zeke, you're just going to have to keep me around, because I'm all that's left of him, and I will not part with a single memory! He left them to *me!*"

Eoduun made a sardonic face and began a slow clap. "What a performance." He looked between Eve and Bo, then over to Isaac. "Are any of you buying this? Obviously, he has Eve fucking fooled, but you two know better, right?"

Dagon stood next to Eve. "You're not going to like this," he mumbled to her, "but trust me." And then he stepped past her – beyond the bounds of the devil's trap.

Everyone pulled their weapons except Eve. She still hadn't gotten into the habit of always strapping a knife to her before leaving the apartment. Isaac and Bo both had knives, but Eoduun had pulled a gun, and he had it aimed right at Dagon's head.

"What the fuck, Dagon?!" Eve blurted as Dagon stood there, outside the devil's trap, his hands held wide.

"That trap has been compromised since last night." He pointed at where Eve had broken the mirror, and there was a small spot in the floor where the glass had scratched the paint from the elaborate sigil. The solid ring around the trap had been broken in a thin, one-eighth-inch strip. "I could've walked out of here at any point. *I didn't.*" He looked down the barrel of the gun Eoduun pointed at him. "I could've crushed you the moment you walked in here. *I didn't.* Asshole." He stalked back to his chair inside the trap and sat down again.

"You could've told us the trap was compromised. *You didn't,*" Bo pointed out.

Dagon smirked and shrugged his shoulders. "I never needed a trap to keep me here anyway. If Eve is here, I am here. But if she tried to leave without me…well, I wasn't going to let that happen again."

Bo said, "If you think this proves we can trust you, it doesn't. It only proves you're still deceitful."

Dagon just grinned devilishly, and Eve hated how good it looked on him.

Eve exhaled in exasperation and turned her eyes to the ceiling. "Dagon…fucking hell." She raked her fingernails over her scalp. "Why can't you ever make anything easy?"

Eve and Bo both suddenly snapped to attention, their heads swiveling toward the apartment door.

Luc's scent. He was home.

Oh, and he was *not* going to like this.

26
Typical Skullduggery

Luc did not like it. He stood with his arms folded, scrutinizing Dagon from behind his sunglasses. "We don't have time for your shit right now. You know that, don't you?" Luc reprimanded.

"By all means, let me know when it would be a more convenient time for you to deal with me," Dagon said sarcastically. "Or you all could put aside your animosity and let me help. I'm sure there are better ways I can pay my penance than rotting away in here."

"You could rot away in the ground instead," Eoduun suggested.

"Only if you join me."

"Shut up, children," Luc scolded. He scrubbed his hand down his mouth and sighed heavily. "Too many spinning plates, goddamn it." Then, after a moment, the corners of his mouth quirked up, and his expression lightened. "Bo, be a buddy and go find us some more paint." He pointed at Eoduun. "Go clean your apartment. I hear it's ground zero." Then, to Isaac, he spoke and signed, "Go…read or something."

When everyone left, Luc's attention settled on Eve, and he grinned.

"Uh oh," she said apprehensively.

"You, my love, are going to stay right here and practice your mental espionage skills on me until Bo gets back with the paint."

"Ok…but are we really going to just patch up the devil's trap and see how long it lasts this time?"

"Do you have a better idea?"

"You know what I'm going to say."

"I said *better* idea. Not terrible idea." Luc slipped off his sunglasses and stuck them in the pocket of his suit jacket.

Dagon's curiosity piqued. "What's your terrible idea?" he wondered.

"To make you *my* ward," she said.

He nodded approvingly. "I second that idea."

"You don't get a vote," Luc said.

"Why? Wouldn't you rather me be under twenty-four-hour supervision by the one monster who has guaranteed power over me? Well, at least until she needs a recharge," Dagon added slyly.

Electricity crackled through the air in the room as Luc's eyes flared. He captured Eve's gaze. "Excuse the fuck out of me? Care to tell me what the fuck he's talking about?"

Eve cast her eyes to her feet. "I tried to kill him last night. I have his powers."

Luc pressed his eyes closed and clenched his jaw, inhaling through his nose. When his gaze settled on her once more, he asked, "Does Bo know? Did he condone this?"

"I acted alone. But Bo sensed it and came in and stopped me." She chewed her lip nervously. "So…yeah, I have all the power I need to keep this fucker in check."

"Hey!" Dagon snapped.

"You are a fucker," Luc agreed with a brief glance toward Dagon. Then, to Eve, "And now you've decided that instead of killing him, you'd rather be his babysitter?"

"Because of Zeke, like I told you. And because of his merits."

"Yes, Lucius. My merits," Dagon taunted.

Eve shot him an incredulous look. "*Really?* You just can't fucking help yourself, can you?"

"While I have your ear, might I request some clothes that fucking fit?" Dagon asked. He gestured to his bare torso and the tattered cargo pants that tapered to shreds above his ankles and bare feet.

Luc looked him up and down with distaste. "Sorry, Gigantor, we're fresh out of your size. Too bad *merits* don't buy you clothes."

"I'll see what I can find in Zeke's closet," Eve offered.

"I know exactly what he has that will fit," Dagon said. Then he disappeared.

"Goddamn it!" Luc shouted, and then he was gone, too.

Eve followed suit, teleporting to Zeke's room, placing herself directly between Luc and Dagon. Dagon was pulling a pair of dark grey sweatpants from Zeke's dresser while Luc scowled at him with his arms crossed.

"This behavior isn't helping your case any," Luc informed him coldly. He glanced at Eve. "Is this how you mean to control him?"

"He's not hurting anything."

Dagon shucked off the old pants, and Eve made a point to look away, for Luc's sake.

"Except maybe Lucius' pride," Dagon mused as he slipped on a clean pair of Zeke's boxers and the sweatpants. He crossed the room and grabbed a cotton t-shirt from Zeke's closet, and before he put it on, he folded his wings in. Eve watched as two long, vertical slits opened in his back, and his wings receded into them. Then his skin sealed back up again, hiding the extra appendages completely. He tugged the shirt down over his torso, the fabric stretching taut across his chest.

Eve stared at the black shirt, the breath stalling in her lungs. Her heart was caught in a ruthless vise, because she could still see Zeke in it. *She'd* worn that shirt, and she remembered how it had smelled of him. Citrus and sunshine.

Before she realized what she was doing, her feet were propelling her forward, and her fists were bunching in the shirt. She buried her face in the fabric, inhaling, and a shuddering breath caught in her throat. Dagon's scent was already mixing with it, erasing that last trace evidence of Zeke.

A wave of fury passed through her, followed by a flood of despair. Dagon would never be Zeke, no matter how much of him resided within him.

She shoved Dagon away, then used her own shirt collar to dab the stupid tears from her eyes as she turned away from him.

"Eve?" Luc's voice was filled with concern as he moved closer to her.

"I'm fine. I just need a minute."

Dagon's voice was in her head. *I'm not trying to erase him, princess.*

Stop reading my mind! And get back to your chair! She slammed the door on him in her mind. She needed to do a better job of putting up mental shields when she was around him.

He vanished from Zeke's apartment.

"Fucking fuck," Luc lamented in exasperation. He looked at Eve indecisively.

"Go. I'll be there momentarily," she assured him.

He gave her a sympathetic smile before teleporting from the room as well.

Eve knew time was not on her side today, and she had preparations to make before Ramil returned, but goddamn it, she was still in fucking mourning. She climbed into Zeke's bed and wrapped his blankets around herself.

Citrus. A hint of fresh pine needles. Pure sunshine.

Her throat constricted with grief. Zeke's presence was fading from her world already, and it killed her. There would come a day when they would have to strip this bed and clean out his things. Someone else would live here – maybe not for years, but eventually, it would happen. Eventually, she would have to move on. She would have to leave Zeke behind, because he resided now only in the past, and she couldn't stay there with him.

She was needed here and now.

But, goddamn it, so was Zeke. He had so much life left to live. So much love left to give. So many jokes, laughs, smiles that she'd never see.

And she was terrified of this happening to anyone else she loved, and she realized that perhaps *that* was the real reason she wanted to keep Dagon around. If they had to go into battle against Apep, or even Ramil, she wanted to use Dagon's immense power to protect everyone else.

She wouldn't survive another loss.

I would do anything to bring you back, Z. You were the best of us.

When Eve popped back over to Ruth's old apartment...Dagon's apartment, she noticed that teleporting had suddenly become so much easier. Almost effortless. Was this Dagon's ability? With Bo and Luc's space-bending power, teleporting was exhausting.

She found Luc and Dagon just waiting for her in silence. Dagon was in his chair, as she'd directed him, and Luc was leaning against the wall with his hands in his pockets.

"Are you all right, love?" Luc asked gently, pushing off the wall and closing the distance between them with long-legged strides. She shook her head, and he folded his arms around her, pulling her to his chest. He kissed the top of her head. "It's ok to not be ok."

"I need to pull my shit together," she said in frustration. "I have a job to do."

"Hey, hey." Luc pulled back so he could look her in the eye. "You don't have to do anything. We can bide our time and deal with Ramil another way. I'll come up with a different plan."

"No," Eve objected. "Don't bench me just yet. I can do this." She sniffled and wiped her face, clearing her throat loudly as though it would clear out all her doubts, all her fears. She pushed down the grief and swallowed it. She lifted her chin and drew her shoulders back. "Tell me what to do. What's the plan?"

Luc studied her. "You're sure?"

"Fully."

"I'm going to task you and Ramil with repainting the devil's trap. While you three are alone in here, Dagon is going to go in like a battering ram and break through Ramil's barriers, and you're going to slip in unnoticed while Ramil is distracted with Dagon."

"You're going to put me alone with Ramil?"

"Not alone. Dagon will be here, and if he has one redeeming quality, it's that he won't let anyone else harm you."

"While that may be true," Dagon said, "I never agreed to this plan. What is the purpose of this?"

"Ramil's a traitor," Eve said.

"We need to see the extent of his betrayal," Luc added.

"So I'm supposed to provide the assist while I'm painted into another trap? Hardly seems like a fair tradeoff."

Luc crossed his arms. "Show us you can be a team player, and it'll only improve your reputation. As you know, most hunters don't look too favorably upon you. This could help turn that around, and maybe, eventually, lead to a more active role in this organization."

"I need more than 'maybe, eventually.'"

"And I need more than just a promise you'll behave if not contained, so here we are."

Dagon sucked his teeth. "Very well. But your plan puts Eve at risk. I have a better one."

"Pray tell."

"She joins me in here," Dagon said, gesturing to himself. "I let her possess me, and we can sync our mental capabilities. Send Ramil in here alone, and keep Eve's body safe in her apartment. Even if he detects us in his head, he won't suspect Eve of anything. He'll just think I'm up to my typical skullduggery."

"I love that word," Eve mused. "It's a close second to 'scallywag.'"

"I'm partial to 'tomfoolery.'" Luc remarked.

"You *are* partial to tomfoolery," Eve teased. Then she looked over at Dagon. "If I do this, do you promise not to fuck with me while I'm inside y—Nope. Nope. Let me rephrase. Do you promise not to fuck with me while we're sharing your bodily space?"

"I solemnly swear," he replied, but the gleam in his eye suggested otherwise.

With his hands in his pockets, Luc walked up to Dagon, bending at the waist so his eyes were level with Dagon's in his seated position. His expression was menacing. "If you *do* give her any grief or mentally molest her in any way, I *will* leave you lifeless in the bottom of a crater the size of Rhode Island." Luc straightened and smiled brightly. He rubbed his hands together eagerly. "Let's do a practice run, shall we? You can break into my mind, love."

Luc brought her a chair from the kitchen table and placed it in front of Dagon. She sat down and looked up at the hulking god seated before her, and nervous tremors quaked through her body, causing her to shiver as if she were chilled. She'd been in his head, but she'd never been in his body with him.

"You aren't afraid he's going to fuck around in your head?" Eve worried, turning to look up at Luc standing next to her.

"He's not getting into my head. He's just blazing a path for you." He fixed Dagon with a meaningful glare. "Right?"

Dagon scoffed. "Don't overestimate my interest in your puny little mind."

"See?" Luc said, looking back down to Eve. "No worries."

Eve focused on Dagon, opening the familiar, swirling black and red portal into his mind. This time when she dove through, though, it was more like falling in. She'd come running at the door full force, expecting the same resistance as last time, but this time he simply opened it before she made impact. Instead of having to try to subdue him and distract him with emotional memories, as she did when she tried to possess Luc and Ruth, she was pushed straight into the control room. She was looking at herself through his eyes, and she felt his essence guiding her energy throughout his body, like some twisted version of that famous pottery wheel scene in *Ghost*.

Go ahead, stretch out, Dagon said.

Why is this so easy? she wondered as she moved his enormous arms, flexing his thick fingers.

Because this is mutual. I'm not fighting your possession. And, you may remember, I'm well versed in sharing a body with someone else.

I still feel you, like you're spooning my fucking soul, Eve noted. *It wasn't like this with Luc.* Then again, Luc was training her in how to take possession by force. This was an entirely different situation.

Exactly. It is different, because I'm helping you, not training you, Dagon said, responding to her internal thoughts to herself. Apparently, there were no thoughts to herself in here. *I'm trying to help you reserve energy.*

Eve looked over at Luc's eager face through Dagon's eyes.

"Are you settled in?" he asked.

"I think so," she said aloud, Dagon's deep, grumbling voice speaking her words. "Oh, wait. I want to see something first." She stood up and looked down at Luc. Deep laughter shook her broad chest, and she reached out and patted him on the head with her huge hand. "Now who's the Oompa Loompa?"

"This is mildly disturbing," Luc grumbled, pushing Dagon's hand away.

"Would you still love me if I looked like this?" she jested. "Would your love for me still be *ineffable*?"

"Forever is forever, love," Luc said with a shrug.

Can I try the wings? Eve requested excitedly.

It'll rip the shirt. There are no slits cut into it to accommodate releasing my wings, Dagon responded.

"Can we focus now?" Luc suggested. "Let's see how well you can work together."

I need you to take a backseat for this part, Dagon instructed. *That way, once I break through the shield, you can slip into his mind and focus solely on your own task.*

Eve felt the shift, and Dagon navigated his own body back to the chair and sat in front of Eve's vacant body.

What are you going to look for in his head? Dagon wondered as he began to exert pressure against Luc's mental barriers.

Eve paused. Mira's words from Grand Rapids still haunted her: *"I don't know if there's even a real person behind those beautiful eyes, or if it's just a collection of carefully curated personalities."*

Dagon picked up the memory as it flashed through her mind. *You're going to see if she was right?*

I'm going to prove she's wrong, Eve replied.

27
That Ass

Eve could feel Dagon's power working against Luc's mental barrier, but he wasn't quite making it through. They were evenly matched. Eve channeled a little of her energy into the effort, imagining that she was helping to push the door open, and it was just enough to tip the scales. When the barrier broke, Eve rushed in.

She knew what she wanted to see. She sought out memories of his first impressions of her. If anything could prove to her that his feelings were real, that *he* was real, it was experiencing how he fell in love.

Luc stood across the street from a small-scale art gallery. This was where the girl displayed and sold her paintings, according to Celeste.

Celeste had done some of the footwork for him already, giving him whatever information she could glean from the internet and social media, public, and not-so-public records.

His phone chimed, and he saw he had a text from Mira.

Wyd tonight?

He was busy tonight, like most nights. He knew she was only texting him because she wanted to fuck, but he was fine with that. That was what he liked about Mira – she scratched an itch when he needed it, and she was discreet. And convenient. She may have the personality of a cheese grater, but that was also convenient, because there was no chance of him catching feelings. She never asked for or expected more from him, because she knew he wouldn't give it.

Maybe he *couldn't* give it. He wasn't sure that bothered him, though. He'd seen what love could do to people. How it twisted them. Look at how losing Shira had destroyed Bo. He didn't need problems like that.

He left her on 'read' and crossed the street, entering the gallery to the announcement of tinkling bells over the doorway. A colorful woman with piercings and wild blue hair greeted him. "Welcome! I'm Gwendolyn. Can I help you find anything special today?"

Gwendolyn. It sounded like the name of a fairytale dragon.

From the way she was looking at him, he knew she could smell his money. Most people could, often to his advantage.

"Do you have anything by…" he consulted his phone quickly, having already forgotten her weird ass name. "…Evrys Alarie?"

"Oh, Eve? Sure." Gwendolyn guided him to the back of the gallery and showed him several large canvases along the back wall. "These are hers. Do you know her?"

Luc shook his head as he scrutinized the oil paintings. Landscapes with wildlife and rustic cabins. Calm lakes with canoes and fall trees. Birch trees and birds. Lighthouses.

Boring. Not at all his style. He preferred art that was unusual. Unexpected. He liked art that evoked feelings. This was…just boring. Pretty, but boring.

"Is she popular?" he asked.

Gwendolyn hedged. "Um…she does ok. She sold a gorgeous piece last week of the Tahquamenon Falls."

"Was it for a hotel? A bank lobby?" he replied superciliously.

"Um, no. It was a private buyer." She licked her lips and keenly eyed Luc's hands as he adjusted his sunglasses. "I like your sunglasses. They look like Daredevil's."

"Blind lawyer slash vigilante is exactly the look I was going for," he quipped, flashing her a charming grin. He turned on his heel. "Thank you Gwendolynn, that will be all."

She hurried after him. "If there isn't anything you're interested in here, she'll be coming to drop off some more work in about half an hour."

Luc didn't slow down. "I appreciate it, but I think I've seen enough. Oh, and if you could keep it to yourself that I was inquiring, that would be much appreciated. I don't want her to be offended that I didn't make a purchase. Thank you," he called behind him as he opened the door, making the little bells chime again.

He sat at a coffee shop across the street and waited, watching out the window as he sipped his latte. Her artwork was technically good, but it was too real. Life is real enough. She painted the world as it appeared on the surface, rather than the way she *felt* about it, or maybe the way she'd *like* to see it.

He wanted to see a blue duck.

He dragged his phone from his pocket once more and opened his files from Celeste. She'd sent him an old picture of Eve from an Instagram page she never posted to, and a driver's license photo. He had an idea of what she looked like, yet, when the pink-haired woman in baggy grey sweatpants and white high-tops strolled by and walked into the gallery carrying a huge portfolio bag, he was surprised by the weird spark that suddenly ignited in his chest.

Briefly.

She was prettier than her pictures.

And that *ass*.

When she left the gallery, she got into a rusty old Subaru with a noisy exhaust leak and drove off.

As he finished his latte, he considered her work. Her art revealed nothing about her, but maybe that told him everything about her. She was closed off. She didn't pour herself out for just anyone. Maybe she was an oyster to be cracked.

Or maybe she was just fucking boring. What a disappointment that would be.

Celeste had conveyed to him that, not only was this potential recruit an artist, but she was also heavy into the local MMA circuit and was a well-trained fighter. He wanted to see it for himself. She didn't express herself on the canvas, but maybe she would express herself in the octagon.

Oh, how she did. When he went to watch her fight that night, he was mesmerized by her brutality, her swift delivery, her complete lack of hesitation, her confidence. She was a beautiful monster. She would make an efficient killer.

Was this really his new blood healer?

The ref held her hand up high in victory as blood dripped down her nose, a jubilant, yet ferocious smile showcasing bloodied teeth. If only she knew what that sweet, crimson nectar could do. Her feminine muscles and round curves glistened with sweat as her chest heaved, and for just a moment, he wondered what that sweat tasted like.

There was that feeling in his chest again, tugging at him.

Shit.

Well, this was inconvenient.

He found her apartment the next day. He acquired use of the apartment next door for the next few months using a fake badge, claiming official Bureau business and waving a wad of cash. People ask fewer questions when you throw lots of money at them and act like they have no choice but to do what you say.

As he checked out the layout of the place, he heard a ruckus from outside. He moved to the sliding door that led out to the tiny balcony, nudging it open.

"Shut up, this is *my* space! You came into *my* space, yelling at *me,* asshole!"

Chitter chitter chirp!

He glanced discretely out from behind the slats of the vertical blinds in front of the sliding door.

Jesus fuck, she was arguing with a squirrel.

"Fuck you!"

Chirp! Chirp!

"No, fuck *you!*"

The squirrel was braced for a battle at the corner of the rail on her balcony, facing her with its fluffed tail arched, quaking with every chirp. She was standing in a stained, oversized t-shirt and fluffy pajama pants, her pink hair piled messily atop her head.

"What's your name?!"

Chitter!

"What?!"

Chirp!

"Fuck you, Tony!"

Chitter chitter!

"Don't you fucking bring my mother into this! Fuck you!"

She threw an enthusiastically vicious middle finger up into the air at the sassy little critter, and the sudden motion startled it, sending it scurrying down the rail, and it disappeared from view.

Eve leaned over the balcony rail, looking down at the retreating squirrel. "Good thing you ran away, or I would've taunted you a second time!" She smiled smugly as she plopped down onto the single patio chair on her tiny balcony and sipped coffee from a mug.

A grin lifted the corner of Luc's lip.

She wasn't boring.

He opened his briefcase and spread his work out on the kitchen table. Might as well get some work done while he waited for her to leave her apartment.

Which she didn't do the entire day.

At 2AM, he stuck his ear to the wall, and no longer heard her television. Finally. He warped the space between them, and he saw her lying in her bed, all the lights off in her apartment. He stepped through into her living room. He found a device charger plugged into the wall, and he replaced it with his own – one with a tiny camera in it.

There. Mission accomplished. Yet…he slowly made his way toward her closed bedroom door. He stood outside it, conflicted. She definitely had a charger in there that he could replace, but that was crossing a line, wasn't it? Well, maybe he should just *see* what was in here. He silently moved through the closed door, then paused inside, listening to her breathing.

Slow and even.

He looked around the room in the dark. Her illuminated clock on the nightstand cast a deep orange light through the room, and it was just enough ambient light to see that Eve's bedroom was also her art studio. Canvases were stacked against the walls, and an easel stood in the corner with a half-finished work perched on the ledge. There was a small table next to the easel that was littered with paint bottles and brushes and empty cups. It smelled strongly of mineral spirits and oil paint.

This woman was lucky she couldn't get cancer.

He ambled slowly toward the bed, but before he got there, she stirred, and, like a panicked idiot, he dropped to the floor at the foot of the bed.

Fuck, why was he even still here?

She rose from her bed and padded past him toward the door, tugging her boy-cut shorts out of her ass crack as she walked away. He saw the bathroom light click on.

She hadn't seen him.

But, even in the dark…that *ass*.

He watched her on the hidden camera over the next few months from his phone – even when he was back at the compound or in a different state. Even when he was supposed to be working. She was so goddamn distracting. And so fucking weird.

He loved it.

He found any excuse to return to the apartment next to her. And when he was there, he found any excuse to go into her apartment and snoop every time she left to train. He was already quite certain she had no ties to the supernatural community, and she had zero inkling that her blood was anything special, but he wasn't quite ready to bring her in yet. He so rarely got to stalk someone so worthy of stalking.

Ahem, *scouting*.

Maybe he wasn't quite ready to share her, either. Right now, he had her all to himself. She had no boyfriend and no real friends that he could discern. One night when she was sleeping, he went through her phone, and the only people she talked to were Gwendolyn from the art gallery and the guy who scheduled her fights. She had "Mom" in her phone, but there was no history of her ever connecting with it.

Eve was alone in the world.

But from what he saw, she excelled at being alone. She talked animatedly to herself all day long, sang and danced to the music on her headphones, laughed obnoxiously at her own lame jokes, and fell asleep on the couch watching the most heinous murder documentaries and horror movies. She would turn on audiobooks or podcasts on her headphones and then provide running commentary as she went about her business. She would flex at her own reflection in the sliding glass door to the balcony, then sometimes twerk at it. Once, she performed the sign of the cross at it as she passed by.

She was a one-woman show.

Then she would disappear to her room for hours, and an odd sense of loneliness would squeeze at his chest. Like he missed her.

Fucking pathetic.

When he was in the apartment next door, he would wait all night until he saw her check the door and turn the lights out, and his adrenaline would spike. He would wait thirty more minutes, then teleport straight into her room – after checking to make sure she was in bed. Most nights he only stayed for a few minutes, just to be near her and see her in person. But there was one night he accidentally fell asleep on the floor beside the bed, listening to her breathe, wondering what she would feel like tucked next to him in that bed. He dreamed about what she felt like beneath him, his dick buried deep in her pussy, until her blaring alarm woke him. He narrowly escaped discovery, teleporting out just as she rolled over to grab her phone.

He was loathe to leave that shitty little apartment because it meant leaving her proximity, but whenever he was summoned to attend to his family's business, he went. He knew better than to defy his father's demands. Meetings, presentations, grand openings, appearances – whatever was asked of him, he obliged. He didn't have it in him to disappoint his father. His was the only approval that had ever mattered, the only validation Luc never seemed *quite* able to obtain, regardless of how hard he strived for it.

Someday, he would be enough. Someday, his father would be proud of him. Someday, his father would love him.

"Distracted, per usual," his father derided Luc in the middle of the quarterly projections presentation. Luc's attention jerked from his phone screen, where he'd been watching Eve trying to teach herself how to juggle oranges in her living room. She'd been at it for half an hour, at least. He shoved down the affection that might be lingering in his expression as he calmly slid his phone into his pocket.

Emotion was weakness. The Straw Man didn't have emotions.

"My apologies, sir." He felt everyone's eyes on him, and he hated it, but he couldn't let it show. The Straw Man was never uncomfortable.

"What's more important than our projected profits, Lucius?"

"I was simply checking on a potential…" he considered the mixed company before continuing, "…recruit. A potential game-changer." He allowed a tinge of pride to color his tone, but was careful to keep the warmth from his voice at the thought of her. The Straw Man doesn't carry warm regard for anyone.

His father's countenance reeked of superiority, and in a condescending tone, he said, "How about you work on your side projects in your free time, hm? It's time to do some big boy work now. Try to keep up, boy."

"Yes, sir." He limited his expression to only the appropriate level of resignation, refusing to let his father see the pathetic shame he felt. He shouldn't have been looking at his phone. He knew better.

His father needed him to be the perfect businessman, the perfect son, the perfect heir. He would accept nothing less, and certainly nothing *human*. Humans make mistakes. Humans let their emotions get the best of them. Humans have feelings and doubts and regrets and the occasional whimsical aspiration. But not the Straw Man. The Straw Man surpassed human. The Straw Man was his father's perception of perfection. The Straw Man was everything his father needed him to be, so the Straw Man was who he became whenever he was confronted with his father's presence.

The Straw Man didn't get distracted by pretty little pink-haired, orange-juggling clowns, regardless of how amazing their asses looked in scrunched booty shorts.

His fingers tapped lightly on his knee under the long conference table, his hand hidden from the critical eye of his father. The Straw Man didn't fidget, but Luc did, and Luc was itching to check his phone again. Had Eve figured out how to juggle yet? Had she given up on it? Was she going to eat those bruised oranges or toss them in the trash? Maybe she'd put them out for Tony, the asshole squirrel.

Nah, probably not. Fuck you, Tony.

Then, one night, a little over three months into his stalki—*scouting* assignment, Luc almost took it too far. He was watching on the camera when Eve answered the door for a pizza delivery, and he was surprised when she struck up a conversation with the delivery man. She never did that. She didn't like strangers, so she must have known him from somewhere else, apparently. The delivery man stepped inside her apartment and closed the door behind him, and a wrathful inferno ignited in Luc's chest when he saw the man's eyes drop to her ass as she walked away from him to place the pizza on the table. She turned back to him and reached out for a hug.

Luc pushed up so quickly from the table, he overturned the chair he'd been sitting in. *Don't you fucking touch her, she's MINE!*

The lights flickered through the whole apartment building as Luc slammed his fist on the table. He was already looking through warped space at Eve and the stranger in her apartment as they looked around at the flickering lights in confusion. He was ready to jump in and cause a scene, but the bewildered expression on Eve's face stopped him from doing something completely insane. She didn't know anything about the stranger side of the world they lived in. She didn't know *him*. His obsession with her was a one-sided affair. He had no right to this feeling brewing in his heart.

That was when he realized his fascination with her had slipped into dangerous territory. His father's approval was no longer the only thing that mattered to him.

He couldn't watch from afar any longer. He needed to *touch* her. *Talk* to her.

He called Veris. "I need your powers of persuasion. But get a sedative from Mira for backup, just in case. This recruit could be tricky."

28

Stripped Bare

Eve pulled back, retreating from Luc's mind and returning to Dagon's body.

"You *stalked* me!" she blurted in Dagon's voice. "Like, you actually *stalked* me!"

"I'm going to assume that's you, Eve?" Luc replied. "I prefer the term '*scouting*.' I had to vet you before I brought you to the compound and persuaded you to become a hunter."

"God, all the embarrassing things you saw me do!" She wasn't sure if Dagon's body was capable of blushing, but her face felt as crimson as his eyes.

"You were my favorite reality show," Luc admitted. He returned his sunglasses to his face. "Is that what you were looking for? Me before you?"

She crossed Dagon's giant arms as she considered her answer. "I was looking for something…real."

Luc was quizzical. "Are you suggesting I'm not real?"

"You're not always real, no. The Straw Man isn't real."

Luc sighed wearily. "He's a necessity. Just an optimized version of me to keep my father off my back."

"Not to keep him off your back. To make him love you," Eve said, taking a step toward him.

Discomfort settled in Luc's face, and he pushed his sunglasses up his nose. "I'm not having this conversation with you in mixed company, love."

"It wouldn't be *you* he loved, though. You understand that, right?" Eve pointed out, pressing on despite Dagon's presence. "He'd love the fake version of you, and that's not real love. It's a lie."

Luc folded his arms over his chest, mirroring Eve's stance in Dagon's body. "Is that what you think I've done with you? Made a special Straw Man just for you to make you love me?" He looked away, embarrassment tinging his angular cheekbones. "Please return to your own body if you want to continue this conversation. This is weirding me the fuck out."

Eve ignored his request. "I used to wonder that – if you were just being the kind of man you thought I wanted. I wondered if I was just a passing amusement to you, a brief obsession that would eventually be replaced by a new one. But I felt it in your memories, that these feelings were new to you. That they were, *are*, genuine. And whether or not you've tried to build a Straw Man for me, it doesn't matter, because I see the real you shine through all the time. I see the truth behind the jokes, the insecurities hiding in the nonchalance, the feelings masquerading as amusement. When you stood in front of me, covered in blood, holding Dizzy's ripped-off head, asking me to love you again, I saw you. *You*, stripped bare of your usual pomp and circumstance. That was real. You need me to love you, but you also know you don't have to pretend to be someone else to achieve that."

Touching, Dagon interrupted in her thoughts.

Eat glass, she retorted.

She smiled at Luc, and it felt strange on Dagon's bearded face. "I would kiss you right now, but I'm guessing that's a no-go."

Don't you fucking dare, Dagon warned at the same time Luc took a step back, palms facing her.

"As tempted as I am to feel that luxurious beard against my mouth, I'll have to pass for now," he jested.

Dagon overrode Eve's control to his mouth and said, "Fuck the feelings. Did it work? Did you detect her in your memories?"

"Ah, Dagon. Always so tactful," Luc quipped. "Well, it mostly worked. As long as you were distracting me, I didn't notice. But the moment you let up, it was obvious Eve was in my head. I could see the memories she was pulling up. So, if this is going to work with Ramil, you're going to need to do a better job of distracting him. Draw him into conversation, bringing up subjects about secrets and betrayal. Bring up his affiliation with a cult. Question his loyalty to Knighco. Pick at him. Push his buttons. You know, work to your strengths."

Luc's phone chimed, and he dragged it from his pocket to check it. "The jet just landed." He looked up at Eve and Dagon. "Ramil will be here shortly."

Bo returned with a gallon of white latex paint and a couple of brushes. When he saw Eve's catatonic body sitting in a chair in front of Dagon's chair, Luc filled him in on the plan, to which he was predictably apprehensive.

"And if he detects the deception?" Bo asked. "What then?"

Dagon answered, "Then I take the blame for it, obviously. Eve is in no danger." He smirked. "She's in very capable hands, boys."

Eve sighed internally. *Tell me when Ramil shows up. I'm taking a little trip down memory lane while I'm in here.* She didn't wait for a response before she buried herself in the memories Zeke left behind.

It broke her heart all over again as she perused them, like she was looking through a photo album that didn't have nearly enough pictures. She desperately wished she had more memories with Zeke. Decades. She wanted decades. She wanted to see him with graying temples and wrinkles around his eyes. If any of them were to have kids, it should've been Zeke. He would've been a great dad. A loving husband.

He never belonged here in the first place. He wasn't like the rest of them. There wasn't a hint of darkness in him. He was only here because of a specialty he had to learn to control, and then he was stuck here because he sacrificed his body to save a little boy from becoming Dagon's vessel. Zeke wasn't a natural killer. Of all of them, he was the most likely to have been able to function normally in civilian life. Fuck, he would've thrived in civilian life. He *had* thrived in civilian life, before his powers awakened.

She looked back at his childhood, and saw that he wanted to be a firefighter. Even when he was in high school, he had plans to eventually get into the Hotshots. He had already taken the initial steps and had been training for it.

Then, in that cruel twist of fate, his specialty became activated, and it ruined everything.

He would've been an amazing firefighter. He *should've* been a firefighter. He deserved that opportunity. If he had to die, he should've died saving someone, doing something noble – not disappearing helplessly into the body of an ancient god.

He never belonged here among the monsters.

You resent me again, Dagon noted.

It's hard not to.

Well, you're going to have to stow it. Ramil is here. It's showtime, princess.

Eve shifted focus, looking out of Dagon's eyes at Ramil and Luc. Bo was gone, and so was Eve's body. He must have taken her to one of their apartments to watch over her.

Ramil studied Dagon as Luc instructed him to fix the devil's trap. Ramil narrowed his unusual eyes skeptically, and they began to glow iridescently, revealing his monstrous nature to the sight Eve had borrowed from Dagon. Eve irrationally feared that Ramil could see her inside Dagon's eyes.

"Where's Eve?" Ramil asked Luc. "She helped me with this last time."

Eve noticed the small changes in Luc's posture, the tick in his jaw, the change in the tone of his voice as he said, "You seem quite taken with her." Shit, he was going off-script. "Is this a new development? Someone to take my sister's place? Or has this been going on for a while?"

Ramil smiled amicably at Luc, completely unperturbed by Luc's accusation. "Oh, nothing of the sort, I assure you. And Eve would never give me the time of day. I suspect I lost any chance I may have ever had when I underestimated her on the mat."

Luc dragged his hand through his hair and smirked. "Oh, you never had a chance. I already know that. But that wasn't what I asked."

"I would never step on any toes, Luc. I'm not interested in Eve."

"Excellent. Now, do a better job of making me believe that." He gestured to the paint bucket and the devil's trap. "Your canvas awaits, Picasso." With one last glance between Ramil and Dagon, he said, "Behave, you two," then left.

Eve suspected he meant that for her and Dagon.

Ramil looked down at his business casual outfit, then began to make his way past the devil's trap toward Ruth's bedroom, unbuttoning his black shirt.

Eve's words blurted from Dagon's mouth. "Where are you going?"

He turned, surprised. "Wherever I please. I'm not the prisoner here."

Eve and Dagon watched him continue on to Ruth's room. When he returned, he was wearing casual jeans and a t-shirt, and he had a spellbook, bottle of holy water, and a few other ingredients from Ruth's stash cradled in his arm.

"You have clothes here?" Eve asked.

Ramil didn't spare Dagon a glance as he set to work on opening the paint can. He opened the spellbook on the floor, and began to recite the incantation as he combined the ingredients. He produced a small dagger from the sheath at his ankle and cut his arm shallowly, allowing a few drops of his blood to drop into the paint can. Then he brought the can to Dagon and held up the knife.

"If you'd be so kind to me as you were to Eve last time we did this, it would be greatly appreciated," Ramil implored.

"I only ask that you indulge me in a little conversation, and I'll cooperate. It gets stale in here by myself," Dagon said, taking over control of his mouth once again.

"Deal." Ramil drew a small amount of blood from Dagon and allowed it to fall into the bucket.

"You had clothes here. You were fucking Ruth?" Dagon guessed.

"A gentleman doesn't kiss and tell," Ramil replied without hesitation. "But…I think it was fairly obvious. She may not have been my first choice, but she was persistent, and my first choice was unwilling to reciprocate." He dipped a brush in the paint and began to follow the pattern already laid on the floor.

"Your first choice?"

Ramil was silent.

"You knew what Ruth was planning," Dagon pressed.

Ramil shook his head. "I did not." He pinned Dagon with an accusatory glare. "But you must have."

Dagon's temper flared. "I did not! It is not my fault he is gone!" Then, internally to Eve, he said, *I'm going in, but I may need help breaking through his shields.*

"Would you bring him back if you could?" Ramil asked.

Dagon and Eve both paused. Dagon finally answered, "Of course. But it's pointless wishing for things that can't happen."

"There is a way," Ramil revealed. "Possibly." He continued to paint, but he glanced up at Dagon, gauging his reaction.

He's fucking with you. He must be, Eve reasoned, but she could feel Dagon's heart racing with the possibility, and she wasn't sure if that was her fault or his. The original plan was suddenly shoved to the backburner.

"You're lying," Dagon hissed.

"I'm not. But…it would require use of resources I no longer have access to." He glanced up at Dagon. "And I would need Eve."

Dagon leapt to his feet and snarled, "Never!"

Ramil reeled back. "Not forever. Calm down. I just need her ability to, well, *consolidate* power. And read the grimoire."

"Why is this the first we are hearing of this?" Eve demanded through Dagon's lips, standing over Ramil.

Ramil paused, narrowing his eyes at Dagon again. Scrutinizing.

He sees me, Eve worried.

He can't, Dagon assured her.

Ramil balanced the paintbrush on the paint can and stood up, dusting off his knees. He stared deeply into Dagon's eyes, the copper-green of his irises shining strangely. "Hello, Eve."

29

As Trustworthy as Week-Old Sushi

Son of a bitch!

Eve shrank back inside of Dagon, trying to hide from Ramil's probing gaze, and Dagon's essence curled around her protectively.

Dagon laughed derisively. "Eve? Are you on drugs?" He bent at the waist to bring his eyes level with Ramil, and in a childish tone, he pointed to himself and said, "Me, Dagon. You, Ramil."

Ramil frowned, studying Dagon's face. "Why are you in there, Eve?"

Dagon spoke in a silly falsetto, "I just wanted to be close to Dagon. He's so big and strong." Then, in his regular voice, he said, "Fuck off, little genie," and returned to his chair, crossing his ankle over his knee casually.

Ramil wasn't buying it. "Why is she in there, Dagon?"

"She isn't."

Eve felt a probing presence pushing at her and Dagon's mental space. *He's trying to get in,* she warned Dagon, but he was already fortifying his shields before she finished her thought.

Anger flashed through Ramil's eyes, but he tamped it down quickly. "Why are you hiding from me, Eve?" He tilted his head and quirked a brow. "Is it because you're afraid I know you and Bo and Isaac were in my apartment?"

How does he know that? Eve fretted.

He's baiting you, Dagon replied calmly.

He's not going to let this go.

"What makes you think anyone was in your apartment?" Dagon asked.

"Oh, just the surveillance footage I have of them rummaging through my things. Come on out Eve. Let's talk. I'm not angry."

"You sound a little angry," Dagon remarked, tilting his head to the side.

Then Eve's words burst from his mouth, her indignation expressed on his stern face. "If anyone's angry, it should be me, you fucking thief!"

Dagon sighed internally, and a victorious expression brightened Ramil's features. "There she is. You *almost* had me doubting myself."

Fuck, princess. Way to play it fucking close to the chest, Dagon chastised. *He'll never let his guard down now. There's no way we're getting past his mental barriers.*

Well, if this confrontation is going to happen, I'm glad I have your body as a shield, she thought bluntly.

My body will always be your shield.

"Why are you in there?" Ramil wanted to know, his tone distrusting.

"Training," Dagon replied for her. Believable. Reasonable. Much better than admitting they planned to break into his mind.

She elaborated, "I wanted to see if I could control Dagon if I needed to. Apparently, I can." She quickly shifted focus. "You stole from me," she accused Ramil. "And you sent me photos you never should've had in the first place. You set Luc up and deceived me."

Ramil held his palms up defensively. "Whoa, whoa. I didn't mean to deceive you, and I didn't mean to set Luc up. I was myself deceived, truth be told. I thought it *was* him. I was trying to warn you about him…anonymously. I didn't want blowback. I was trying to look out for *you*."

Dagon interjected skeptically, "You can detect Eve inside of me, but you couldn't tell a shifted Dizzy from Luc?"

"I suppose if I'd really suspected it *wasn't* Luc, I would've looked a little closer. But, Luc being Luc, it was easy to believe it was him."

Eve didn't appreciate that insinuation about Luc's character, but the twinge of guilt in her heart reminded her that she'd made the exact same assumption. "How did you get cameras in all those places?" she interrogated.

"I have acquaintances from my old life who still owe me favors."

Eve contemplated his explanation. It was too easy. But…also reasonable. Fuck.

"What about the shit you stole from me?" she demanded in Dagon's gravelly baritone. "You broke into my apartment and took things from me!"

Ramil's face flushed crimson. "You broke into my apartment and took them back. *And* snooped on my laptop."

"Why did you take my things? Who else have you stolen from?"

"I'm sorry. I have a problem. I know you saw my treasures. But I haven't taken anything from anyone else here."

"So why me? They weren't even valuable things. They weren't *treasures*."

Discomfort tensed Ramil's forehead. "Let's discuss this later. Privately. There is one thing you missed, and I will return it to you."

"If it is her underwear, I will gut you right here and now," Dagon threatened.

Ramil rolled his eyes. "It isn't underwear." He knelt down and picked up the paintbrush again, resuming his work on the devil's trap. "It was a book. Come to my apartment later, Eve, and we can discuss everything, including Zeke."

"I want to discuss Zeke now," Dagon said, but Eve was beginning to feel utterly exhausted. She knew what that meant.

I have to return to my body now, she told Dagon. *I can't hold the possession any longer.*

She barely had the words out before she felt an irresistible tugging, and she was ripped from Dagon's body and slammed back into her own. She bolted upright and clapped her hands to her face, digging the heels of her hands into her eyes.

"Ah, fuck, my *head!*" she cried. It felt like someone had struck her between the eyes with a driving wedge.

"Evie," Bo fretted, his hands worrying over her face and shoulders. She felt another pair of hands on her knees. "Is everything ok?"

She groaned in reply, but the pain quickly dissipated, and she blinked her eyes open. Isaac was crouched in front of her, and Bo was sitting next to her with his mask down around his neck. She was in Isaac's living room, sitting on the couch that was a perfect clone of hers.

Were he and Bo *willingly* spending time together?

Isaac raised his brows and signed, *You ok?*

"I'm good," she said, brushing their hands away. She looked around. "Where's Luc?"

"He went to see Celeste about Ramil's laptop," Bo supplied. "So, how did it go?"

"Ramil figured out I was there."

Bo's eyes widened. "How?"

"I don't know, but he knew." She gave them a quick rundown of what transpired, but she didn't mention the part about going to his apartment later. They would want to go with her, but she had a feeling she would get more information if she saw Ramil alone.

Isaac began to sign, but after a quick glance at Bo, he asked aloud, "You didn't get into his memories?"

Eve shook her head.

"Do you believe him?" Bo inquired. "About Zeke?"

"I don't know." A crease formed between her brows. "I don't *trust* him, but is it stupid for me to want to believe him?"

"Maybe," Bo admitted. "He's obviously using it as a bargaining chip to earn back favor after being caught doing shady shit. It could all be bullshit. It probably is bullshit."

"But you want to believe it, too," Eve surmised.

He didn't deny it.

She reached out to Dagon. *What did he say?*

Dagon's voice was in her head instantly. *Nothing. As soon as you made your exit, he stopped talking. He's just ignoring me now, and I can't get past his mental barriers. Come back and help him finish this stupid fucking trap so we can interrogate him some more.*

When Eve returned to Dagon's apartment, Bo and Isaac refused to let her go alone. Ramil watched them all walk in, smiling pleasantly at Eve, and offered her a knife and a brush. She added her blood to the paint mix and began to work on the devil's trap alongside him.

Eve, Bo, and Dagon all tried to pry more information from Ramil regarding Zeke's resurrection, but he wouldn't say more about it. All he would say is that he needed to look into it a little more, and he didn't mean to get anyone's hopes up just yet.

Bullshit.

Later that evening, Eve found herself with a little free time to herself. Rather, she orchestrated it. She told Bo she was craving Chinese food from a restaurant twenty miles away and sent him on his way. She made Luc promise to work on whittling down the workload he'd accumulated. Isaac went back to his apartment of his own accord. And Eoduun? He was holed up in his apartment, likely still furious with her, and she had no expectations of him coming to find her tonight.

She knocked quietly on Ramil's door, looking over her shoulder for the fifth time to make sure no one was in the hallway. When she turned back, Ramil was standing there in the open doorway.

"Jesus," Eve blurted, jerking back.

"Not quite," Ramil teased, smirking. He stepped back and gestured for her to enter. "Please, come in." He glanced out into the hallway behind her. "No entourage?" he asked.

"You said you wanted to speak privately," she replied.

"And they agreed to it?" he inquired skeptically as he closed the door.

"I don't need permission. Now, give me what you stole from me," she said curtly, holding out her hand.

Ramil nodded sheepishly. He turned and gestured for her to follow. "This way." Eve followed behind him, but stopped in the doorway to his bedroom as he entered. He grabbed a book off his nightstand and turned to her, noting her hesitation. "Are you afraid to come into my room? You've already been through every inch of it."

She dipped her head toward the book in his hand. "Not every inch, apparently."

Ramil chuckled, the sound low and surprisingly enticing. He sauntered up to her and stood *just* inside her personal space, holding the book up casually. He gazed down at her with his strange eyes and replied in a sultry tone, "No, not *every inch*."

Fuck, her cheeks were flushing. She could feel them burning under his gaze. Her eyes flicked to the foot of his bed, to the padded holes meant for wrists and a neck, and the image of herself locked into that stockade suddenly popped into her mind. She was on her back, her head tipped back. She saw Dagon standing at the foot of the bed, fucking her mouth with his giant hands tangled in her hair, and Apep on top of her, driving his hips into her with hard, deep thrusts, her legs wrapped around his waist. Ramil was next to her on

251

the bed, his mouth working over one nipple while his hand cupped her other breast.

An unholy trinity.

Ramil's eyes suddenly glanced up at her within the erotic reverie, and she was snapped back to reality.

"Is something wrong?" Ramil inquired with kindly concern.

"I'm fine," she lied, ignoring the pulse in her core. She snatched the book from Ramil's hand and moved back a step, diverting her attention to its cover.

Myths and Monsters in Modern Times. It was a book from the library that she'd taken back to her apartment her first day at Knighco. She'd forgotten she even had it. There was a tiny space in the pages in the middle of the book, so she flipped it open. The pages splayed open to the Wendigo section, and Eve's heart dropped into her stomach when she saw the bookmark wedged between the pages. It was a little piece of torn notebook paper with a familiar, messily scrawled message written on it.

> *I'm so sorry. Please don't be afraid of me. I won't let him out*
> *again, I promise.*
> *-Zeke*
> *P.S. I swear I'm not a pervert.*
> *P.P.S. Your pretty.*

Eve covered her mouth with her hand, Zeke's words blurring through the tears welling in her eyes. She blinked them back, refusing to lose her composure in Ramil's presence. She looked up at him.

"Tell me how to bring Zeke back," she demanded.

Ramil held her gaze. "It won't be easy, and no one will agree to it."

"You'd be appalled at what I would agree to do to bring him back."

Ramil's eyebrows darted up, but a slow smile spread across his face. "Good. Because the ritual isn't for the faint of heart, and you're the only person on earth who can complete it."

"Because of my ability to 'consolidate power,' as you so eloquently put it?"

"Because if you're the Abomination, you can raise Lilith. And if you have the power to raise Lilith, you have the power to raise *anyone,* including Zeke."

Eve frowned. "But I thought that was just some crazy zealot nonsense from the Locusts. Now you're telling me you believe it?"

"I believe it's a possibility."

"And what about the grimoire? You said we need the grimoire, and, I'm not sure if you've noticed, but we don't have it."

A pensive expression creased Ramil's brow. "I said I needed your ability to *read* the grimoire. Maybe you should sit down."

Eve's eyes widened. "Do you have the fucking grimoire?!"

Ramil shook his head. "No, I don't have it. But…I know where it is."

Alarms blared and red flags flew in Eve's mind. She took a step away from Ramil. What was his angle? "Where is it? Why haven't you told anyone?"

"You think I'm lying," he surmised.

"I think you're about as trustworthy as week-old sushi."

Ramil smirked. "That's fair. I earned that." He tilted his head and knowingly added, "But you came to speak to me anyway. You want to trust me."

"I want Zeke back. That is the *only* reason I am here," Eve shot back.

"Then we share the same desire," Ramil said. "I only wish to rectify my mistakes with Ruth. I should've seen what she was up to, or perhaps limited her training so she didn't have the skills to do what she did. I am partially to blame for Zeke's untimely demise, because I was unknowingly helping prepare Ruth for the ritual."

"You weren't just helping her train." Eve eyed the kinky stockade-style footboard on his bed again. "You were fucking her. You were spending most of your time together. I don't believe you didn't know she was up to something." Eve narrowed her eyes. "And now that I'm thinking about it, why don't you care that I decimated her? Didn't you care about her?"

Ramil's expression was unchanging. "I'm not sorry she's dead. She betrayed all of us. She made her choice, and it was the wrong one. I don't begrudge you for taking revenge. I only regret that I didn't see her deception sooner." He gestured toward the living room. "Now, please, let's have a seat and discuss where to go from here."

30

Sacrifice

Eve sat across from Ramil in his living room, gold ornamentations glinting all around her as she stared him down.

Ramil steepled his fingers and crossed one long leg over the other. "I'm going to reveal things to you that I would prefer you keep to yourself. I am trusting you, as I hope you will eventually trust me. I ask that you please listen to all I have to say before passing judgement."

Eve circled her hand, indicating he should just get on with it.

He inhaled deeply. "I haven't *completely* cut ties with the Locusts." He held up his palms when Eve's eyes widened confrontationally. "That is not to say I am still part of their organization, cult, whatever you'd like to call it. I'm not. But I have a few close friends that I have secretly kept in touch with – friends whose loyalty to the Locusts is questionable. The Locusts don't know they still talk to me, and Knighco doesn't know I am in contact with them. Our interactions are usually of a personal nature, and we aren't out to trade secrets. But yesterday, I contacted one of my friends and asked about Stacey Rose."

Ramil paused, his penetrating gaze fixed on Eve, watching for the reaction she was trying to hide. She kept her expression impassive, though she was impatient for him to keep talking.

"And?" she pressed.

"I was told she betrayed them…And she was your mother."

Eve's mask slipped, her eyes widening.

"You truly are Eno's Abomination. Stacey Rose ran away from the Locusts to give birth in secret, then hid the child - you. She tried to pass off another baby as hers, hoping the Locusts would leave her be when the girl's powers didn't activate at thirteen. And they believed it, right up until she gave herself away by going Newbury to check on you, to see if you'd started the activation phase. She led them right to you, and when they realized what she'd done, she was killed for it. I remember it."

Ice crystalized in Eve's veins. "I thought you didn't remember Stacey." She used Dagon's powers to tentatively prod at Ramil's mind, desperately wanting to see behind his barriers, to see what he was hiding, but she hit a solid wall. Now that he knew the powers she possessed, he was keeping his guard up around her. There was no sneaking in now.

His eyes snapped to hers, as though he sensed her attempted intrusion. "I didn't. I had forgotten her name, but I remembered the ordeal around the mother of the Abomination and her betrayal. I was just a teenager myself then, and not privy to more sensitive matters, but it was a big deal in the organization and people were talking about it. It caused a rift in the Locusts, actually. Those who set out to collect you never returned. And then, you disappeared, and they lost you."

"I couldn't have been that hard to find. It wasn't like I changed my name."

"But you were a teenager, with no bills in your name, credit history, bank account, or lease, I assume? That makes it a lot harder to track someone down when they don't leave a paper trail. But that's not the only reason they didn't find you. They stopped looking."

"If I was that important, why would they stop?"

"Forgive me for putting it this way, but you never showed any signs of being *special* after you survived your activation phase. By the time you disappeared, most Locusts believed you were a dud. Eno still believed you were the Abomination, but he also believed that you would be led back to them by fate once all the prophecies of Revelation had come to pass."

She crossed her arms and shot an accusing look at Ramil. "Did you tell them you found me? Do they know about me now?"

"Relax, they don't know anything. But I did use the trajectory of the conversation to segue into questions about the Abomination and the ritual to raise Lilith. That was when I found out that the Locusts have the grimoire – and Apep."

Eve was floored. "*What?!* They have it?! And Apep's working with them?! We have to tell Luc!"

"We can't tell Luc yet. I haven't figured out how to explain how I came across this information without compromising my fragile relationship with the Locusts," Ramil reasoned. "And Apep isn't working with them. He's their prisoner. They believe him to be the serpent from Revelation Twenty, bound for a thousand years, then released onto the earth to deceive nations."

"How did they capture him?!"

"I don't know. No one I spoke with knew."

Eve frowned. "How many 'books' or 'sections' of Revelation are there?"

Ramil gave her a knowing look. "Twenty-Two. Which means Eno will be expecting you soon. This could be a perfect opportunity for us. They should already have some preparations made in anticipation of finally resurrecting Lilith."

Eve shifted uncomfortably in her seat. "What are you suggesting?"

"We can't just take the grimoire and run. We have to do the ritual *there*. They should have everything we need. Well, most everything we need."

Eve's ears perked as she heard the Toyota pull up outside. Bo was back. She had to wrap this up quickly.

She rose from the couch and studied Ramil. She didn't trust him, but if there was any possibility of bringing back Zeke, she had to explore it. "How do we get the others to agree to this? Because I won't go behind their back to do it. It never ends well when I do."

"Leave that to me. I think I can convince them, if they know it's for Zeke."

"What do I need to do?"

"You need to choose a vessel for Zeke. I will take care of everything else."

"A vessel? Wait, is he just going to possess someone else's body?"

"No, they will only provide the clay. He will take his own form."

Eve's stomach dropped. "Like Dagon did." Ramil nodded. "So you're not asking for a vessel. You're asking for a sacrifice."

"You can't expect a feat of this magnitude to come without a hefty price." Ramil pushed off from the chair and stood in front of her. He looked down at her with an intensity that made her uncomfortable. "I think we both know who the clear choice is, given the circumstances."

The color drained from her face, and she turned on her heel and headed toward the door without giving a response.

Ramil followed her to the door, and as she opened it, he caught it and held it partially closed, obstructing her exit. He leaned close to her and said, "I would appreciate it if you could keep our conversation to yourself until I can work out the details. I don't want to bring Luc a plan that's half-baked, and I don't want him shooting it down before I can even present it to him."

Eve simply nodded. Satisfied, Ramil opened the door the rest of the way and Eve walked out. She didn't want to be the one to present this to Bo and Luc anyway. It was insane. Of course they would shoot it down.

And even though she knew who the clear choice was for the sacrifice, the thought of offering up Dagon to meet the same fate as Zeke made her feel sick. She'd been ready to kill him for taking Zeke's body, but now that she actually had the opportunity to turn the tables and deliver Zeke back into his own body at Dagon's expense, she knew she couldn't do it.

She couldn't trade one for the other. Fair or not, she couldn't, and she wouldn't let anyone else choose Dagon, either.

But she desperately, *selfishly* needed to bring Zeke back, so they *had* to choose someone. But who?

Bo, Luc, Isaac, and Eve all gathered around her kitchen island, eating the subpar Chinese food she'd sent Bo out to get.

Luc scrunched his nose after one bite. "Bo, what the hell is this?"

Bo looked equally unimpressed as he dropped his chopsticks back into the container he was eating from. He looked at Eve with his mask still down. "*This* is what you were craving?"

Eve gave an apologetic shrug. "Sorry. I thought it would be better."

Isaac coughed and shoved his container away, touching his chin and arcing his hand away, flipping his flat palm downward. *Bad.* He pointed to his chest, swiped one pointed finger down across the tip of the other pointed finger, touched his closed fingers to his lips, then indicated the container with a Y-handshape. *I can't eat that.*

Eve circled her fist over her chest. *Sorry.* Then, to the group, she said, "At least Eoduun isn't missing much."

Bo sighed. "I don't know what to do with him. I thought he was starting to come around, and now he won't leave his apartment again."

"It's my fault," Eve said. "I shouldn't have gotten his hopes up that Zeke might still be alive in Dagon. And I shouldn't have promised to kill Dagon if he wasn't. Now he feels like I've betrayed him."

Luc leaned down and crossed his arms on the counter, looking at Eve over the top of his sunglasses. "Speaking of Zeke, what do you make of Ramil's sudden confession that he knows a way to bring him back?"

Eve's eyes darted down to her unpalatable noodles. "I don't know. He didn't give us enough information about it to make anything of it."

"I think he's bluffing," Bo said, and Isaac nodded in agreement.

Luc lifted one hand from the counter to rest his chin in it as he turned his attention to Bo. "You're not hiding," he noticed, a hint of amusement in his voice as he nodded toward Bo's unmasked face.

"He's being considerate," Eve said, flitting her eyes briefly toward Isaac.

Luc's brows hiked up. "Oh, so you and Isaac are besties now?" he asked Bo, a smirk on his lips.

"Leave him alone," Eve chastised, feeling a tinge of Bo's self-conscious embarrassment in her chest. "This is a *good* thing. Don't fuck with him."

"It won't last," Luc asserted as he stood upright. "The moment Isaac steps out of line with you again, this little bromance," he wagged his finger between Bo and Isaac, "will be over." His head tipped slightly to the side. "And we'll both be back to wanting to murder the little priest."

Isaac stared back at Luc coolly, seemingly unaffected, but Bo was irritated. He snipped, "Can we get back to the issue at hand? Ramil? Zeke?"

"Touchy. Fine," Luc said, pushing his sunglasses up his nose. He turned his attention to Eve. "So, you and Dagon got jack squat from Ramil's memories? No indication of whether he was being truthful or not about Zeke?"

"Sorry. The whole plan got completely derailed. But…there was one thing he said that kind of bothered me. He suggested that Zeke would need a body. A sacrifice." She couldn't keep it to herself any longer. It was eating at her.

"You didn't mention that before," Bo said.

"I'm mentioning it now. If it were true, and we *did* have to choose someone to sacrifice to bring Zeke back…"

"Dagon, obviously," Luc interrupted.

Eve glanced at Bo and Isaac, and she could see the assent on their faces.

"No," she dissented. "Not Dagon."

"He's the obvious choice, love," Luc replied. "The only one, really."

"He's not the only choice. Pick someone else," she argued.

There was a knock on the door, and Eve recognized the scent immediately. "Ramil."

The room fell silent, and Luc whispered, "Speak of the devil, and he shall appear." Then, loudly, he yelled, "Come in!"

A moment later, Ramil walked into the kitchen, an unopened bottle of Johnnie Walker in his hand. "Do I smell Chinese food?"

"You do," Eve said. "And it tastes like it really came all the way from China. On a fishing boat. In a dirty, unrefrigerated shipping crate."

"Surely, it can't be that bad," Ramil said.

"Oh, it is, and don't call me Shirley," Eve jested. It was a joke she remembered her asshole stepfather using, and it was one of those stupid little things she couldn't help saying. "I *wish* it wasn't that bad."

Ramil moved next to her, his arm brushing hers, and grabbed up the container in front of her. He used her chopsticks to lift some noodles to his mouth, then slid the container back toward her.

"That's not so bad. Perhaps you should try another bite," Ramil urged, ignoring the incensed glare Luc was giving him.

She picked up the chopsticks and took tentative taste of the noodles.

…And they suddenly tasted better. "I swear, this tasted like shit just a minute ago," she mumbled, staring down at the container in confusion.

"Sometimes the palate needs time to adjust to new flavors," Ramil reasoned. He glanced around at the others. "Perhaps you should give yours a second chance, too."

Bo looked at his food skeptically, but ventured one more bite, quickly pulling his mask up over his face as he chewed. His eyebrows rose. "Huh," he muttered. "I guess it isn't so bad."

Luc took a bite, and surprise flashed across his face. Then he dropped his takeout in the garbage can. "Hm. Seems I've lost my appetite, unfortunately."

Isaac stood with his arms crossed, his suspicious dark eyes following Ramil's every move, ignoring his noodles. He went to the fridge, grabbed two beers, then rounded the kitchen island, sliding forcefully between Ramil and Eve. He twisted the cap off both bottles and set one down in front of Eve, then took a drink of the other. He rested his elbows on the counter next to her, effectively blocking Ramil from any further physical contact with her.

Subtle.

"To what do we owe the pleasure, Ramil?" Luc inquired, faint annoyance lacing his tone.

Ramil raised the bottle of Scotch in his hand. "I come bearing gifts. A peace offering. An apology." He went directly to the cupboard that contained the tumblers and pulled them out, lining up five glasses on the counter. He poured two fingers into each glass, then placed one in front of Luc, Bo, Isaac, and, finally, Eve, retaining the last for himself.

Isaac slid the glasses offered to him and Eve back toward Ramil. He rocked a K-handshape between himself and Eve and touched his thumb to his chest with his fingers up vertically. *We're fine.*

"So be it." Ramil raised his glass to his lips and sipped, his eyes on Eve. "I *am* sorry about the photos. I stuck my nose where it didn't belong, misunderstood the situation, and passed that misunderstanding on to Eve. I thought I was doing the right thing, but I grossly misjudged." He glanced between Eve and Luc. "You both have my deepest apologies. I may have been harboring a little crush that clouded my judgment, but I assure you, the cloud has lifted. It will never happen again."

Luc stood with his hands in his pockets, his expression stern behind his sunglasses. "Hm." He took the glass of Scotch, downed it in one gulp, and said curtly, "I drank the Scotch. I heard your apology. Anything else?"

"I also wanted to assure you that I will do all that I can to bring Zeke earthside. I know there is a way. A ritual. I need to do a little more research, but, rest assured, I will figure it out and bring a solid plan to you. Team Alpha *will* be complete again."

Bo took a sip of his Scotch, then scowled at Ramil. "And why the fuck should we believe a word out of your mouth?"

Ramil was unrattled. "I understand your mistrust. But I've fought alongside you for years, Bo. The Knighco hunters have been like family to me. This was one little indiscretion, and, as I stated, I *thought* I was doing the right thing. I thought I was saving Eve from a bad relationship, from deception. Please, let me make it up to you all. Let me give you Zeke back."

The kitchen was quiet, save for the soft tapping of Eve's fingernails on the glass beer bottle in front of her.

"I think it's time for you to go, Ramil. We'll speak more tomorrow," Luc said flatly, leaning back against the counter behind him, his attention focused on his empty tumbler on the island instead of on Ramil.

Ramil gave a resigned nod. "Certainly." As he walked past Eve, he rested his hand in the middle of her back and leaned in. Her curse snarled and surged inside her, like a taunted beast charging the bars of its cage. She fought to hide the sudden burst of arousal and aggression. "Please, enjoy the Scotch," Ramil said smoothly. "I noticed you were running low."

Eve watched him walk away, and the monster inside her relaxed again.

She glanced up at the almost-empty bottle of Johnnie Walker she kept on top of her fridge. Grief swelled in her heart. Memories of Zeke swam in that amber liquid. She glanced down at the tumbler Ramil had poured for her, and wondered if it would taste of Zeke. She remembered the way it tasted on Z's tongue, and the way it smelled on his breath when he moaned in pleasure. She remembered the burn of it in her nose from a time Eoduun and Z made her laugh when she was taking a shot because they were taking turns trying to recreate the one-person fight scene in *Fight Club*.

Zeke had a penchant for cult classics.

"I am Jack's broken heart," she mumbled to herself as she snatched up the tumbler, lifted it to her lips, and emptied its contents.

31
I'll Do It

"I want to believe him just as much as I don't," Luc sighed.

"I think we all feel that way," Bo agreed. He stood up and finished his drink. "I'm going to go talk to Eoduun. He needs to be part of this conversation."

"Is it a conversation?" Eve wondered. "Are we actually entertaining it?"

Luc shoved his hands in his pockets. "I won't disregard it until I hear his plan. I don't want to squash a real opportunity to bring back Z, if that's what this turns out to be."

Hope dared to flutter in Eve's heart.

Twenty minutes later, Bo returned to Eve's apartment with Eoduun in tow. As Eoduun stepped into the kitchen, Eve noticed how gaunt he was beginning to appear, like he'd lost weight and aged ten years. Dark circles shadowed the bloodshot eyes he cast her way, a hollow expression on his face. His grief was eating him alive, and it made Eve's heart hurt.

If they promised him Zeke, and it fell through again, he wouldn't survive it.

"I'm here," he intoned lifelessly.

Eve pushed the container of noodles in front of her toward him. "Eat," she urged.

He barely spared her a glance as he took up the container and inspected the contents. "This smells like shit."

"It isn't half bad after a few bites," she said.

Eoduun dug the chopsticks in and lifted some noodles to his mouth, then immediately spit them back into the container. "That's fucking foul," he spat, shoving the container back at Eve.

"Ugh, really, dude?" Eve complained. She took the container back and dug out the noodles Eoduun had spit out, flinging them into the garbage can next to the counter. Then she took a bite of the untouched noodles – and did exactly what Eoduun had just done. "What the fuck? It tastes like shit again!" She threw the box in the trash with an exasperated sigh.

"I didn't come here for shitty Chinese food," Eoduun said impatiently. "I came to find out what news you have about Zeke."

They relayed what they'd been told by Ramil, and Eve watched Eoduun's face slowly coming back to life. They'd barely finished speaking when Eoduun blurted, "We're going to try, right?" He looked to Eve. "We have to do it. Give him Dagon and get Zeke back."

"Easy, boy," Luc interrupted. "We haven't decided anything yet. Ramil hasn't brought us a solid plan. We'll decide what to do when we know what we're getting into. We just wanted you to be aware of the situation."

"We're doing it," Eoduun asserted as he turned away from them and headed toward the door. "I don't care what it costs us."

When everyone gathered in Eve's living room the next day to hear Ramil's plan, however, no one was quite prepared for what it would entail.

"I need to bring Eve into the LOA compound and make the Locusts think I've returned to them. They need to think we're raising Lilith," Ramil disclosed.

Isaac shook his head and closed his thumb and first two fingers together while Bo and Luc both scoffed. Eoduun sat silently on the floor, resting his back against the edge of the couch.

"Just wait," Ramil pleaded, holding his palms out. "The ritual is complicated, and I need the Locusts' help and resources to complete it. I've made contact with someone I believe I can trust at LOA, and I've discovered that they have both the grimoire *and* Apep in containment, and they are already making preparations for the ritual. But I've insinuated that we'll be performing the ritual for Lilith, when in reality, it'll be Zeke we're resurrecting. They won't know any different until right at the end, and by then, it'll be too late for the Locusts to do anything about it."

Eve frowned. "And what happens when they see Zeke standing there instead of Lilith? They're not just going to let us walk out with him."

"I can handle the Locusts," Ramil replied.

Bo crossed his arms. "If you think we're letting you just *take* Evie with you, you're fucking insane. If we do this, we're all going."

Ramil was hesitant. "That could be tricky."

"I don't give a fuck," Luc interjected. "We're going."

"Eve won't be in any danger, if that's what you're worried about. They revere her. That'd be like worrying about Jesus in a church full of Catholics."

"We're going," Luc repeated more firmly.

"I want to be there for Zeke when he returns," Eoduun added. "You're not leaving us behind."

"Fine," Ramil relented. "We'll figure it out. But you can't interfere in any way until the ritual is over."

Eve leaned forward on the couch between Bo and Luc. "What do I need to do? What *exactly* do I need to do?"

A strange air of pride colored Ramil's features. "What you were made to do, of course."

Bo's hand tightened on Eve's thigh, and she felt his possessive fury burning in her chest.

Luc rolled his fingers together absently while little arcs of electricity danced over his hands. "Elaborate," he commanded with deadly calm.

Ramil gave them a nervous, placating smile. "I think you know what that entails. She will need to obtain certain powers."

Luc's fingers stilled. "Yours?"

"…Yes."

Eve's heart thundered nervously in her chest, and the image of her in Ramil's bed sprang up in her head again. "Yours, and who else's?" she ventured slowly. She again tried to surreptitiously breech his mental shields, trying to get a peek inside his head without him noticing, but it was like tickling a brick wall with a feather.

Ramil fixed his unusual eyes on her. "The three beasts of Revelation. The serpent, the dragon, and the beast out of the sea. Apep, myself, and Dagon, as the Locusts see it."

How had she known that already? How had she *seen* that already?

Ramil scrutinized her. "You don't seem surprised."

"But you wanted to use Dagon as the sacrifice," Eve said.

"You possess his power already, as it would appear. He is of no further use," Ramil reasoned.

Bo gave Eve a worried look. "You don't have to do this. Please, don't do this," he pleaded.

When she turned to look at Bo, she saw Isaac shaking his head at her. He signed, *I don't like this. This is Zephlyn's vision. A serpent, a dragon, and a sea monster. You must be the goblet.*

Ramil interjected, "Zephlyn mentioned his vision to me as well, looking for input. I'm not oblivious to how bad it looks, but Zephlyn's visions are difficult to interpret and not always as they appear on the surface. Yes, Eve *could* raise monsters like Lilith if she so desired. But we aren't raising monsters – we're raising Zeke."

Eve looked at Luc, but he didn't notice. She could see his eyes behind his sunglasses, and he was staring vacantly at the wall across the room. "Luc?"

He blinked, but he didn't look at her for a long moment, just staring at the wall. When he finally turned his head her way, his tone was full of resignation. "If you trust we can bring Zeke back, I will follow your lead, love." He took her hand and lifted her knuckles to his lips. He leaned closer to her, and his gaze shifted to Ramil as he whispered conspiratorially to her, "And if you decide you want me to kill anyone, I will gladly oblige."

She turned to Bo and Isaac, already noticing the knots in her chest from Bo's unease. Isaac shook his head and touched his middle finger and thumb together at his chest, then flicked his hand away. *I don't like it.*

Bo's brows drew upward in the center, apprehension etched on his face. His mismatched eyes searched hers for reassurance. "I don't want you to do this…but I won't stand in your way. I know you can handle yourself." He kissed her forehead, then stood to face Ramil. He toed up to the taller man, his wolf eye blazing threateningly. "If any of you harm a hair on her head, I will send you all to Hell myself, and there will be no resurrecting you from the mess I leave behind."

Luc raised his eyebrows and nodded approvingly as Bo retreated to the kitchen, taking up his perch on the barstool in his spot at the island. He needed space from the conversation at hand.

"Noted," Ramil acknowledged, seemingly unbothered by the threat. He continued, "I think our biggest obstacle is how we're going to get Dagon on location for the ritual."

"We're not sacrificing Dagon," Eve said.

Eoduun swung his head in her direction, but she didn't meet his accusatory glare. "Are you fucking kidding me?" he seethed.

Eve pleaded, "Pick another monster." She looked to Ramil. "Pick a Locust, for all I care. Tell them they'll be given the *honor* of becoming Lilith's vessel."

"No, Eve," Eoduun argued. "Dagon stole Zeke's body, and now he has to give it back! And we can finally be rid of him!"

"I don't want to be rid of him!" she snapped back.

The room went silent.

"I will find someone else," Ramil offered. "If that's what you truly wish, I will find someone else."

"Please," Eve said appreciatively. Ramil nodded.

Eoduun suddenly announced, "I'll do it."

Everyone shot him an incredulous stare.

"Absolutely fucking not!" Bo countered from the kitchen.

"I have to," Eoduun insisted. He turned his onyx eyes toward Eve and Luc, and she saw how full of purpose they were. "Don't you see? It's what I'm meant to do! *I* can give Zeke his life back!"

"No, Eoduun. And it's not up for discussion," Luc said.

"If you won't use Dagon, then it has to be me. I *want* it to be me."

Ramil's eyes suddenly flashed iridescently as he regarded Eoduun. "Do you truly wish to become Zeke's vessel?"

"I wouldn't fucking say it if I didn't mean it," Eoduun snapped.

Ramil arched a dark brow at Eve. "Is this what you had in mind?"

She scowled at him. "No! Of course not!"

Eoduun argued, "You don't get to decide everything, Eve! This is *my* choice. I'll become a part of Zeke. He and I will become one." He gave Eve a pleading expression, a rogue tear rolling down the side of his nose, and Eve's heart broke. "Are you going to deny me that? After everything we've seen, you're really going to try to deny me a happy ending?"

Eve's reply was a whisper. "It will break Zeke's heart."

"But at least he will have a heart to break. That's more than he has now."

Bo and Luc began to try to reason with Eoduun, but he had stubbornly made up his mind and wouldn't be swayed. While they argued, Ramil looked at Eve.

"Are you willing to sacrifice Eoduun over Dagon?" he wondered.

She didn't want to lose either of them. But Eoduun *wanted* to be sacrificed, and Dagon was never given the option; everyone else just assumed that they would sacrifice him.

She connected with Dagon. *Eoduun wants to be the sacrifice to bring Zeke back. Everyone else wants it to be you.*

Dagon replied, *And what do you want, princess?*

I want it to be someone else. Someone I don't know or care about.

Dagon's voice took on a smug quality in her mind. *You care about me.*

Eat shit. I just don't want you to die. You're useful.

He laughed. *Then find someone else. Though, for the record, I'm not opposed to using Eoduun. Anyone but me, ideally.*

"Let's use Apep," Eve suddenly blurted, and everyone paused to look at her. "Why not? If we could use Dagon, why not Apep?"

Ramil shrugged. "Apep could work."

"Yes, Apep," Luc agreed with an exasperated sigh. "Finally, a plan I can get behind."

Ramil glanced over at Eoduun. "We'll use Apep."

Eoduun scowled and crossed his arms, another tear streaking down his cheek. He wiped it on his shoulder and didn't answer.

"It won't be you, Eoduun," Bo asserted. "I won't allow it." He walked to the back of the couch and rested his hands on the headrest behind Eve. "So...when do we leave?"

Ramil grinned. "I'll make contact with Eno."

32

My Little Abomination

A deep knot of anxiety twisted in Eve's chest as she sat next to Bo on the Knighco jet, her head resting on his shoulder. His feelings were tangled so deeply with hers that she sometimes had a hard time deciphering whose belonged to whom, but in this case, she knew the apprehension was a team effort.

Everyone had agreed that the sooner they got this over with, the better, especially considering she needed Dagon's power to complete the ritual and she was already in possession of it. So, everyone but Luc had boarded the jet and were on their way to Kentucky. Luc, however, was already there, having made the jump alone so he could survey the situation. Eve opted to ride with everyone else on the jet.

Eve looked over at Isaac sitting across from her and Bo. His eyes were fixed on the scenery out the window. When he noticed her staring, he glanced at her. She was beginning to realize that the face she once considered to be inscrutable, was, in fact, *entirely* scrutable. On the surface, he looked as impassive as ever, but she knew better. He was uneasy, and he didn't want her to do the ritual. He wanted to turn the jet around and go home.

He was worried about her.

She graced him with an empathic smile, and he exhaled heavily and returned his gaze to the window.

Bo's voice was soft but tense. "This could all go sideways in so many ways," he warned.

"I have Dagon's power. I have your power. I'm not helpless."

"I know. But if the Locusts could trap Apep, what kind of power must they have at their disposal?"

"Good thing I'm their Jesus," Eve retorted. "And that power is going to bring Zeke back." Her eyes shifted to Eoduun, who sat by himself across the aisle, staring out the window with his earbuds in. "We need this. We need a win."

Bo cupped the side of her face and kissed the top of her head through his mask. "I need you to walk away from this unscathed. I would love to have Zeke back, but not if it costs me you."

"Don't worry, Daddy," Eve consoled.

His eyes tracked Ramil across the cabin as Ramil made his way to the coffee machine. "It's all I do when it comes to you," he confessed with a sigh. "You're a fucking magnet for trouble, little girl."

When they landed in Kentucky, Luc met them at the airport, swinging keys to a rental vehicle on his finger as he watched them deboard the jet. Once they were all packed into the SUV, he drove them toward the remote compound in the mountains where LOA was headquartered.

"I can't bring you all into the compound, for obvious reasons," Ramil said from the passenger seat as the SUV climbed higher and the road became narrower. "But my acquaintance has set up a place for you on the outskirts of the property in an unused storehouse. TV, sleeping bags, food, the works. You should be comfortable and unnoticed there until we need you."

"How long do you expect it will be before the ritual?" Luc wanted to know.

"We'll need to perform it as soon as possible, while Eve still possesses Dagon's power. I wouldn't be surprised if Eno wants to make it happen tonight."

Eve's heart stalled. "My father is going to be there?"

"He's the leader of LOA," Ramil said, turning in his seat to look at her. "Of course he's going to be there."

"Is he going to be a problem?" Eve wondered.

Ramil grinned at her. "For you? No. He'll be elated when he sees you."

"And how elated will he be when we raise Zeke instead of Lilith?"

"I have a feeling we won't have a problem handling him when the time comes," he replied.

"Isn't he unkillable because of the Mark of Cain? Won't we be punished 'sevenfold' for trying to kill him?" Eve worried.

Ramil hiked a dark brow at her, his copper-green eyes glinting. "The mark is powerless against another mark." His eyes dropped to the exposed skin of her stomach, the slightly miscolored patch delineating a portion of her mark revealed by her cropped, baggy shirt.

Eve's eyes sprang wide as she wrapped her arms around her middle. "You *knew*?!"

Ramil laughed and faced forward in his seat again. In a mildly condescending tone, he said, "I have eyes, darling."

Luc's hand leapt from the steering wheel and struck Ramil smartly across the cheek with a loud *smack*. Eve gasped, and Ramil

274

whipped his head toward Luc, his own hand rubbing his accosted cheek. "Hey! What the hell!?"

"Mosquito. Buggy out here in the backwoods, isn't it, *darling*?" Luc replied cheerfully, smiling widely at Ramil.

The rest of the ride was quiet, save for Luc singing along to Chappell Roan's "Pink Pony Club" on the radio.

When they were close to the compound, they were met in the road by a large, portly man in tan coveralls. He looked like a custodial worker. Luc slowed the SUV, and the man came to Ramil's window.

"Darnell," Ramil greeted him, reaching his hand out the window to shake the other man's hand. "I trust we're all set?"

"All set. If you wanna drive through with the girl, I can take the others to their quarters on foot. It's not far from here, but we oughta be quick about it." Darnell looked around nervously.

Everyone piled out of the SUV, and Ramil walked around and got behind the steering wheel. Luc opened the passenger's door for Eve, but instead of allowing her into her seat, he hoisted her up in a suffocating embrace, burying his face in her neck.

"I love you, Eve. I trust you to be safe and take no shit. I'll keep an eye on you from afar," Luc promised, tapping the side of his sunglasses. "If something doesn't seem right, do not hesitate to go nuclear. I'll be there in a flash to help you finish it."

Eve hugged his neck and kissed him. She touched her forehead to his. "I'll do whatever I have to," she avowed.

When Luc released her, Bo snatched her up, pulling her against his chest. His arms surrounded her shoulders, his hand pressing her head against his hard pecs. He rested his cheek on top of her head, then kissed her head through his mask. "You are my heart," he mumbled against her hair. "The only thing you *have* to do, is return to me."

Eve rose up onto her toes and pulled his mask down, planting a kiss on his bare lips. "I will return to you. Always. And this time, I'll bring Zeke back with me."

To Eve's surprise, as she stepped away from Bo, Isaac's arm curled around her, and she felt his heavy-knuckled hand fisting in her shirt as he pulled her against him. His other hand curved gently over her throat as his lips came to her ear. "Trust no one. You're entering a den of vipers, and Ramil might be the most venomous of them all," he whispered. "If you've changed your mind, give me one word, one sound against my hand, and I will put you in this car and take you away from here right now, no questions asked."

Eve shook her head and snapped her first two fingers against her thumb. *No.* She stepped back so he could see her sign, *I need to do this. For Zeke.*

She could see that he wanted to argue, to *make* her leave with him, but he didn't. He simply pleaded with his eyes.

"I'll be fine. I promise," she mouthed.

He stepped close again, stroking his thumb down her trachea. "You fucking better be," he mumbled.

As Eve turned and was about to climb into the passenger seat, she felt a hand pat the top of her head. She glanced behind her.

"Bring him home. Please," Eoduun beseeched in an uncharacteristically soft tone. "And if this ends up being my last chance to say it, I need you to know that I'm sorry. I do love you, Eve. I've just been so buried in all this hate and grief and... I was an asshole. I am an asshole. And I'm sorry."

Eve gave him a soft smile. "I forgive you...asshole."

As Eve climbed into the SUV, Darnell pulled a can of what looked like bug spray from a pocket in his coveralls and handed it to Luc. "Y'all need to spray down so's the wolves don't scent ya." He reached over and closed Eve's door, then thudded his fist twice against the side of the SUV. Ramil drove away, leaving the rest of Eve's team in the dust.

The compound was much more expansive than Eve was expecting. There were buildings all over the grounds, and when Ramil pulled up to an enormous, foreboding concrete building, she got the distinct impression of militarism. This wasn't a friendly, inviting environment, and nothing about it boasted of religion and spirituality.

Ramil parked the SUV and turned to her. He reached over and rested his hand on her knee, and she stared down at the act of familiarity with furrowed brows. She knew it was meant to comfort her, but her mind was suddenly imagining his hand sliding up her thigh, wondering what his hands would feel like between her legs. Wondering what his cock felt like.

"Are you blushing?" he asked with a tinge of amusement.

She brushed his hand away. Why was she thinking about him like that at a time like this? "I'm nervous."

Ramil inhaled deeply as he looked at the building in front of the SUV. "Yeah. Me too." He gave Eve a comforting smile. "But we can do this, right? Me and you, we can resurrect Zeke. Put all your effort into trusting that we can do it."

In that moment, Eve felt her resolve fortified. She smiled back at Ramil. "Of course we can."

When they climbed out of the SUV, Eve noticed people – monsters? – were beginning to gather in groups, their eyes following her and Ramil's every move. Ramil held his hand out to her as they faced the front doors of the concrete building, and she took it.

"Why are they staring?" she asked as he led her through the heavy doors.

In an amused tone, he replied, "Maybe they think you look different from your portrait."

Eve was about to ask what he meant by that, but when she looked about her, she saw a huge oil painting hanging on the wall of the otherwise-minimalist lobby they had walked into, and *she* was the subject. Her hair was its natural brown, not pink, but every other feature of her face and body were identical. She was wearing an elegant red and purple dress with spiked heels, and she sat upon a creature with seven heads. She was holding a golden goblet, and blood dripped from the brim. Her painted brown eyes gazed down at her and Ramil with smug satisfaction.

"Jesus Christ," Eve murmured, staring up at herself.

Eve scented a man approaching, and she turned. He looked to be in his late forties, early fifties, with a smattering of grey mixed into his dark beard and the loose, dark curls on his head. He was a mildly attractive man, with a severely aquiline nose and dark eyes that sparkled with delight.

"As I live and breathe," he said, awestricken as he beheld her. "My little Abomination has finally found her way home."

33

Do You Owe Me Three Wishes?

"Eno," Ramil greeted the man, holding his hand out.

"Handshakes are for strangers," Eno replied warmly, grabbing Ramil's hand and using it to tug him into a bearhug. "You've claimed your bride and returned to us. I couldn't be happier, kid."

Eve's blood halted in her veins. "Bride?" she choked.

Ramil offered an apologetic, almost embarrassed expression as Eno turned his attention to Eve. "My daughter. I've waited so long to meet you, but I knew my patience would be rewarded." He hugged her affectionately, then held her out at arms' length. "Let me look at you, my beautiful child." He looked her over, but his gaze faltered when he cast his eyes over her bare stomach. His eyes sprang back to hers in surprise. "You bear the mark."

"So it would seem," she replied coolly.

"I wasn't informed of this," he said, his jovial demeanor slipping slightly. There was something in his eyes that made her instantly uneasy as he looked back down at her stomach. Was he...afraid?

Ramil's words came back to her: *The mark is powerless against another mark.* He should be afraid.

"What did you do to my mother?" Eve demanded.

Eno was taken aback. "Excuse me?"

"You killed my mother," she accused venomously. "You killed Stacey Rose and left her desecrated body in a fucking cemetery in Michigan. You killed her for trying to protect me."

Eno placed a hand on his chest and shook his head. "That wasn't my doing. That was a small group of former Locusts acting independently, contrary to our wishes. I never wanted to see my Stacey get hurt, let alone killed. I loved your mother, even when she left. The whole debacle almost broke LOA, and we lost several members over it."

Eve looked to Ramil for feedback, but his expression was impassive. Did he know if Eno was telling the truth? Or wasn't he involved enough in the matter to know?

Eno took her hand and gazed at her earnestly. "It's important to me that you believe me, and that you trust me. I need to know that you don't harbor hate toward me over something I had no hand in. Please."

"Then show me." Using the power she still retained from Eoduun, she stared into Eno's eyes and pushed her mind through the swirling golden tunnel that opened up. There were thousands of years of memories to sift through, and she saw fleeting images of what must've been biblical times, but she moved forward on instinct, seeking out her mother.

And she found her. She watched Eno fall in love with Stacey, and she watched him bring her into his realm. But she didn't accept it, accept *him*, the way he had hoped. Even when she became pregnant with his child, the prophesied Abomination, and became the Mother of Abominations herself, she still pulled away from him. He'd made her special, and she rebuked him for it.

Ungrateful.

He'd misjudged her. A part of him still loved her, but another part loathed her for her rejection of him, his monsters, and his grandmother, Lilith. She didn't understand what he was trying to do. He wanted peace! He wanted all creatures to live freely in the sunlight, exposed and unafraid, and hated that his beastly brethren were sentenced to live in the shadows and darkness. He could achieve harmony, if only he could bring Lilith back from the Abyss and make the whole world take notice.

Make the world believe.

Make Stacey believe.

But she fled from him, from the Locusts of Abaddon, and with her, she took his only chance at peace. He'd waited thousands of years for the time to be right, for the *woman* to be right, and for all the pieces on the chessboard to finally fall into place. The grimoire had been explicit, and he trusted the word of Lilith over any other. She was the only one who wasn't afraid to go against the powers that be, to stand up for her own convictions, even in the face of persecution.

He didn't chase after Stacey. He had his people looking for her, and they eventually found her, but he only watched her from afar and waited. He knew the prophecy would come to fruition, because Lilith had foreseen it.

When the child's thirteenth birthday came around, they were watching. Eno stayed close to Stacey's home, waiting to see if the child would bloom into the Abomination. But when Stacey suddenly packed up and headed to some obscure little town hundreds of miles away, the day before their daughter's birthday, some of his fellow Locusts followed her, unbeknownst to Eno.

Then the truth was discovered. The Locusts that had followed her to Newbury became outraged at the betrayal. It was one thing for her to have left the compound, but it was quite another to hide their savior from them. They made her pay, and when Eno found out, he was furious.

Eve stopped digging at that point and withdrew. She had her answer. "You didn't kill her."

Eno's eyes lit with pride. "You are truly a wonder. The power you hold is immeasurable."

Eve's face reddened with discomfort under his admiring gaze.

Her father was praising her. *Proud* of her.

This feeling was...new.

She curled her lips into a smile and pushed away the discomfort. "Great. Well, as long as you had nothing to do with it, we're fucking golden."

Eno chuckled. "Your mother had a real way with words, too." He turned and motioned for them to follow. "C'mon. I'll show you to your new place."

He led Eve and Ramil back out the front doors and joined them in the SUV, directing Ramil's driving from the back seat. He glanced in the cargo space behind him. "Not much luggage?"

Ramil shook his head. "We left in a hurry. Knighco probably doesn't even know we're gone yet," he lied.

Eno leaned forward. "So...what made you defect?" he asked Eve, his eyes fixated on her face.

She was caught off-guard. She looked to Ramil for aid.

"I thought she was ready for the truth," Ramil answered for her. "And when she was brought into the know, we both agreed that she didn't belong at Knighco any longer."

"I'm a monster," Eve added. "Knighco kills monsters."

"You're not *a* monster," Eno said as Ramil drove toward a long row of small, identical structures across the way. "You're *the* monster. You will breathe new life into our entire existence. When you raise Lilith, our whole world is going to change."

"How so?" Eve asked.

"Lilith will lead us to peace," he replied simply.

"But...how?" she pressed.

"She will unite our kind and inspire the rest of the world to accept us. And those who refuse will be eradicated."

"That doesn't sound like peace."

"Peace comes only in the wake of horror. It rips and tears its way into existence. That is the nature of peace." He glanced over at Eve. "No great nation of prosperity, great *races,* were ever birthed from gentle origins."

Eve didn't argue. Instead, she asked, "Why have you joined forces with monsters? From what I understand, you also have mixed blood, and you're the reason I am what I am. But you could've just as easily sided with the good—" she caught herself, "—with the other guys. With the Blood of Eve."

"Could I have?" He shook his head. "I'm tainted. Even my 'good' blood, as you consider it, is tainted because of my father's sins, just as yours is. The curse he was plagued with, the mark that you and I both bear, was placed by Adam himself. It's not a punishment, but rather a promise of protection for his son, because there were many who were out for his blood for what he had done to his brother. Regardless of how heartbroken Adam was by Cain's actions, he still loved him, and he cursed him with life rather than death, and sent him away from those who wanted to harm him."

"Wait, is Cain still alive, like you?" Eve interrupted.

Eno shook his head. "Who knows. He was banished from interacting with humankind forever. Actually, it was in his exile that he was seduced by my mother, Maziki. She was a lilim, a first daughter of Lilith, one sired by a celestial named Samael. After she gave birth to me, she took me from him and gifted me to a coven of witches as a favor for their fealty." He shrugged. "I've been around monsters my whole life. I've seen their struggle. I've *lived* their struggle. I think it's time to end their struggle."

Before she could think better of it, she blurted, "Monsters hurt people. Doesn't that ever bother you?"

Eno scoffed and sat back in his seat, stretching his arms across the backrest. "And people hurt monsters. But people hurt other people way more often than monsters do. *That's* what bothers me."

Eno directed Ramil to stop in front of one of the little buildings lined up along the dirt road, and Eve realized they were trendy, tiny houses. Eno gestured toward the one closest to them. "Welcome home, Eve."

Eve followed Eno and Ramil into the little house. It felt like a camper. *I won't be here long,* she reassured herself as she looked up at the bed tucked away in the loft. "It's…cozy," Eve remarked.

Eno grinned. "I hope you two are comfortable here until we can build you a home worthy of your status."

You two?

"You'll like your neighbors. Bryleigh on this side," Eno continued, pointing, "and Jayden and Callie on the other side. They're young and know how to have fun." He looked at Ramil. "You remember Jayden? Young vampire who used to have that green mohawk? Now he's sporting a mullet."

"I remember him," Ramil answered with a nod. "I remember Callie, too. I'm a little surprised to hear they ended up together. She was so straightlaced, and he…wasn't."

Eno chuckled as he stepped back toward the door. "Well, I'll let you two get settled. I'll have Leslie get some supplies together for you from the donation closet at the church." He smiled with genuine affection at Eve. "I'm so happy to have my little girl home. You have no idea how proud I am of you, and I can't wait to stand with you at my side as we *finally* raise the Great Mother from the Abyss tonight." His attention shifted to Ramil as he placed his hand on the doorknob. "You'll find the serpent in the solitary chamber. Do you have the sea beast?"

"There was no need to collect him. Eve is already in possession of his power, and I've brought an offering of his blood."

Eno nodded. "I suppose that'll do. But we still need a vessel."

"I have it covered," Ramil assured him, but didn't elaborate.

"Excellent. Please be sure Eve is ready for tonight. The ritual commences at moonrise." Eno suddenly grinned with a wild, demented excitement, and he lunged at Eve and Ramil, throwing his arms around them both and hugging them aggressively. "Everything changes tonight, kids. The world will finally be ours."

When Eve and Ramil were alone, she hammered him with questions. First and foremost, "What the fuck did Eno mean when he called me your *bride*?! Why does he have us here *together*, like we're a couple?!"

Ramil gave her a sheepish look. "You were betrothed to me. It was decided before you were even born."

"How long have you known this?!"

"Years." When she shot him an incredulous glare, he added, "But, as you recall, I *left* the Locusts. I didn't think anything of it after that."

"Why the fuck didn't you tell me?"

Ramil leaned back in his seat across from her at the small table in the tiny house. "When would have been a good time to do that? *How* should I have broached that subject?"

Eve groaned and dropped her forehead onto her folded forearms on the table. "This is so fucked up."

"Maybe, but we're here, and we're doing this for Zeke," Ramil reminded her.

She lifted her head enough to rest her chin on her arm as she looked at him. "You told Eno you had an offering of Dagon's blood. How did you get Dagon to give you blood?"

Ramil pointed out to the SUV. "I took some of the paint from the can we used to create the devil's trap. His blood is in it."

"Oh. Will it be enough?"

He nodded.

"How are we going to trick them into raising Zeke instead of Lilith?"

Ramil reached into the breast pocket of his shirt and withdrew a familiar piece of torn notebook paper. "I'll switch out the Lilithian relic for this. It's something of his. It will call to his soul instead of Lilith."

Eve snatched the paper from his fingers. It was Zeke's note.

The note Ramil had *returned* to her.

"How the fuck did you get this again?!" she snarled.

Ramil smirked. "We needed it."

"Then tell me to bring it, don't just steal it again! Stay out of my shit, Ramil!"

He held his palms up and leaned away from her. "Ok! Ok. Sorry! But I need the note back for the ritual."

Eve slid it aggressively across the table to him. "You'll be lucky if I don't kill you when—" Ramil's finger brushed her hand as he took the paper from her, and her mouth abruptly snapped shut, cutting off her tirade. Her mind was suddenly writhing with erotic visuals of Ramil, one cascading into another in rapid succession. On top of her. Beneath her. Inside of her. Hands in her hair, around her neck, on her breasts, between her legs. His breath in her ear. His lips on hers. His teeth in her flesh, her blood on his tongue. His hips slamming into her. His thick, hot cock filling her with toe-curling pleasure.

"When what?" he asked, challenging her to finish her sentence.

Eve swallowed, then choked on her own saliva and began coughing and sputtering.

"When this is over? Or do you mean when you take my powers?" he taunted as she tried to catch her breath.

"I'm going to enjoy hurting you," she finally spat.

Ramil smirked. "I have no doubt." He stood and held his hand out to her. "Well, darling, are you ready to go visit Apep and get this over with?"

"Ew, stop calling me darling."

"My betrothed?" he quipped. Eve scowled at him and stood without touching his offered hand. He moved to the door and opened it for her, and as she walked out, he asked, "All joking aside, are you prepared for this? Are you truly willing to do this?"

Eve took a cleansing breath. "I told you already. You'd be appalled at what I'm willing to do to bring Zeke back." She looked him straight in the eye. "Don't you dare underestimate me again."

Ramil smirked. "Never. I remember what happened last time." A few moments later, as they strolled back toward the building where they first met Eno, opting to walk rather than drive since it wasn't that far, he asked, "Am I really that appalling?"

Eve's eyes involuntarily flitted from his face to his feet and back again before she forced her gaze to the road in front of her. There was nothing appalling about his appearance. She gave him a short, indecisive hum, then slipped her phone from her pocket and averted her attention to it. No messages. She sent both Luc and Bo a quick text to check in, but they never switched from "delivered" to "read."

"Can we check in with the boys?" Eve asked Ramil. "Just to let them know I'm ok?"

Ramil shook his head. "They'll be fine. You need to worry about yourself and only yourself right now. Focus on the task at hand." Ramil glanced discreetly behind him. "Besides, we have an audience."

They were starting to accumulate a gathering behind them. Eve leaned closer to Ramil. "Why are they following us?" she whispered.

"It's not every day their holy savior arrives and walks in their presence. They're starstruck."

"Do they know we're supposed to be raising Lilith tonight?"

"Probably. Word travels fast around here."

A flashback of the carnage after Ruth's ritual flashed in Eve's mind. She whispered, "Are they going to end up like Ruth's army?"

Ramil's expression was unchanging. "Probably."

She looked down at her feet as she walked. "And Eno?"

"…Is your responsibility."

She thought about how adoringly he had treated her today. She'd never gotten even a fraction of that kind of affection from her stepfather. What if Eno really did love her as his daughter? He would be upset by her betrayal, but…maybe, if she had a chance to explain it to him, he would understand why she had to do it.

"He won't," Ramil stated. "Eno isn't always the kind and affectionate man you met today. He can be harsh and cruel when it suits him. He won't forgive you for this."

Startled, Eve slammed down the barriers in her mind. She hadn't meant to let them slip. Then, she blushed. "How long have you had access?"

Ramil's heated gaze slid to her. "Long enough to know you aren't dreading taking my power as much as you pretend to be."

Her face was on fire.

"Your ears get just as red as Bo's," he noticed.

"Shut your face," Eve hissed.

"Just an observation."

"Your face is not shutting."

Ramil sighed. "As you wish, darling."

Eve was fuming, but his use of the word "wish" caught her attention. She switched gears. "I do wish. So…*are* you a jinn? Do you owe me three wishes?"

"I don't owe you any wishes, and Knighco hasn't confirmed that I'm a jinni, either. But my abilities do overlap with those of a jinni, so it may not be outside the realm of possibilities."

"Jinni?"

"It's the singular form of the word," Ramil replied.

"Oh. So, do jinn…jinni…really make wishes come true?"

Ramil was elusive. "They've been known to reward humans that are good to them. But jinn can be benevolent *or* malevolent. They aren't your typical 'monster.' They're complicated."

"What about the dragon accusation? I've seen your obsession with all things gold and shiny, Smaug."

Ramil's tone became stony. "Dragons are extinct."

"What do you know about dragons?"

"I know I'm not one."

"How do you know?"

"Because if I were, I would've been able to kill Luc," Ramil snapped. His eyes blazed strangely as he stared ahead. "A dragon losing to a human would be a disgrace and would leave him forever dishonored in the eyes of his kind."

"Oh. Well, good thing they're extinct, then," Eve placated.

"Indeed."

"...But if they weren't, what *would* their powers be?" Eve pressed.

"Elemental."

"Like, Earth, Wind, Fire, Water?"

"Just like."

"Which are you?"

"Fff...unny," Ramil stuttered, then chuckled. "I got you, didn't I?" he derided sarcastically. "You thought you were being clever."

But Eve didn't laugh. "Fire, huh?"

"Guess you'll find out soon enough," he replied ominously.

34
Drink My Poison

Eve and Ramil stood outside of a plexiglass enclosure in the basement of the concrete building, staring at Apep.

The entourage they had acquired fell back and didn't follow them through the doors into the building, thankfully. Eve wondered if they would be outside waiting for them when they were finished here.

She wondered if they knew what was supposed to happen in here.

Did *she* know what was supposed to happen in here?

Apep's arms were outstretched, his wrists shackled to the wall on either side of him like a burgundy-haired savior on a cross. His tattooed torso was bare from the waist up, with only a loose-fitting pair of beige, cotton pants hanging from his narrow hips. His bronze eyes shifted between Ramil and Eve, and finally settled on Eve.

"The poisoned apple," he murmured, sneering at her. He tilted his head and stepped forward, his bare feet padding over the intricate lines and sigils stained in blood on the floor, the chains of his shackles rattling as they drew out of two holes in the cinderblock wall to allow him freedom of movement, like a retractable leash. His hands dropped to his sides as he approached the glass opposite of Eve. "Fancy meeting you here, little devil." He glanced over at Ramil before adding, "You were supposed to kill the dragon."

"Why did you want me to do that?" she wondered, her eyes narrowed.

Apep looked Ramil up and down. "Because his kind should've been extinguished a long time ago. Dragons don't belong here anymore."

"This isn't about me," Ramil deflected.

"You and I have unfinished business," Eve told Apep, looking up at him defiantly.

Apep leaned down to the glass so his face was level with hers. "Still aching for my cock, is that it?"

Ramil reached over and hit a button on the wall, and Apep was yanked backwards, his chains retracting quickly into the wall. His back slammed against the wall, and he glowered at Ramil from the position he'd started from, his hair hanging messily over his eyes.

Apep curled his lip in agitation. "What's the purpose of keeping me trapped here like some kind of interactive art piece?" The agitation shifted to amusement. "I'm the god of chaos. I will escape these enchanted chains and juvenile spells sooner or later."

Ramil gave a low chuckle. "I don't think so."

"You got lucky when that witch betrayed me. But luck shifts."

Eve was given pause. "Wait. The witch – Ruth? Ruth trapped you?"

Apep's amusement faltered. "She used the grimoire to temporarily rob me of my powers, then sent me here. Not the 'thank you' I was expecting for returning her memories to her."

"Why did you do it?" Eve snarled, slamming her fist against the plexiglass. "Why did you give her those fucking memories?! She betrayed us *all!*"

Apep grinned, then stepped forward, his chains loosening again. "I knew she'd find that grimoire. You fools gave her unfettered access to that compound. But when I came to retrieve it from her in Montana, she had a trap set for me."

"And she sent you *here*?" Eve looked to Ramil. "Ruth was associated with the Locusts?"

Ramil frowned. "This is news to me."

Eve skimmed Ruth's old memories in her head, but there was nothing relating to LOA. Her connection to them must be recent.

"Did you tell her about them when you were helping her train?" Eve asked Ramil.

He shook his head. "I don't think so, but…I suppose it's possible it may have come up."

Eve scrunched her face in concentration. "How did they get the grimoire, then, if Apep didn't have it? She was *using* it when she pulled Dagon out of Zeke."

"Someone must've escaped with it," Ramil reasoned, "like Dizzy did. Someone at the Montana ranch must've been in cahoots with the Locusts."

Something was nagging in the back of Eve's mind, but she couldn't peg it down.

"But we can worry about that later," Ramil changed the subject. "We have pressing matters to attend to now." He reached over and ran his finger down the back of her neck, his eyes shimmering iridescently, and her curse surged forward, bursting free from its cage in an instant.

Eve gasped and braced her hands against the plexiglass as that familiar, violent sexual urge raged through her.

Ramil's hand closed around the nape of her neck. He leaned close, his lips brushing her ear as he whispered, "It's time to feed the

292

beast." His hand slid up to the base of her skull, and he angled her head toward Apep. "You want to devour him, don't you?"

Apep watched with keen interest as Ramil hit a button on the side of the enclosure and led Eve through the door that opened. It closed behind them with a loud click, and Eve was alone, locked in with Ramil and Apep.

The dragon and the serpent.

Subdue them.

Crush them.

Devour their power.

"Wolf eyes again," Apep remarked as Eve stalked toward him. "He must be your favorite."

"I still need to punish you for trying to kill him," she retorted. She held her palm out as she approached, and using Dagon's power, she telekinetically forced Apep's back against the wall. He laughed down at her when she toed up to him.

"I didn't *try* to kill him. I succeeded," he retorted.

"All the more reason for me to kill you," Eve said, tracing a finger down between his pecs.

"A fuck to the death?" he asked breathily, grinning at her.

Eve allowed her eyes to rove his fit body and intricate tattoos. She flattened both palms onto his chest and pressed her body into his, dragging her breasts against him as she raised herself up on her toes, whispering, "Doesn't that sound like fun?" Heat unfurled in her belly, and she felt her core begin to weep with need.

Ramil moved in behind her, trailing his knuckles down the back of her arms. He looked over her at Apep. "She won't kill you today. She simply needs your power."

Apep was intrigued. "Is that right?" He cast his eyes down to Eve. "Whatever for, little devil? Looking to spread a little chaos along with those legs?"

"I need to right a wrong," Eve replied, sliding one hand up from his chest to mold her hand lightly over the base of his neck. "One you set in motion by returning that bitch's memories to her."

Apep looked over at Ramil. "And why are you here?" His lower lip rolled between his teeth as he appraised Ramil. "You may be a disgusting dragon, but you're quite a specimen as a man. Are you here to participate? Or maybe *you're* planning to try to kill me?"

"I'm here to make sure everything goes as it should." Ramil brushed Eve's hair from the side of her neck and kissed the sensitive spot behind her ear, and she reached one hand back and thrust her fingers into his hair. In a low voice, he added, "And yes, I'm here to participate." He suddenly fisted his hand into Eve's hair, yanking her head back, exposing her neck.

Eve felt a cool blade slide shallowly over her throat, but the edge was so sharp she barely felt the sting of it.

Drink it.

Drink my poison.

Give me every drop of power.

Ramil's tongue dragged over the warm trickle of blood, and unbridled euphoria vibrated through Eve's whole body, drawing a low moan from her throat. She turned on Ramil, Apep temporarily forgotten in her need for relief. She grabbed Ramil's neck and pulled his face down to hers, her teeth digging into his bottom lip, her other hand ripping open the fly of his jeans.

Just one taste of her blood drew from him a need as desperate as hers. He buried his hands in her hair and shoved her roughly against the wall next to Apep, pushing his jeans down over his hips as his mouth devoured hers. Eve eagerly kicked out of her pants as she caught his tongue between her teeth, biting him viciously. The bitter, coppery taste of his blood spreading over her tastebuds only fueled her frantic desire, urging on the depraved monster inside her.

Ramil hoisted her onto his hips, and she wrapped her legs around him, her slick center pressing against the hot, bare length of his cock. She reached between them and angled the crown of his cock at her entrance, and he thrust his hips forward, slamming her against the wall as he buried himself inside of her.

Eve gripped his hair and tipped her head back against the wall, gasping with the overwhelming sensations surging through her body. He radiated with power, with *unique* power she'd never felt before, and he was just begging for her to take it. To take *him*. To destroy him.

She should have more control than this, but her curse was ravenous for the immense power he was so freely offering. His length drove into her, over and over, her calves on his ass, urging his pace as her nails clawed into his back.

"Fuck, Eve," he groaned against her neck, his cock deep inside of her. His mouth covered the cut on her neck, his tongue tasting her blood once more, and another jolt of pleasure pulsed between them.

"As much as I'm enjoying the show, I'm feeling rudely excluded," Apep complained. He pulled against his chains and reached over, grabbing Eve's jaw with rough fingers and tugging her mouth to his. He kissed her aggressively, biting and sucking her lower lip and tongue, while Ramil fucked her against the wall.

One hand still clawing at Ramil's back, Eve pressed her other hand to Apep's throat as their mouths moved voraciously together. Rage tingled through her fingertips, and her hand closed tightly around the cabled muscles of Apep's neck.

Kill.

Destroy.

Annihilate.

Ramil's grip was bruising on her thighs as she felt him swell inside of her, a low sound rumbling in his throat.

It occurred to her at that moment just how much the sound of pleasure resembled the anguish of pain. The whimper of fear. The cries of prey between the teeth of a predator.

The ache building in the base of Eve's core intensified, pleasure welling up and spilling over as her thighs clenched around Ramil's hips. She rocked her pelvis, her walls tightly wringing Ramil's cock as it spasmed, his hips jerking violently against her as a roar of utter bliss tore from his throat.

Power shot through Eve's body, the base of her teeth tingling with a rage she unleashed onto Apep. She bit down on his tongue in her mouth, catching her own lip in the bite, and their blood mingled in their mouths. She pushed off of Ramil, kicking him away, then tackled Apep to the floor, his chains rattling and tangling round them.

Eve shoved Apep onto his back and yanked his loose, cotton pants down and settled her hips over his, lowering herself onto his awaiting length.

"I can see why another god would claim you," Apep marveled as he looked up at her with his bronze, snakelike eyes, blood smeared over his lips. "If Dagon hadn't, I'd be tempted to make my own mark on your soul a permanent one. You are positively monstrous."

"You already belong to me," Eve hissed, fisting her hand in the wine-red hair falling back from his forehead. She rolled her hips, grinding against him, taking him deeper. Her body hummed with power, rage, and desire.

Ruin him.

Her curse's cravings were running rampant through her veins as she held him down and rode him. When he reached his hands up to grab her hips, she used Dagon's power to restrain him, slamming his hands to the floor without ever touching them. Pleasure began to grow in her core once more, and she had the sudden desire to see Apep wrapped in his chains. Immobilized. Bound. She held her free hand out, the other still fisted near his forehead, and she telekinetically guided the loose chains to move at her behest. They snaked over his arms, wrists, legs, and around his neck and torso.

The chaotic delight in his eyes began to color with something more primal, something akin to fear, and it only served to further fuel Eve's bloodlust. The rapacious need for violence surged through her, rising with her pleasure, and she squeezed her hand, watching the chains tighten around Apep's body.

Ramil came up behind her. "Eve." His hand touched her arm, but she jerked her chin at him, and he flew across the room, hitting the wall with a pained grunt.

Apep thrust up into her, and she began to grind harder on him, feeling his power almost at her fingertips. It was like luring the cobra from his basket with every swivel of her hips, drawing his power to her as her curse raged.

With a strained groan, Apep released his immeasurable power into her, and she threw her head back, allowing the violent euphoria of her climax to crash over her. She clenched one hand in his hair, the other hand curling into a tight fist as she unleashed her rage.

The chains around Apep squeezed and pulled, and in an instant, they tore through his body, ripping him asunder in an explosion of blood and gore.

As Eve blinked through the blood all over her face, her pleasure pulsing and receding, she raised the hand that was tangled in Apep's hair, lifting Apep's severed head from his bloody, mangled remains. She leapt up, staring down at the mess she'd made, horrified.

Her curse settled back into its cage, leaving her alone to cope with the aftermath of what she'd done.

35

I'm Khaleesi

Eve stared at what was left of Apep's lifeless body, the chains weaving gruesomely through the bloody carnage. She whirled around and leveled a deadly glare at Ramil, who was wincing as he picked himself up off the floor.

"You let me kill him!" Eve accused.

"I couldn't stop you. I tried!"

"You didn't try hard enough! What are we going to do now?! We needed him to bring Zeke back!" she panicked.

"We have his blood..." He glanced at the mess. "...Everywhere. And you have his power. We can do the ritual even if he's dead. He can't be the sacrifice, but Eoduun still can be."

Eve's heart dropped to the floor. "I will not sacrifice Eoduun."

Ramil took a tentative step toward her. "It was his wish."

"Well, it isn't mine!" She studied Ramil's face, noticing the complete lack of distress in his features. "...Did you *plan* this?"

Ramil furrowed his brow. "Not at all."

Red flags sprang up in Eve's mind. She'd been warned not to trust him, and, foolishly, in her pursuit of Zeke's resurrection, she'd ignored every warning sign. Oh, she'd seen them. But she'd ignored them.

She'd wanted to believe him, so she had. Now, she tasted the bitter flavor of deception on her tongue.

Instinctively, she knew how to get the truth from him, using his own powers against him. The power of the jinn. She looked into his eyes. "What is it you wish, Ramil? What do you desire?"

His eyes widened. "I wish to bring Zeke back for you, to do anything to please you, so you will want me. You were supposed to be mine. You were promised to me. You are the one I need to pass on my legacy, because I am incompatible with anyone else."

Eve stared in disbelief. What the fuck?

She didn't bother with more questions. She was brimming with power she could feel but didn't fully comprehend. Power over him. With only the simple desire to see into his memories, she was instantly in his mind, his barriers useless against her now.

And it became immediately apparent that Ramil *was* deceiving her.

She saw the world below him, mountains rolling by like they were no greater than ant hills. She felt his expansive, leathery wings flex and pump, and his long, powerful tail twitch. His immense body moved gracefully through the sky, his armored scales shifting and shining in the sun. The freedom of taking to the air in his true form was invigorating. He so rarely got to stretch his wings.

But the loneliness that hollowed his heart was almost unbearable. No one could quite understand him, because he wasn't supposed to exist. Even surrounded by fellow monsters, accepted and beloved for his power, he was utterly alone.

The last dragon.

And a half-breed, at that.

He knew nothing of his parents, only that they died when he was a toddler. The Locusts took him in, knowing nothing about him other than the fact that he wasn't human. But when Eno first laid eyes on him, he knew exactly what he was, and he knew he was special. Eno had told him he'd been waiting for someone like him for centuries. Millennia, even. And then, when Ramil had grown into an adult, Eno had promised him a mate.

"Someday, Ramil," Eno told him, "you will be my son. It was decided by myself and the elders long ago, before the Abomination was even born, but I feel it's time you knew. You are the only one worthy of my daughter. Your kind is rare and exquisite, as dragons are an *original* being, not borne of Lilith. You may be mixed with jinn, but the dragon blood burns like fire in your veins, allowing you to retain the ability to access your true form. You are a marvel, Ramil. You will be a well-suited mate for the Abomination when she returns to us."

The prospect of a companion filled Ramil's heart with hope. He wouldn't be alone forever. Someone would love him. Understand him. Be an equal to him, and not fear him. Everyone in LOA revered his power, but he was an untouchable. Only a select few knew what he truly was, but everyone knew he was *different*, and it scared them. If they knew he was a dragon, they would've avoided his presence completely.

From what Ramil had learned in his time at LOA, dragons were part of an original bloodline, in the lineage of the Leviathans, and the Leviathans were hated by all other bloodlines. Their power was tremendous, and they once ruled the land and sea before Lilith unleashed her monsters onto the world. The Leviathans were tyrants, hated, and they had been hunted into extinction by gods, monsters, and man.

Ramil wasn't supposed to exist.

When LOA had taken on Knighco, Ramil chose to accept defeat rather than expose his true nature to the world. If he had shifted to his beastly form, he could have defeated Luc, but then every Locust would know what he was. They already feared him. What would they do if they saw that he wasn't even one of them? That he wasn't fully of Lilith? That he was a Leviathan?

He didn't belong with the Locusts.

So, when he got a chance at a fresh start in Knighco, he lied about what he was. He feigned ignorance, and the strength of his mental barriers was great enough to keep his secret safe from Eoduun and Luc. He quickly befriended the shy, quiet guy who possessed the power to compel. Through Veris, Ramil found the acceptance he'd always longed for. Veris was intrigued by him rather than fearful. He liked to sit and listen to his stories about LOA and the lore of Lilith, and they were soon inseparable. When the other hunters saw that Veris trusted him, they were more willing to trust him as well.

He'd found family that didn't fear him, as long as he kept his true self a secret.

But something was still missing.

…Until Knighco's new blood healer arrived on the scene. He didn't understand his immediate, all-consuming obsession with Eve, but he knew better than to pursue her when Luc had already made his intentions clear. Yet he couldn't leave her alone. He took glimpses into her mind every chance he could, trying to figure out her desires and what he might do to gain her favor. But all he ever saw in her thoughts was Luc. Bo. Zeke. Eoduun. Dagon. And later, Isaac. There was no room for him in Eve's heart.

When she wasn't around, he would sneak into her apartment and nick things. He'd always had a predilection for petty theft, but it was typically geared more toward gold and jewels. But with Eve, he wanted things that would make him feel closer to her. The chapstick that had caressed her full, pouty lips. The notepad her skilled hand had graced a pencil over, filling the pages with art and doodles. The book her pretty brown eyes had been poring over, learning about the monsters she shared this world with. An elastic band that had tied her long, soft pink hair into a pony tail that still smelled of her shampoo. He never took anything lewd or inappropriate or valuable. They were just *things*, but they were things that had touched her. Things she'd left an impression upon.

And then, one day in the gym, he'd offered to spar with her, and everything changed. He felt a spark, and the curse inside of her reacted to the Leviathan inside of him, and she showed herself. Finally. The immense power of the monster within.

The Abomination.

She'd found her way to him, after all this time. He could scarcely believe it. But...was it really her? Was she really the one he'd been promised?

And if she was, why didn't she want him? She was supposed to be the one who would finally love him for what he was. *Truly* love all of him. But the more he tried to get to know her and read her desires, the more she put up barriers. The warier she became. The less she trusted him.

Was it because Luc stood in his way?

He could fix that.

If there was one thing he was certain of, it was that Luc didn't deserve Eve, and it didn't take him long to find proof of it. All it took was a phone call to a couple of acquaintances who specialized in gathering intel for the Locusts, and he had videos and photos that proved Luc was unworthy.

But when he showed her Luc's true colors, all it did was break Eve's heart and drive her away from him rather than closer to him. He had been prepared to offer a shoulder to cry on, to help her through her heartache, but instead, his actions had only brought her closer to the *exorcist*, Isaac.

Isaac was a problem as well. He could *see* Ramil's jinn powers at work when he was near Eve, but Isaac had no way of telling whether Ramil was using his powers for benevolent or malicious purposes. He must have assumed they were malicious, and he warned Eve to be distrustful of Ramil. He knew Isaac could sense there was something darker beneath Ramil's surface, but he couldn't see the dragon lurking there.

And then Apep showed up in Eve's kitchen, and he made Eve choose someone. For the first time ever, she chose Ramil. Too bad she was choosing him to be the one to die. He didn't begrudge her for it, but it hurt.

It ripped his heart out.

Ramil changed tactics. He took Ruth under his wing, hoping the distraction of a beautiful, powerful witch would keep his mind off Eve. Perhaps she could be a suitable partner for him. If she was able to wield Lilith's grimoire, maybe she was powerful enough to become his mate.

But there was no spark between them. The darkness in her didn't speak to the darkness in him the way the Abomination had. He didn't love Ruth, and he found his attention still drawn to Eve. His obsession made him bolder, and he began to pursue her more openly. Not so openly as to draw the wrath of Luc, but openly enough that she would understand his intentions without question.

Still, she shunned him.

Then Ruth betrayed them all, and his loyalty to Knighco was questioned. He was suspected of aiding Ruth, even though he was just as blindsided as everyone else was. He hadn't seen even a hint of her intentions in what he could access of her mind. He'd been certain she was on the path to redemption. How had he so misjudged her?

He felt the distrust in the eyes turned his way, saw it in their thoughts when they interacted with him, felt the sting of their accusations. Yet again, he'd become an untouchable.

If they didn't trust him, then he couldn't trust them. He put up the cameras in his apartment to protect himself, and set out trying to figure out how to fix everything.

But how?

Then Eve started asking questions about LOA and Stacey Rose, and the answer hit him like a freight train.

He would bring Zeke back, and everything would be set right. He would give Eve the one thing she most desired, and maybe she would finally love him.

He would grant her *every* wish if she loved him, not just her wish for her Chinese takeout to taste better.

Eve withdrew from Ramil's mind, her own mind reeling from what she'd seen.

She'd had him wrong this whole time. She thought her curse reacted to him because it was trying to warn her, but it was simply rising to meet the Leviathan power inside him. She'd misjudged him egregiously. She'd been breaking his heart since she met him, slowly destroying him from the inside out.

It seemed to be the only thing she excelled at. She wanted to think of herself as a creative force, proof of the artist inside of her. A healing force. But no, she was all destruction. The fighter that broke bones and spilled blood, the so-called healer that used her curative blood to steal powers and kill through the guise of intimacy.

She wasn't the cure.

She was the disease.

She stared at Ramil, not knowing what to say to him. He stared back, and Eve could finally see the hidden anguish in the depths of those copper-green eyes. He held his hand out to her. "Let's go. We should help prepare for the ritual so I can swap Lilith's relic for Zeke's."

Eve took his hand and glanced back at Apep's mutilated body once more before following Ramil out of the enclosure. "You *are* a dragon," she said quietly as they left the room and started down a dark corridor.

He nodded, then glanced down at her. "Please don't tell anyone."

"I don't think you're giving the hunters enough credit. I think they'd be stoked to know they had a dragon on their side."

He sighed and shook his head. "You still don't get it. They won't believe I'm on their side. Dragons were notorious for taking no side but their own. No one trusts a dragon."

Eve arched a brow at him. "I trust a dragon."

He scoffed as he led her down a long, spiraling stone staircase. "You do *now*. But you didn't. If they find out I've been hiding it all this time…"

"I won't let anything happen to you."

"You do realize you don't run Knighco, don't you?"

Eve smirked. "Don't I?"

"But the *Vatican* has its hands in the mix, and they won't let a dragon go free. A Leviathan is the highest form of evil, and they tried to stamp us out two thousand years ago. If they learn a bloodline persists, the church will show no mercy."

Eve steeled her expression. "I won't give them a choice."

The expansive room at the bottom of the staircase smelled of old blood and rot. It looked like it had been dug out of the bowels of the Earth back when the Earth was still young, and made into a cyclopean cathedral. Locusts rushed about in a mild frenzy, preparing for the ritual, setting up an elaborate altar, painting sigils and runes on the walls and floors. Eve looked up at the ceiling, but it was bathed in darkness, beyond the reaches of the soft, ominous firelight cast by the sconces on the walls and the torches in the aisles.

This is where she would raise Zeke from the dead.

Eve felt a tingling in the base of her spine, and her whole body trembled with a harsh shiver. She felt like ants were beginning to crawl beneath her skin, and hornets swarmed in her chest.

Something was wrong.

Her curse had gorged itself on power, like some great, hungry black hole. Had she taken too much? She was supposed to be built for this, wasn't she?

"You look like you're about to be sick," Ramil noted.

"It smells like shit in here," she deflected. It wasn't *untrue*.

"Death," Ramil corrected.

Eve felt a burning in her throat, and she coughed into the crook of her elbow.

There was a sudden burst of heat and flame from her mouth, and the edge of her t-shirt sleeve singed and glowed orange briefly.

"Oh, fuck!" Eve shrieked and frantically swatted at her sleeve. She inspected her arm, but it was unscathed. She turned wide eyes up to Ramil.

A grin lit his whole face. "You took the power of the dragon, too," he marveled. "You *can* wield the power of a Leviathan."

Eve looked back down at her arm. "It didn't burn my skin."

"I'm a Fire dragon. I'm immune to heat and flame. Things still *feel* hot, but it doesn't hurt me. Ergo, *you* must be immune to fire now, too."

Eve raised her brows and grinned. "I'm Khaleesi."

Ramil gave her a quizzical look.

Eve's smile faded. "Luc would get it." She took her phone from her pocket once more and checked her messages. Nothing. Bo and Luc still hadn't seen her texts. She looked around to make sure no one was within earshot. "When will I be able to see the boys?"

"They will come when it's time, don't worry," Ramil assured her.

But she did worry. And so did Bo. Her bond with Bo had been strangely quiet, and it unsettled her. He should be beside himself with anxiety. She should be feeling *something* from him. She wished she could talk to him the way she did with Dagon.

And now that she was focused on it, she realized there *was* something stirring in her gut.

Dread.

"What if this doesn't work?"

Ramil's eyes were fixed on the ancient, leatherbound grimoire Eno was placing on the podium overlooking the altar. "It will work. Don't let doubt creep into your heart."

Eno spotted Eve and Ramil, and he smiled brightly and gave them a small wave. She wondered what kind of expression he would be wearing when he saw Zeke appear where Lilith was supposed to be.

She would soon find out.

36
I Chose This

Eve's heart thundered with anxiety as she watched Locusts filing into the unholy underground cathedral from behind her designated place at the podium. Her guts churned, twisting into painful knots as a creeping fear crawled through her veins.

The plan will derail. Everything will go to shit. Zeke will stay dead forever. Everyone you love will suffer and die. They'll die. They'll DIE. They're going to DIE. But not you. They'll die, and you'll be left behind. You'll be all alone again. Unloved and alone. Alone. Broken. Ruined. Useless. You're garbage. Trash. Shit. Worthless. A fucking waste of space. What the fuck are you even trying to do here? You're going to get everyone killed, you stupid fucking bitch.

Eve started humming some stupid, random tune, trying to banish the terrible thoughts swirling in her head.

Stop, stop, stop!

Don't think it, don't say it.

Don't think it, don't say it.

Don't think it, don't say it.

Her vision blurred with unshed tears as she looked down at the grimoire in front of her, her hands trembling as she skimmed her fingertips over the strangely supple, odd-smelling leather of the binding.

"Open it."

Eve startled at Eno's voice so close to her. He was standing right next to her. She hadn't even heard him approach. She did as he asked, and stared down at the odd characters covering the first page. She didn't recognize the language, but…somehow, it felt familiar. As she turned the page, she immediately noticed the strange texture of the pages, and rubbed it gently between her fingers.

"Human skin," Eno explained, and he chuckled when Eve yanked her hand back. "The cover is made of Leviathan leather. The spine was stitched with my grandfather's hair." Eno caressed the book reverently. "The first mortal blessed with holy powers," he noted.

"Adam?"

"The one and only. Lilith's first husband. If not for her gift of manipulating the metaphysical, her ability to bestow others with the supernatural abilities most suited to them, he wouldn't have learned her skills and given Eve the powers Lilith gave him. I believe that's where the myth that Eve was made from a part of Adam originated from. He gave her the power that made her like him, but it didn't originate from him. Ironic, isn't it? Without Lilith, there would be no Blood of Eve. They are two sides to the same coin."

Eve was at a loss for words. Then, she wondered, "What was Adam's power? Eve was the first with Panacea Blood, wasn't she?"

"Yes. Eve's affinity for mending, her desire to fix and heal, were the very traits that made her an ideal companion for Adam after

Lilith. And those traits are likely what manifested in her as Panacea Blood. But Adam was an innovator, with great intelligence and an affinity for planning, so his power manifested as a kind of seer. He could see things beyond their physical boundaries, like their future, their past, and sometimes, even their purpose. Perhaps that's how the tree of knowledge myth arose. Except it wasn't Eve who led him to it. It was Lilith."

"Do *you* have powers?"

Eno smirked. "I share my grandfather's abilities. It's how I knew you would be special. It's how I knew Ramil was special. I see things most people can't."

Eve hesitated before asking, "Can you see how everything will turn out tonight?"

He barked a laugh. "You will raise Lilith. Trust in it."

Eve's adrenaline spiked. That wasn't what was going to happen. How much could he *really* see? "Are you sure?"

"Do you doubt your own abilities?"

Every fucking day. Especially now.

Eno tapped the open pages of the grimoire in front of her. "Do you see the words written upon the pages?" he asked, hope gleaming in his eyes.

Eve nodded. "Yeah. Can't you?"

He shook his head. "The words remain hidden from men, from masculine, male energy. Only a select few women have the power to be able to see the words in Lilith's grimoire, and even fewer can understand those words." He arched a brow at her. "Can you understand the words?"

Eve shook her head as she skimmed her eyes over the passages. "This language *feels* familiar, but I know I've never learned it. I don't know what any of this means, yet I know how I'm supposed to pronounce every character." Was this knowledge from Ruth's memories? She looked at Eno.

"It's Ancient Sumerian. Your connection to Lilith, the gift that lives inside you, is guiding you." He graced her with a proud smile and hugged her to his side. "You'll do wonderfully tonight. Trust your instincts, and you'll be just fine."

Eve suddenly scented a familiar oud noir aroma, and her head shot up. Her eyes frantically scanned the crowded room as more Locusts poured in from the twisting stairwell, and her heart stopped when she saw Eoduun moving through the crowd toward the altar.

No.

Ramil was right next to him, leading him to the altar, his copper-green eyes meeting Eve's as he shook his head in resignation.

NO.

Eve left Eno at the podium and rushed to Eoduun. She crashed into him, gripping his biceps tightly. "What the fuck are you doing here?!" she panicked.

Eoduun's eyes were dead. Lifeless. Resigned. "I'm doing what I said I would do. I'm giving my life for Zeke's, and you *aren't* going to stand in my way."

Tears pricked Eve's eyes. "I won't do it. I will *not* trade."

Eoduun's tone was suddenly wrathful as he roared, "It isn't your choice! It's my life to give, and I'm giving it!" He brushed her hands away and lowered his voice. "Go play your role, and let me play mine."

"We can find someone else. Please," Eve pleaded. "*Anyone* else."

Eoduun gritted his teeth as he leaned into Eve. "I won't leave Zeke with someone else's memories. If it happens for him like it did for Dagon, I don't want anyone else's memories haunting him but my own. Maybe he'll finally realize just how much I loved him." His voice broke as he added, "It wasn't just a crush for me."

"Eno." Ramil loudly announced the Locust leader's approach, cuing Eve in on his proximity. Eoduun and Eve immediately stopped arguing. "Is everything ready?"

Eno looked down at his smart phone. "I believe so. It's almost time." He quickly assessed Eoduun, then looked to Ramil. "Is this our sacrificial vessel?"

"I am." Eoduun answered flatly.

Eno stepped close to Eoduun, producing a small glass vial from his pocket, and pressed the vial to Eoduun's lips. "No turning back. Drink."

"No, wait!" But before Eve could act, the liquid was down Eoduun's throat. "What was that?!" she fretted, snatching the bottle away far too late.

"A potent elixir. It'll open his mind and body to the other realms. A mortal body isn't meant to withstand the effects, so we have a limited window to work the spell before he…" Eno gave Eoduun a mildly sympathetic look. "…Expires."

Eve's heart filled with molten lead.

Eoduun saw the horror in her eyes, and his determined expression softened. "I chose this. My happy ending, remember?" He forced a smile.

She didn't return it. Tears streamed down her cheeks, and using a power she didn't even realize she had until now, her mind flickered through all the different possibilities before her, like a slot machine. Apep's power. Chaos. She immediately knew what paths would lead to the most destruction and chaos, but it did her little good in this situation. She wanted the path where Eoduun walks away from this unscathed, but she now knew she'd already moved beyond a point in time where that possibility was still on the table.

Every path forward led to the same outcome: Eoduun dies.

He dies.

He is going to die, and there's nothing she can do to stop it. The only thing she will have accomplished after everything is said and done, is traded one hell for another.

Eno placed his hand gently on her back and began to usher her toward the podium. Her feet shuffled forward numbly. "We need to begin," he insisted. "You need to use your intuition to find the correct spell in the grimoire, and we need to get to work."

Eve flipped through the grimoire with clumsy fingers and watery eyes while Eno stood beside her. He instructed her to hold in her heart her desire to raise Lilith, seeking out the section of the book that spoke most loudly to her. But she didn't want to raise Lilith, she wanted to raise Zeke. She *had* to raise Zeke.

Because if she failed, Eoduun would die for *nothing*, and she would lose them both.

But she knew the spell she needed to raise Zeke was the spell to raise Lilith, so that's what she focused on.

When she approached the end of the grimoire, she began to worry that it wasn't speaking to her in the way that Eno suggested it was. Nothing jumped out at her. Nothing felt right.

But then she turned to the last page, and her adrenaline spiked. *This one.*

She skimmed the words. She could hear them in her head, but she had no idea what any of it meant except for one name: Lilith.

She looked up at Ramil, who was helping Eoduun onto the altar. Eoduun was quickly becoming sloppy, falling in and out of consciousness like he was drunk, his eyes bleary and unfocused.

This was all wrong. It wasn't supposed to be like this.

Undo. Unsend. Rewind. Skip back.

Please.

I want to move back three steps.

She wondered if Bo could feel her anguish. Why couldn't she feel him? She wondered if the boys had all agreed to just let Eoduun go, or if he had given them no choice. She found it hard to believe that Bo knew what Eoduun was doing, because he wasn't twisting her guts with his grief right now.

There was nothing.

He must not know.

"Read the page aloud to me," Eno instructed, snapping Eve's attention back to the grimoire. She did as she was told, and Eno listened closely, nodding. When she had finished, he took the book from her and guided her down to the altar, placing the book on the ledge near Eoduun's now unconscious, prone body.

Eve chewed her lip as more tears spilled down the sides of her nose.

"No need to cry, sweet child," Eno comforted her. "He will be rewarded for his sacrifice. Just you wait and see."

Eve felt a warm hand brushing her elbow, and Ramil's fingers slid down her arm and intertwined with hers. "It's all set," he whispered. "I'm sorry about Eoduun, but…he wanted this. It was his wish. I couldn't deny him his wish."

Eno stepped around the altar and looked out over the crowded room. He raised his hands and clapped them loudly over his head, and the entire room fell deathly silent.

"Tonight, my Locusts, you shall meet your creator. Your mother. The blood of our blood. The Spirit of the Darkness. She will rise, and with her, so shall we. If the world will not embrace us in the light, we shall bathe it in darkness so that we may thrive." After a long applause and cheering, Eno raised a hand to silence the crowd. His voice echoed off the stone walls as he bellowed, "Let us begin!"

A ring of flame was suddenly ignited, and it circled the altar and met around the other side, enclosing Eve, Eoduun, Ramil, and Eno inside its borders. Eno nodded to Eve, his eyes flicking to the opened grimoire in front of her, and Eve's heart threatened to clog her throat.

She read aloud, but she didn't hear her own words as she saw Ramil pour two small vials into Eoduun's mouth before slicing his own hand and dripping blood onto Eoduun's tongue. He took Eve's hand, and with only a small smile and nod, he cut her hand as well, adding her blood to the collection. When he was finished, he gingerly tucked a folded piece of paper into Eoduun's mouth, which Eve assumed must have been Zeke's note.

As Eve neared the end of the spell, she could feel the powers inside of her begin warring, like a pack of fighting dogs all locked in the same cage. She tried to swallow it down and ignore it, pressing on. She could handle it. She had to handle it.

And then the last word spilled from her tongue, and everything inside of her stilled, as though standing at attention.

Waiting.

Eoduun's body trembled, and his back arched up off the altar. His limbs twisted and contorted, and his body began to reshape itself. For a moment, Eve's breath stalled in her lungs. Her heart raced. This was it. She was going to see Zeke again.

Eoduun's silky black hair began to fall out, and in its place, short, tight black curls erupted over the deepening brown skin of his scalp. His nails lengthened, and his chest swelled into breasts. His hips widened and his lips grew full and plump.

Horror thrashed in Eve's guts and ripped through her chest. In the breadth of a moment, Eoduun had transformed not into Zeke...

...But into Lilith.

37

I Just Want to be *Normal*

Eve didn't need anyone to tell her who that beautiful, ebony-skinned goddess rising from the altar was. Pure energy radiated from her like rays of light from the sun. Eve could *feel* it.

Lilith's eyes were pools of black as she cast her gaze around the room. Locusts fell to their knees in reverence, a hush settling over the crowd. When Lilith's gaze settled on Eve, the black, demonic pools of her eyes shifted into dark irises that were much more humanlike. She stood before her, still dressed in Eoduun's black jeans and purple and black sweatshirt, and smiled. It wasn't exactly an *unfriendly* smile, but there was a dark cunning behind it.

"My Abomination has finally freed me," she declared in a rich, deep, powerfully feminine voice. It was like melted dark chocolate for the ears.

Eno moved to Eve's side. "Welcome back, Lilith," he greeted warmly. "There is much work to do, and we anxiously await your guidance."

Eve's stomach twisted and flopped, and her skin crawled and prickled. Her knees shook, and she gripped the side of the altar to steady herself. The power inside her seemed to be absorbing the energy radiating from Lilith, but she felt weak.

This is wrong.

All wrong.

Wrong.

I failed.

I failed.

I failed.

Before Lilith had a chance to respond, another voice spoke. A voice Eve didn't know well because she didn't hear it often, but one she recognized.

"I'm the one who raised you, Lilith."

Rising from his knees in the back of the crowd, Veris stepped forward, slowly moving toward the dying flames around the altar. "I am the one who set all of this in motion. I orchestrated everything. I raised you, hoping you would grant me one favor. A reward, if you saw fit."

Eno began to move forward, but Lilith raised a hand to halt him.

Eve could scarcely believe what she was hearing. Why was *he* here? What the hell did Veris have to do with...*anything*? She tore her eyes from Lilith to look at Ramil. Veris was Ramil's best friend. Had Ramil betrayed her after all? Had he been working with Veris to raise Lilith and somehow hidden it all from her prying mind?

Ramil didn't meet her eyes because he was staring out at Veris, mouth agape, eyes wide and brows pinched in disbelief. No, the shocked expression on Ramil's face seemed genuine. Veris had betrayed him, too.

They needed backup. "Where are the boys?" Eve whispered to Ramil while Lilith assessed Veris.

He dragged his eyes from Veris and Lilith to look at Eve. "They didn't respond to the message I sent them. They should've been here by now, but I don't see them." He looked back out over the scene before them, a hopelessness settling in his features. "It all went wrong. We were betrayed," he mumbled, and Eve wasn't sure if he was talking to her or himself.

It was time for a Hail Mary. Eve had one last ace up her sleeve, and he had giant, leathery wings and a violent disposition.

Dagon, I need you here. NOW.

Before she'd left the compound, she'd taken a risk and surreptitiously nicked the paint in his devil's trap, ordering him to remain within its bounds unless she called to him. She hoped her trust in him would pay off, and not bite her in the ass.

Wind tussled her hair as Dagon appeared next to her, wings stretched wide. His vermilion gaze took in Lilith. "Oh, fuck."

"Go find the boys," Eve commanded. "I'm afraid something's happened to them." She wouldn't allow her mind to ponder all the awful possibilities. "I need to stay here and keep an eye on this situation."

Dagon hesitated as Lilith turned away from Veris to inspect the godly newcomer.

"Dagon," she purred, a light amusement in her tone. She wasn't remotely intimidated. "It's been ages."

"Lilith." Dagon's wings were suddenly all Eve could see as he put himself between her and Lilith. "You will not harm this one," he warned.

Lilith laughed. "I wouldn't dream of harming her. She is blood of my blood."

Eve placed her hand in the middle of Dagon's bare back, between his wings. "Go find my boys, Dagon. That's *not* a request. I can handle myself."

He growled in frustration, but then he disappeared.

"Listen to me!" Veris shouted, and everyone but Eve and Lilith whipped their head in his direction, as though instantly enraptured by whatever he had to say.

"The God Tongue," Lilith smirked. She hopped up onto the altar and sat with her legs crossed over the edge of it. She leaned back on her hands, completely at ease. "That's a rare and impressive power. Shame to see it wasted on a man."

"Then take it," Veris begged. "Please, take it and make me normal so I can go and live a normal life." Despair painted his face. "I just want to be *normal.*"

Lilith canted her head to the side. "Why should I?"

"Because I did all this for you!" he declared, arms outstretched.

Lilith studied Veris for a long moment. "Interesting," she remarked. Then she turned to Eve. "I think you'd be interested in taking a look through his memories."

"Why?" Eve asked tremulously. Her chest felt like it was churning with bees.

Lilith looked down at her long nails. "Because I'm not sure what to do with him, and I think after you see what's in his head, you'll have some ideas."

Eve barely needed to work to bore straight into Veris' mind, and she needed only to feel what she wanted to see, and the memories were at her fingertips. His mind was an open book to her.

Veris' deceit began even before Eve was brought to Knighco. It wasn't Mira and Celeste who found her. It was Veris who had tracked her down, and he had used his powers to convince Celeste and Mira that *they* had stumbled upon a new blood healer. He'd listened raptly to Ramil's stories about the Locusts of Abaddon, and their belief in the power of Lilith. He became obsessed with raising her, because he knew she was the only one with the power to cleanse him of his cursed tongue.

He hated his power. It controlled him, not the other way around. It robbed him of a normal life. It condemned him to silence for much of his life. He never knew just how much of his power seeped out in regular conversation, so he never *quite* knew what was a real interaction, and what might have been influenced by his powers of compulsion.

His powers had activated at a young age. Much too young. When he was nine, he noticed that, when he really wanted someone to do something, he could *make* them do it. But when he tried to tell his parents about it, to show them, they weren't amazed. They looked at him like he was the most monstrous thing they'd ever seen, and that upset him. They tried to silence him, and told him he was never to use that power again. They were terrified of what he could do.

He thought they'd be impressed, but they were mad at him? How was that fair?

He would show them.

In a fit of anger, he told them to walk into traffic.

And they did.

He was taken into a secret detention center run by the Vatican, because they believed him to be possessed by a demon. His ability was too powerful for someone so young. He was fitted with a gag and kept separated from other people. They feared his ability so much, there was only one exorcist they dared to send in to handle him.

Isaac D'Angelo, the Angel of Death. The exorcist who could never fall victim to his cursed, spoken words, and the one who wouldn't hesitate to put him down if he tried to escape.

He was kept as a kind of prisoner, spending every day for the next seven years reliving the moment he watched his parents step in front of a bus. He desperately wished he could take it back. He was haunted and horrified by the consequences of his childish, impulsive anger. And when the exorcisms didn't work, he began to believe that he wasn't just possessed by a demon.

Maybe he was one.

He loathed himself and his unnatural ability.

Then, he was rescued by Sister Fiona and brought to Knighco to undergo training. They didn't usually take anyone under the age of eighteen, but Sister Fiona convinced Victor Fagerberg, who was running Knighco at the time, to take him in.

Veris was no longer a prisoner, per se, but he was informed that he had to earn his place at Knighco, or he would be sent right back to the Vatican's detention center. He was kept in a special sound-proof room and trained by Roy and Levi, who were fitted with sound-canceling earmuffs, and he worked his ass off to learn to control his powers.

He finally earned his own apartment after a year and a half of isolation training, but even outside of the containment room, he was still lonely. Victor had lied and told everyone he'd grown up voluntarily mute, afraid of his own powers, hoping it would garner sympathy and acceptance. But everyone knew he was dangerous, that one word from him could ruin them, so they kept their distance.

Until Ramil.

Ramil was new. He didn't know to fear him yet, and everyone seemed to be avoiding him as well. What better companion than a fellow outcast?

And then, through Ramil, Veris learned about the LOA belief system, and about the Abomination and the ritual to raise Lilith, and his whole purpose shifted. If Lilith could give power, could *make* monsters, she could take power away, couldn't she? The more he researched, the more he became convinced that Lilith was his ticket to a new life.

A normal life.

And better yet? She would wreak havoc on the religious institution that took his childhood from him. His revenge would be glorious.

So he began scheming.

He got to work finding out what was needed for the ritual. He discovered that the Locusts believed they needed a dragon, a sea beast, and a serpent, and they believed Ramil to be the "dragon." He had seen the gills on Dagon when he took over Zeke's body, which made him believe Dagon would suffice for the sea beast. After some research, he concluded that the Egyptian god Apep was fitting for the serpent.

But he would need their blood, so he needed them to be freed and in their own bodies. He knew of only one witch powerful enough to raise a god, because she'd already accomplished it. She just needed the right tools to perfect it.

Veris contacted one of Ramil's few remaining friends at LOA, and he used his vocal powers to make Darnell his pawn. Darnell became his spy, and soon informed him that the leader of the Locusts, Eno, had access to a powerful spell book. He kept it in a locked box in the LOA compound in Kentucky.

Lilith's grimoire.

Darnell was compelled to make sure that the grimoire found its way into Ruthlys Fagerberg's hands, by any means necessary.

But Veris was still missing a big piece of the puzzle. Darnell had little trouble tracking down and relaying to Veris the location of Evrys Alarie, the suspected Abomination. But he warned Veris that there was some uncertainty as to whether she was truly the monster of prophecy. He wasn't even sure if she was a blood healer. Some suspected she was a dud.

He had to take his chances.

Veris passed the information regarding a possible new blood healer on to Celeste, who passed it on to Mira, and he made them think it was their own discovery. Then, when Eve was brought in, he kept a close eye on her to make sure she was what she was supposed to be. He was the one who compelled Mira to send Eve's blood and DNA samples to the Vatican, to verify that she was the Abomination.

Once he knew for sure, he realized he would need a liaison to make contact with Ruth. Someone simple and easily manipulated, but useful. Someone no one would suspect of such a betrayal. A loner who wouldn't be missed when he disappeared for a few hours, maybe a day.

Dizzy. He was perfect! There was no greater spy than a shapeshifter. He would get Dizzy's hands dirty, and steer clear of danger and suspicion himself.

He compelled Dizzy, and made Dizzy believe that he wanted to help Ruth because it would finally make him feel useful. Appreciated. Important. He compelled Dizzy to approach Ruth, and she took the bait. She couldn't resist having a doting Knighco mole.

Once Dizzy had earned her trust, Veris compelled him to suggest that Ruth raise Apep and bind him to her.

But instead of raising Apep, she kidnapped Eve in the hopes of creating an entire army of monsters, and it almost derailed Veris' plans. Eve was resourceful, though, and more powerful than Veris had realized. She killed Ruth's titan and slipped through Ruth's fingers, and *finally* Ruth had the good sense to raise Apep, binding him to herself so she could control him.

In turn, Veris could control him through her. As powerful as his powers of persuasion were, they didn't work on originals. Gods.

Now, he had only one more god to free.

When he saw how desperate Dagon had been to get Eve back, it gave him an idea, and he switched gears.

He wanted to get Eve back into Ruth's hands. He suspected that if Ruth promised Dagon Eve *and* his freedom, he would willingly switch sides. He needed Dagon freed. He was the last basic ingredient required for the ritual.

But then the Angel of Death came back into Veris' life. The Vatican sent him to evaluate Eve, and if he deemed her to be dangerous, he would kill her. Oh, what Veris wouldn't have given to be able to compel Isaac. He would have to keep a close eye on that situation. He couldn't let Isaac kill his Abomination.

Luc called a meeting and presented his half-baked plan to capture Ruth, and Veris saw Eoduun's irises turn purple as he scanned the other hunters at the conference table in the War Room. So, they suspected a mole. They were onto him. He had no mental barriers against Eoduun, and he couldn't block him from seeing his deceptions, but he *could* compel him to forget. At the conclusion of the meeting, Veris passed behind Eoduun and whispered, "Forget what you saw in my memories. My memories were clean. You will never read me again."

That was too close for comfort.

Later that day, Luc invited Veris to Eve's apartment for a secret meeting, where the Angel of Death stood with his back to the wall, barely sparing Veris a second glance. He wondered if Isaac remembered him at all. If he did, he didn't show it.

Veris was informed of the *real* plan to trap Ruth, and Luc wanted him to compel Ruth to come alone to the papermill. He didn't. He said the words, but he didn't put any power behind them. Ruth played along, likely thinking *she* was playing *him*. Probably thinking she was immune to his power.

She wasn't.

She still had no idea that he was the one pulling all the strings.

Veris made sure that Dizzy warned Ruth about the real plan before it was executed, knowing she would bring backup. She wouldn't dare underestimate her brother.

But they underestimated Eve. And then Dizzy took the grimoire and went awol, Apep disappeared, and Ruth lost all of her memories, making her totally useless.

Veris' plans were fucked.

3.8
Eve is My God

But he wouldn't give up that easily. He'd already come too far, and his heart was set on someday being free of this cursed tongue.

He needed to adapt. He hadn't failed. He'd just been delayed.

He "suggested" Ramil should help train Ruth so she could relearn her skills. She still had all that power. She just didn't know how to use it anymore.

Veris got to work trying to track down the grimoire, but before he made much headway, he learned that Luc had killed Dizzy and was himself in possession of the grimoire.

It was somewhere in the compound, safe from Apep.

Perfect.

Then, when he saw Ruth walking down the hall one morning, carrying herself with an air of superiority, her bracelets jangling and rings and earrings sparkling brightly, he was given pause. Something was different. She seemed like the *old* Ruth. He stopped her, using his powers to persuade her to tell him the truth. "Do you have your memories back?"

"Yes."

He could scarcely believe his luck. He glanced around to make sure no one else was in the hallway. He whispered, "How?"

She whispered back, "Apep. He gave them back to me in exchange for the grimoire." She looked uncertain. "I'm supposed to find it and meet him in Montana. But…"

"Tell me."

"I don't want to leave Knighco. I…I think I actually like it here. Maybe I *should* find the grimoire, but instead, use it to seal Apep away. Luc would be impressed that I single-handedly eliminated a threat as powerful as Apep. He would trust me again."

Veris considered his options, and on a whim, he pushed his power through his throat. "You have no allegiance to Knighco or any of its hunters. You will find the grimoire, and you will take Zeke back to Montana and free Dagon. When Apep comes to retrieve the grimoire…" He paused. Where would the safest place be to keep Apep, now that he was no longer bound to Ruth? Who was capable of containing him, but also wouldn't try to kill him? Whose motives aligned with his own?

He grinned. "You will use a spell to incapacitate him and send him to the Locusts of Abaddon compound in Kentucky. I will send you the coordinates."

He would advise Darnell to make sure the Locusts were ready for their new guest.

And once Ruth had fulfilled her purpose and released Dagon, he could remove her from the equation, because she was no longer needed. She would only get in the way.

When he saw Ramil, he instructed him to go after Ruth and kill her once she freed Dagon. He was then to fetch the grimoire and bring it back to Veris, and forget he ever did so.

But when Ruth sent out her urgent meeting message that night, Veris didn't know what she had up her sleeve. If Eve hadn't returned when she did, the fire Ruth set in the bunker would've killed them all, including Veris.

"You have no allegiance to Knighco or any of its hunters."

Perhaps he needed to choose his words more carefully next time. But everything was in motion. Dagon had been freed, Eve had destroyed Ruth before Ramil even showed up on the scene, Apep was in Locust custody, and Ramil had managed to snatch up the grimoire before anyone noticed. It was in the back of Veris' closet, waiting for him to deliver it to Darnell. He had everything he needed for the ritual.

Shame about Zeke, though. He had always liked the guy. But he wasn't letting anything get in his way. Maybe he would ask Lilith to erase his memories before she took his powers, too. He wanted a fresh start, free of his curse, but also free of the burden of guilt that gnawed at him with increasing frequency.

He'd broken a lot of eggs to make his omelet.

All he needed to do now was find a way to get Eve, Dagon, and Ramil to the LOA compound.

When he heard that Eve tried to kill Dagon, but changed her mind because Zeke's memories had left an imprint on him, he realized just how important Zeke had been to her. To all of her team. Dagon was still alive simply because they loved Zeke.

Inspiring.

Zeke was his answer. Their love for him would be their downfall.

When Luc contacted Ramil while Team Beta were on a case in New York, ordering him to return to the Knighco compound for some other nonsense he'd gotten involved in, Veris sent him with a mission.

"You believe Eve can bring Zeke back by performing the ritual to raise Lilith. You'll use a trinket of Zeke's, because you believe that will make Zeke come back instead of Lilith. Convince her and her team to agree to it. Contact Darnell at LOA to arrange it as soon as possible. Forget we had this conversation."

And then Veris compelled Mira to believe he went elsewhere to follow a lead, and he met with Darnell at the LOA compound. Darnell put him up in an unused outbuilding on the edge of the property where no one would notice him.

That should've been it, but he hadn't foreseen that Eve's entire entourage would accompany them. When Darnell informed him of the complication, Veris instructed him to bring them to the outbuilding Darnell had intended for him, but he compelled Darnell to drug them with a handy little sedating spray the Locusts had access to. He didn't want to take any chances.

He hid and waited until Darnell informed him that the team had all passed out in the small outbuilding. He found them all slumped in various places inside one room, like they'd all had too much to drink and had simply passed out where they sat. One by one, he whispered in their ears, "You will remain asleep until someone comes to wake you." He would make sure no one bothered them until he was long gone. He didn't want to have to kill them. "When you wake, you will tell everyone I was killed by Lilith, and you will believe it yourself. Even if you see evidence to the contrary, you will always believe I was killed by Lilith."

He needed a different approach to Isaac, however. He couldn't compel someone who couldn't hear his words, so the priest had to be tied up. Darnell helped him secure Isaac to a support beam, binding him in cuffs and chains.

Now he just had to sit and wait.

It felt like hours before Isaac began to stir. Veris sat forward in his chair, studying the exorcist's face, waiting for the moment he realized he was trapped.

Vatican scum.

Isaac's dark eyes met his, but surprise never shaped his features. His steady gaze focused acutely on Veris in the most unsettling way, like he could see every sin, every awful thing Veris had done, and he was simply biding his time until he could cleanse him in blood.

"Don't look at me like that," Veris spat with a scowl. He sat back in his chair, trying to put a little space between himself and Isaac without being obvious about it.

Isaac's expression remained unchanging as he stared right back at Veris.

"The Angel of Death," Veris taunted. "I remember you. Do you remember me? You don't, do you? The Vatican wanted you to exorcise my *demons*, because most nine-year-olds don't compel their parents to kill themselves. They thought I was too young for abilities, that it had to be a demon. You knew it wasn't, though, didn't you? Instead of killing me because I had an irrevocable, dangerous ability, you just let them keep me there. You let them continue with the prayers and rituals, which, let's face it, are no different than spells and enchantments. Witchcraft is for monsters, but holy prayers are for the righteous, right? The hypocrisy," Veris said venomously. "You think you're righteous, don't you? Your beloved Catholic church isn't holy. It's an evil institution. It's a lie told over and over again. It's a way to control people, to make them fear powers they don't understand. *The devil. Demons.* Did you know that after your exorcisms didn't work and you left, they began torturing me, trying to beat a demon out of me that was never there to begin with?" Veris scoffed. "The Catholic church brainwashes people into hating things they have no reason to hate, then has the audacity to claim to be a religion of love and forgiveness and meekness. Then they turn around and threaten their own believers with fire and brimstone if they misbehave; if they love the wrong people; if they don't live the righteous and holy life the church has dictated for them. It isn't about love. It's about control.

"And now that Lilith is coming, people will open their eyes. They're going to realize they've been lied to for centuries, that the real monsters aren't the ones hiding in the shadows, but rather the ones standing right in front of them in the pulpit in their stupid hats and robes, dressed like kings while preaching about the holiness of simplicity." He shook his head. "Your time is over, priest. *You're* the monster here, not me, so quit looking at me like I'm the evil one." After a brief pause, he added, "And if I *am* a monster, it's only because your stupid fucking church made me one."

Isaac's hands twitched behind his back as he glanced around the room, his nostrils flaring briefly. To Veris' surprise, he spoke one simple, impatient question.

"Where's Eve?"

He didn't know what he had been expecting, but this wasn't it. He honestly didn't expect Isaac to speak to him at all. But he did, and he offered no defense of the church? No condemnation for his blasphemy?

Curious.

Veris canted his head. "What if I said she was dead?"

Something flashed briefly in the priest's eyes before being smothered by the blackness. "Then you'd see what true evil can come out of a Catholic priest. If you've harmed her, your blood will stain my white collar red. I won't just torture or beat you. I will utterly annihilate you."

Veris raised his eyebrows. "What would your so-called God say?"

Isaac's eyes darkened, his features shifting to a deadly calm. "Eve is my god."

Veris could hardly believe his ears. He leaned forward again. "Isn't she considered the Antichrist to your church? A false idol? That kind of talk will land you in Hell, won't it, priest?" he scoffed.

Isaac leaned forward against his restraints. "Hell *is* my domain, little boy, and I will show you the devil himself if you've laid a hand on Eve."

A shiver of fear rolled up Veris' spine, and he was grateful for the chains keeping Isaac in place. This was a bear he didn't want to poke, after all. Something in Isaac's eyes told him that he would hunt Veris to the ends of the Earth if he dared to hurt the Abomination.

Apparently, the Locusts weren't the only ones who worshipped her.

"Relax. She's fine. Once Lilith is raised, you can have her back."

He didn't care what happened to Eve after that, honestly. In truth, he hadn't thought much about anyone else *after*. All his effort had been put into orchestrating Lilith's ritual, getting *here*, getting *his* happily ever after. He figured he'd just make everyone believe he was dead before Lilith took his powers.

She *would* take his powers away, wouldn't she? She would be so grateful to his efforts, she would have to grant him one request, right? He would sell his soul to her just to be normal, if that's what it took. This power was too heavy a burden. He dreamed of a day when he could carry on a normal conversation without the constant vigilance and effort required to keep cursed words from slipping out.

But even if he compelled everyone else to believe he died, he couldn't make Isaac believe it.

The door suddenly swung open, and Darnell entered the outbuilding. "We hit a snag," Darnell announced. "She killed the serpent. Ramil told me to see if the long-haired one still wanted to be the host and, if so, to bring him to the pit."

Fine. But he had one last task for Eoduun. He whispered in Eoduun's ear, "Wake up. Erase me from Isaac's memories. Then you will be the host for the ritual."

Eoduun's eyes sprang open, and he rose to his feet. Isaac tried to clench his eyes shut, but Eoduun used his fingers to peel them open, and Veris saw Eoduun's irises turn purple and begin spinning. Veris stepped outside and waited for him to finish, not wanting to risk Isaac getting a glimpse of him after having his memories erased.

He then quietly followed Eoduun and Darnell to the ritual, staying out of sight. He slipped silently in with the other Locusts, unnoticed by Ramil or Eve, as their focus was entirely on Eoduun.

Eve withdrew from Veris' mind, still unable to fully believe what she'd seen. *Veris*? The innocent, quiet, boyish-looking hunter who'd been completely off her radar was the one behind almost *everything*? It was incomprehensible.

Realization hit Eve like a sledgehammer. Ruth hadn't wanted to leave Knighco. She *liked* it there, and she had no interest in killing Zeke. She was truly working toward reformation when Veris compelled her to betray them.

And Eve killed her. Horrifically.

Veris may not have bloodied his own hands, but he was responsible for so much death. And even though he couldn't directly compel Eve, he'd used her, just the same. He'd manipulated her decisions and turned her into a pawn in his game.

All just to be *normal*.

Fire burned in her chest.

Eve stepped forward and directed Lilith, "Go ahead. Take his power from him." Veris may have played an elaborate, well-crafted game, but he was an idiot if he thought she would let him simply walk out of here alive.

Lilith arched a sculpted brow at her. "You'd grant him his happy ending?"

A sinister smirk curled Eve's lip. "Everyone deserves a happy ending."

Lilith studied her briefly, then a wicked, knowing grin lit her face. "Delightful," she said in a low tone. Then she turned back to Veris. "Come here, puppet master," she commanded, curling a finger at him. She leaned forward, uncrossing and recrossing her legs, still perched on the edge of the altar. To Eno, she ordered, "Bring me my grimoire."

"You'll take my curse from me?" Veris asked.

"You will be free of your God Tongue."

As he stepped forward, he shouted, "Everyone will believe I am dead as soon as I leave this room. But if anyone tries to hurt me before then, you will attack them and defend me with your lives."

In unison, the entire room replied, "With our lives."

Even Ramil and Eno.

Shit. So he wasn't as naïve as she'd hoped. She could kill him in an instant with Apep's power, stopping his heart like Apep had done to Bo, but then she would have this whole room after her.

She glanced over at Ramil. No, not the whole room. Ramil couldn't harm her. She had his power.

As Eve watched Eno deliver the grimoire into Lilith's hands, panic suddenly gripped her. She dropped to her knees, clutching her chest.

It was Bo.

And then he was there, crouching in front of her, his hands framing her face as he tilted her head to frantically inspect her. "Evie...you're ok," he breathed, his relief spilling through both of them. He crushed her against his chest, holding her there protectively.

The tattoo on her wrist tingled, and she heard the crackle of electricity as Luc appeared at her side, assessing the situation before them. "Tell me who to kill first," he seethed.

Dagon was last to arrive, and he tossed Isaac aside. He must've carried him here. If shit wasn't completely fucked right now, she would've laughed about that.

Isaac quickly recovered his balance, drawing his knives and positioning himself in front of Bo and Eve, ready to defend them from everyone else in the room.

Dagon spread his wings and stood at Eve's back, looming over her like a demonic hellhound, his gaze challenging anyone to dare to approach her.

A calm settled over Eve. She was on the frontlines, teetering on the brink of all-out war with the promise of untold carnage and life-changing consequences, but she felt safe.

These men surrounding her would do the most monstrous things to protect her, and it was the most loved she had ever felt. But she needed to protect them, too, and if that meant letting Veris walk out of here alive...

...she would do it. She wouldn't risk their lives for her revenge.

But after all this, she *would* track him down and kill him quietly. Even if everyone else could be forced to forget him or think he's dead, she would never forget what he'd done.

39
For a Price

She stood up and dusted off her knees. "Don't kill anyone just yet," she instructed. "Let's just see what happens."

Eno took notice of the strangers around Eve. "Who are they?"

Eve couldn't be bothered with Eno right now.

"What the fuck is going on?" Luc inquired, his icy gaze scanning the room. He saw Lilith with the grimoire, standing over a kneeling Veris. "Is the ritual not finished? Who is that? It can't be Veris. Veris is dead."

Bo's brows furrowed. "Why were we passed out? Where's Eoduun?"

Her heart broke all over again. "I made a mistake," she said, her voice just a whisper. "Eoduun is gone, and Zeke isn't coming back." She choked on the words. "I've lost them both."

Lilith spoke in a hushed tone as she held one hand out over Veris' head, reading from the grimoire. She used her long, sharp thumb nail to gouge a small slice into the side of her middle finger. "Open your mouth," she commanded him, and he did. Lilith held her hand above his mouth, allowing the blood to drip down her fingertip onto his tongue.

Veris began to shrink, and hair sprouted all over his skin. In an instant, were Veris once knelt, there was a cute, fluffy, odd little animal that looked like a mix between a dog and a cat.

Dagon let out a small chuckle. "Never trust Lilith."

Lilith picked up the little animal and held it up for all to see. "He is unharmed," she assured them.

Under Veris' orders, they had no reason to defend him.

Lilith turned and began to approach Eve with the critter in her arms, but the men around her raised their guard. Lilith stopped and looked at them with a bored, annoyed expression. She then looked past them to Eve. "A gift." She held the squirming furball out, offering it to Eve. "Do with him what you see fit." Then, after a pause, she added, "*After* you leave here with him. He is mostly harmless now, but they aren't." She tilted her head to indicate the crowd of Locusts.

Eve moved past Bo and Isaac and gathered up the soft little bundle into her own arms. She looked down at it with its floppy ears, flat, pug-like face, and big, reddish-brown eyes. Its fur was the same pale yellow as Veris' hair. The tail wasn't as long as a cat's but neither was it as rigid as a dog's. It was quite round, like a small pet who had been excessively overfed. It wasn't quite dog *or* cat. Or maybe it was *both*.

It was fucking cute.

"What is it?" she asked Lilith while still looking down at the critter.

But Bo answered first. "Sunekosuri," he marveled. Everyone gathered around Eve and looked down at it.

"It's a yokai," Lilith added. "Keep him, give him away, kill him... That's your call to make. But if you keep him, don't take him out in the rain or he's sure to trip you."

Eve stared into the round eyes looking up at her. "Is there any of him still left in there? Does he remember who he is?"

Lilith grinned widely and reached out and scratched under the sunekosuri's chin. He closed his eyes and stretched his neck, welcoming more scratches. "Maybe, but his sense of self has been...simplified."

"He doesn't have his powers anymore?"

"Well, he still has them, in some capacity. But he cannot speak, therefore he cannot command."

Veris' warm, soft weight in Eve's arms was pleasant, but she hated to think of him using that name. She wanted to squeeze him and bury her face in his silky fur, yet she hated Veris for what he'd done. Then again...how could she kill him now? How could she harm this cute little fucker?

Goddamn it.

"You killed Zeke and Eoduun, you little bastard," she said to him, hoping that saying the words aloud would make her hate him. "But... how the hell am I supposed to kill you now?"

He chirruped happily at her, nuzzling into the crook of her elbow, and her vision blurred with tears.

Fuck.

"If you want him dead, I'll kill him," Dagon offered.

Eve hugged him closer to her chest and quickly angled him away from Dagon. "Don't!" And then she was instantly irritated with herself. Maybe she should just give him to Dagon after they got away from these Locusts.

She should.

Or...

Maybe she should just give him a new name.

"Why couldn't you turn him into something ugly and slimy and gross, like a slug?" she complained to Lilith.

"This is what he turned into. I didn't choose what he would be. It was what his soul chose to be."

Luc stared warily at the sunekosuri. "What the hell does that mean?"

Eno interrupted their huddle. "Great Mother, I was wondering if I might have a few moments with you to discuss where we should go from here. I've been waiting for your arrival for millennia. I have so much to discuss with you."

Lilith studied him with curious eyes. "What do you wish to discuss with me? What concern do I have with where you go from here? I hardly know what you expect of me."

"You'll lead the revolution, of course," Eno declared. "Our time has finally come to emerge from the shadows. It's time for your children to rise to power and crush our enemies into the dirt!"

Lilith laughed, the sound both musical and terrifying. "I can sense you are blood of my blood, but do not mistake our familial bond for anything more. You do not command me. I will do as I wish, when I wish, and I certainly will not seek your counsel."

Eno was taken aback. "But…but everything we've done, we've done for you, Lilith. We've been waiting for you, preparing for your return."

Lilith tilted her head. "I fear you've mistaken me for someone who can be manipulated."

Eno was speechless for a moment. "What will you do, then? Are you forsaking us?"

"I owe you nothing. I answer to no man. Speak again, and I will cut out your tongue."

His eyes went wide, his mouth clamping shut. He turned to Eve, clearly hoping for sympathy or for her to intercede on his behalf.

Not bloody likely.

Lilith held her hand out to Eve. "Come, child. I have much to teach you. Together, you and I shall want for nothing in this world."

Eve stepped away from her, backing into Bo's arms, and Bo growled, "Evie's not leaving with you."

Lilith ignored Bo, instead studying Eve's face. She dropped her hand. "You will not go with me?"

"Why would I?!" Eve asked incredulously, holding the sunekosuri tighter.

"I can teach you my ways, and help you understand the things you still can't fathom. I can offer you everything. You are part of me and I of you."

"You can't have her," Luc said, his tone threatening. Ramil crossed his arms and moved closer to Eve. Dagon's wings flexed wider, and Isaac's knuckles whitened around the handles of his knives as they watched Lilith's every move.

Lilith didn't spare them a glance when she warned, "Quiet, boys. The ladies are speaking."

Eve scowled at her. This was *Lilith* she was talking to. She'd almost forgotten that. "I want nothing from you. You...you're a monster. You make monsters. You filled this world with evil."

"Did I, now?" Lilith raised a brow, amused. "The way I see it, I simply made new life. *Humans* made them monsters. And I certainly didn't fill the world with evil. Evil has always existed, in man, monster, god...everywhere, from the beginning of time."

"Your monsters kill people!"

"Animals kill people. The elements kill people. *People* kill people."

"Most people don't kill people," Eve argued.

Lilith crossed her arms. "Do you know why so many of my monsters go so long in society without ever being noticed? Why most of them blend in so well?" She gestured to the Locusts in the room, which all looked just as human as any true human. She then raised her hand to indicate Bo. "Why half-breeds are even possible?" When Eve didn't answer, Lilith continued, "It's because we're *all* monsters. I simply took different aspects of humanity, of primal human desires, emotions, fears, and put form to them. I didn't make monsters. I just showed humanity its real face."

Eno chimed in, "Please, Lilith, help us remove the false mask mankind has been hiding behind for far too long. Let us show them what we truly are. What *they* truly are."

Lilith shook her head. "You can show a dog its own reflection, and all it will do is bark at it. Your endeavor is pointless. If you want to start a war, start a war. You don't need me for that."

"We need your power, Great Mother. The world will listen to you. You can *make* them listen!"

To that, Lilith threw her head back and laughed. She chided, "Mankind does not listen, and if I am not mistaken, it is still *man*kind that rules this world, is it not?"

"You could rule the world," Eno suggested hopefully.

Lilith rolled her eyes. "Enough," she said impatiently, then made a small gesture with her finger, slicing it through the air and whispering an incantation.

Eno's mouth gushed blood and his tongue plopped between his feet. He stared down at it in horror, a low moan rising from his throat. He tried to speak, but blood spurted from between his lips instead of words. The crowd of Locusts began to stir, fear and unease saturating the air as they whispered among themselves, but several Locusts rushed to Eno's aid. They helped him to find a seated position on the floor, one man ripping the sleeve from his own shirt and shoving into Eno's mouth to staunch the bleeding.

The sunekosuri squirmed out of Eve's arms, startled by the sudden swarm of activity around him. He hid behind her legs.

Eve could heal Eno if she wanted to.

But did she want to?

Lilith scrutinized her. "You came here for a reason, child," Lilith said to Eve, ignoring the dramatics over Eno. "I saw it in that boy's mind. He tricked you. You didn't come to free me. You came to resurrect a dead man." She smirked. "The Blood of Eve runs deep in your veins. She was always a sentimental one." Lilith returned to the altar and leaned back against it.

Ramil glanced at the grimoire on the altar next to her. "Can he still be raised?" he asked. "Can you do it?"

"And what about Eoduun?" Eve added, hope daring to edge into her heart.

A devious grin graced Lilith's lips. "For a price."

"Name it," Eve blurted.

Lilith chuckled wickedly, then hooked her finger at Eve. "Come."

"Don't do it," Bo advised Eve, then scooped up the sunekosuri that had wandered from behind her feet and was making his way toward Eno's tongue on the floor.

Eve hesitated. "Are you going to turn me into a catdog, too?"

"I want to see what's in your heart," Lilith answered. "What on earth would possess you to blindly agree to my price...for a *man*?" she said disdainfully.

"My heart gets to stay in my chest, though, right?"

"Just come here, child. I will never hurt you. You're special."

"You're special." Eve remembered Luc saying that to her the very first time they met. Well, the very first time *she* met *him*.

"You're here because you're special."

If she had known everything that would happen because she was *special*, would she have run the other way? Would they have *let* her run the other way?

When Eve stood before her, Lilith reached her hand out and rested it over Eve's heart, closing her dark, almost black eyes. Her face scrunched as though she were in mild pain. "My, my, child. A heart torn in so many directions." She opened her eyes and looked down at Eve, her hand still on Eve's chest. "You're a bubbling cauldron of emotions. There's so much *love*. I almost forgot what love felt like." She pulled her hand away, adding, "I forgot how much it hurts. It really is the most wicked curse of all."

Eve didn't argue. "Will you do it? Will you bring Zeke and Eoduun back?"

Lilith sighed, and for a brief moment, Eve thought she saw something that resembled sympathy in those immortal eyes. "No."

Eve's heart shattered.

"But you can do it yourself," Lilith continued, "if you are willing to accept my powers."

Her eyes widened. "Really? Tell me what to do! I'll do it!" she begged eagerly.

Lilith held a hand up. "Wait. You must understand the curse that comes with *my* powers, child. When you take someone's power or steal a curse, it will be yours forever. It will no longer fade. And the more you collect, the more powerful you become, the more you will become like *me*."

"What do you mean, *like you*?"

"All that love in your heart? All those human things that make you *you*? They will begin to slip away. Little by little, your ability to *feel* will diminish. I used up all of my humanity to create my monsters. Where do you think I got the inspiration? After Adam, I wanted nothing to do with humanity, with the complicated emotions. So I put them into my monsters. I put my desire into the vampires, my greed into the wendigo, my contempt for men into the lilim and succubus, my primal instincts into the werewolves and skinwalkers, my indecisiveness into the shapeshifters, my rage into the gorgons and basilisks, my need for control into the witches…the endless collection of human emotions made for a wide array of creatures, as you well know. I traded my humanity to reign over my beasts. That is the price you will have to pay to wield my power."

"What about your love, your positive emotions?"

Lilith tilted her head toward the sunekosuri in Bo's arms. "Not all of my monsters are born of darkness." When Eve looked back at her boys, Lilith informed her, "I've made it so they can't understand this conversation. To them, we're speaking a language no one has ever heard. This doesn't concern them."

"I don't want to make this decision without them," Eve said.

"You must. You are the only one who *can* make this decision. What will you do? Will you throw away your humanity for two mere men? And if you do, will they still love you after the sacrifice you made for them?"

"What if I choose not to steal abilities anymore? Would that keep me from turning into you?"

"You would squander such power?"

"If I had to."

The condescending smile on Lilith's lips was knowing. "Even if you needed those abilities to protect the ones you love?"

Eve hesitated.

Lilith sighed. "Yes, you could keep the curse at bay if you chose not to acquire any abilities or curses. But you're already holding onto an overabundance of power, and this offer will expire when you leave this room. It's now or never, child."

Eve was crippled with indecision as she stared at all those concerned faces looking back at her. And then her gaze landed on Isaac.

The exorcist.

Eve turned back to Lilith, her eyes gleaming with renewed hope. "A priest was able to exorcise my stolen abilities once. He wiped the slate clean. If I had your power, would he still be able to do that?"

Lilith considered the question. "He might be able to cleanse your stolen powers, but he can never cure you of my curse."

"But if I didn't *accumulate* powers, if I got *rid* of them regularly, would it be like I never had them at all? Would I stay myself, or would I still become like you?"

Lilith looked off to the side, contemplating. Finally, she admitted, "It's very possible you could remain as you are. But are you willing to risk it? And what happens if the priest who could work such magic were to die?"

"I won't let him die," Eve avowed. She set her shoulders and steeled her expression. "I've decided."

40

Raise Your Monsters

"Give me your curse," Eve implored.

Lilith canted her head. "As you wish, child. But know that I can never revoke this gift. It will be with you forever. No turning back."

"I'm aware."

Lilith pushed away from the altar and stood before Eve. "One more thing. Once you have this power, your abilities will surpass even my own. You will have the power to destroy me. You must vow to never use your power against me. A blood pact."

For as much as Eve had feared Lilith, she had no desire to destroy her. She felt connected to her. A kinship. But if she threatened Knighco? That was a different story.

"I'll agree to it on one condition," Eve said. "You can never use your powers against anyone I care about."

Lilith shrugged. "You leave me be, I'll leave you be. I am not here to mindlessly wreak havoc."

"What about the Book of Revelation in the Bible? These Locusts of Abaddon believed you to be the second-coming described there. They believed you were going to bring the Apocalypse. Are you?"

Lilith shook her head and chuckled. "Ah, yes. The Apocalypse. Do you know what 'apocalypse' actually means? It's simply another word for 'revelation.' Mankind twisted it to mean catastrophic destruction. They took liberties with the story I planted in that man's head back in that cave on Patmos."

"How were you able to do that? I thought you were trapped, sealed away."

"That cave touches dangerously close to the borders of the Abyss. Many call it the Veil. A nothingness between worlds. Imagine my luck when some poor fool stumbled into it, his mind wide open for manipulation. I fed him a story, little by little, piece by piece, through the cracks in the Veil. I gave him the ingredients needed to release me, the ingredients I inscribed in my grimoire when I became aware of the plans the other gods had for me. See, they weren't pleased with my growing powers, or my distribution of power to mortals. Power that rivaled theirs. They hated me from the moment I gifted Adam with 'knowledge.'

"So, when I saw my chance, I gave that list to the man in the cave, woven into a story that would trick the world into thinking it would bring the return of whatever beloved god they most worshipped at the time. The rest? The parts about punishment and destruction and the end of the wicked world? That was their own addition."

Eve felt like the whole world of black and white, good and evil, monsters and mankind, had been tipped on its head, and Lilith's revelation only deepened that sense.

There were only varying shades of grey, and righteousness was relative.

Lilith used her long fingernail to slice a gash into her own wrist, the crimson blood quickly pooling to the surface and dripping from her arm. She held up her bleeding arm. "Are you satisfied I'm not going to destroy the world? Shall we continue?"

Did she believe Lilith?

Did she have a choice?

"Yes."

Lilith took Eve's hand and swiped her sharp nail over Eve's wrist, drawing blood. She pressed her own bloody wrist to Eve's and grasped her forearm, holding tight. "Vow you will never use your power against me, and I vow to never use mine against you or those you care about."

Eve gripped Lilith's strong forearm. "I vow."

"I vow," Lilith followed.

Eve felt a brief surge flow through her, and she knew the pact had been completed.

Lilith released her arm and raised her wrist to Eve's face. She chanted under her breath, then said, "I gift my power to you. Drink."

Blood spilled over Eve's tongue as she took Lilith's wrist to her mouth, and with the first swallow, there was a shift inside of her. The monster she kept caged began to change. It no longer felt like something *other*, like a parasite she was simply host to. It grew and morphed, melding with the very fiber of her being. Its power swelled, but with it, a sense of control.

The cage ceased to exist, but it was no longer needed. The wild, untamable curse she had struggled with matured into something more sophisticated as it fused with her. Her will pushed into it and its will into her, and they finally understood each other.

The war inside was over.

Lilith stepped back and picked up the grimoire from the altar. She flipped it open to a page in the middle of the book and handed it to Eve. "Pick two bodies and raise your monsters."

Eve frowned. "My monsters?"

"Yes. But then I will be taking my grimoire back, and you will no longer have access to it."

"Wait, what do you mean *monsters*?"

"I mean precisely that. If you want your boys back, you must raise them as monsters. That is my power."

Eve's heart stopped. "You never said I had to make them into monsters."

"I thought it was implied."

Eve stared down at the grimoire, the words on the page now fully within her understanding. It was no different than reading a book written in English. At the top of the spell page, it was labeled "Binding Lost Soul to Form."

"What will they become?" Eve asked.

"Whatever their soul decides."

Lilith sashayed into the uneasy crowd and selected two Locusts near the front, and they regarded her with awe. "You two have been chosen by your queen," she told them, then guided them to the altar. She directed the first onto the altar, then the other, and instructed them to lie back.

Luc, Dagon, Bo, Isaac, and Ramil all moved to Eve's side.

"What's happening?" Bo demanded, shifting the weight of the sunekosuri in his arms.

"What was she telling you?" Luc inquired.

Dagon assessed Eve. "She changed you."

Isaac just stared at the aura around Eve, wide-eyed.

"What is she doing?" Ramil asked, watching Lilith drip blood from her wrist into the first Locust's mouth.

Eve looked down at the grimoire. Part of the dead body was required for the spell. Lilith must be supplying it, since Eoduun's body had become hers. She would need Dagon's blood for Zeke.

Luc furrowed his pale brow. "Is she making monsters?"

Eve looked up at him. "No. I am. If we want Eoduun and Zeke back, they have to come back as monsters." She looked at Dagon. "I need you to offer your blood to the other Locust on that altar."

"As you wish, princess."

Bo frowned as he watched Dagon walk past, and Eve felt his discomfort in her own chest. "Is that what they would want? To come back as monsters?"

"As long as we love them, it won't matter what they are," Eve answered. "We're all monsters anyway."

Eve performed the ritual as her entourage and the crowd of Locusts looked on nervously. Eno watched from behind her, still seated on the floor, the blood-soaked shirt sleeve stuffed in his mouth.

This was wrong. Stealing the lives of two strangers to bring back her own loved ones wasn't something the *good guy* would do. She knew that. They all knew that, yet none of them were stopping her.

As she'd said before: she'd do the most appalling things to get Zeke back. She'd meant it.

When Eve read the last word of the spell, the Locusts on the altar began to writhe. The first arched his back, his mouth gaping open. Two long fangs sprouted, then receded back into normal-looking canines.

Vampire.

The body bulged and bent, slowly morphing into the familiar shape Eve knew well. Silky black hair fell over his face as Eoduun sat up. He swiped his hair from his eyes, looking around in confusion.

The second Locust was only a moment behind, his body swelling with muscles, his jaw widening and his neck thickening. A grotesque, monstrous face formed, two great horns erupting from his skull and curling back. His skin took on a strangely stony appearance, and when he sat up on the altar, two great, stony wings unfolded behind him with the sound of scraping granite.

Though Eve had never seen such a creature, the powers she'd accepted from Lilith allowed her to sense what Zeke had become.

Gargoyle.

Deep-golden eyes blinked open. He looked over at Eoduun.

"...Zeke?" Eoduun questioned fearfully, staring at Zeke's changed appearance. "Zeke, is that you?"

"What happened?!" Zeke panicked as he looked down at himself. His voice was rough and gravelly. He opened and closed his huge, clawed hands, marveling at the unusual texture of his skin, but as he did so, the texture faded. His strange eyes shifted to a soft caramel color, and his horrific visage shifted and shrank, taking on the handsome, athletic form Eve knew.

Well, almost. His wings hadn't disappeared. He glanced behind him, widening his eyes at the protrusions on his back, and as he turned to try to get a better look, one of his wings knocked Eoduun off the altar.

"Jesus, dude!" Eoduun grunted, clambering up off the floor. "Watch it!"

Eve's heart lodged in her throat, joyful tears welling in her eyes. She rushed to them, leaping into Zeke's lap and throwing her arms around his big neck. She squeezed him so tightly, if he were anyone else, she would've broken him in half. His huge arms encircled her, and her heart swelled with such love she feared it might burst. Her sweet, sunshine boy. She grabbed his face and peppered kisses all over him.

"Babe," he chuckled, scrunching his nose.

"I missed you so much, Z," she cried.

Still holding onto Zeke with one arm, she reached over to Eoduun as he dusted off his pants. She fisted his shirt, yanking him back onto the altar to join in the hug. "Come here, fucker," she blubbered, then pressed their faces to either side of hers, wetting their cheeks with the tears streaming from her eyes. She was smiling so hard it hurt.

Eoduun turned his face to her neck, inhaling deeply. "You smell fucking delicious," he whispered. "Fuck, I'm so thirsty. Why am I so thirsty?" He sat back suddenly, fear in his eyes. "Why do I want to eat you, Eve?" He curled his lips back, and the fangs were back. He touched them gingerly with his fingertips, then made a panicked sound. "Eve?!"

Eve framed his face with her hands and bumped her forehead to his as the rest of the team surrounded them. "I know. I know," she comforted. "Don't be scared. I will feed you. I will always feed you. We will work through this. It's all going to be ok."

Luc ruffled Zeke's hair. "It's good to have you back, Z. Love the wings."

"What's going on?" Zeke wondered, slightly dazed. "What was wrong with my face and hands a minute ago? Why do I have wings?" His eyes widened. "Am I an angel? Am I dead?!" He frowned. "I did die, didn't I? In that circle. Ruth released Dagon. I...I died."

Eoduun grabbed Zeke and hugged him, kissing him on the cheek. He answered, "You did die. We were here to bring you back." He released him from his embrace, then looked at Zeke's wings again. "But I don't understand what happened. Or why we're like *this*." Then he saw the fluffy critter in Bo's arms. "What the fuck is that?"

Eve took the sunekosuri from Bo and held it out to Eoduun. Eoduun took it from her, hooking his hands under its forelegs and holding it up in front of his face as it studied him with big, reddish-brown eyes.

"Don't eat it," Eve warned, only somewhat jokingly.

"Whatever," Eoduun grumbled, then placed the sunekosuri on the floor.

As Eoduun climbed down from the altar, he gave Lilith a wary glance. He turned to Eve. "Who is that? What happened? Why are we like this, Eve?"

"We were betrayed. This was the only way I could fix everything"

"I'm a vampire, aren't I? And that's *Lilith*," he spat. He looked at Zeke again. "What is he?"

"Am I a Weeping Angel?" Zeke ventured in a hushed tone.

Eve laughed through her tears. "No, you're a gargoyle."

Luc ushered Eoduun and Zeke away from the altar, dodging Zeke's stony yet oddly flexible wings. "We'll debrief later." He gave

Eoduun a wary glance. "Just focus on keeping your thirst under control for now."

The rest of the crowd began to erupt in protests. "What is this?!" they demanded. "This isn't what we were promised! You're supposed to make more monsters, not change us!"

Lilith's eyes turned fully black, shouting, "You dare to question your *Great Mother!?!* You dare to question your *queen?!*" Her voice rang thunderously through the room, and the Locusts fell to their knees once again, silence on their lips. She turned back to Eve, the blackness of her eyes fading into dark irises. She held out her hand. "I will take my grimoire now. It needs to be destroyed."

Destroyed? But what if she needed it again? Eve stared down at it, and as she considered *not* giving it back to Lilith, she took a step back – and tripped over the sunekosuri, stepping on his foot.

He let out a pained yowl, and all hell broke loose.

41

Kiss My Naked Ass

The grimoire was snatched from her hands as she tumbled to the floor, a swarm of angry, shouting Locusts descending on her and her team. Some were transforming into their true forms, fangs, claws, horns, and wings erupting from the bodies.

The sunekosuri darted under the altar, and when Eve looked to the place where Lilith had been standing only a moment ago, she was gone.

And then Ramil was on top of her, his hands around her throat. He looked like he was desperately trying to tighten his grip, his eyes shining strangely and brimming with rage, but his hands wouldn't cooperate. She still had his power, and he couldn't truly harm her. She thrust her arms up between his forearms and broke his hold on her, then drove her hips up to roll him off of her.

"Everyone will believe I am dead as soon as I leave this room. But if anyone tries to hurt me before then, you will attack them and defend me with your lives."

Apparently, Veris' compulsion was a standing order, even as a sunekosuri.

"What the fuck?!" Luc shouted as he grabbed Ramil by the throat and tried to hold him at bay. The others surrounded her and fought off Locusts who were trying to get to her. Even Eno had forgotten about his injury and was trying to push through the crowd toward her. Eoduun was viciously tearing into necks, his face covered in blood, as Zeke knocked them away with his wings and ripped through their flesh with his huge fangs and claws, having shifted back to his gargoyle form. Dagon was striking them down with his telekinetic forces before they could even get near him, and Isaac and Bo were cutting them down in a flurry of knifes.

"Get the catdog and get it out of here!" Eve commanded as she caught a Locust by the neck and snapped it. Power tingled through her limbs, itching to be used, but she was afraid of her precision if she tried. "He's under the altar! They'll stop when he's gone!"

Bo argued, "We can't get to it! There's too many of them!" He slashed his knife across a Locust's throat, spraying blood all over himself.

"Then just get out! It's me they want, and they won't stop until they're dead!" She could kill everyone in this room, but she didn't want to risk friendly fire. She needed the freedom to rage, unimpeded.

We're not leaving you, princess, Dagon said in her head.

"I don't want to kill you, Ramil, but I fucking will! Do you really want me to use my full power?!" Luc warned, electrical sparks dancing from his fingertips as Ramil charged him, trying to get past him to Eve. When the electricity coursed through Ramil, however, he barely flinched.

Instead, he began to grow, scales forming over his skin.

Oh, fuck.

Eve needed to get her boys out of here. *Now.* Either they would kill Ramil, or Ramil would kill them. She just got Zeke back, and she wasn't about to lose anyone else ever again. But they wouldn't just leave. She would have to *make* them leave.

She drew from Apep's incredible abilities and focused her mind on the god realm. She could see it, faintly flickering all around her, like double-exposure film. She didn't have time to pick a specific reality, but she knew she would find everyone afterward. They were connected in a way that couldn't be severed by space or time.

The air around Luc began to glow brighter, the stone floor and walls vibrating with energy as he gaped up at Ramil's transformation.

He was about to go nuclear.

She couldn't let him do that.

Eve popped up behind him and shoved him, and he disappeared through the thin veil into the domain of the gods. She used Dagon's telekinetic powers to simultaneously shove the rest of them through, too. They would be pissed, but they would be safe long enough for Eve to do what she had to do.

She looked up at Ramil. He had grown so large, she could no longer see the ends of his wings or his head, as they were lost in the darkness above. The Locusts around her closed in on her, snarling and shouting, and she grinned.

Time to rage.

As she inhaled, she called on Ramil's powers, feeling a slight burning in her chest. Then she exhaled forcefully, spewing forth a wall of flame. She spun around, instantly incinerating every Locust within a ten-foot radius. She began to draw another breath, readying herself for the next wave.

But she was suddenly inside an inferno, fire raging all around her. Her clothes crumbled to ash, but her skin felt only the lightest licks of warmth, as though she were standing next to a cozy fireplace. The Locusts that had been barreling down on her barely had time to scream before the flames devoured them.

When the inferno ceased, Eve looked up into huge, angry, copper-green eyes as Ramil lowered his head. My, but he was a sight to behold. When this was all over, she was going to have to get him out to some remote field and make him show her himself in the daylight.

She had no time to worry about modesty as she began to run toward the Locusts still coming at her. "You missed me, darling," she taunted behind her. "Kiss my naked ass!" Flames rushed past her, and the next wave of Locusts were turned to ash.

She bolted for the other side of the room, right between the columns of Ramil's legs, where more monsters of all shapes and sizes were scrambling to get to her. She took a note from Apep's book and focused on the first Locust running toward her, then snapped her fingers, willing his heart to stop with the sound. The Locust fell in a tumbling heap, tripping the ones behind him.

Eve let loose a blast of energy, and the wave of Locusts rushing toward her exploded, as though they'd all had grenades lodged inside their bellies.

Ramil's flames roared around her once again, his wrath meant only for her, but instead descending upon the Locusts that had escaped her blast.

Eve glanced around the demolished room as Ramil took a few thundering steps toward her, his tail sweeping like a wrecking ball through the pews behind him, the enclosed space encumbering the movement of his gargantuan body. The sunekosuri had to be dead, didn't it? The altar was smoldering tinder. But if he was dead, did that mean that Ramil would *never* stop trying to kill her?

Shit.

But if the sunekosuri was dead, wouldn't it be someone else who harmed it? If it was dead, and it wasn't her who killed it, wouldn't the Locusts have attacked the one who did?

Was it still alive somewhere in here?

Ramil was still coming for her, and another wall of flames erupted around her. She teleported to the other side of the room, dodging the huge, clawed foot he swiped at her. She began searching through the rubble and overturned pews, trying to catch any scent that could be the cute little catdog.

As she whispered, "Here, little critter," she heard a shuffle behind her. She whipped around, hoping to see round, curious eyes, but instead, she found herself face to face with the last Locust left. The one that only she could kill.

Eno.

He lunged at her, and she threw her hand out to stop him, unwittingly casting a powerful surge of energy at him. His head snapped all the way back, his bones cracking with sickening, muffled snaps, and he dropped to the floor. She stared at the broken pile of flesh and bone that landed at her feet, shocked at the immediate consequences of her lack of control.

Thousands of years of life, and she'd just extinguished him in the breadth of a moment. Her own father. She didn't even know if she really wanted to kill him.

But...

He'd lived long enough.

Eve looked up at the dragon in the middle of the room, Ramil's snakelike neck twisting around, his enormous head turning from side to side, searching for her.

She had to stop him, but she couldn't kill him. She *wouldn't* kill him. He was quite possibly the last dragon in all of existence, and he didn't deserve to die like this, under the compulsion of a weaselly little shyster Ramil thought was his best friend.

She needed to find that cute little tripping demon.

Dagon suddenly appeared in front of her, startling her, and her fist flung out and punched him in the ribs. He doubled over, wrapping one giant wing around himself. "Ouch! Fuck, princess!"

"Sorry!" she apologized. "What the fuck are you doing here?!"

"You can't trap a god in the god realm," he answered, his gaze roving her naked form. "Why are you naked?"

Eve gestured to the dragon in the middle of the room as Ramil's eyes found them. "It got hot in here. I took off all my clothes."

"Why haven't you killed him yet? You have the power to do so."

Eve grabbed at Dagon as he turned to square up against Ramil, who was now advancing on them.

"Don't fight him! Help me find the stupid catdog!"

Then Eve heard a helicopter outside. What the fuck?

Ramil unleashed his fiery breath once more, and Eve allowed it to engulf her while Dagon teleported out of its path. She reached out mentally, *Go see what that helicopter is doing here. I will take care of Ramil and the fucking catdog. He can't hurt me, but he can hurt you.*

Aw, are you worried about me?

Go!

Eve heard an exasperated sigh through their mental connection, and when the flames ceased, he was no longer in the room. But her eyes caught a flash of movement.

The sunekosuri!

He was darting from cover to cover at an unbelievable pace. Eve teleported to where he was, but he had already scampered across the room, running straight between Ramil's feet. He was going to get himself killed, and Eve didn't know what would happen if he did.

"Be careful, you little shit!"

She tried to cut him off, teleporting to the location he was headed, but he veered around her and dodged her hands. Everywhere she popped up, he was one step ahead.

This was pointless. She couldn't catch the little fucking gingerbread man. Maybe if she could guide him to the stairs, he would run up them of his own accord.

The other hunters are here. They're climbing out of the helicopter, but they haven't seen me. Should I go give them a surprise welcome?

Goddamn it, no! What are they doing here?! How many are there?

All of them, Dagon answered.

In one helicopter?

It's a big helicopter.

Shit. Ramil wouldn't want them to see him like this. *She* didn't want them to see him like this. They couldn't interfere or someone would get hurt. She needed to do something fast, and catching the damn catdog was proving impossible.

Distract them, she told Dagon. *But don't hurt anyone! And don't get yourself killed, got it?*

I knew you loved me.

Fuck you!

Eve gave an angry groan and rolled her head back as Ramil's fire hit her once again. "Just stop! You're wasting your breath, you dumb bastard!" She looked up at him when he was finished, and an idea struck her. She teleported, landing on top of his snout, and she dropped down to onto her belly and clung for dear life to his rough scales.

She glanced down. Fuck, she was really high up. She hated heights. She focused on the big eyes staring back at her, and dove straight into his mind.

Confusion roiled, his thoughts consumed only with his desire to destroy her. She needed to bring order to his chaos, calm to his storm. But first, she needed to physically stop him. She pushed her will against his, stretching out in his enormous body. She fought for control of his neck, then his legs, his wings, and finally, his tail. She blinked her eyes, *his* eyes, and saw herself lying limply on his snout.

She wrested control from him and slowly, gingerly, she lowered his massive head and deposited her body onto the floor next to the stairs, where she wouldn't accidentally step on herself. His left hind leg stamped angrily as he briefly took control of it, his fury flowing through her, but she forced him down again.

She quickly sorted through his memories, seeking out a sense of serenity. She needed to calm him and bury him in his own mind until she could usher the sunekosuri to the stairs.

There! She heard singing, and a cozy, sweet feeling warmed her. She saw an old woman with white hair tied back in a bun walking into the room. Ramil was lying in a soft, comfortable bed, blankets tucked up to his chin, and he smiled when Tillie sat next to him, her weight shifting the mattress slightly.

"What's wrong, Ram?" she asked, her voice surprisingly rich and smooth for her age. "Can't sleep?"

Ramil loved Tillie, and Eve understood from his memory that she was the one who took care of him as a small child. Other than Eno, she was the only one who didn't look at him with fear in her eyes. Just kindness and love.

"I had a bad dream. I turned into Godzilla and ate everyone."

Tillie gave him a sympathetic smile. "Oh, my poor darling, that is scary. Would a happy song make you feel better?"

He nodded his little head.

Tillie ran her thin, wrinkled hand over his head in slow, soothing strokes, and she began to sing. The song was soft and joyful, and Ramil was instantly at ease, as though Tillie were casting a calming spell on him.

He didn't know it at the time, but he would learn later that Tillie was a Siren, and her songs could make people feel whatever she wanted them to feel.

She always used them to make him feel happy.

Eve pulled away from the memory, leaving Ramil to calm down with Tillie. She clumsily moved her dragon body, scanning the room for the sunekosuri. She slowly swept her long tail from one side of the room to the other, and finally, the little catdog leapt out from behind some debris and ran toward the other side of the room, toward where the stairs were. Eve moved forward, keeping her tail curved to provide a barrier to keep the critter from retreating back to where he came from.

As she got closer, he ran again, even closer to the stairs. Eve shifted her body so she was facing the stairwell, and she lay down, stretching her forelegs out to block in the sunekosuri. But he still wouldn't run up the stairs. He ran to them, then panicked and huddled at the bottom step, flattening himself out like a scolded pet.

She was afraid to use her enormous taloned toe to nudge him up the stairs, but how was she going to get him to move? If she were in her body, she could reach out and grab him now. But if she relinquished control of Ramil's body, would he stay calm, or would he be wrenched from his memory and rage again?

She lowered her head and huffed, and the gust of wind swept up the stairwell and rattled a dry leaf midway up the steps. The sunekosuri's head twisted in the direction of the sound, his pupils blowing wide. His short little tail trembled. Eve huffed again, and when the leaf rattled, the catdog bound up two steps and huddled down, peeking up over the next step, waiting. One more huff, a few more steps. Eve lowered her head more and huffed up the stairs, blowing the leaf up several steps, and the sunekosuri darted up the stairs for it.

Eve meant to make a small sound of victory, but coming through the throat of a dragon, it was roar. It startled both Eve and the catdog, and he bolted the rest of the way up the stairs, out of sight.

42

Compromised

A splitting headache drew a pained groan from Eve when she returned to her own body. She stood up slowly, dusting the dirt and ash from her naked skin. She looked over at Ramil, and he was already shrinking, morphing back into a man.

What's going on up there? Eve asked Dagon.

I'm sitting on the ground with guns pointed at my head. They want to know where Luc is. They said he sent a cryptic message telling them you all might be in danger and to come at once, ready for battle. They refuse to listen to anything I say. Can I hurt someone now?

No. Give me a minute to retrieve the boys, and I'll be up.

I am dangerously close to unburdening Ruger of his vocal cords. You'd better hurry if you want your hunters to remain intact, princess.

You leave him alone! Fucking bully.

He keeps calling me Batboy!

Eve didn't bother with a response, as Ramil had fully returned to normal.

"I am so sorry, Eve! I couldn't—"

"I know, I know," she interrupted. "No time for apologies. I need to go get my team. The rest of Knighco is outside holding Dagon at gunpoint. Can you handle that until I get back?

He nodded and headed for the stairs.

Eve stepped into the god realm, using her bond with Bo to guide her to her team. When she appeared before them, they were equal parts relieved and pissed, right after they got past the initial shock at her disheveled, naked state.

She was just as shocked at their battered condition. She hadn't noticed how rough they looked when she ejected them from the fight.

Bo and Isaac both quickly grabbed her and began to inspect for injury while Luc unbuttoned and shrugged off his shirt, draping it over Eve's shoulders. As he buttoned it up for her, he looked down at her from over top his sunglasses, his aquamarine eyes full of fear.

Fear for her.

"Don't ever fucking do that again," he reprimanded. "How the fuck did you get like this?"

"Forget me. Look at you guys!" Bo's tactical vest and shirt were both ripped and covered in blood. She reached over and lifted Isaac's bloody shirt, and gasped at the gashes and ugly purple bruises blooming over his torso. He was lucky he couldn't feel pain, because if he could, he'd be in agony. She turned to Luc and grabbed his jaw, angling his face so she could see the black eye and cut across his eyebrow. "Fuck, guys," she lamented.

"I'm ok," Zeke remarked, looking down at his unscathed flesh. "I think my skin turns to rock when I'm in my monster form."

Eve looked him over. "Not a single scratch." She cupped his handsome face in her hands and smiled at him. Was it wrong of her to be a little disappointed that she didn't get to heal him?

She grabbed one of Isaac's knives and sliced it across her hand, shoving the bloodied injury into Bo's mouth first, before he could protest. She bit her lip and squeezed her thighs together as pleasure crashed through her, again and again, as she healed her team.

"So what happened?" Luc inquired. "Where are we? Why the fuck can't I teleport out of here, yet Dagon can?"

"The situation has been handled." Eve replied, checking over Isaac's injuries again to make sure they were healing. "I'll explain later. But we need to get back, because the other hunters showed up and they're threatening Dagon."

"Back from *where*?" Luc persisted.

"The god realm! Where anything is possible!" Eve answered in exasperation, waving her arms wide.

"Disneyland?" Zeke questioned, confused.

"That's where dreams are made of, genius," Eoduun snapped.

"No, *that's* New York, Jay-Z." Luc said. "Disneyland is where dreams come true."

Isaac huffed and impatiently pushed Eve's probing hands away. He signed, *Can we go now?!*

"Yes!" Eve agreed. "Let's go! We need to convince the other hunters not to kill Dagon."

"Do we, though?" Luc hedged.

Eve narrowed her eyes at him.

"He showed me how to put away my wings before he disappeared," Zeke offered in defense of Dagon, and Eve only then noticed that he was no longer sporting the stony appendages. "That was pretty nice of him."

Isaac pointed to the side and shook his head as he brushed his thumb under his chin and swiped one palm over the other. *He's* not *nice.*

"Nice is not a word I would ever use to describe Dagon," Bo retorted at the same time.

"He doesn't have to be nice," Eve argued. "He's an asset to our team. I think he's proven he's safe to keep around."

Eoduun scoffed. "An asset. Is that the *only* reason you want to keep him around?"

Eve shoved them all out of the god realm before they could notice the blush on her cheeks.

"He was free to roam this whole time?!" Roy barked in his gruff, grouchy tone as Luc led the team out the front doors of the building into the cool, night air. Dagon was no longer sitting on the ground, but lying on his back with his ankles crossed and hands behind his head, his wings tucked away, and a bored, annoyed expression on his face while Roy waved the barrel of his shotgun at him.

The other hunters warily watched the sparse assembly of curious Locusts and children who hadn't been at the ritual as they looked on from a distance, concerned. They had no idea what had transpired in that underground cathedral.

"Eve!" Cassie exclaimed when Eve walked out the door behind Luc wearing only his shirt, her body still smeared in blood and ash. Cassie sheathed her katana and ran to her. "Are you ok?! What happened?!" she fretted, pulling Eve into a bearhug. "Who do I have to kill?!"

"What the fuck is going on here?" Mendal demanded.

Zephlyn frowned. "It was my vision, wasn't it? The beasts and the chalice and the monsters rising from the pit." He looked to Eve for confirmation.

Then Zeke walked out of the building behind the rest of his team, and everyone fell into a shocked silence.

"Dude, I know it's dark, but that looks like Zeke," Ruger whispered loudly to Remi.

"Yeah," Remi replied, drawing out the word.

"I thought he was dead," Ruger continued, and Cassie elbowed him in the ribs.

"He is," Remi replied slowly, a deep furrow in his brow.

Kai approached and sniffed Zeke. "Not a shifter," he marveled. "You smell like Zeke, but…something's off." He scrutinized Zeke briefly. "Zombie?"

"He's a gargoyle," Eve answered. "It was the only way to bring him back. We had no choice."

Luc revealed to the other hunters that they originally came here to try to resurrect Zeke.

"*That's* what this whole thing was about?" Mira seethed. "To bring back *one* team member?" She held a hand up to Zeke. "Not that I have anything against you." She then turned to Luc. "We've lost people who were way more valuable than him, and no one has ever suggested trying to bring them back. But your whore says she wa—"

Mira's words were cut off as a crack of thunder peeled, the ground quaking beneath their feet. Luc toed up to Mira and looked down at her, lowering his sunglasses. "My *what*?" His tone was low and threatening.

Mira looked off to the side, cowed. "This was a poor use of resources," she replied, her tone suddenly timid. "You sent a helicopter to collect us all from our missions, just to get us here, but for what? I feel like you didn't think this through, that you may be…"

"I may be what?"

Mira twisted her lip in her teeth. "Compromised," she whispered.

Luc's spine straightened, his eyes widening. "You wouldn't."

"It's my job to report back to him, Luc. It's your ass or mine, and I'm incredibly fond of my ass."

"You know what he'll do, Mira. I can't allow you to do that," he warned.

"You've made a mess of things. You can't deny it. Or, rather, you've let *her* make a mess of things. Even if I don't tell him, he's going to find out." Mira crossed her arms and took a step back, looking Luc in the eye. "Your father is not one to be trifled with."

"And neither am I," he growled between clenched teeth.

Eve interjected. "Let me speak with Victor. Maybe I can make him see things our way." And by that, she meant she was going to threaten him.

Mira scowled at Eve. "And why would he listen to you?"

Ramil chimed in, "She can be very persuasive."

Celeste cleared her throat. "Speaking of persuasive, where's Veris?"

Ramil and Isaac both looked confused, but in unison, Bo, Luc, and Eoduun all said, "He's dead."

"Lilith killed him," Bo added.

The hunters all began to speak at once in shock and outrage, wanting to know how it was possible.

Eve didn't bother to argue. Let them all believe it. "Veris wasn't who you thought he was," she said. "He was using his specialty to manipulate us all. He wanted Lilith raised, thinking she would take away his powers and make him normal. But she didn't do it the way he thought she would."

"And where is Lilith now?" Zephlyn inquired.

No one answered.

"Beautiful," Ruger groaned.

"Should I start looking for her?" Levi offered.

"How big of a fucking mess did you guys make?" Mira demanded, glowering at Eve.

Rain started to sprinkle down on them.

"I refuse to sit in the mud," Dagon said as he pushed up off the ground. He towered over the whole group, and everyone took a step back, shouldering their guns once more. Dagon ignored them and sauntered over to Eve. "Game's over. I'll see you at home, princess," he announced, pressing a kiss to the top of her head before disappearing.

Everyone stared at her in horror. Except Cassie. Cassie looked horrified, *and* intrigued.

Kai pointed at Eve. "Did he just—"

Luc dragged his hand down his face and interrupted with, "Let's get back to our own compound." He eyed the remaining Locusts, mostly the elderly and children, who were slowly moving closer to the helicopter and hunters, trying to see what was going on. "We can hash this all out there." He held his arms out and swung them toward the helicopter as the rain picked up. "Load up."

"'Get to the choppa!'" Ruger exclaimed, doing his best Schwarzenegger impression.

"Oh my god," Cassie complained, rolling her eyes.

Zeke was the only one who laughed out loud, but Eve may have snorted a little.

A lot had changed, but these were still her people.

Except Mira. Mira could choke on a pinecone.

As Eve made her way to the helicopter, something snaked between her legs, tripping her up. Isaac caught her arm, stopping her fall, and Eve looked down.

The sunekosuri rubbed against her legs, looking up at her sweetly. He made a strange little chirpy bark. Isaac picked it up and held it in front of him, studying it with a cigarette hanging between his lips. Eve saw the tiniest hint of a smirk lift the corner of his mouth. He tucked the critter under his arm and turned to Eve, signing with one hand, *His mist is bright.* Then he raised his brows and added, *Can we keep him?*

Eve chuckled and bobbed her fist. *Yes.*

They boarded the large, luxury helicopter, and Luc took his seat next to Eve. Bo sat on the other side of her, and Isaac sat next to him with the sunekosuri curled up in his lap. Ramil, Eoduun, and Zeke sat across from her. As much as Eve was desperate to be near Zeke, to touch him and make sure he was still real, she knew Eoduun needed his proximity more than she did. She knew he had a *right* to Zeke's proximity more than she did. He deserved to have Zeke's attention to himself for a while, so she gave them space, even though she wanted to plant herself between them and revel in the knowledge that they were ok.

She shifted her focus to Luc, asking him the question that had been burning in her mind since the hunters arrived. "When did you have time to call everyone here?"

Luc held up his phone. "Deadman's switch. I had a message set up that, if something happened to me and I was unable to cancel it, it would go out to all the teams, directing them to show up here, guns blazing."

"And you bought a helicopter just for that?"

"I didn't buy it. I borrowed it without permission. But to be fair, I didn't expect to have to borrow it at all. I told my pilot yesterday to be ready in case he got a message today, but—"

"You *stole* a helicopter?!"

Luc pointed to the cockpit. "Technically, my friend Harvey here stole it, but he doesn't know he stole it. He thinks we have permission."

"Whose is it?!"

"My father's. But he hardly ever uses it anyway. He'll never know it's missing." He draped his arm along the backrest, and when his hand accidentally brushed Bo's shoulder, Bo turned and gave it an irritated glance.

Luc flicked him in the ear.

"Ow! Asshole!" Bo hissed, cupping his hand over his ear.

"Luc!" Eve chastised. She leaned over and kissed Bo's ear, and he rested his hand on her ashy, naked thigh.

It suddenly occurred to her that it wasn't *just* ash. "I'm covered in remains," she pointed out. She swiped her finger through the dusty grey material coating her leg, then held it up. "Cremated bodies."

Luc draped his hand over her shoulder and tugged at a lock of her hair. "Will you rub my cremated remains all over your body when I die?"

She gave him a disgusted look. "No!" Then added, "I'm not cremating you. I'm keeping you in my closet, remember?"

"Mmm, yes, your sex corpse. How silly of me. You can't fuck dust."

"You two are fucking ridiculous," Bo sighed.

Eve heard Cassie trying to talk to Isaac. "Is that some kind of cat? Where did you get it? It's so cute!" She wandered from her seat and plopped down next to Isaac. She reached over and stroked the sunekosuri's soft fur, and it climbed out of Isaac's lap and into hers.

"Awww! It likes me! What's its name?"

Isaac looked over at Eve. He tapped two H-handshapes perpendicularly across each other, then pointed toward the sunekosuri, raising his palms with his brows furrowed. *What's his name?*

She couldn't just call him Veris. She *wouldn't* call him that. Everyone thought he was dead or had forgotten he existed, and she was content with letting it stay that way.

After brief consideration, with a grin, she answered, "Bitches."

Cassie made a face. "His name is Bitches?"

"Yeah. Because Bitches be trippin'," Eve replied.

43
I Do Belong Here

As everyone climbed out of the helicopter and began the trek from the training field to the apartment complex, Eve, Bo, and Kai all paused, sniffing the air.

"Strangers," Eve announced. No, wait. One of them was familiar.

"My father," Bo corrected. "And Sister Fiona."

"Someone's in trouuubllllle," Kai sang ominously. "Sister Fiona almost never comes here."

Eve called out to Dagon, *Where are you?*

He replied immediately, *Your apartment.*

Luc's father and the Knighco leader are both here. You need to make sure they don't see you, Eve urged.

They haven't. But if they come looking for me, I will not hide.

Just stay put, please.

As you wish, princess.

Eve turned her attention to Bo. "I know your father can teleport, but how did Sister Fiona get here so fast?" Eve wondered.

"I feel like we're in fucking Hogwarts," Ruger remarked. "Everybody suddenly apparating and disapparating all the time."

"Can she do that?" Eve asked.

"No. But, like you, my father has been known to occasionally take a passenger with him when the situation calls for it. Apparently, this calls for it." He held a hand out to stop her from moving forward. "Maybe you should hang back, Evie."

"Why? I'm not scared of them. I could kill them if I wanted to."

"Exactly," Bo answered, giving her a look.

Luc's jaw ticked as he looked down at his phone. "They want a meeting," he said. "They're in the common room." He dragged his hand through his hair and grumbled, "Mira must have contacted them before we got into the air. I should've smashed her phone." When he turned to look at Eve, she could see the worry lining his face, even through his sunglasses. "Bo's right. Let me handle my father."

"You *won't* handle your father," Eve shot back, irritated. "He'll handle *you*. Maybe you should let me handle him. I have a few things I'd like to say to him."

"That's a supremely terrible idea," Bo said. "I love you, Evie, but your mouth doesn't know when to quit."

"And as much as I love that about your mouth," Luc agreed, "I have to side with my brother on this one. My father doesn't appreciate sass the same way that I do."

"Someone needs to put that tyrant in his place," Eve argued. "And I'm just the bitch to do it."

She left them behind before they could stop her, teleporting to the common room in the apartment complex. Victor Fagerberg was seated in the middle of the couch, his arms outstretched along the top of the backrest. A plain, older woman in a habit and simple black dress stood next to the couch, her hands clasped demurely in front of her. She unclasped them to push her glasses up her mousy face, and she studied Eve.

Luc and Bo appeared on either side of her before she could speak.

"It's the middle of the night, sir," Luc said. "This couldn't wait until tomorrow?"

"It's morning in Vatican City," Sister Fiona pointed out.

Victor rose from the couch, standing with his feet wide, crossing his arms, and Eve felt Luc shift back ever so slightly. "You fucked up, Lucius. Are you trying to start a war? Don't you remember what happened last time Knighco clashed with LOA? I was cleaning up your mess for weeks!" His voice grew louder with every word. "And now look what you've done! Mira informed us that, because of your asinine little adventure, *Lilith* is free!"

"The Vatican set express rules, and you know this," Sister Fiona added, her voice sweet and soft. She sounded like she was gently reprimanding a small child. "You cannot engage with an organization like that without the Vatican's consent. That is part of our agreement. They let us operate freely as long as we keep our heads down and our noses clean." Sister Fiona shook her head. "The powers that be are most displeased with the outcome of your endeavor."

Luc began to reply, but Eve spoke over him. "We took down an organization of monsters. They should be thanking us."

"Lilith is out walking the earth because of you!" Victor roared.

Sister Fiona was right behind him, adding softly, "This is not an outcome we should be celebrating."

"She isn't the villain she's been made out to be," Eve rejoined. "She isn't *evil*. She's a scapegoat."

"Of course you would side with her," Victor sniped, disgusted. He looked at her bedraggled appearance, her bare legs, and scowled. "You and Lilith are both cut from the same cloth. You don't belong here. We should've disposed of you as soon as we knew what you were."

Eve felt Bo's fury erupt in her chest, and he stepped in front of her protectively.

Luc began to laugh, but it was a strange sound. It was higher pitched than usual, and Eve glanced over at him. He slipped his sunglasses off and tucked them into the neckline of his undershirt, and Eve saw how wild his eyes were. He grinned, but it was anything but charming.

Something inside had snapped.

His smile fell and his face went completely flat as he challenged, "Go ahead and try it. If she doesn't kill you, sir...I will."

Victor and Sister Fiona both stood in stunned silence, eyes wide.

Isaac burst through the door, Ramil and the rest of the hunters hot on his heels. They poured into the common room, anxious to see what was going on. Isaac lowered the sunekosuri to the floor, and it scampered off, frightened by the commotion.

Victor watched the odd creature depart, but quickly returned his attention to Luc. "You're unfit," he told him. "You've let her get into your head and compromise you. I'm revoking your position. You aren't ready to be in charge of anything, let alone an organization like this. You're a fucking child."

Eve pushed past Bo and toed up to Victor, looking up at the face she wished didn't look so much like the faces of his sons. "No, *you're* a child. *You're* unfit. I refuse to stand—"

"You will not speak to me!" Victor interrupted, jabbing a finger in her face.

Bo's hand shot out and caught Victor's finger, yanking it from Eve's face. "She will speak," he growled.

Eve drew on Apep's powers and focused on Victor's vocal cords, paralyzing them as Apep had done to her. When he tried to shout back at Bo, nothing but a tiny squeak came out.

Sister Fiona only stood by and watched, her expression of surprise slowly shifting to one of interest.

"Better," Eve smiled, and Victor's face reddened with anger and...maybe a little fear? "As I was saying before you so rudely interrupted me, I will not stand here and let you talk to Luc like this anymore. He loves you, despite the fact that you are, as far as I can tell, an insufferable bastard. But I won't let you hurt him anymore. I will give him all the love and support he's always deserved, and you will fade into the background, like the unremarkable asshole you are. If you want to fight me, I'll gladly go to war with you. But that's a war you will not win." Then she looked into his eyes and pushed past the considerable barriers in his mind. *I think it's time for you to step down, Victor. You don't need to be involved in this world anymore. Stick to Fagerberg Enterprises and leave the monsters to us. This isn't a suggestion.* Then she recapped her most horrific kills, allowing them to play through in vivid detail in Victor's mind.

Rending the head from Varghrir's shoulders with her bare hands.

Blasting Ruth with enough electricity to blow her into a bloody mist.

Trapping Apep's body in chains and tearing it asunder, his severed head dangling from her hand.

Gleefully incinerating a group of monsters with dragon's fire from her own throat.

Effortlessly reducing her own father to a pile of flesh and bone with a flick of her wrist.

The highlight reel.

His future, if he doesn't heed her warning.

But she followed up by conveying her fierce feelings of loyalty to his sons, and to Knighco, showing him that, despite his beliefs, she wasn't their enemy, and she would protect them all with her life. She *did* belong, and he would never extract her from this place she called home. These hunters were family, and Victor knew nothing about the meaning of family.

Victor Fagerberg was an unnecessary cog in the Knighco machinery, and it was time for him to go.

When she retreated from his mind, she unparalyzed his vocal cords, allowing him to speak. He looked down at her, then leaned close to her ear and whispered, "One day, Luc will bore of you. I know my son. You'll make a mistake you can't reconcile, and this family you think you have? They'll turn on you, because you *are* the thing they should be hunting. The truth always finds the light. And I will be there to smile in your face as they put you down." Then he stood straight and gave a dismissive wave of his hand. "You can handle this, Sister," he said to Sister Fiona. "Do what you want."

And then he was gone.

There was a shrewdness in the nun's eyes that Eve hadn't noticed before as she studied the hunters in the room. "Who is responsible for what transpired at the LOA compound?" she asked calmly.

Ramil raised his hand and stepped forward. "It was me. I was the one who convinced Eve and the rest of her team to come here. It's all my fault. I thought we could bring Zeke back from the dead using the LOA's ritual to raise Lilith." Shame clouded his handsome face. "I was wrong."

Sister Fiona looked past Ramil, noting Zeke's presence behind him as he and Eoduun stood next to Isaac. "Yet there he stands…?"

Eve answered the implied question. "I brought him back with Lilith's grimoire." *And her power. Oh, and he's a monster.* "But this wasn't Ramil's fault. It was Veris."

Sister Fiona glanced at the group, noting Veris' absence, but she didn't look surprised. She only folded her hands, awaiting elaboration.

"He set us up," Eve explained. "He was manipulating everyone. He compelled Ramil, Ruth, Dizzy, and even someone at LOA. He wanted Lilith raised so she could take his power away and make him normal. He resented his abilities, and, from what I saw in his memories, his time in the Vatican's detention center didn't do him any favors." *Your precious institution shares the blame, Sister.*

"And where is he now?" Sister Fiona asked.

"Lilith killed him," Luc answered.

"How convenient for you," she remarked with pursed lips.

"Who's Veris?" Ramil whispered to Zephlyn, and Zephlyn stared back at him in confusion.

Eve answered for him, "He was your best friend, and he used you. He used all of us. He compelled you to forget him before he died. It was part of his plan to make sure no one would look for him when he left to live his 'normal' life."

"And what of the grimoire?" Sister Fiona inquired. "Where is it now?"

Eve looked at the floor. "Lilith took it and vanished when the Locusts attacked us. Veris compelled them to attack, trying to protect himself, and our hands were tied. We didn't go to the LOA compound with the intention of killing them."

"I see." Sister Fiona looked at Luc. "Well, Lucius, what do you propose we do?"

"Lilith will turn up. A presence like hers in this world won't remain hidden for long," he replied.

"Not about Lilith," Sister Fiona clarified. "She will be dealt with in due time. What do you propose we do about the Abomination?"

Eve scowled. "The Abomination has a name, you know. It's Eve, and I'm right fucking here."

"Indeed you fucking are," Sister Fiona replied, surprising Eve with her language. Were nuns allowed to swear? "Why?"

Eve was puzzled by the question. "Why what? Why am I here?"

"Yes. Why are you here, with us? What is keeping you here? You could leave, vanish, go off on your own whenever you please…and, as I recall, you did so recently. But you came back. And here you are now. I'm vaguely aware of the lore around the power needed to raise Lilith, and I know only the Abomination can do so. You've fulfilled the unholy prophecy, unleashing the prisoner of the Abyss onto the world…and you came back *here*. I can only imagine the power you possess now. Why destroy the cult that worshipped you as a goddess to come back to the organization that, under any other circumstances, should've hunted you…and may still?"

Tears pricked Eve's eyes. "Why *wouldn't* I come back here? This is my home." She looked back at the hunters behind her, and at Luc, Isaac, and her team. "This is my family. I'm finally strong enough to make a difference, to protect them. How can I protect them if I run away?"

"Who do you think you need to protect them from?" Sister Fiona queried. "Are you unaware that your very existence is what has put them in the most danger? That *you*, in fact, are the greatest danger to them?"

Those words shot like fire-tipped arrows through Eve's heart, and she clenched her teeth and willed the tears in her eyes not to spill over. "Maybe that was true once. But it isn't now." With Lilith's power, she had control that she didn't have before. But she wasn't about to tell anyone from the Vatican that. If they knew she had Lilith's power, it *would* start a war.

Isaac signed at Sister Fiona, *She isn't a threat. She belongs here with them.* Then, after a brief pause, *With me.*

Sister Fiona raised her thin brows and signed back, *You're not returning to the Vatican?*

Isaac shook his head and snapped his thumb and first two fingers together. *No.*

She pursed her lips. "This is why you're dangerous," she said to Eve. "You inspire fealty to *you* over loyalty to this organization. You change people. You draw them in, put them under your spell, and encourage them to do your bidding, man and monster alike." Sister Fiona narrowed her eyes, turning her attention to Luc. "Speaking of monsters, where is Dagon?"

Luc shoved his hands in his pockets and answered nonchalantly, "Secured."

"Is that true, Mira?" Sister Fiona asked. "Because you indicated otherwise."

"He is not secure, ma'am," Mira spoke up from the back of the group. "He's completely untethered."

"He is tethered," Eve countered. "Tethered to *me*."

Sister Fiona sucked her teeth. "Again, we come back to you. All problems center around you."

Luc spoke up. "You're looking at this all wrong, Sister. Eve isn't the problem. She's the solution. She's powerful, loyal, and compassionate. With all due respect, she cares about Knighco more than the Vatican or my father ever did. She's the keystone that makes us the strongest we've ever been."

"And what happens next time you two have a little spat? What happens when you break her heart, Lucius?" Sister Fiona eyed Eve. "How loyal will you be to us then?"

Eve gritted her teeth. "I know I don't have the best track record. Yes, I ran off and threw a temper tantrum last time that happened. I know. It looks bad. But I didn't hurt anyone. I never had any ill-will toward Knighco or anyone else. In fact, I *missed* everyone. I came back because I do belong here. I came back *with* a broken heart, and everyone was there, welcoming me home, ready to help put me back together." She smiled. "I've found myself here. It's going to take a lot more than a broken heart to pry me away from Knighco now, ma'am. I've put down roots, and I intend to keep growing here."

Sister Fiona studied her, and she watched Bo's fingers interlace with Eve's. Luc placed a comforting hand on Eve's lower back, and Zeke, Eoduun, and Isaac moved closer to her. Sister Fiona's perceptive gaze scanned the hunters around Eve, and an expression of resignation shadowed her face.

"I see." Sister Fiona glanced down at her sensible shoes. "I will talk to my superiors, but I can't promise they won't require more of an assurance than your 'roots.'"

"The assurance of their Angel of Death should be all they need, shouldn't it?" Eve pointed out. "He was, after all, the one they sent to assess me, was he not?" She looked back at Isaac, and he nodded at her. "He says I'm not a threat."

Sister Fiona didn't look satisfied. "Yes, I am aware. I will pass along his assessment, and we will see what comes of it." She gave Eve a softened expression. "In the meantime, please try to keep yourself out of trouble. I will do my best to shift their focus to Lilith, but that will be difficult to do if your name keeps coming up in reports."

Eve saluted the nun. "I'll do my damnedest."

Sister Fiona sighed. "See that you do." She turned to Luc. "Lucius, be a dear and drive me to the airport. Your father seemed rather in a hurry to abandon me here, and it sounds like your helicopter has already departed." She smiled warmly at Luc. "But I can't say I'm disappointed at having some time to chat and catch up with you, my boy."

"Of course, Sister," Luc said, then kissed Eve on the temple. "I'll be back shortly, love."

Sister Fiona followed Luc toward the door, but as she passed Eve, she patted her on the cheek. "Behave, dear," she said softly. "I know you aren't a bad person, and I can see how much you and your team care about each other. But you're still young, still finding your place in this world. If you want that place to be here, with them, you need to learn to play by the rules. If you step out of line, it may not be only you who is punished. Keep that in mind. I am quite fond of Babhdán and Lucius, and I don't ever want to see them pay for your mistakes."

Eve nodded. "Yes, ma'am."

Sister Fiona smiled at Eve in that motherly way that said *I'm disappointed in what you've done, but I know you will do better next time.* And then she walked out the door to join Luc.

44

I've Been Licking a Lot of Cupcakes

Dagon was sprawled out on Eve's couch when she walked into her apartment, watching *Lucifer* on Netflix. "You didn't call for help, so I'm assuming everything went well?" he surmised.

"I really couldn't tell you," Eve replied with a heavy sigh. "I think so?"

As her team followed her in, Zeke suddenly tripped and fell into Eoduun, who fell into Isaac, who grabbed onto Bo for support, almost taking him down as well.

"What the fuck?!" Bo barked, turning to the wreckage behind him.

The sunekosuri skittered from the tangled limbs and jumped up on the back of the couch. He headbutted Eve's hand, demanding attention.

"Bitches be trippin'," Eve snorted as she scratched his short, yet somehow still floppy ears.

"Bitches is getting a bell," Zeke complained as he stood and helped Eoduun to his feet.

Ramil popped in behind them, looking uncharacteristically unsure of himself. "Can I come in?"

"Only if you know the password," Eve teased.

Team Flannel was right behind him. Ruger yawned loudly and stretched. "So, do we go to bed and sleep for a few hours, or do we get out the booze and pull an all-nighter?" he asked, already heading to the kitchen for the bottle of Johnnie Walker on the fridge.

"Did I hear someone say 'all-nighter'?" Kai called from the hallway. He walked in with Zephlyn, Mendal, and Celeste.

Dagon rose from the couch, and everyone finally took notice that he was there. The crowded room went silent.

"You all chatter like fucking monkeys. I can't hear my show. I'm returning to my quarters," he announced, giving them all a dark glare. Then he looked at Eve. "You're welcome to join me, princess."

"He has *quarters*?" Mendal blurted. "Here?!"

"Don't bother me, and I won't bother you," Dagon stated. He glanced at Eve again. "You know where I'll be." Then he disappeared.

"Fucking Hogwarts," Ruger remarked as he took a swig from the Johnnie Walker. He picked up a chopstick sitting on Eve's counter and pointed it at Remi, shouting in a deep, strangled, husky voice, "Avada Kadavra!"

"Are we really just going to let Dagon live here with us?" Mendal complained. "Or are we all forgetting what he did to Shira?"

Eve felt Bo's anger surge as he turned on Mendal. "No one has forgotten what he did to Shira!" Bo lashed out. He took a breath. "But the Dagon we have now isn't the same monster who did that."

Celeste snatched the bottle of Scotch from Ruger. "Are you trying to tell us he's *changed*?" she chided as she raised the bottle to her lips.

"Maybe. He's saved our asses more than once."

"I've been in his head," Eve added. "He might be a selfish asshole, but he isn't going to betray us. When he was freed from Zeke, it changed him. He basically has a copy of Zeke's soul imprinted on his own."

"I can say one thing for him," Cassie smirked. "He sure isn't hard on the eyes."

"Down, girl," Ruger said, pointing at her as he moved to the door. "I'm going to get more booze from our apartment. Too bad I can't just disapparate like everyone else in this fucking place."

Zephlyn watched Ruger leave, then continued along the topic of Dagon. "If what you say is true, then I'm not opposed to giving Dagon a chance. But I think he should have some kind of probationary period. I don't like the idea of him having free reign just yet."

"That sounds fair to me," Kai agreed. "I have to say, I'd rather have that big fucker on our side than make an enemy of him."

"I vote we give him a chance," Zeke said. "I literally shared a body with him. He's a dick, but he's not evil. Plus, he'd do anything for Eve, and we all know she would never let him hurt us."

"Who *wouldn't* do anything for Eve?" Kai said slyly, giving Eve a playful wink. It made her fully aware that she was still only wearing Luc's shirt.

Bo bristled from his seat at the kitchen island, looking up from his phone with a blazing yellow eye. "Careful, kid."

Kai stole the bottle of Scotch from Celeste. "Just sayin'," he mumbled, then took a swig.

"If I may," Ramil spoke up. "I was in a similar position as Dagon when I first came here. Hell, I killed Remi and Ruger when I was a Locust. I tried to kill Luc. But you all eventually accepted me, and I will forever be grateful for it. I fully believe in second chances, and after Dagon came to our aid tonight, I trust he deserves one."

Ruger burst back into the room holding up a bottle of tequila. "Expecto PATRÓN-um!" he shouted.

Cassie grabbed the bottle and popped it open. "Give it a rest. You're *not* a wizard, Harry."

Eve stepped away from the merriment to take a quick shower and dress in comfortable joggers and a baggy t-shirt. It felt good to be fully clothed again and not be covered in the ashes of monsters anymore.

"So what the fuck happened with Veris?" Remi wanted to know as soon as she returned to the party.

Eve gave a brief and highly censored recap of what transpired as everyone passed the bottles around, and she shared what she saw in Veris' memories. She didn't tell them she had Lilith's power, but she did tell them she had to raise Zeke and Eoduun as monsters. Ruger looked wary when she revealed that Eoduun was a vampire now, but she assured them that she would slake his thirst when needed since she was immune to vampire venom.

Everyone had a hard time believing the quiet, innocent-looking little blond guy was the one causing the chaos this whole time. Eve let them believe that Lilith killed him, though, and told them that she found the sunekosuri at the LOA compound.

She glanced over at Isaac while everyone split off into their own conversations. He was settled into his usual chair with Stacey's journal in his hand, and she watched Bitches hop up into his lap and curl up there. Isaac absently stroked his fur while he perused the journal, and Bitches made a rumbling sound that was a cross between a contented groan and a purr.

It was better they didn't know the sunekosuri's true nature. She didn't want anyone to try to hurt him because of who he used to be.

She shifted her attention to Zeke. He was on the couch with Eoduun sitting on the floor in front of him. He raised his brows at

Eve and patted the seat next to him, and Eve plopped down beside him.

She rested her head on Zeke's shoulder, and she felt like the grinch at the end of the movie when his heart grew three sizes. "I missed you more than you will ever know," she confessed. "I'm sorry I had to bring you back as a monster, but...I'm not sorry I brought you back. Maybe I should be, because it was selfish and you didn't ask for this, but I'm not. I couldn't stand how much it hurt to not have you here, and I couldn't stand how much agony Eoduun was in. It nearly broke us. It might've broken us, eventually."

Zeke rested his temple on the top of her head. "Never apologize for needing me. I'm not mad about being a gargoyle. I don't know anything about gargoyles, but I guess I'll get the crash course," he chuckled. Then he sighed. "I'm used to being seen as a monster. At least this time it's all me, and not someone living inside of me."

Eoduun leaned his head back onto Zeke's lap and looked up at Eve. "Why am I not going completely bloodthirsty? I've seen people who've been infected with vampire venom, and they completely lose their minds."

Celeste overheard the conversation as she rested her elbows on the back of the couch on the other side of Eve. "You weren't infected, though, were you?" she pointed out. "Given the circumstances, I'd think you're basically a natural vampire. A born vampire. You have control over your curse, just like a natural werewolf versus an infected werewolf."

Cassie and Ruger squeezed onto the couch next to Eve, and Cassie passed the bottle of tequila to her. "So...Dagon, hm?" She nudged Eve with her elbow. "He seems keen."

Eve chuckled and took a sip of the burning liquid in the bottle. "Yeah, I've been licking a lot of cupcakes."

Cassie glanced at Isaac in the chair adjacent to them. "I'm going to have to give up on the holy cupcake, aren't I?" she whispered.

"I don't think that cupcake wants to be licked," she admitted. "But, hey, you gave it a hell of a go, Cass. If he were any other cupcake, he wouldn't have been able to resist you."

"Right?" Cassie agreed. "I'm pretty damn irresistible."

Ruger took the bottle from Eve. "I think you're both forgetting that I never got my end of the bargain anyway, so it's a moot point," he reminded them, a hint begrudgingly.

Two scarred hands gripped the couch on either side of Ruger's head. Bo lowered his head next to Ruger's ear and whispered, "And you never will." Eve hadn't even noticed him leave his seat in the kitchen. Bo straightened. "God, it's like swatting flies tonight."

"You know, I'm not opposed to a group setting," Cassie suggested, looking up at Bo mischievously.

"Not. Happening," he replied firmly.

Eve couldn't resist. "What if I said *I* wanted to?"

She felt the burn of Bo's possessiveness. He stood behind her and slid his hand into her soft pink tresses, gripping at the roots. He angled her head back and looked down at her with eyes of fire and ice. His voice was low and dark when he vowed, "I would drag you back into the woods and remind you who you belong to."

A shiver of need pulsed through her core.

"Lord have mercy," Cassie cried with delight, fanning herself and crossing her legs.

Ruger stared at Bo like he had a new-found respect for him. "Damn, Bo. I think you just made *my* panties wet."

Zeke gaped at Bo like he didn't recognize him. "What the hell did I miss while I was dead?"

Eoduun sighed in annoyance. "It's been right in front of your face this whole time. You're just too oblivious."

Bo ignored them all, his possessive gaze softening as he looked down at Eve. She watched the gold shift back to charcoal. "My pretty little menace." He leaned down and pressed a masked kiss to her lips, then one to her forehead.

He'd sufficiently marked his territory, so he returned to the kitchen island to browse manga smut on his phone.

By the time Luc walked in, the bottles of liquor being passed around had taken quite a hit, and the merriment was at its height. The only two not partaking were Bo and Isaac, but they seemed satisfied to just be there, where Eve was.

Eve leapt over the back of the couch, interrupting a lively game of Cards Against Humanity she, Zeke, Eoduun, Mendal, Celeste, Cassie, and Ruger were all playing around the coffee table. The black card said "Run, run, as fast as you can! You can't catch me, I'm ___!" and she'd played the card that said "Gary."

She lifted onto her toes and pulled him down for a quick kiss.

Luc looked around the room and groaned. "They've multiplied," he complained.

Eve surveyed the room with satisfaction. "They have, haven't they?"

"I shouldn't be annoyed. You'll have everyone to keep you company while I'm gone."

Eve gave him an exasperated sigh. "You have to leave again? Now?"

He gave her a tight-lipped smile. "Sorry, love. I promised Sister Fiona I would meet her in Vatican City to help her smooth things over. We did make a rather monumental mess, and she'll need all the reinforcements she can get."

"Did she have anything interesting to say on the way to the airport?"

"She has concerns, but she's willing to put her trust in us. She thinks she can keep the Vatican focused on Lilith and off our backs for now, as long as we lay low for a while." A smile graced his face. "She admired the way you got in my father's face. She said it made her whole week."

"She doesn't like him?"

"No one likes him, not even my own mother, but no one else would dare tell him that. Only you, love."

Eve remembered the story Bo told her about his own origins. "Well, someone loved him once. Maybe what happened to Bo's mother broke him, turned him into the uncaring asshole he is now."

Luc considered it. "Maybe. I never really thought about it."

"Would you be the same if something happened to me?"

A scowled darkened Luc's face. "I wouldn't survive it."

"Maybe that was the only way he could survive it. He just…shut it all off. Threw away his ability to love and empathize."

Like Lilith.

She glanced down at her hands nervously, knowing this conversation was going to have to come up eventually. Time to rip off the band-aid.

"I had to make a deal with Lilith to resurrect Zeke and Eoduun. I took her power, and with it, I can keep stolen abilities forever." She watched his face light up, and regretted that it wouldn't stay that way long. "But there is a price. The more power I hold, the less human I become. My emotions will…fade."

The brightness disappeared. "You'll stop loving me."

"But I think there's a way around it." She gave a pointed look toward Isaac, and realized he was watching them out of the corner of his eye. "I think my stolen powers can be exorcised."

A tiny smirk lifted the corner of Isaac's mouth as he stared down at the journal in front of him.

Emotions warred on Luc's face, and an unamused chuckle rose from his throat. Then he sighed heavily. "Good thing you didn't let me kill the exorcist, I guess."

Eve smiled up at him. "He's not an outsider anymore, Luc. He's one of us. Even you have to admit that."

Luc eyed the sunekosuri in Isaac's lap. "You have a terrible habit of bringing in strays and turning them into your pets, love," he mused.

She heard Eoduun's voice from her memories. *"Lapdogs."*

Eve looked around the room at all the people, the *monsters*, she'd grown to love. They weren't her lapdogs. They were family. "I like to think I just have a lot of love to give. No one really gave a shit about me my whole life, and I'd learned to take any bit of love I could get. I don't think I can ever shut that off."

Luc kissed her temple. "Don't ever try to shut it off. You're perfect as you are, and you deserve all the love in the world."

But she didn't deserve it. Not really. Maybe someday she would grow into the person who did deserve it, but she wasn't that person yet. She still had a lot of baggage stacked in the corners of her soul that she needed to sort through, broken bits she needed to mend, and a lot of trash she needed to dispose of.

But it would come. Eventually, she would sort herself out and become someone worthy of them all.

Luc interrupted her thoughts. "Just know that *I* will always love you most."

Eve's eyes found Bo's, and though Luc fully believed what he said, she wondered if there was one man who possibly loved her more, broken bits and all.

After most of the hunters had passed out in various places around Eve's apartment, Eve sat at the kitchen island with Bo, munching on some rice chips and watching the room spin. Isaac was snoring lightly in his chair, Bitches snoozing with his feet up in the air in Isaac's lap. Ruger and Remi were asleep on the couch with Cassie sprawled out on top of them. Kai had his head on the coffee table, drool pooling under his face, with Celeste and Zephlyn in a heap on the floor behind him. Mendal was curled up in the bathtub.

Eve furrowed her brow. "Where did Zeke and Eoduun go?"

Bo looked up from his phone. "They probably went to bed. I think that's where I'm headed, too," he said with a yawn. "I'm fucking spent." He slid from the barstool. "You need to get some rest, too."

He cupped the back of her head and pulled his mask down to kiss her forehead. "I love you, Evie. Goodnight."

When he pulled away, Eve grabbed his face and pulled him back, planting a kiss on his delicious lips. "Is that all I get?"

"For tonight…this morning…yes," he said. "I'm asleep on my feet at this point. You and I both need rest."

Eve pouted. "I forgot my boyfriend was an old man."

Bo cupped her chin and tilted her head up. "Boyfriend?" he mocked. His tone dropped and his eye shifted to gold as he said, "We're a bonded pair, sweetheart. In the world of wolves, I'm your husband. Save the boyfriend bullshit for the boys."

Eve's heart fluttered. "Yet you're going to neglect your husbandly duties?" she taunted.

He tucked her hair behind her ear. "I'm not what you need tonight. You just got Zeke back, and I can feel how much you want to be close to him. You should go to him."

There wasn't an ounce of jealousy radiating from him. "You're not jealous? You were puffing your chest and acting all possessive earlier with Kai and Cassie and Ruger."

"I wasn't *jealous*. I was being *territorial*," he reasoned. He smiled down at her. "The longer we share all of our most intimate feelings, the harder it is for me to be jealous. You loving someone makes me feel that affection for them, too."

Eve raised her eyebrows at him.

His cheeks flushed. "Not like that!" He crossed his arms. "I just mean when you need something, some*one*, I need you to have it. Our needs and affections are aligned." With a disgruntled huff, he added, "I think you've even made me mildly fond of Dagon."

When she laughed, he uncrossed his arms and gave her a satisfied grin. He rested his hand on the counter next to her, leaning close to her ear. "But the main reason I don't get jealous about them anymore, Evie, is because I know your heart. I know you love me most of all. More than Zeke and Eoduun. More than Isaac – and yes,

I know you love Isaac. And you love me even more than you love Luc. You love me *most*, and it's *almost* as much as I love you."

Eve hugged her arms around his neck. It was true. She did love him most. Maybe it had always been true, and she just refused to admit it. Luc wanted to be loved the most, but for as much as he loved Eve, she knew he was incapable of loving her as much as Bo loved her.

No one would ever love her the way Bo did.

He untangled her hands from behind his neck. "Now that we've settled that, go be with Zeke. I'm guessing he needs you just as much as you need him."

45
It Is You and You Are It

When Eve went to her room, she found Zeke and Eoduun both passed out in her bed. She crawled up from the foot of the bed and snuggled in between them. She curled up around Zeke's wide back, draping her arm over his side, her hand fisting between his pecs. She kissed his shoulder, then pressed her cheek against it, inhaling his scent.

Her eyes welled with tears. She got him back. He was here. He was really here. Her mind replayed the image of him in the moments before he died. The fear. The desperation. A part of her had died when he did, but now, lying here, holding him, she was whole again. She squeezed him harder, and a soft sob escaped her throat.

Zeke roused, turning his head. "Babe?"

She sniffled and cleared her throat. "Sorry. I didn't mean to wake you," she whispered thickly.

He shifted onto his other side so he was facing her, and he wrapped his enormous arms around her and hugged her against his chest. He kissed the top of her head and whispered against her hair, "Why are you crying?"

"I'm just happy to have you back. I missed you so fucking much."

Zeke hugged her a little harder. "I'm sorry. But I'm here now, and I'm not going anywhere."

After a quiet moment, Eve asked, "Where did you go when you died?"

Zeke shrugged one shoulder. "I don't know. I don't remember anything about it. The last thing I remembered before waking up on that altar was feeling myself fading as Dagon took over, and I looked over and saw you."

Eve's throat tightened. "You looked terrified."

His voice became quiet. "So did you. I was afraid my death was going to…well, do exactly what it did, from what Eoduun told me. So I held on as long as I could to tell Dagon to protect you. To be better than everyone expected him to be. He was going to have to take my place, and I needed him to help you all move on. I needed to leave a piece of myself behind for you to find in him."

Eve smiled through her tears. "I found it. But it wasn't enough. I needed you. *We* needed you."

Zeke stroked her hair. "You have me. I'm right here."

"Don't ever die again."

He chuckled. "I don't think I can promise that, babe."

"I don't care. Do it anyway," she demanded petulantly.

He grabbed her face and angled it up to his so she could see his falsely serious expression in the darkness. In a monotone voice, he declared, "I promise. I will never die."

Eve laughed, because she recognized the line. "Did you just quote that stupid old marionette movie you made me watch?"

"I'm so proud of you for recognizing it."

She rested her hand on his cheek. "It's so fucking good to have you back. I'll watch whatever idiotic movies you want me to." She wriggled up so she could reach her lips to his, kissing him softly.

"You know, there is one perk to everything going down the way it did," Zeke mumbled against her lips. "You can sleep with me now without worrying Dagon is going to cause trouble for you."

Eve smiled and pulled away just enough so she could look at his face. "Ever Mr. Brightside."

His hand stroked her hair. "You have to admit, this is pretty nice. We haven't slept next to each other since our first case together when you tried to molest me."

"I did do that. I will own up to that. But I was drunk, and you were cute."

"*Were* cute? I'm not cute anymore?"

Eve laughed. "You're still cute. And here again, I'm a little drunk."

"But you're not trying to molest me. I'm offended."

Eve smiled and kissed him again. Her hand glided from his cheek, down his chest, over his hard abdominals, and she ran her finger along his waistline. "You want me to molest you, Z?"

He grabbed her hand and pressed her palm against the hard ridge in his pants. "I'll be heartbroken if you don't."

"What about Eoduun?" she reminded him as she rubbed him through his pants.

"He can sleep through anything. He's fallen out of his own bed and slept through it. Besides, I don't feel like sharing tonight. I want you all to myself."

He raised himself up on one arm and used the other to drag Eve beneath him. She wrapped her legs around his waist, and he thrust his hardness against her, the friction on her clit through her clothes urging her to rock her hips against him. His mouth was on hers, their tongues tangling desperately for a moment before he moved down the column of her neck, nipping at her collarbone, then lifting her shirt off her and taking her pert breast into his mouth. He teased her

393

nipple with his tongue while his other hand slid down the front of her joggers.

She was already wet for him. He pressed two fingers inside of her, burying them to the knuckles, and she moaned as he thrust them in and out, his warm palm cupping her pubic bone. She rocked her hips, pressing against his hand as his mouth moved down the shallow valley that ran down the center of her abs. He yanked her joggers down with his free hand, and she kicked them off the rest of the way, not caring where they ended up.

His mouth descended upon her, his tongue circling her clit as his fingers continued to fuck her, and she arched her back, pressing her head back into the pillow. "Fuck, Zeke," she moaned.

She reached down and gripped his hair, riding his face while he fucked her with his fingers, panting as the pleasure rose to its precipice. She threw her other hand over her mouth and bit her knuckles to try to muffle her cries as she came, her core clenching around Zeke's fingers as she pulsed against his tongue. Her thighs trembled against his shoulders as she came down.

Zeke pulled his shirt off over his head and quickly shucked his pants off. He notched his engorged cock at her entrance, one hand next to her head as he leaned over her. He watched her face as he slowly sank into her heat, and Eve's eyes rolled back, reveling in the way it felt to have him inside of her again. She threw her arms around him and pulled him against her, wrapping her legs around his waist. She needed to feel his whole body against hers as he fucked her. She needed to know he was really there. He was really back.

And then Eve felt fingers lightly dragging down her arm, and she looked over. Eoduun looked like he was still sleeping, or at least half-asleep. In any case, he wasn't in full control of himself. He took her hand from Zeke's back and brought it to his mouth. Eve let out a small cry of anguish as his fangs sank into her wrist, but it turned into a moan as a wave of euphoria ripped through her.

Giant wings suddenly burst from Zeke's back, as a vicious snarl tore from his throat. His muscles and skin were solid as stone against her flesh, and his cock swelled and hardened like a hot steel rod inside of her. He braced his stony arms on either side of her, and he held himself over her like he was trying to shield her. She looked up at his face, but it wasn't Zeke.

Two horns had erupted from his forehead, curling back along his head like a ram, and his face had become grotesquely yet somehow beautifully monstrous. Huge fangs protruded from his mouth, his granite-like lips curled back as he snarled, his deep-golden eyes trained on Eoduun.

The gargoyle.

Eoduun's eyes snapped open in terror, and he sat bolt-upright, dropping Eve's hand. He was wide awake now. "The fuck?!"

"Don't touch her!" a deep, terrifying voice roared at Eoduun.

Eve clung to Zeke, wrapping her legs tightly around his solid hips, her hands fighting to force his face back toward her. Fuck, he was strong. "Zeke! Stop!"

He thrust his rock-hard cock into her, making her bite her lip, fucking her while he glared at Eoduun. "Don't. Fucking. Hurt. Her."

"Zeke!" Eve slapped his cheek, but it was like slapping a statue. She grabbed him by the horns and finally was able to force him to face her. His monstrous gaze on her thrilled her in a way it shouldn't have. "What the fuck, Zeke?"

He growled down at her, "You are mine to protect. No one will ever hurt you."

Then she understood. Eoduun had triggered the protective instincts of the gargoyle Zeke had become.

"He's not hurting me, Z. Calm down." She caressed the rough angles of his face. "Focus on me. He's fine. I'm fine. You're fine." She glanced over at Eoduun's horrified expression. "We're all good," she said calmly.

Zeke's eyes roved her body as he pushed into her again, but when he saw the blood trickling down her arm, a deep growl resonated through his chest and his fiery gaze snapped back to Eoduun, his wings twitching with rage. Eoduun backed away to the edge of the bed, unsure what he should do.

"Hey!" Eve barked, dragging Zeke's gaze back. "Eyes on me. Stay with me, Zeke." She lifted her head from the pillow and ran her tongue along one of his massive fangs, cupping his face in her hands. She rolled her hips and flexed her thighs, lifting her lower back off the mattress, riding him from beneath at a slow, languid pace. "Show me how much you love me," she whispered against his lips.

That got his attention. "I do love you," he rumbled, and he touched his horned forehead to hers as he met her pace. "I won't let anyone hurt you."

Eve panted as he pressed her back into the mattress with the force of his thrusts. She rasped, "But sometimes I like it when it hurts."

He sat back on his haunches, hauling Eve up with him, still inside her. She straddled him, wrapping her arms around his neck, and rode him slow and hard. He was solid everywhere, like she was fucking a living, breathing statue. His wings cocooned around them, hiding Eve's naked body from Eoduun.

"Well, I don't," he growled in response. "You should only feel pleasure."

"Sometimes pain *is* pleasure," she countered. She gripped his horns and pressed her chest against his, grinding harder in his lap, taking him deeper. "Now shut up and fuck me," she demanded as she threw her head back, the sweet ache of pleasure between her legs just beginning to crest.

He grabbed her hips and slammed her down onto his cock while he thrust up into her, and she keened as her orgasm exploded through her body.

"Fuck, Zeke," she cried as he drove up into her with a guttural groan, emptying himself into her as her inner walls squeezed and spasmed around him.

Slowly, as they came down from the high, Zeke's horns receded, his skin softening back to normal, and his face morphing back to the sweet, innocent man she knew. The deep-golden eyes shifted back to soft caramel brown. Only his wings remained, and when he realized they were still out, he awkwardly folded them away, obviously still getting used to the process.

He and Eve stared at each other, still panting, and Eve laughed breathlessly. "Well, that was exciting," she mused.

Eoduun spoke up from the edge of the bed. "That was hot *and* terrifying."

"I didn't mean to lose it," Zeke apologized. "But..." He took Eve's bitten wrist into his hand, inspecting the quickly healing puncture wounds. Then his eyes met Eoduun's. "I don't like it when you hurt her."

"I didn't know what I was doing, dude," Eoduun explained, moving back to his original spot in the bed and lying back. "I wasn't even awake."

Eve patted Zeke's chest and climbed off his lap. "You're going to have to work on controlling that, because Eoduun is going to have to bite me occasionally." She pulled her underwear and joggers on, and Zeke handed her her shirt. "And what about training? Bo and Isaac don't hold back. You can't hulk out every time I get hurt."

"Sorry. I couldn't stop it. I'm not used to this new ability, and the need to protect you was overwhelming." He scratched his head and gave Eve and Eoduun an apologetic smile. "Sorry."

Eve smirked at him as she climbed back into bed. "Well, like Eoduun said, it was terrifying, but it was really fucking hot."

Zeke lay down next to her, pulling her to his chest. "You wanted to be with *me*, though. Not that monster."

"You *are* that monster, sweetie," Eve reminded him softly. "This isn't like Dagon. It isn't something else that lives in you. It is you and you are it." She swallowed. "This is what I made you, and I love every part of you."

"I don't know how much I love it," Eoduun chimed in. Then he looked over and gave Zeke one of those smiles he saves only for him. "I'm kidding, Z. We're both monsters. At least we get to be monsters together."

Eve closed her eyes, exhausted, and fell into a deep, dreamless sleep between the monsters she'd created.

46

I Like You on Your Knees

It took several days for things to finally calm down after the excitement at the LOA compound. Eve still held on to her powers, knowing the other hunters were more comfortable knowing that she could destroy Dagon if she needed to, but she was already beginning to notice changes in herself.

Changes like not caring about little things that would've mattered before, and not even caring that she didn't care.

She'd been put in charge of monitoring Dagon, which seemed to please him when they were alone, but, to his chagrin, that was rarely the case. Bo, Isaac, Zeke, and Eoduun were constantly at Eve's side. Luc still had some business matters to attend to, and on top of providing backup for Sister Fiona at the Vatican, he ended up also meeting with her and his father about Victor's sudden decision to resign from Knighco.

Luc was also working to arrange for Mira to be moved to Fagerberg Enterprises on a full-time basis, no longer trusting her discretion in Knighco matters. He'd sent her a notice that she was officially kicked out of the compound the morning after the LOA incident, while most of the other hunters were passed out all over Eve's apartment. Unfortunately, Mira was indispensable at his father's company and she couldn't be completely kicked to the curb.

With Mira gone and Veris becoming Eve's house pet, Ramil no longer had a team. He had been coming to hang out at Eve's apartment more often because, in many ways, he had no one but Eve. She knew he still had feelings for her, and he still believed they were destined to be together, but for now, he accepted whatever attention she would give him.

Between Dagon's constant presence and the other hunters coming in and out of Eve's apartment, there hadn't been much opportunity for her to be alone with any of her boys since the night they returned from Kentucky. Thankfully, her curse didn't seem to be as hungry as it used to be, and she no longer feared losing control. The past few nights, she'd fallen asleep the moment her head hit the pillow, completely exhausted after spending the day working with Eoduun and Zeke, helping them to master their new powers.

It wasn't difficult for them, considering the monsters they became were the ones that most suited their souls. Eoduun had taken to his powers like they were second nature, learning to use his new mental manipulation abilities to convince Zeke to slap Bo. It took him a little longer to get used to using his speed, agility, and strength, and the joke, "You better hold on tight, spider monkey," was used more than once.

His ability to erase memories had taken a hit in the resurrection, but it wasn't gone. He no longer took memories, but instead made them fuzzy. When he used it on Zeke, Zeke said it was like trying to remember something someone said to you after having a root canal.

Zeke's abilities were new to everyone at Knighco, however. No one had ever encountered a gargoyle, and Roy, their aging cryptologist, grumpily agreed to assist in the training to help Zeke understand what kind of power he was working with. He had trouble transforming into the beast without provocation at first, but he was starting to get the hang of it.

He was something to see in broad daylight, standing out in the middle of the training field. His skin looked like stone, and when Roy tried to pierce him with a small knife, it glanced off his skin, breaking the tip of the blade. His strength was still inhuman, as it was before, but he could extend claws from his fingers and toes that allowed him to scale trees and other vertical surfaces with ease. His bite force was off the charts, making his jaws and fangs deadly weapons that could tear a neck in half.

His most remarkable new ability, however, was in his wings. Zeke could *fly*. Dagon had to show him how, and it took a lot of coaching to get Zeke into the air. He was clumsy and slow, but after a few tries, he was able to make it to the top of a tall pine and alight in the crown. And, in true Zeke fashion, he joked, "I can see down your shirt!" But it sounded a little threatening when he said it with his gargoyle voice. It was like his vocal cords were made of gravel.

But when Eve told Eoduun to bite her, to test Zeke's control, the snarl that resonated through the trees chilled Eve's blood the moment Eoduun's fangs sank into her flesh. Zeke leapt from the top of the tree, expanding his wings as he glided quickly through the air, straight for Eoduun. Eve stepped in front of him just in time to stop Zeke, making him veer to her left and crash epically to the ground. He was up in an instant, his deep-golden eyes full of rage as he focused on Eoduun.

Dagon stepped in, shoving Eoduun away. He grabbed Eve's hair and yanked it, making her yelp.

"Ouch! What the fuck?!" she cried, rubbing her scalp.

Zeke lunged at Dagon, his huge teeth bared. They clashed like two titans, and Dagon grabbed Zeke's jaws, keeping them pried open as Zeke tried to tear into his neck.

"She's not in danger, Zeke," Dagon said calmly as he tussled with the stony beast. "Control yourself."

"You hurt her!" Zeke growled, his words loosely articulated with his jaws held open.

"She likes it when I pull her hair," Dagon taunted, amused.

"She cried out!"

Dagon chuckled. "Yes, she does that quite a lot when she likes something." He held Zeke back and added, "You know the difference, Zeke. You need to get control of yourself. You know she's not in danger from any of us." Dagon leaned close and looked into Zeke's eyes, and Zeke immediately stopped fighting.

"What did you just do?" Bo asked, relaxing a little now that Zeke had calmed down.

"I pulled him back to reality." He released his hold on Zeke. "You good?" he asked him.

Zeke nodded.

Dagon reached over and pinched Eve's arm. Hard.

"Ow! Fucker!" she shouted.

Zeke snarled at Dagon, but this time, he didn't lunge.

Eve reached over and grabbed Dagon's bare nipple, since he had his shirt off to allow free movement of his wings, and twisted.

"Fuck!" he roared, shoving her hand away.

Zeke's eyes were still watching Dagon, a scowl on his face.

Roy sighed. "Well, I reckon we know who his protective instinct is focused on."

Dagon rubbed his sore nipple. "He'll get it under control. He just needs to fight the instinct and not allow it to overtake his reasoning." He turned devious vermilion eyes to Eve. "Let's see how he handles sparring."

Eve smirked at him, holding her arms wide. "Come at me, bro."

Bo crossed his arms and stepped back to enjoy the show, a smug grin on his face, knowing Eve had every advantage. He pulled his mask down and turned to Isaac. "This should be good."

Isaac nodded in agreement, lighting up a cigarette.

When Dagon teleported, suddenly appearing behind Eve and grabbing her in a rear naked choke, she threw an elbow back into his ribs. She felt a crack, and he hissed between his teeth. She grabbed his arm and spun around, twisting his arm behind his back and kicking the back of his knee, dropping him to the ground. She shoved the back of his head, throwing him facedown into the grass. He swept his foot out and caught her ankles, landing her flat on her back, and in an instant, he was on top of her, pinning her hands over her head with one hand, his other hand wrapped around her throat.

Zeke attacked with a vicious roar, and Dagon was tackled off of Eve, rolling over the grass with Zeke. His teeth sank into Dagon's neck, but Dagon caught his fingers between his jaws, preventing him from biting down too hard.

Eve threw her hand out toward Zeke, suddenly afraid for Dagon's safety, and Zeke was thrown off him, landing on his back. "No!" Eve reprimanded, appearing next to him and standing over him intimidatingly. She pointed an accusatory finger in his face. "Bad boy!"

Zeke stared up at her incredulously, and she saw the reason return to his monstrous face. Then, to her surprise, he laughed. "I'm not a dog, babe."

She pursed her lips and glanced at the amused expressions around her, embarrassed. "Shut up. You *were* being a bad boy."

Then Eve felt a huge hand tangle in her thick mane, and she was pulled back. Zeke's twitched forward, as though he were about to lunge, but caught himself. Eve clamped her hands down over top of Dagon's fist on her scalp, intertwining her fingers to hold his hand in place, then pivoted around to face him. His wrist twisted at an unnatural angle, and Eve felt a snap. He released her hair with a roar of pain, and she took that opportunity to grab his shoulder, hoisting herself up to drive her knee into his gut.

A whoosh of air accompanied the groan that Dagon expelled as he doubled over, dropping to his knees. "Fuck, princess," he rasped. "You're a little fucking monster."

"Thank you," she grinned.

"Glad she's on our side," Roy mumbled.

Eve stood in front of Dagon, gripping his long dark hair and angling his head back to make him look up at her. "I like you on your knees," she remarked darkly. Tendrils of heat wove their way between her thighs.

Zeke cleared his throat, but she ignored him, her mind singularly focused.

Since taking Lilith's power, she no longer had uncontrollable urges she needed to act upon. The monster she'd become still needed to be fed, but the hunger manifested differently now. Instead of wild, acute desire, her mind was clouding with increasing frequency, wandering to fantasies about the men around her.

Like right now.

She had tunnel vision, and all she could think about was Dagon's thick, delicious cock pounding into her while he pulled her back by her hair. She imagined pushing him onto the ground and riding on top of him, her hands around his throat. Her core pulsed and wept at the vivid mental image.

Dagon's vermilion eyes bored into hers, and a devilish grin spread over his face. "Anything for you, princess."

Eve released his hair and ran her hand down the side of his face, under his jaw, and cupped his chin as he looked up at her.

"Beg," she whispered.

"Evie," Bo warned.

She glanced up at Bo, pulled from the fantasy, and he shook his head at her, his arms crossed. *No.* She looked over at Isaac standing next to him, and he wore an expression of concern. She furrowed her brow and raised her palms. *What?*

He tapped the ash from his cigarette and signed back, *You need your powers expelled.* With a pointed look, he tapped the curled fingers of an F-handshape to his chin. *Soon.*

She pushed into his mind to see what he was seeing, and it snapped her back to reality. Her massive aura wasn't just black. It was a slowly growing void.

Her humanity was beginning to slip.

The desire pooling between her legs wasn't fading. She might as well seize the moment. While still in his mind, she purred, *No time like the present.*

47
I'm Your Fucking God

She returned to her own perspective just in time to see Isaac arch a brow at her, then glance hesitantly over at Bo.

Eve popped up in front of them, grabbing Isaac's hand and flicking the cigarette from it. "I think it's time for confession," she informed Bo. "I'll be back in a bit."

He gave her a knowing look, then nodded. He'd already been made aware of the circumstances regarding her new powers from Lilith.

She warped space around her and Isaac, stepping through into Isaac's apartment and dragging him along with her.

She'd barely completed the transition before Isaac's hand was on her throat, yanking her toward him, her body crashing against his.

"Finally," he murmured, his mouth descending upon hers, sucking her bottom lip between his teeth. His thumb stroked along her jaw as she tilted her head, allowing him to deepen the kiss, tasting the smoke on his tongue.

She wanted to tell him she'd heard what he said to Veris about her, but she didn't. He wouldn't remember it anyway, since Eoduun had erased all his memories of Veris. But she knew how he felt about her. *"Eve is my god."*

This wasn't just an exorcism.

Isaac dropped his hands to her ass, hooking under her hamstrings and hoisting her onto his hips, drawing a startled sound from Eve. She wrapped her legs around his waist and threw her arms over his shoulders to steady herself. His cock was already hard, his bulge pressing between her legs.

He carried her to his bedroom, kicking the door closed and pressing her back against it. His hands gripped her thighs as his lips traced along her jaw, dipping down to taste her pulse when she tipped her head back against the door. She rolled her hips, grinding herself against him, *needing* to feel him inside her. She ran her hand up the back of his neck and closed her eyes as he released his grip on one thigh and slid his fingers down the front of her sweatpants. He reached between her legs and stroked her through the thin cotton of her underwear, stirring her pleasure. She knew he could feel her arousal already saturating the fabric. His lips crashed against hers once more, devouring her whimpers as he slipped aside her underwear and pushed two thick digits inside of her.

She tightened her thighs around his waist, riding his hand, shamelessly succumbing to the need to chase the high his fingers offered. But she needed more. *Now.* She took his face in her hands and made him look at her, her hips still rolling.

With hooded eyes, she begged, "Fill me with your blessing, Father, before the devil takes my soul."

The corner of his lip quirked up as his eyes narrowed. "The devil? You *are* the devil." He withdrew his hand from her sweatpants and spun them both around, taking her down to his bed, his hips pushing hers into the mattress. He pulled her shirt off over her head, and her skin heated beneath his eyes as they feasted on her body beneath him. "And I think you've taken *my* soul."

Her hand fisted in his shirt as she raised her head off the pillow. His eyes followed her lips as she declared, "I'm no devil. I'm your fucking god." He might not remember saying it, but she would never forget.

The fire in his eyes only confirmed the truth of her declaration. He hooked his fingers in her waistband and dragged her sweatpants down her thighs. His gaze raked her naked body, then his deep brown eyes clashed with hers. "I'm beginning to think they're one and the same."

He pulled his shirt off and tossed it aside, leaning over and grabbing a rosary from his nightstand. He brought it to his lips and kissed it, mumbling a short prayer, then snatched up Eve's hands and wrapped it around her wrists, binding them together. Once bound, he kissed her knuckles and raised her hands above her head, using one hand to hold her wrists against the headboard. He reached his other hand down to unfasten his fly and lower his pants, his impressive cock finally bursting free.

As he pressed his hips between her thighs, his thickness sinking slowly into her, stretching her walls, he whispered, "You are my damnation *and* my salvation." He kissed her jaw and ran his hand up her neck, pushing himself deeper. "You show me heaven, then drag me through the fires of hell." He pulled out, then pushed harder, deeper, Eve's back arching off the mattress as his hand gripped her throat. His teeth nipped at her earlobe. "I cleanse your soul, likely at the expense of my own." She felt his lips smile against her neck as he buried himself to the hilt inside of her, making her gasp. "But when I'm with you, I'm alive. In moments like this, the white whale isn't dragging me under, and I can breathe."

Eve opened her mouth, but Isaac's searing kiss stole her reply. With his hips thrusting against hers, his massive cock driving into her, she couldn't string together a cohesive thought. All she could focus on was the sweet heat coiling in her belly, like a cobra tensing, ready to strike at any moment.

Latin words fell from Isaac's tongue as he fucked her, one hand firmly holding her wrists to the headboard, the other hand on her throat. She cried out as the tension in her core snapped, her voice vibrating against his palm as her body thrashed, a torrent of pleasure rushing through her.

His last words rushed out in a breathless prayer as he grasped for control, and the emotions Eve didn't even realize were being suppressed came crashing through the dam Lilith's power had erected in her heart. She knew her emotions had dampened, but she didn't know they had faded to this extent. Love, guilt, joy, anger, desperation...they all swarmed and collided in her heart with unbearable intensity.

The exorcism worked. Thank the Fates.

And then she sensed him. Through the blurry tears in her eyes, Eve saw Bo appear next to the bed. She blinked to clear her vision, her hips still gyrating against Isaac's in the aftermath of her climax, and her gaze fused with Bo's. He stood, captivated, his wolfish, heterochrome gaze taking in the scene before him.

"Bo..." she rasped, and she was slammed with a fresh wave of desire, not all of it hers.

Isaac's head turned, aware of Bo's presence, but he didn't stop fucking Eve, issuing a silent challenge.

Bo's chest rose and fell with heavy breaths as he tugged his mask down around his neck. He moved to stand at the edge of the bed. "Hands and knees, Evie," he commanded, pointing to the spot on the bed in front of him.

Submit. Obey.

Isaac withdrew and sat back, and Eve crawled clumsily across the bed, the rosary still wrapped around her wrists. She looked up at Bo on her fists and knees in front of him. Bo looked over at Isaac. "Keep going," he ordered.

Warily, Isaac positioned himself behind Eve, lining his cock up to her entrance. He glanced questioningly back up at Bo, and Bo gave him a slight nod.

Eve whimpered and screwed her eyes shut as Isaac slammed into her, his hands gripping her hips.

Bo cupped Eve's chin, and she looked up at him. "Do you like his cock, Evie?"

She nodded.

"Words," he demanded.

"Yes," she panted.

"But you want more, don't you?"

"Yes."

Bo unzipped his pants and released his engorged cock. He buried his fingers in her hair and touched the crown of his cock to her lips. "Open up, baby."

Eve parted her lips, and Bo's hot length slid over her tongue, into her mouth. His fingers tightened against her scalp as he pressed his hips forward, making her eyes water as he hit the back of her throat. He looked down at her, fucking her mouth as Isaac fucked her from behind, falling into a mutual cadence.

"Such a good girl," Bo praised, watching her swallow his cock.

The pressure in Eve's core was building once again, her walls tightening around Isaac's thick shaft. He began to thrust harder, his fingers bruising Eve's hips as he pulled her against him, and she moaned around Bo's cock, panting through her nostrils.

"Come for us, Evie," Bo growled, his eyes darting up to watch Isaac pound into her.

She heard Isaac groan and felt him swell inside of her, pushing them both over the precipice into pure bliss. She ground her hips against him, her core pulsing and spasming.

"Fuuuck," Bo groaned, tugging on her hair and jerking his hips forward, pouring himself down her throat.

Isaac sat back on his haunches, panting, and Bo withdrew from Eve's mouth and tucked himself back into his pants. He raked his fingers through her mane and smiled breathlessly down at her, showing her his beautiful fangs.

She wiped her mouth on the back of her hand and smirked up at him. "Babhdán Fagerberg, I never thought I'd see the day you learned to share."

Bo's golden wolf eye darkened back to charcoal grey. "That makes two of us."

Eve flopped onto her back in the middle of the bed as Isaac pulled his pants up over his hips. He and Bo both looked down at her, and she looked between them. "What, no cuddle session?"

Bo's cheeks tinged pink as he picked her clothes up off the floor and held them out to her. He glanced at Isaac. "Too far, Evie."

She scoffed as she grabbed her clothes and began to put them back on. "Oh, *that's* too far. Ok," she mumbled sarcastically.

A look of satisfaction sat comfortably on Isaac's face as he gazed at her. He began to sign, then paused, considering Bo. "It worked," he said. "You're bright again."

"Powerless, you mean," she derided as she combed her hand through her tangled hair. But she wasn't powerless, was she? Isaac couldn't exorcise Lilith's power. She called on Ruth's memories, something she hadn't done in a while, and focused on the papers sticking up out of the trash can in the corner of the room. She mumbled an incantation, and the trash can burst into flames.

Bo turned toward the burning trash, eyes widening. "Evie! What the fuck?! Don't start fires in Isaac's apartment!"

She laughed at his panicked tone, then said another incantation to put the fire out. Smoke curled from the blackened refuse, and the smoke alarm began to screech, prompting Bo to clamp his palms down over his sensitive ears.

"Goddamn it!" he complained while Isaac jumped up and began waving the shirt in his hand in front of the smoke detector.

"Dinner's ready!" Eve shouted, still laughing. She pushed up off the bed and headed to the door, ducking under Isaac's wildly swinging arm. "I'll leave you to it!"

Then she paused. Lilith had teleported out of the LOA compound. Maybe she could still teleport, too.

And then she was standing in her own apartment.

"Fuck yes," she whispered to herself. She looked down at Bitches, who had roused from his nap on the couch to come rub against her legs. "Hear that?" she asked him as she crouched down to pet him, listening to the faint drone of Isaac's alarm still going off several doors down. "This girl is on *fire*."

48

The Scar of the Incident Remained

Eve was sitting at the kitchen island, eating the last of the chicken nuggets from her freezer, when Bo and Isaac walked in. Bo still had his mask down. She grinned at them. "You cuddled without me, didn't you?"

Bo shot her an annoyed glare. He pointed at her and raised his brows as he instructed, "No more fires inside the complex! Got it?"

Eve took a bite of a nugget and watched him settle into his spot on the barstool next to her. "Yes, Daddy."

Isaac tripped over Bitches on his way to his chair, then huffed and scooped up the little furball and sat down with him. He scowled at the catdog and touched his chin, turning his palm out as he drew it away, then he made a B-handshape and curled his fingers near his chin. It was similar to Eve's name, but with a B-handshape instead of a middle finger. That must be Bitches designated sign name. He shook his head and brushed his thumb under his chin, then swiped one palm over the other.

Bad Bitches. Not nice.

Bitches twitched his stubby little tail and butted his head up under Isaac's chin, and Isaac's scowl melted away.

As Eve raised another nugget to her mouth, the tattoo on her wrist burned and tingled, and Luc appeared across the counter from her. She paused with the nugget halfway to her mouth, staring at him, thinking about what would've happened if he had done that about fifteen minutes ago.

He smiled at her. "What's the matter? Sunekosuri got your tongue? Or had you just forgotten how dazzling my devilishly good looks were?"

She popped the chicken nugget into her mouth and smiled around it. "Color me dazzled," she said as she chewed.

Luc leaned over the counter and kissed her head. "I missed you, love." He glanced down at the remaining nuggets on her plate. "Do you want me to make you something to eat? Maybe something that *doesn't* taste like mushed up assholes?"

Eve faked surprise. "You mean you *do* know how to make something that doesn't taste like mushed up assholes? You've been holding out on me all this time?"

Luc laughed. "Rude," he chastised playfully. He leaned his elbows on the counter across from her. "And here I came home bearing good news. Maybe I shouldn't tell you."

"Is Mira gone for good?" she asked excitedly.

"Well, gone for good from Knighco. She'll still be involved in Fagerberg Enterprises, but you'll likely never have to see her again."

"Good. Stupid bitch. How did everything go at the Vatican?"

Luc raised a shoulder. "As well as can be expected. Sister Fiona presented them with the edited-for-TV version of events, and they accepted it. They were more than happy to accept that Veris was to blame for everything because they already had a heavy bias against him anyway. Apparently, they had some history with him I didn't know about. They seemed to be relieved to hear he was dead. So, we're in the clear for now. But they do expect our help in taking care of Lilith."

Eve frowned. "I won't help with that."

Luc rested his chin in his hand. "You really believe she's not evil? That she's not going to cause problems?"

"She's not evil. Well, no more evil than I am. I think she just wants to enjoy her freedom."

"Zephlyn hasn't had any visions about her," Bo offered.

"If the Vatican finds her, we can't refuse to hunt her unless we want to make a very dangerous enemy," Luc said.

Eve ate her last nugget. "I'm already on their shitlist. I won't hunt her, and I couldn't, even if I wanted to. We made a blood pact that I would never use my power against her. It was part of the deal I made so I could raise Zeke."

Luc took her empty plate from in front of her and walked it to the dishwasher. "You don't have to participate."

"I don't want you hunting her, either. I don't want her hunted," Eve said firmly. "Period."

The dishes clattered in the rack as Luc found a place for the plate in the overly-packed appliance. He closed the door and furrowed his brows at her. "Why?"

"Because we hunt the monsters that hurt people, and I don't think she fits that description. I won't just blindly hunt whoever the *Vatican* feels threatened by." She gave him a pointed look. "Especially since I'm on that list, and likely always will be."

"She has a point," Bo said, staring down at his phone screen.

Luc sighed and leaned back, resting his hands on the edge of the counter behind him. "Fine. As long as she doesn't stir up trouble, we'll allow her to remain one step ahead of us. I've gotten rather adept at falsifying reports lately anyway."

"If you are anything, you are an excellent bullshitter," Bo agreed.

Then Dagon appeared in the open area between the living room and kitchen. Ruger wasn't wrong when he said it was like Hogwarts around here these days.

"Oh, joy," Luc said flatly.

Dagon ignored him, his eyes only on Eve.

"How did the rest of Zeke's training go?" Eve asked him.

"He flies with the grace of a wet fucking bumblebee. He's an embarrassment to all winged-kind."

"He'll learn. No more outbursts?"

"When you left, apparently his protective instincts honed in on Eoduun. Z tried to rip my arm off when I shoved him."

"Interesting. He went from trying to kill him to protecting him? Glad I'm at the top of the hierarchy," Eve mused. "Why did you shove Eoduun?"

Dagon shrugged. "He's an annoying little prick."

"That's no way to make friends, Gilly," Luc chastised sarcastically.

"Wow, clever. Think of that all by yourself?" Dagon shot back. He crossed his arms. "I don't need friends."

"You do if you're going to join a team. No one will work with you if you're a dick."

"They work with you," Bo pointed out, glancing up at Luc over his phone.

Eve could tell Luc's eyes had widened behind his sunglasses. "Are you seriously siding with him?"

"No. Just saying." Bo replied nonchalantly. His attention returned to his phone.

"I'll join Team Alpha," Dagon said decisively.

"Team Alpha is full," Bo replied without looking up.

"Ramil doesn't have a team anymore," Luc said, rubbing his chin thoughtfully. "I could put Dagon and Isaac on Team Beta."

Eve and Bo both jerked their heads up. Eve protested, "But Isaac is already with Team Alpha."

"Team Alpha already has four hunters," Luc contested. "And Ramil can translate for Isaac. It's perfect."

Eve looked forlornly at Isaac sitting in the living room with Bitches sleeping in his lap, his attention on the opened book in his hand. It was Eve's copy of *Pride and Prejudice*. She wondered if he could tell they were talking about him.

She didn't want to be separated from him. If he was sent with another team, who would heal him when he got hurt? Who would pay attention to the fact that he *was* hurt? Because he certainly didn't. Who would he talk to? She and Bo were his only friends, and he refused to speak to anyone else. Sure, he could sign with Ramil, but he didn't seem to like Ramil.

He didn't really like anyone else, even Cassie.

"You can't move him to another team. He needs us," Eve said quietly.

"He's a grown ass man, love. I assure you, he will be fine."

She turned puppy-dog eyes to Luc. "He'll be lonely."

Luc took off his sunglasses and dragged his hand down his face. "Eve. Love. He is the *Angel of Death*. Everywhere he goes, he is preceded by his reputation. He will be fine."

She looked out at Isaac again, and this time his eyes met hers. He signed, *I will be fine. Don't worry about me.*

But she did worry about him. She couldn't help it. She didn't worry about Dagon so much, with his godly powers, but she worried about *all* of her mortal boys. They were breakable. She wanted to gather them all up with her and keep them safe from everything. After what happened to Zeke, and then Eoduun, the fear of losing one of them filled her with crippling panic. Her blood could bring someone back to life if she was quick enough, and if there was a body to heal, but what if she wasn't there? What if she couldn't get there in time? What if they were blown to bits, or incinerated, or... She'd never considered that they would be separated from her.

Eve clutched her hand to the sudden ache in her chest, her throat tightening, making it hard to breath. Her scalp and ears tingled, and her vision blurred. "You can't take them away. What if they die?" she mumbled in a rushed panic, tears pricking her eyes. "I can't protect them if they aren't with me. I can't save them if I'm not there. You can't take them. You all have to stay with me. They have to stay with me." Her glazed eyes looked toward Luc, but she had a hard time focusing on him. "You have to stay with me. I can't lose anyone. The grimoire is gone, and death will be forever. I can't lose them forever. You forever. I can't..." Her voice trailed off as she began to hyperventilate, tears streaming down her face.

Two strong hands cupped her face, and Bo's mismatched eyes filled her blurred field of vision. Light and dark. "Evie." He took her hand and pressed it to his chest.

Thump-thump...Thump-thump...Thump-thump. His heartbeat was strong and steady beneath her palm, and she felt a soothing wave of calm envelop her rapidly racing heart and mind. Her vision cleared, and she gazed back at Bo, her ragged breaths slowing. The panic slowly subsided.

He'd used his calm to override her storm.

She still wasn't ok, even after bringing Zeke and Eoduun back. The scar of the incident remained.

Now that her head had cleared, she realized Dagon was standing behind her, his fingers lightly playing with her hair, and Isaac stood on the other side of her with the sunekosuri in his arms. He handed Bitches to Eve for a cuddle, and she hugged the furry yokai to her chest, feeling the light rumble of his version of a purr.

Concern etched itself into Luc's face as he regarded Eve. "I understand your fears, love," he said softly. "It's the same way I feel every time I send you out on a case. But we gotta let our peacocks fly, right? It might be dangerous, but we have a job to do, and all of us...we're very good at it. We have a responsibility to keep people safe."

"And I have a responsibility to keep all of you safe. *I* have a job to do, too, and I can't do it if I'm not there." She sniffled. "I finally have everyone back. Everyone is safe. I'm not ready to let anybody go yet."

Dagon exhaled an exasperated, defeated sigh from behind her. He gently rested his palm on the top of Eve's head. "You know you don't have to worry about me. I'm not some mere mortal. I will keep your priest and your dragon alive. You have my word."

"See? You have his word," Luc said cheerfully, his face brightening. "And for once, I actually believe him."

Eve chewed her lip uneasily. She looked over at Isaac as she squished her cheek against Bitches' head.

He gave her a smug smirk and signed, *I'm hard to kill. I'll be fine.*

She spun around on her barstool and looked up at Dagon. "If anyone gets hurt, you tell me—" she tapped her head— "immediately. I will teleport there and heal them."

He grinned down at her. "Yes, princess. As you wish."

Voices in the hallway heralded the approach of Ramil, Zeke, and Eoduun, and moments later, they all filed through the door. Roy must've fucked off already.

Zeke pushed between Dagon and Bo and pressed a kiss to Eve's cheek. "Did Dagon tell you I'm getting the hang of flying?" he asked excitedly.

Eve smiled at his sunny expression. "Something like that."

"These powers are actually pretty cool. I mean, once I'm able to stop hulking out over stupid shit, I'll be like a fucking X-Men! Er...X-Man?"

"I'm glad you're happy," she beamed. She turned her attention to Eoduun. "You seem to be taking well to your new abilities. Any cravings?"

"Nothing crazy," Eoduun replied, resting his elbows on the counter adjacent to Bo. "But I kind of binged at the LOA compound before you sidelined us. Roy said I need to feed a little bit every four or five days if I want to maintain control of my thirst, though, so I'm probably almost due for a top-off." He licked his lips as he eyed Eve's pulse point.

"I'll keep you fed, don't worry," she assured him.

"Good news, Ramil!" Luc announced, changing the subject. "You have a new team!" With a flourish of his hands, he gestured to Isaac and Dagon like they were the prize in a gameshow.

Ramil nodded, seemingly satisfied.

Now that Eve had a moment to process the fact that she couldn't keep everyone on her team, she was glad Dagon, Ramil, and Isaac would be on a team together. Who stood a chance against a god, a dragon, and the Angel of Death? They would be all right.

They had to be.

She felt Ramil's presence pressing on her mental barriers, so she let him in. He asked, *Can I speak with you in private?*

Eve excused herself and Ramil just as Team Flannel barged in, Ruger laughing obnoxiously about some prank he just pulled on a red-faced Remi, Cassie trailing in their wake with an exasperated look. Eve promised Cass she'd be back shortly to provide backup in that room full of testosterone.

Eve followed Ramil into his apartment and sat next to him on his couch, tucking one leg under her so she could face him. "What's on your mind, *darling*?" she teased.

He sat angled slightly toward her, looking uncomfortable. "We never really talked about what happened between us," he said.

Eve's stomach turned. She knew this conversation was coming. "I don't know what to say. We did what needed to be done to resurrect Zeke. But, I mean, I'm happy we got to know each other better, and I feel like we bonded over the experience."

Ramil clasped his hands together in his lap, his striking eyes fixed on hers. "I can't stop thinking about you, Eve."

Words eluded her as she stared stupidly back at him. What was she supposed to say to that? She knew he was harboring feelings for her, but she had also hoped that her lack of reciprocation in the matter would have cued him in that she didn't feel the same way. Yes, he was wildly attractive, and he stirred something carnal and primal in her, but her affection for him extended only into friendship.

She cared for him, but she wasn't *in* love with him. But, god, she couldn't go with that old cliché line.

Let's just be friends.

So, she just stared mutely at him.

After a long, awkward silence, he gave a defeated sigh. "Yeah."

Eve's heart broke for him. "I'm so sorry, Ramil." She leaned forward and placed her hand on his. "I care about you. I really fucking care about you. But I'm happy with what we have now, and I want you to be happy with this, too." She gave him a playful smirk. "And hey, I'm sure I'll need to borrow your power from time to time, so we'll always have that, too, if you're still willing to lend it to me."

He smiled at her. "Anything for you."

"But no more spying on anyone, or breaking into my apartment to steal things, got it?"

He chuckled. "I'll do my best to refrain. But I am a hoarder. It's in my nature, unfortunately."

"I've noticed, Goldmember," she jested.

They smiled at each other, but it was bittersweet. She had a feeling Ramil would still hold out hope that she would grow to love him in time, but her boys had stolen her whole heart, and they hadn't left a scrap of it behind for anyone else.

49

You Don't Have to Be What They Wanted You to Be

When Eve and Ramil returned to Eve's apartment, Eve found that Celeste, Zephlyn, Mendal, and Kai had all stopped by as well. Her place was beginning to resemble a college frat party on a daily basis while all the hunters were home. The only two who never came to hang out now were Roy and Levi.

She supposed the zoo didn't appeal to middle-aged men.

"We're gonna need a bigger boat," Eve mumbled as she weaved through the crowded space. She saw Zeke sitting on the floor by the coffee table, dangling the string from the hood on his sweatshirt while Bitches swatted playfully at it. She made her way over and sat on the floor next to him just as Bitches caught the string in his mouth, tugged on it, then let it go, causing it to spring back and whack Zeke in the eye.

"Ow!" Zeke clapped his hand over his eye, and Bitches stopped, taking a moment to bump his head affectionately against the back of Zeke's hand. "Aw, you're sorry, I know," he crooned, rubbing the sunekosuri's back.

Eve picked up her mother's journal from the coffee table in front of her, opening it in her lap to the torn-out section around her birthday. She fanned the short, jagged edges with her thumb.

"What's that?" Zeke asked, nodding toward the journal as Zephlyn came over and sat on the couch across from them.

"Stacey Rose's journal. My origin story." She frowned down at it. "But a chunk is missing."

Zephlyn leaned forward. "Do you want me to give it a go?"

"Give it a go?" Eve echoed.

He held out his hand. "Maybe I can get something from it. A vision, or a fragment of a memory."

Eve extended the book across the coffee table to him. "Please."

As soon as the journal rested in Zephlyn's hands, his face went slack and his eyes turned completely white. Eve's heart leapt. Was he seeing something? She desperately wanted to see whatever it was he was seeing.

Lilith had been able to see into Veris' memories, and into Eve's heart, so did that mean that Eve also still possessed the power to get into someone's mind? Was that a power that was hers to keep, like her ability to perform witchcraft?

She focused on Zephlyn, reaching into his head. He had strong mental barriers, but she pushed through with little effort.

Flashes of memories raced through her mind like a flipbook. Stacey had left her mental imprint on each page, and as Zephlyn's fingers traced lightly over the torn edges of the ripped-out pages, the memories she left behind rose to the surface.

Running. Stacey was running through the woods in the dark, holding her swollen belly with one hand, her other hand clasped tightly in

Moira's as branches whipped across her face and arms. She could hear the wolves howling in the distance behind them, indicating the discovery of her escape. But the wolves sent to track her would be confounded, at least for a short time. They couldn't scent her and her best friend thanks to Moira's cloaking spell. But it wouldn't last long, so they had to run. Moira left her car about a mile up the road to avoid alerting anyone of her presence, and all Stacey had to do was *get to it,* and she was free.

But running a mile at eight-months pregnant was no easy fucking task. It was more like speed-waddling. In school, she remembered running the mile in around seven or eight minutes.

This felt infinitely longer.

"Baby still in there?" Moira asked breathlessly as they weaved around a tree.

"She hasn't fallen out yet!" Stacey replied, the air burning her exhausted lungs.

"Keep clenching! We're almost there!"

When they broke through the trees and Stacey beheld the ugly beige Ford Taurus parked there, she laughed, tears of relief welling in her eyes.

She fucking made it.

Stacey was sore everywhere as she stared at the passing trees and small towns from the passenger seat, wondering where Moira was taking her. She hoped to fuck that the baby was ok after her frolic through the woods.

Maybe after all that, the baby would come a little early. Would that be so bad? If she didn't arrive on All Hallow's Eve, maybe she would grow up to be a normal, regular girl.

Not this 'Abomination.'

Stacey rubbed her sore belly, and she felt a little foot press up against her palm. "You'll be ok, baby girl. Whatever comes, whatever fate throws at you, you'll be ok. You don't have to be what they wanted you to be. You be what *you* want to be. I didn't run a mile through the woods with you on my bladder for you to grow up and live for anyone other than yourself."

Moira drove all through the night and into the next day, stopping only for gas, food, and bathroom breaks. When they were getting close to the Canadian border, they stopped in a sleepy little town called Newbury to get gas. They saw a paper on the wall by the bathroom advertising a rental cottage with a short-term lease.

It was perfect.

They stayed.

But as the days dragged on closer to Halloween, Stacey grew anxious. She hoped the baby would come earlier. Or later. Anything to thwart the damned prophecy.

When Stacey's water broke at 7AM on October 31st, however, she cried.

Labor wasn't easy, even with Moira's spells and herbal concoctions and the home birthing tub, but they made it through it, and at 2:43PM, Stacey's baby girl was born.

She fed and swaddled her and held her close as she lay in bed to rest afterward while Moira cleaned up the birthing area.

"I wish I could keep you and raise you as my own, little peanut. But life's not fucking fair. You'll learn that soon enough, and it breaks my heart to know that I won't be there to help you through it. You might have a darkness in you, and I won't be there to help you understand it. Monsters may come looking for you, and I won't be there to protect you from them. But this is the best way I know how to keep you safe. Keep you hidden. I'm going to find a new mommy for you, and she will take care of you and love you and make you feel safe. You'll never even know about me, and that's the way it has to be. But maybe somewhere in that sweet little head of yours, you'll remember my voice and know that there is someone out there who loves you so, so much."

The next day, Moira and Stacey brought the baby to the nearest hospital, dressed as nurses with fake ID badges Moira had enchanted, and switched her out for another baby girl who had just been born that morning. Moira took the new baby and left, while Stacey brought her baby to the new mother.

"Here's your little bundle of joy, ma'am," she said as she held her baby for the last time. She passed her off to the new mother, Sylvia, who looked down at her as though she didn't know what to do with her. There was no joy on the woman's face.

God, Stacey hoped she hadn't made a grave mistake.

"Have you thought of a name?" she asked Sylvia.

"I had some picked out, but...nothing seems quite right."

"She looks like an 'Evrys' to me. Maybe 'Eve' for short," Stacey suggested hopefully as Sylvia studied her face. Eno wanted to name her 'Lilian,' after Lilith, so Stacey had her heart set on 'Eve.'

"Evrys, huh?" She looked down at the baby in her arms. "Eve. Hm. I kind of like it."

"Is this your first child?"

"Yeah." Sylvia looked up at Stacey, admitting, "I'm terrified."

Stacey gave her a sympathetic smile. *Me too.* "I'll let you two get acquainted," she said softly, patting Sylvia's hand. She looked at her baby one last time, then turned and walked out of the room before her tears could fall.

When she returned to the car in the hospital parking lot where Moira and the new baby were waiting for her, Stacey's face was red and blotchy from crying. She sat in the back seat next to the car seat that held her new daughter, Emma.

"She'll be ok, Stace," Moira assured her. "But we need to get far away from here. I checked the files on your daughter's new mom, and she lives in Newbury, too. The address isn't far from the cottage, over by Black Lake."

"We're out of money. Where are we going to go?" She sighed. "Let's just go back home to Grand Rapids. That should be far enough away from here. You still have your house there, and I can move back in with my mom for a bit. We'll lay low. Besides, I don't want to be too far away. I still want to be able to check in on Evrys."

As Moira pulled the car out onto the road, she glanced at Stacey in the rearview. "Are you sure that's wise? Checking in on her?"

"I need to know she's ok. I can walk away, but I can't live my life not knowing how she's doing." Stacey buried her face in her hands. "God, what if they find her? What if they figure it out?"

When they got back to the cottage, Moira plopped a heavy, ancient-looking book on the counter. "This has been passed down in my family for generations. It's…for dire circumstances only. The spells in here are dark, powerful, and potentially dangerous. It's in Gaelic, but I think I remember enough from what my grandma taught me to be able to work a spell. I'm not sure if I have the *power* to do it, but if you want…we can try the spell to bind a supernatural guardian to the girl."

"Evrys. Her name is Evrys."

They looked through the fragile pages of the old tome, and when Stacey saw the image of the fearsome nuckelavee, she jabbed her finger to the page. "That one. No one would fuck with that."

"They're only in Scotland, and only in saltwater," Moira told her.

"I want that one. You said Evrys' new home is by a lake. It isn't saltwater, but it's water. Can we make it happen?"

Moira twisted her mouth contemplatively. "I don't know. There is a summoning spell, but I don't know if there are limitations on distance. I have the spell to bind it, but I need an enchantment that would allow it to survive here."

Moira and Stacey sat up all night with the fussy new baby and the book, and finally, in the early hours of the morning, Moira yelped with excitement.

"I found it! This should work!" She turned to Stacey with a wide grin.

That night, at 3AM, Stacey and Moira drove to the public access, and while Emma slept in the car seat in the Taurus twenty feet away, they summoned Mòrag. The beast was both awe-inspiring and disgusting, and Stacey's hands trembled as she placed the tiny, blood-soaked tuft of Evrys's newborn baby hair into its mouth. She watched it step back and sink slowly into the water, and she felt hopeful.

No one would dare mess with Evrys with that thing around.

Stacey and Moira packed their belongings that morning and drove to Grand Rapids. Stacey moved back in with her mother for a time, until she found a little house that she could afford.

She fought the urge to go check on her daughter, uncertain if anyone from LOA had tracked her down and was watching her. Coming home probably wasn't her smartest move, but, financially, she didn't have another option. She'd gotten Evrys safely away, and that was what mattered. Stacey wasn't worried about herself, because it wasn't her they wanted anymore. She'd served her purpose. No, they wanted Evrys.

Even so, she was constantly looking over her shoulder, never allowing Emma out of her sight. Emma would never have the powers they were after, and the trackers they would send would likely smell that she wasn't the right child, but she couldn't be certain they wouldn't harm her simply out of malice.

The week before Christmas, Stacey convinced Moira to make a trip to check on Evrys and the nuckelavee, and she was relieved to hear that all seemed to be well. Quiet. Normal.

The Locusts hadn't found her.

But it was then that she realized that if they found Stacey and searched her belongings, her journal would be damning. She couldn't allow her own words to lead the Locusts right to Evrys' doorstep. She rushed to find it in her desk drawer, grabbed a lighter, and brought it to the kitchen sink. She held the flame to the corner of the book, but a sudden feeling in her chest stopped her. Something told her she shouldn't destroy the whole journal. She couldn't explain why, but she knew someday, someone would need it. So, instead, she tore out the entire section she wrote in Newbury and burned the pages in the sink, washing the ashes down the drain.

Eve withdrew from Zephlyn's mind as the vision ended, and she saw his eyes return to their normal dark brown.

"Are your visions always that vivid?" Eve asked him as he returned the journal to her.

He looked surprised. "Did you see it, too?"

"I was in your head, watching it through you."

His naturally narrow eyes widened.

She immediately added, "Don't worry, I wasn't rummaging around or anything. I just wanted to see what you were seeing."

"Have you been working to hone your own powers of premonition?" he asked.

"Oh yeah," Zeke chimed in. "What is it you call it? Don't Ask, Don't Tell?"

Eve laughed. "Don't Think It, Don't Say It. And no, it just happens when it happens. I don't seem to have any control over it."

Zephlyn cleared his throat. "Is that…is that something you could borrow from me, if it helped you to control it yourself?"

"She can take anybody's abilities," Zeke replied for her, dangling his hoodie string in front of Bitches again.

Eoduun was sitting on the floor next to Zephlyn, but he pushed up and sat on the couch, leaning closer to him. "She doesn't need your power, so keep it in your pants."

"Eoduun!" Eve chastised. She saw that Zephlyn's eyes were fixed on the fangs Eoduun was showcasing simply for the intimidation factor. "Put those things away."

She turned her attention to Zephlyn and held up the journal. "Thanks for doing this. I think…I think I needed that closure."

She now had the full story, and even though she never got to meet her mother, she felt closer to her. She felt like she *knew* her.

She took the journal and slid it onto the small shelf on the wall where she kept the other books she'd brought back from her old house. It belonged there, with the other stories from her past. Stacey's story was finally complete.

50

You Won't Ever Be Alone

That night, after Luc ushered everyone out of her apartment, Eve went to his apartment and properly welcomed him home.

As she lay in the afterglow in his bed with him, her head on his bare chest, listening to his heartbeat, she remarked, "We have a fucked-up life."

"Isn't it grand?" he replied with a contented sigh. "So much better than a boring old regular life."

"I used to have a regular life. What the fuck happened?"

"I'm shocked you don't know. You were there for most of it. You were responsible for at *least* half of it."

Eve laughed. "But how did I live the last thirteen years not knowing my blood could heal?"

"How many times in your life did you ever have someone suck your blood directly from you? Lick your bloody lip or bloody tongue? Before coming here, that is."

He had her there. "Never. But I had to have gotten my blood in another fighter's mouth at least once."

"Spray, maybe. Not the same."

"True," Eve conceded. She thought about her days as an MMA fighter. An artist. Fuck, she hadn't picked up a brush in ages, other than to paint devil's traps. She still sketched occasionally, but nothing worthwhile. She didn't even miss it. It was hard to reconcile who she was now with who she was then.

"So much has changed," she said. "I'm a completely different person, yet...not."

"You're just an evolved version of the old you. All the same old quirks, with some shiny new features." He grinned. "And maybe a little less sanity." He reached over and booped her nose. "I knew you had a crazy little psychopath in there somewhere. I'm glad you found her."

"Found her? I'm pretty sure you sculpted her."

"Oh, you give me too much credit. I was but your humble guide."

After a long silence, Eve asked, "So...what now? What comes next in this fucked-up little life of ours?"

Luc hummed. "Monsters. Mayhem. ...Marriage?"

Eve sighed. "I don't think that's in the cards, Luc."

"Why not?"

"Because Bo," she replied as though it should be obvious.

"I didn't say you had to marry only me."

Eve paused. "Are you suggesting I marry *both* of you? That's illegal."

Luc chuckled as he absently played with her hair. "I'm not sure if you've noticed, love, but pretty much everything we do is illegal."

"How exactly would that work on paper? That could make taxes hell," she joked.

He was quick to reply. "Marry me on paper, marry us both in ceremony. You'll get the safety of my assets, and either way, you'll still be Mrs. Fagerberg. Win-win."

Eve sat up and looked down at him, admiring that chiseled chest and that annoyingly perfect, beautiful face. "You've thought about this."

He smiled up at her, his expression so full of love and adoration as he simply said, "A lot."

"And the others? My 'boyfriends,' as Bo put it? Where do they fit in this master plan of yours?"

"They stay just that. You can't marry a god or a priest, and Zeke and Eoduun should just marry each other and get it the fuck over with." He reached up and brushed the hair from her face. "You can keep your boy toys."

"Even *Dagon*?"

Luc rolled his eyes. "I couldn't keep him away from you when he was trapped inside another human being. How the fuck am I going to keep him away from you now? Besides, he'd level a city for you. He's...maybe he's not so bad."

"Lucius fucking Fagerberg, did you really just say that?!"

"I know I'm good at it, and I know by rights it *should* be, but 'fucking' is not my middle name."

Eve stopped to think. "Wait, what *is* your middle name?"

"Xavier."

An incredulous gasp escaped her lips. "They wasted that on a *middle* name?! That's first fucking name material."

"It was my grandfather's name."

"It's a cool name."

"He was a dick."

Eve rested her head on his chest again. "You come from a long line of dicks."

"And a line of long dicks."

"Delightful," she intoned.

"Look at that, you don't even laugh at my jokes anymore. It's like we're already married."

Eve fell asleep to the sound of Luc tapping away on the keyboard of his laptop, surrounded by papers, because he had one more report to finish up for Fagerberg Enterprises. But her sleep was interrupted a short time later by a female voice.

She sat up, a paper crinkling under her palm, and looked around for the source. All was quiet, and no one else was in the room. She looked over at Luc. He was sound asleep with his laptop still open on the bed, papers everywhere. She closed the lid on the computer and moved it to the bedside table, then began gathering up the papers.

A rich, female voice filled her head. *I'm lonely. Come chat with me, child.*

Lilith.

Where are you? Eve asked.

You're connected to me. Just think of me and come to me.

Eve stacked Luc's papers on top of his laptop and tucked the covers up over him. She jotted a note in the blank space on the top page, letting him know she would be back shortly, but didn't specify where she was going.

She hoped Bo was fast asleep and wouldn't notice her absence.

She dressed and put her shoes on, then brought Lilith up in her mind, and she could *feel* her location.

And then she was there, standing in a cozy little cabin, a crackling fire burning in the hearth, the scent of aged wood and herbs tickling her nostrils. Lilith was sitting in a rocking chair by the fire, dressed in a long, cotton dress with a shawl over her shoulders and a mug wrapped in her hands, steam rising from the hot liquid. Her smooth, ebony skin shone warmly in the firelight.

She looked comfortable.

Content.

Lilith gestured to a steaming mug sitting on the wooden table next to Eve. "Grab your tea and come sit with me."

Eve picked up the mug and sat in the empty wooden rocking chair next to Lilith and looked around at the rustic log cabin, noting the snow-covered evergreens reflecting silver in the moonlight. "I pictured you living in luxury."

Lilith took in her surroundings. "This is luxury."

"This is a witch's hut in the middle of the woods."

A deep, musical laugh rose from Lilith's lips. "Exactly."

Eve studied her. "Why am I here? What are *you* doing here?"

Lilith sipped her tea. "I'm living, dear child." She looked Eve over and smiled, her beautiful white teeth glimmering. "You look well. Are you happy?"

Eve nodded, rocking in her chair. "I am. But I'm terrified." Lilith's dark eyes remained fixed on her, waiting, so Eve elaborated, "Happiness is always short-lived. There's always horror waiting around the corner."

"All the more reason to relish in it when you have it."

"How can I relish when I'm busy bracing for the next hit? When I have to sit and wonder who I will lose next?"

"Life is loss. Love them while you can. If you don't learn to enjoy the moment, you'll not just live with fear, but also regret, wishing you had allowed yourself to feel your joy when you could."

"Easy to say, hard to do," Eve retorted, sipping her tea.

"Well, you may have a very long time to learn."

Eve stopped mid-sip, her eyes flicking sideways to Lilith. "What is that supposed to mean?"

"It means, you may live longer than you expected." She studied Eve. "You are the Abomination. You have my power. Your blood is ichor. You are the son of Enoch, and my great-grandchild. You bear the Mark of Cain. Child, you aren't fully human. Did you really think you were on the same timeline as one?"

She could live as long as Enoch had. She could be immortal.

She would outlive everyone.

Panic surged through her at the realization. "I'll have to watch them all die." Her eyes burned with tears. "No matter what I do, I'll have to watch them die, one way or another."

Lilith nodded slowly, never taking her eyes off Eve. "They will fade, and you will not. So enjoy them now. Live in every moment of happiness you are gifted. Their lives may be ephemeral, but heartache is rarely so. Make the most of your time with them."

"Can't I do something? Can't I make them immortal, too? Can't I somehow make them into monsters that live for centuries? What about a spell? What if I give them my blood to keep them alive? There must be something!"

The fire crackled as Lilith leaned forward and adjusted a log with the iron poker, her demeanor calm. "Your blood is meant to repair injury, cure diseases and curses, to fix what a body wishes to heal. But all mortal creatures reach a point of natural, bodily degradation that no amount of your blood can fix. An old tapestry can only be repaired so many times before the very fibers disintegrate with age. They cannot be changed into immortal beings. It is something they must be born with."

"I wasn't born immortal."

"You were. It was always in your blood. It was simply dormant, waiting to be awakened."

"Then make it dormant again!" Eve cried.

Lilith's expression didn't change. "It cannot be undone."

"Then what do I do? Without my boys, my friends, my *family*, what do I have to live for? My soul will be an empty shell, broken and hollow. What's the point of keeping my emotions if all I have is loss and heartache waiting in my future for me?" She shook her head, wiping her tears on her sleeve. "I should just let them fade, like you did."

"That is your choice to make. But it is not what I would advise. I wish I could get back what I threw away. That flood of emotion I felt through you...all that love...I'd forgotten how it felt." She sighed. "I regret no longer being able to experience that for myself."

"Except I won't feel love anymore, not once they're gone. I'll just be alone and broken." She hugged her arms around herself. "When Isaac is gone, I won't be able to exorcise my powers anyway."

"You have time to find a solution to that. He can't be the only exorcist who can perform such a feat."

"He's the only exorcist I *want* to perform it." Eve looked forlornly at the fire. "Maybe it's best if I just let my emotions die with them. Maybe that's how it should be."

"No need to be so dramatic, child. You're acting as if they are all going to die tomorrow. They are all young and healthy, in the prime of their lives. You'll likely have a lifetime together. And let's face it, even if you weren't immortal, they would all still be destined to die, and in all probability, before you did. This is an outcome that your immortality does not change. You would still need to learn to accept their loss. You would still need to learn to live without them." Lilith gave her a knowing look. "Or would you rather be the first to go, and let them all suffer your loss instead?"

Eve's head jerked toward Lilith. "No. I would never want to put them through that."

"Then you see that, if you love them as deeply as I believe you do, this is the best thing for them. They will never have to watch you fade. Never have to watch you struggle for life. Never have to live in a world where you no longer exist. Your immortality is a mercy to them, even if it is a curse to you. And as long as you are alive, a part of them will always exist in you."

Eve sat in silence for a long time, staring at the fire. "Being immortal doesn't mean I can't be killed, though, right? It just means I won't die of old age. I killed Apep, and he was an immortal god. If I wanted to, when they die, I could still find my end so I wouldn't have to be alone, couldn't I?"

"You won't ever be alone. I will always be here whenever you wish to talk or seek company. My home will always be open to you, my child. And I believe you are forgetting, even after the others are gone, there is one other that will remain."

Eve raised her eyes to Lilith's. "…Dagon."

"He awakened your true nature and marked your soul. I can sense his mark in you. He bound himself to you in a way only gods can. In the world of the immortals, you belong to each other. He has *promised* himself to you." Lilith looked down at her tea, a small smile creeping over her lips. "You could've done worse."

Eve didn't know how to feel.

Lilith smiled at her. "If you bore of him, you can always come live with me. We can read books by the fire, put hexes on everyone who annoys us, and eat all the delicious things until we're as round as prized pigs." She reached over and patted Eve's hand. "I may not feel love, but I do appreciate this familial bond we share. You intrigue me and amuse me, and I enjoy your company. That's as close to love as I can get. I'm not the family you wanted, perhaps, but I am here if you need me."

Lilith sat back and gazed at the fire as she continued, "You won't ever be alone, not by a long shot, child. You will live more lives than you can count and have more adventures than you care to remember. But you will always remember this life. This first century – this is the one that shapes you." Lilith appraised Eve carefully. "So far, you are being shaped into a truly amazing creature. I'm proud to claim you as my kin."

Kin. Eve glanced over at Lilith's beautiful ebony skin, her long graceful limbs, and her short, tight curls. She was built so differently from Eve. Despite the revelations scattering her mind and the emotions churning in her chest, she just *had* to know. "You are my great-grandmother. Why don't I look anything like you? Why didn't Eno look anything like you?"

Lilith laughed. "I'm not human. My children bear no meaningful resemblance to me. They come in all colors, shapes, and sizes." She looked at Eve with fondness. "And they are all beautiful, in all their variations."

Eve sat with her thoughts, staring into the fire, sipping her tea with unsteady hands. She was still shaken by Lilith's revelations, but she understood that Lilith was right. She shouldn't panic, because she still had time with her boys. And maybe in that time, she would find a way to keep them around a little longer. If she could raise people from the dead, surely she could find a way to extend their lives beyond their natural limits.

And, Fates forbid it, when her world did finally fall apart, and her heart was shattered into a million pieces, she was slightly comforted in the knowledge that she would still have Dagon. He could be an insufferable prick, but she remembered the way he held her when Zeke died. The uncharacteristic patience and understanding he showed. He wouldn't let her suffer alone. He would be there. He would catch her when she fell and wrap her in his strong arms and use his enormous wings to block out the world outside.

Even when she had no one else left, she wouldn't have to take on the world alone. She would still have her hellhound to watch over her, for better or worse.

51
I'm Right Here

When Eve returned to Luc's apartment, she found him still sleeping in the same position she'd left him in. She admired his handsome face, so peaceful and serene in his sleep, and she smiled. She never stood a chance against his charms. She leaned down and kissed him on the forehead, and he stirred and hummed at her, but he didn't wake.

She walked out of his apartment and made her way across the common area to her own hallway. She stopped in front of Dagon's door and knocked.

The door swung open on its own, and she saw Dagon lying on his couch, watching *Lucifer*. He sat up. "Come in, princess."

"Why aren't you sleeping?" she questioned as she stepped in and closed the door behind her. She went to the couch and sat next to him.

He draped one big arm across the back of the couch. "Maybe I was waiting for you to join me."

She stared at the television, not taking the bait.

"Why aren't *you* sleeping?" he inquired. "Something on your mind?"

Eve sighed. "I'm immortal."

Dagon looked over at her, a hint of delight on his face. "That's excellent news. I suspected, but I couldn't tell for sure. How do you know?"

"Lilith told me."

"When did you see Lilith?"

"Tonight. She was lonely, so I went to visit her."

Dagon scowled, his red eyes incensed. "Alone?!"

Eve waved a dismissive hand at him. "Get over it. She likes me. We're family. We made plans to make these visits a regular thing."

"She's dangerous."

"Not to me," Eve argued, and she knew it to be true. Lilith *was* dangerous, but she would never be a danger to Eve. "I'm her Abomination. She adores me," she said playfully. Then, in a more serious tone, she added quietly, "And someday, you two will be all I have left."

Dagon studied her face. "You have time, princess. The world isn't ending tomorrow."

"Are you sure? We did usher in the Apocalypse, after all," she said with a hint of sarcasm. Then, in a more serious tone, "But I need some assurance." She pinched her brow at him. "I need to hear it from you. I need to know I won't be alone when it does end."

Dagon's expression softened. "I've known you were my destiny from the moment I first laid eyes on you. Mortals may throw promises and vows around like paper airplanes, but I *branded* my loyalty on your heart. Your *soul*. That's a covenant that will last forever."

"But you must know that I will never love you most, Dagon. You are special to me, but Bo and Luc are *everything* to me. I loved them first, and I will always love them first."

To Eve's surprise, Dagon looked smug rather than upset. "You loved them first, but you will love me last." He took her hand and kissed her palm. "If there's one thing I've had to learn since you came along, it's how to be patient."

"So, what, you're just going to sit and twiddle your thumbs until I'm all yours?" she asked dubiously.

"Fuck no. I'm going to torment you every chance I get until I have you to myself for all of eternity." He winked one vermilion eye at her. "How else would you know I cared?"

Eve rose to her feet. "You know I can kill you," she warned.

"But you won't. That's how I know *you* care."

Eve turned on her heel and walked toward the door, but as she reached for it, Dagon's hand slammed against it. His powerful arms caged her between him and the door, his huge, muscular body pressing into her back. Hot breath caressed down her neck, and she was reminded of the dream she had about him the first night she arrived here.

She wasn't supposed to like this.

His voice rumbled in her ear as he leaned over her. "Stay with me." It was a command, not a request.

But she wasn't someone who could be commanded anymore. She turned and looked up at him, pressing her back to the door. She reached up and slowly ran her finger down his nose, over his lips, and under his bearded chin. She rolled her bottom lip between her teeth…then patted him smartly on the cheek, surprising him.

"You used to be so much scarier," she mused, then nudged him away and walked out the door.

Her feet carried her straight to Bo's door, and she didn't even bother to knock or announce herself. She passed through the door, kicked her shoes off and let them land where they may, and went to his room. She slipped under the covers and tucked herself against his chest, under his chin.

"Mmm, Evie," he murmured sleepily. He wrapped his arms around her and sighed into her hair. "Why do you smell weird?"

"Words every girl dreams of hearing," she replied sarcastically. She looked up at him, trying to see his face in the darkness, but settling for the feeling of the rough scruff of his cheek under her fingertips. "I went to see Lilith tonight. And before you freak out, she's not a danger. She's just...lonely."

Bo sighed. "I think I need to start using reverse psychology with you, because telling you *not* to do shit isn't working."

Eve grinned, but her smile faded quickly. "She told me something." Eve shared the news of the night with him, and, much like Dagon, he didn't seem shocked. A little surprised, but it didn't blow his mind.

"Is it weird that I'm relieved?" Bo wondered.

Eve furrowed her brow. "*I'm* not. If anything, I'm more terrified than ever," she admitted, curling into his chest once more. "Now I don't just have the possibility of losing you, I have the *certainty*."

"I'm right here. I'm not going anywhere anytime soon, Evie," he comforted her, kissing the top of her head. He stroked her hair gently. "Think of all the time we have, and all the things we will get to do with our life together. This isn't the time to be worrying about the end. We're still at the beginning! Please trust that by the time I'm ready to go, when I'm old and grey and withered, you'll be ready for me to go, too. I'll be so tired by then, Evie, and you'll be ready to let me rest. But I'll be happy, and completely at peace with the knowledge that you get to keep going, to live a thousand lives and do all the things that can never be accomplished in one lifetime. You'll meet new people, new hunters, new friends, new family. You'll travel and see new places. Maybe you'll take a break from hunting and go back to painting, if you wanted. The possibilities are endless.

442

"You'll have an opportunity to change the world, to make it better in ways we never could. You'll have time to make it better without worrying about me, without worrying about all of us. You'll have a freedom you never knew existed. You'll find peace in our peace. And after I'm gone, a long, *long* time from now, I'll watch you from wherever it is that I end up and smile, because I got to have you for a moment in time. You are all I need for this lifetime, but I am not all you need for yours. You'll go on to keep doing amazing things, and I'll be right there with you, always, in your heart."

Eve sniffled. "Stop talking like that. It's making me almost feel excited about the possibilities, and it's making me feel worse, because now I feel guilty."

"Be excited! I'm excited for you! Never feel guilty for living. It's what I *want* for you, Evie. It's what we all want for you. As a matter of fact, it's what I demand of you. When I go, you will fucking live, and you will live well, and you won't let an ounce of guilt sully that beautiful heart of yours." Bo tapped her on the forehead with his finger. "That's a fucking order."

Eve smiled through the wet tears on her face. "Yes, Daddy."

Bo hugged her tightly, smothering her face into his hard pecs. "Now, enough doom and gloom. I still have plenty of good years in the tank, and I don't want to keep talking about myself like I'm already dead."

With her cheek smushed against Bo's chest, Eve's voice was muffled when she asked, "So, what am I supposed to do?"

Bo raked his hand through her hair and sighed. He cupped her chin in his hand and angled her face to his. His fangs scraped lightly over her skin as he kissed her tenderly, whispering against her lips, "Just love me, Evie."

Epilogue
Five Years Later

The chill of autumn had fully settled into the breeze as Eve sat reclined against the trunk of an old oak on the outskirts of the training field, a book opened in her lap. It was a special edition copy of *The Neverending Story*. Isaac had surprised her with it as an early birthday present because he was too excited to wait until tomorrow.

Tomorrow was October 31st. Halloween. Her real birthday. Ever since she found out the truth of her origins, she started celebrating her birthday on Halloween, as it always should've been.

Perhaps it had always been her favorite holiday for a reason.

The sparkling bands on her fingers glinted in the sun, and she looked down at her adorned hands. She wore a wedding band on both hands. The one on the left was platinum, smothered in diamonds, with one huge rock set right in the middle. The one on her right hand was simple, yellow gold, and bore one black moonstone gem.

She smiled as she reminisced about the wedding. The guest list had been small, with only the other hunters and Sister Fiona in attendance. Neither Eve's nor Bo and Luc's family had been invited, but they likely wouldn't have shown up even if they had been.

It had been a grand affair. Luc would have it no other way. The elaborate, gothic black dress Eve had worn had cost a small fortune, and the dinner spread could've fed an army of monsters. They'd held it at The Gutter in the spring, seven months after Luc had made his casual proposal. Cassie and Ramil were Eve's matron and man of honor, and Zeke, Eoduun, and Isaac were Bo and Luc's best men.

It had all gone off without a hitch until it was time to exchange the rings. Isaac handed Bo his moonstone, while Zeke frantically dug through every pocket in his suit. Finally, he reached over and yanked one of the rings off of Eoduun's hand and handed it to Luc, swearing to all the gods that he would find the original one after the ceremony.

And he did. He'd left it on his bathroom sink.

The reception was loud and wild, and the hunters celebrated in true Knighco fashion. The highlight of the night was when a plastered Ruger got up on the bar and belted out an enthusiastic and surprisingly in-tune rendition of "The Zoo" by Scorpions. The song was supposed to be their wedding present, since Ruger had managed to drink the entire bottle of Jack he'd originally gifted them.

It didn't bother Eve that her family wasn't there, because…well, they were. This *was* her family. And at one point after the ceremony, she'd sensed a familiar presence, and her fingers had absently fondled the rose quartz pendant resting on her chest. Lilith had given it to her as a wedding present at her most recent weekly visit, and told her it symbolized everlasting love. Even though she didn't see her, she knew Lilith was there.

Her smooth, rich voice had spoken in her mind, *You look beautiful. I wish you so much love and happiness, child.*

And then she was gone, back to her witch's hut in the forest.

A delighted squeal pulled Eve from her happy reverie, and she looked up to see the silver-headed little girl scrambling from Isaac's lap where she'd been sitting, doing her daily signing lessons with him. She took off running as Bo lunged for her, a wide, toothy grin on her face, her bright, aquamarine eyes sparkling with mirth. She didn't get far before Bo caught her and scooped her up, loudly pretending to gnaw into her belly with his maskless face as the girl shrieked and laughed, trying to push his face away. When she finally wriggled from his grasp, she ran to Luc, hiding behind his long legs, peeking out at Bo with a giggle.

"Are you trying to eat our daughter again?" Luc accused Bo in a playful, lighthearted tone.

They'd decided to embrace the full family dynamic after the wedding, and when Eve had her IUD removed, she had been careful with everyone but Bo and Luc. When Lily Rose Fagerberg was born, they both claimed her as their own, but when that first sharp canine popped through her pink little gums, biting into Eve's breast during a feeding, they all knew whose blood ran through her veins.

But as far as they were concerned, they were both her dad.

Bo curled his fingers like claws at the girl as he prowled toward her and Luc, his sharp canines on display. He'd stopped wearing his mask when he realized that his daughter would have his fangs. He didn't want her to be ashamed of any part of herself, which meant he had to learn to accept the parts of himself that now belonged to her.

"That's what the Big Bad Wolf does," Bo growled. "He gobbles up naughty little children!"

"That's no way to go about it, Bo." Luc turned and looked down at the little girl, a wicked gleam spreading across his face. "We have to put her in the cauldron and cook her first."

"No!" Lily Rose squealed, evading Luc's hands as he lunged for her. She bolted away and ran straight for Dagon, lying on his back in the grass. "Unkoo Dagoo!" She leapt onto his chest and crouched against him. "Dey gown eat me!"

Dagon's wings folded around her, shielding her in a protective cocoon. "Well, we can't have that, little one," he said gruffly.

When she was certain the coast was clear, Lily Rose popped her head out of his wings, her silver-white hair in wild disarray. She saw her daddies had given up the chase, so she climbed off Dagon and, under his watchful eye, made her way over to where Zeke, Eoduun, and Ramil were training.

She wasn't supposed to interrupt training, but they also knew not to go full-out when she was around. They stopped when they saw her approaching.

"Dwagon wide?" she asked hopefully, looking up at Ramil with puppy-dog eyes.

Zeke, still in gargoyle form, offered in his rough, gravelly tone, "I can fly you around, sweetie."

Lily Rose shook her head adamantly. "You no good at it."

She wasn't wrong. Zeke had been practicing for years, but he never quite got the hang of it. He could get from point A to point B, but there was nothing graceful about it.

"Ouch," Zeke pouted.

Eoduun pointed and laughed at him. "You just got burned by a three-year-old."

Zeke and Eoduun had embraced their monstrous natures, and it made for some rather intense encounters when Eve was alone with them. They still held a special place in her life. They would always be her boys.

"Make a wish, and I'll make it happen," Ramil told Lily Rose, smiling and backing away from everyone. The scales were already beginning to appear on his face and arms.

"I wish fo a dwagon wide!" she shouted gleefully.

Ramil's form swelled, his neck lengthening and a tail extending behind him. His huge wings unfolded, and in moments, a giant, reddish dragon stood in the middle of the field.

"Yay!" Lily Rose cheered, running up to his thick leg. Ramil stretched out his forelimb and lowered his shoulder, waiting for the little girl to clumsily climb aboard and settle in the crook between his neck and shoulders.

Not too high, Eve mentally warned Ramil.

Yes, darling, he retorted. With a gusty whoosh of his wings, he was off, Lily Rose shrieking happily.

Ramil still liked to tease Eve with that stupid term of endearment, though Eve knew it bothered his girlfriend, Tamara. She was a recruit they'd brought in three years ago, and she and Ramil had hit it off immediately. She was a jinni, too, and Team Alpha had been sent to hunt her when the wishes she was granting were having catastrophic consequences. She hadn't been malicious, just oblivious. She made Ramil happy, which made Eve happy.

Eve did still occasionally have odd little items go missing around her apartment, however.

Ramil's true nature had been revealed to the other hunters, but with monsters like the Abomination, Lilith, and Dagon walking around freely, what was a dragon? They barely batted an eye.

The Vatican never could pin Lilith down, and Eve was certain they never would. She remained in her witch's hut, content in solitude and simplicity. Eve did notice on her weekly visits that the location of the cabin occasionally changed, but the cabin was always the same. Sometimes Eve would bring Lily Rose to 'Granny Lil's' house on her weekly visits, and it seemed to delight Lilith when she did. Lily Rose loved her Granny Lil, and though Lilith couldn't love her back in the same way, she had obvious affection for the girl.

As Eve watched the huge dragon disappear into the distance with her daughter, Bo and Luc approached. Bo plopped down next to her, and Luc leaned his shoulder against the tree on the other side of her.

"That always makes me nervous," Bo confessed, looking in the direction in which Ramil had disappeared.

Luc shoved his hands in his pockets and crossed one ankle over the other. "Aw, come on, big bro. She's our little peacock. We gotta let her fly."

Bo sighed.

Eve told him, "Ellie says there were some strange biomarkers in her latest lab work that resemble mine. She could be an immortal, too." Ellie was the geneticist they brought in to replace Mira. "And Granny Lil agrees."

Bo laced his fingers with Eve's, kissing the ring on her hand. "I can still worry," he mumbled.

"It is what you do best," Luc remarked. He looked down at the two of them. "Celeste sent me a case this morning. Itching to hunt yet?"

Eve closed her book, and Bitches came sauntering over the grass toward her. He had just been curled up in the sun next to Isaac. He bumped his head up into her outstretched hand. "I am getting a little stir-crazy," she admitted. Then she looked up at Luc and pointed accusingly at him. "But I swear, if I come home and find out you let our daughter watch *It* again while I'm gone, I will beat you to within an inch of your life."

He graced her with a dazzling smile. "Promise?"

"She kept running at me with a creepy smile on her face, yelling, 'We all float! We all float! We all float!' I had nightmares for a week, Lucius!"

"Aw, but it was cute!"

"It was disturbing!"

Luc chuckled. "Fine. We'll stick to *Bluey* and *Scream*."

"She's going to be a psychopath just like you," Eve chastised.

"We can only hope," Luc grinned.

Isaac swaggered over, lighting a cigarette as he dropped down onto the grass in front of Eve. He crossed his ankles and reclined back, resting one forearm on the bent knee of her crisscrossed legs. He pointed his cigarette at the book in her lap, then pointed at her and touched his thumb and middle finger to his chest, drawing it away with his brows raised.

You like it?

Eve smiled and nodded her fist.

"You should've gotten her the movie," Bo criticized.

Isaac rolled his eyes and kicked Bo's foot, blowing a puff of smoke at him. "Asshole," he said aloud.

Ramil returned with Lily Rose, landing gracefully in the middle of the field, and Luc teleported to Ramil's side, ready to help Lily Rose down. Isaac stood up and headed that way as well, and Eve knew he was going to intercept the little girl and make her finish her ASL lesson. Dagon yawned and sat up, then pushed to his feet. He stretched his arms over his head, his wings flexing and trembling slightly, then made his way toward Zeke and Eoduun for a little bit of sparring action. He glanced back at Eve and winked one vermilion eye.

Watch me kick Eoduun's ass, he told her telepathically.

Do it. He ate the last pickle from the fridge this morning and Lily Rose was pissed.

That girl fucking loved pickles.

Vengeance for the little one, then, Dagon avowed as he stalked toward Eoduun.

Eve rested her head on Bo's shoulder as she smiled at the scene before her, knowing that true happiness resided in these moments. But she also knew these moments were short-lived, because the world is dark and full of horrors, so she reveled in the peace she felt right now. Everyone was safe. Everyone was alive. Everyone was fighting for a better world for the little girl climbing off the back of a dragon.

Eve allowed herself to be happy, but she was still always bracing for the kick in the balls. It would come. Someday, it would come.

But until then, she would enjoy the peace she was awarded.

Just Eve and her monsters.

THE END

www.ingramcontent.com/pod-product-compliance
Lightning Source LLC
Chambersburg PA
CBHW030545020726
47494CB00005B/1488